THE
Metaphysical
TOUCH

THE *Metaphysical* TOUCH

by

SYLVIA BROWNRIGG

Farrar, Straus and Giroux ⋮ New York

Farrar, Straus and Giroux
19 Union Square West, New York 10003

Distributed in Canada by Douglas & McIntyre Ltd.
Printed in the United States of America
Designed by Nick Burkett
First published in 1998 by Victor Gollancz, England
First Farrar, Straus and Giroux edition, 1999

LIBRARY OF CONGRESS CATALOGING-IN-PUBLICATION DATA
Brownrigg, Sylvia.
    The metaphysical touch / Sylvia Brownrigg. — 1st Farrar, Straus
and Giroux ed.
        p.   cm.
    ISBN 0-374-19965-5 (alk. paper)
    I. Title.
PS3552.R7867M47   1999
 813'.54 — dc21   98-48755

Acknowledgments

This novel wouldn't have found this shape in print without: the astuteness and generosity of my late grandfather, Jonathan B. Lovelace; the support of the Corporation of Yaddo; the careful early readings of Simon Firth and Pam Thompson; the literate companionship of Claire Messud, Laurie Muchnick, and Pam Dick; the excellent works of Pat Kavanagh and Joy Harris; the good faith and mindful eyes of Mike Petty, Jonathan Galassi, and Christine Kidney; and, from the beginning, the strong-hearted listening and response of Judith Tucker. For all, my great thanks.

with love
for my mother and Philip

and for JAT,
my original reader

But how to stay connected?

THE
Metaphysical
TOUCH

HE WAS THE SUBJECT OF A CONVERSATION HE NEVER EVEN KNEW ABOUT.

At one end of the line, his sister. A clean-hearted person with an instinct for optimism, who knew the mangled joy of owning a brother. At the other end of the line his . . . friend. His interlocutor. His comrade in words. Who wasn't even sure, when she picked up the phone—it was uncanny how evenly it fit into her palm, snug as a gun—who she was asking for. If this man, her "JD," would turn out to exist.

"Is that Cindy—Cynthia Levin?"

"Who's this?"

"Hi—you don't know me. I'm a friend of your brother's."

"Oh, Jesus. Is he in trouble? What is it?"

"No, no." She cleared her throat. "I'm sorry. I don't know where he is. That's why I'm calling you. I just wondered if you might know how I could reach him."

"I'm sorry, what did you say your name was?"

"Well . . ." The friend hesitated. How could this be such a hard question? "He knows me as Sylvia."

"Sylvia?"

"But that's not my real name. My real name is Emily Piper. People call me Pi."

"And how did you say you knew my brother?"

"I didn't say. It's just—it's hard to explain. You see, I've been writing to your brother for the past couple of months. We've been corresponding, and then something changed, and I couldn't get in touch with him . . ." The friend paused; then lied, a little. "And so I was worried about him. I wanted to make sure he was all right."

The sister sighed.

"Listen, Sylvia—"

"It's Pi, actually."

"Pi. I appreciate your concern about JD. I do. I don't know how well you know him, but, you know, we all get worried about him when he disappears the way he sometimes does, because you just never know with him. I mean— you just never know."

The other woman kept quiet. In her mind, the loud thought: *So he is called JD.*

"But I couldn't help you track down his physical whereabouts right now even if I wanted to. All I can tell you is he should be showing up in L.A. pretty soon."

"So he is definitely on his way to L.A.?"

"Well, 'definitely' as far as anything ever is with JD."

"And . . . Will he be staying with your mother once he gets there? I don't want to pry—"

"He should be, yes. Listen. You do sound worried. I'm sorry, it's just there have been all kinds of strange people—I mean, no offense—trying to find out what's happening with him, because of all the Internet stuff. He told me about it, or tried to. I find it all bizarre, I have to admit, but I'm probably a dinosaur. That's what JD tells me. I still believe in books, real books—that's how old-fashioned I am. I read hard copies of stories, on actual pages! Crazy, right? Anyway. Do you want me to give you my mother's phone number? That way you can at least call him there when he arrives."

"That would be great. Thanks."

So his sister, hearing a voice that sounded genuine to her, trusting the faceless person on the other end of the connection, gave out some numbers. Some Southern California numbers. And his friend, nervous with the weight of them, thanked her.

"I really appreciate it. And I'll do as you suggest—I'll call him there just to make sure he gets there OK." This, too, was a kind of lie.

"Good idea." Then the sensible, Western voice hardened with sibling impatience. "It's typical of my brother you know—to go back to L.A. now. Jesus. What timing."

"Right," she replied vaguely. She was looking at these numbers in her hand and thinking of freeways. Would she drive there? Would she find him? Would he be who he said he was?

The emptiness on the phone seemed to be waiting for her to fill it.

"Timing?" she echoed. "Why? What do you mean, exactly?"

"Haven't you been following? L.A., by the looks of it, is getting ready to burn."

Part 1

MARTHA CREPT BY TO SEE WHAT SHE WAS UP TO.

At first Pi didn't see her. She was concentrating on the rough black challenge in her hands. In a small white room with no memories, Pi sliced an avocado clean. It sent its soapy green scent into the air, the smell of guacamole and picnics and oily good sandwiches.

"What are you doing?" Martha asked from the doorway.

"Oh! Shit."

A fold of red appeared on Pi's thumb, staining the avocado brown. Pi brought her thumb to her mouth to suck it clean, but the smell of blood unnerved her stomach and she wiped the cut on her jeans instead.

"You scared me. I didn't see you there." Pi tried to drain her voice of annoyance.

"Sorry," the little brown-haired girl chirped, and skittered back to the kitchen before Pi could readjust and be nice and remember how to talk to kids. Slowly, she figured—with patience and a big smile.

Another missed chance. You had to seize your moments with Martha, which Pi had so far failed to do. It worried her. Martha might be a small person, dimensionally speaking, but she was a big part of this compact household.

The free and full answer to the child's question would have been, *Trying to generate an appetite.* And, to the implicit part of what Martha asked, that is why was Pi making a sandwich in her bedroom instead of in the kitchen, *Because I thought it might be easier if I didn't have anyone watching me.* Pi's elusive appetite: maybe, like sex or philosophy, it needed privacy to flourish.

Her appetite had wandered aimlessly since the fire, much the way Pi had herself. For the first couple of weeks afterwards, Pi's stomach had been bottomless. She'd pushed pizza and salads and french fries and beer into it and nothing ever happened, nothing made it feel better or full. One night she'd gone out for Indian food with her old friend Jen and Pi had eaten an entire livid orange Tandoori chicken. She felt its hot body clucking around in her for days afterwards, but it didn't do anything to satisfy her monstrous appetite.

Up here, though, in post-apocalypse January—her nuclear winter, as Pi thought of it—the distress had sunk deep into the pit of her gut and it seemed reluctant to let any food in there with it. That's the way it goes with distress. It's a greedy guest, hoarding the space in your stomach and in your mind, the places you usually fill with food and companionship and interesting ideas and hunger.

Anyway, her appetite was gone again. The avocado might have coaxed it out; there was something so normal and Californian about avocados, they made Pi think of herself at Martha's age placing the smooth brown egg from inside them in a glass of water, watching over days as it sprouted wormy pale roots as if you could really grow a real tree from such a thing. Her own attempts had never gotten further than the thin scraggle of roots.

But that was it for this effort at eating. Pi put the food away. A blood-smudged avocado and ominous, sweaty cheese; sliced bread that was called Whole Wheat Sourdough Farmhouse, which seemed like a lot to call one little loaf of bread —it was all too much for Pi's stomach, which shrank from the task, and for her dry mouth, which filled with a sour refusal.

"Pi?"

It was Martha again, fluttering out of the kitchen.

"Some mail came. Harry needs to talk to you."

"To me?"

This was ridiculous and impossible. Hardly anyone knew her address here in Mendocino. Pi'd tried to cut herself off from everyone back in the Bay Area for all but the most legal purposes. She had told people—Fran, Jen, Ryan—not to get in touch with her for a while. She claimed the traditional Western need for *personal space*. In fact Pi had been altogether stubborn and stoical about everything, but as she went to talk to Harry now she was secretly thrilled that someone had penetrated her northern fog of mystery.

"Hey, Harry."

A cheerful Japanese man, light blue and eagle-patched, stood on the porch. At the kitchen table Abbie was dealing with the damage of what he had already delivered. Over a sheaf of freshly opened official documents she flapped in indignation.

"Something from Abe?" Pi asked Harry, nodding towards Abbie.

"The lawyers." Harry grimaced. "Doesn't sound good."

Pi left the divorce behind her to see what the mailman had for her. It seemed to be a package. A whole, sweet, unknown package.

"You've got to sign for it. It's registered."

She signed, noticing the zip of the sender. 94720: Berkeley, the university. That stumbled her heart.

"G'ahead. Open it." Harry was too good at his job not to be curious about what he brought people, and not to know that this was the first real mail this girl had received here.

Pi had a dark dread that it could be some personal item of hers that someone had found. Combing through the ashes, maybe. Whatever it was, it was heavy. Maybe someone—she didn't know who, it was hard to imagine who would do this—had found some melted clot of old jewelry of hers. Or a book, something precious that she'd forgotten she kept in a fireproof safe. Maybe it was Zeno's punky chain collar that Fran had given her when Zeno was just a kitten. Pi had nothing left. Had someone contradicted that fact, found her something still to hold and to have?

It was heavy and metal and turned out to be a small piece of equipment. Pi extracted it from the bag in a cloud of padding fluff. She sneezed. A card fluttered to the ground, postcard-sized.

On one side, the familiar letterhead that caused her teeth to clench. DE-PARTMENT OF PHILOSOPHY, UNIVERSITY OF CALIFORNIA, BERKELEY.

On the other side, in Rob's handwriting:

> This is from the body politic. (Didn't want you to think it was an individual thing. There is no private language, don't forget.) We figured it would be more useful than a gold watch. HINT: the non-referential meaning of this gift is: *keep in touch.*

Tears cluttered Pi's vision for a second. But she didn't even know what she was crying over. It was something small, corded, with lots of buttons.

"Did you order it?" Harry asked.

"What is it?"

"What *is* it? It's a modem."

"Oh." It sweated in her reluctant palms. She kind of wanted to drop it. A modem. Who said she wanted a modem?

"I don't even know how to use it. I've never had one."

"They're simple. Did they send you the software? You can always download mine if you want. What system do you have?"

"Can I see?"

Martha stood in her loose purple dress wanting to play with the new toy. Wait! Here it was—another chance for Pi to get the kid thing right.

"Sure! Here, take a look."

Pi was happy to get rid of it. She placed the humming, alien object in Martha's cupped, eager hands. Harry smiled at Pi before turning with his canvas mailbag to the rest of the town's bills and circulars and hefty piles of mail order catalogues.

"You wait." He winked at her. "In about a month she'll be showing *you* how to work it. Like my son. He teaches me how to play computer games. He always beats me, but I don't mind. I tell him, it's when he can beat me at tennis that'll bug me."

Martha looked up into the high foolish faces of the grown-ups. She pulled on Pi's pants leg. There was no time to waste.

"Come *on*," she said to Pi. "Let's go plug it in."

Pi had been living in Abbie's Mendocino house with Abbie and Martha a little less than a month. She was still finding her way around. Around the coastal town, which was small and strange but not hard to negotiate; and around her life, which was unrecognizable, a green dark wood with odd clearings of brightness, a place she hadn't grown up in but had arrived in now, at this age of about thirty, without a clear sense of the north and south of it.

Pi had lost everything in the fire.

It was like death, but the other way around. When you die, it is you, suddenly, leaving all your things behind. Something gets you—a dangerous street, a disease, a blocked heart, or a bullet—and you float off and disappear and become ash. For your "survivors" you leave a heap of things to go through: unpaid bills, embarrassing notes or photographs hidden in drawers, dirty laundry. Small intimate reminders of you—your soap, the contents of your refrigerator, a signed card that will make them cry. The collection of your things is what your survivors have to deal with, but it is also a strange comfort to them because it prolongs their ability to imagine you alive. They move through your youless rooms and they speak to you, because at this late date they've become superstitious and (they swear) they can *feel you there*. They put your clothes up to their faces and inhale the soon-to-be-forgotten scent of you. They look at all the books on your bookshelves, for hours they look at your books and listen to your music, and they think about the worlds of thought and character and song that spoke to you in your inner ear while you were still alive.

It was all the other way around for Pi. All her belongings, all the things that reminded her of herself, even the unpaid bills and dirty laundry—all of that was gone, and she was the one left behind. She was the survivor. She had survived the death of everything she owned. In a single day, actually in a minute or two, her belongings had succumbed to an improbable heat and a ferocious light, had been eaten alive by fire, and Pi was left alone, roomless and objectless, to make some kind of sense of their going.

This did not make her unique. Far from it. The fire had been a public event, the kind watched greedily on television by people somewhere else. The kind nationally remarked, mourned, editorialized, and finally forgotten except by the people disenfranchised by the disaster. Pi was merely one of a group of disenfranchised people; which somehow made the whole thing more humiliating.

Many people in Berkeley seemed to feel differently. In the days and weeks after the great fire there was a tremendous amount of gush, as you'd expect anywhere but especially in California, about how wonderfully the community had pulled together: all the strangers helping strangers and moving photographs of soot-blackened young men helping old ladies, diamonds pulled from the fire and neighbors lending each other their spare Mercedes so they could make their getaways from the flames. Everyone was high on community, after. It lifted people's opinions of themselves. We may think we're all rich selfish folks only watching our own backs, but in a crisis we'll hand each other garden hoses and holler through closed oak doors, we'll help save each other's pets and paintings, and we'll even—under pressure—*carpool*. Because underneath it all we have good hearts and we know how to pull together. Such was the bracing moral taken from the ashes of the fire.

Sadly for Pi this wasn't true. Not that her heart wasn't good—it wasn't bad, anyway—but there was something deep within her that cherished her solitude and uniqueness, and even a fire couldn't burn that part of her spirit away. Pi's impulse, when she learned from her landlord and friend, Jay Dixon, that the Dixons' house, including her "in-law" apartment, had been completely destroyed, was to turn her face to the wall. She hadn't really wanted to run in and help or salvage. She had no desire to see the Dixons or any of her other neighbors. She didn't want to come together and heal. As soon as she could, Monday after the fire and before she'd even talked to Jay, Pi had driven over to San

Francisco to stay with friends there, to push the bay's distance between herself and the wasteland, between herself and all the stricken people gathering to share notes, stories, statistics, and sympathy.

Nonetheless. A couple of months later she found she knew all those statistics in spite of herself. And if one of the whole points of getting away from the Bay Area had been to be referenceless for a while, here in a northern town where she knew no one and no one knew her, where the fire was far away and had happened in a place many locals rolled their eyes over for its arrogance—somehow, in Mendocino, Pi found herself reciting those stats to people who weren't aware of them in order to emphasize the size of the disaster. She wanted and nurtured her private grief. She wanted solitary walks, soundless reflection; she wanted space, water, waves. Time. The things she'd come away for. Yet in conversations—with Abbie, or Harry, or Xander at the store—Pi found herself identifying with the nameless group she had left behind, with the numbers of afflicted left in Berkeley and Oakland.

And the statistics were impressive. On that October Sunday of 1991 over three thousand homes were destroyed. The fire did five billion dollars' worth of damage, placing it in honorable company with that other recent disaster, the '89 quake, which clocked in at eight billion. (Other expensive California disasters were still to come. As always.) Seventeen hundred and seventy acres were laid waste by the blaze. Five thousand people were left *homeless*. Residents who had become used to using that word to describe vagrants and madmen, untouchables even if you pitied them, were suddenly learning to attach the word to themselves. Many spoke of suing. *Somebody* out there had to get sued for this. A hundred and fifty people were injured—bones broken from sliding down muddy hills and falling off roofs and running over broken, desperate ground to safety. Also burns, of course, terrible magenta burns. Heart failures. Strokes. And twenty-five people were killed outright. Suffocated in basements, fried in their cars, a couple lost to heroic acts and the brutal collapse of a burning power line.

Some listeners concentrated on the money. That was what fascinated a lot of people: that billion dollar figure and all the little gruesome stories that made it up, stories of people who'd just bought brand-new homes and hadn't yet insured them, people who'd just built on extensions with elaborate playgrounds to accommodate their six children and had taken out a special loan to do it, people whose fancy cars became black and hollow and whose faxes and PCs and home entertainment systems were transformed through bright fire into dark lumps of nothingness. Often the people Pi met in Mendocino wanted to hear these terrible stories, the personal disasters, or they quoted them back to her from what they'd read, with a certain glitter in their eyes—giving Pi the chance to wonder again as she once had in a Wittgenstein seminar why there wasn't a word in English for *Schadenfreude*, that very human pleasure taken in other people's misery.

Pi didn't know much about the money aspect of the fire. In her own story it was not so important. Yes, she lost a computer and stereo equipment and some fancy jewelry her grandmother had given her before she died, as well as her parents' old VCR they'd shipped up a few weeks earlier for her birthday. And —no. None of it was insured. What graduate student insured anything? They were all used to living cheaply and living with the knowledge that their lives were cheap. That was the graduate student condition. It was demeaning, but it was made up for by the single thing that made you and your home valuable— *in*valuable. That was your mind. Your ideas. Your papers and books, the collection of words that was going to set you on your way into the great human library of thought and endeavor, of intellectual achievement.

This was what Pi had lost. This was her version of everything. Pi was a philosopher: 1991 marked her fifth year philosophizing at UC Berkeley with various grey eminences and other snappy young things like herself, charting invisible worlds in well-appointed classrooms and book-thick apartments all around that pretty, green, worldly institution. Pi had been getting ready her first job applications, having completed about two-thirds of her dissertation on Kant's transcendental idealism. It was efficient of her to have written so much already—some older, lingering students were searching still for thesis topics—and this was one reason people in her department valued Pi. She was quick and also deep. She was one of the ones tipped to go far. She had already had an article accepted for publication in the *Journal of Philosophy*, an achievement more or less on a level with being recruited in your second year of law school to clerk for the Supreme Court, or being nabbed as a junior to play for the NBA. It was the kind of thing that made people envious. Somewhere out there, Pi supposed, some UC Berkeley grad students must be shivering with a little *Schadenfreude* of their own about what had happened to her. It was inevitable. Possibly some of the secretly gleeful included the same people who'd talked about it in the Wittgenstein class, maybe that blond guy Helmut or whatever his name was who'd said, with an unfortunate Teutonic accent, "In a people dzet can name *Schadenfreude* perhaps dzis is a real, vivid emotion, whereas in a people—as it were a language *community*—which cannot name dzis experience it does not so arise. Perhaps in English one sees another's misfortune and has *no* experience because it is not named." Somebody argued with that, Pi remembered. Someone, maybe it was her friend Rob, said, "I think it's that in English we like to deceive ourselves that we're basically nice people. We enjoy other people's misfortunes as much as anybody, we just don't admit it. German doesn't allow you that self-deception."

So perhaps the *Schadenfreuders*, German or American, were now rubbing their hands together to think of what she'd lost. It wasn't that people didn't like Pi. But of course academic departments are dark stuffy rabbit warrens of jealousy, filled with people squabbling in corners, fretting over limited resources, and twitching with anxiety about other people's progress. Pi was famously thorough—or pretentious, if that was the angle you took on it—for having all of Kant's works in German as well as English. In some departmental corners people whispered meanly that Pi had been heard to mispronounce some basic German word like *Dasein* or *Kritik*. On the other hand, you couldn't deny that phrases like *die Dinge-an-sich*, things in themselves, fell musically off her lips or that she spoke of Kant's "noumenal realm" with an absent-minded, easy reverence.

All her Kant was gone. All that German. All of her books, most of them scribbled in either with embarrassingly unsubtle comments in pen when she was an undergraduate or in more cautious pencil from graduate re-readings. She had always corresponded with the philosophers she'd read, ever since she was seventeen and first encountered John Stuart Mill. "What is now called the nature of women is an eminently artificial thing—the result of forced repression in some directions, unnatural stimulation in others," Mill wrote in *On the Subjection of Women*, to which young Pi had penned *Pretty rad stuff John!* The conversations had grown more adult over the years—she was less flippant, at least—but Pi had never lost her urge to engage with these old dead minds. They lived for her in print and she lived with them there, chattering on year after year in the margins of their volumes, in the volume after volume she had stacked on wall-length bookshelves in her converted garage apartment in a low corner of the Berkeley hills. Conversations that were ash or air now. Voices burnt to a crisp. German and English volumes of the *First Critique of Judgment*, of the *Prolegomena to Any Future Metaphysics*, of Wittgenstein's *Philosophical Investigations* . . . and others, others. All dead and buried now, and with them everything she'd ever written or thought about them. Every thought she'd ever considered worth committing to print—which, for Pi, who delighted in the workings of her own mind and who felt most alive when she was burrowed deep within it—for Pi, that meant almost every philosophical thought she'd ever had.

The dissertation was gone, of course. All the notes for it. Disks with all the papers she'd written, files of her essays from college, scores of scholarly volumes of commentary, interpretations. Pi's dissertation was to have been on Kant's metaphysics—on his stark, wisdom-starred vision of what was knowable in the world and what lay beyond the knowable. As a graduate student you had to read around, be ready to teach anything from the ethics of euthanasia to Pythagoras' transmigration of souls; but Pi's loyalty was to Kant. Her heart was floating out there with the German idealist, in the pure ether of his thought, in the deep space of his noumenal realm.

Or it had been, before the fire. Since that October Sunday she couldn't let herself think of him. Pi couldn't see the initial "K" without flinching, without folding in on herself with dread of the memory of what she'd lost. Fortunately, since it all went at once, Pi had lost along with Kant all the other Ks she'd loved—Kierkegaard, Kundera, Kafka. This made the loss simpler, in a way. It meant that she had simply to get used to living in an entirely K-less world, a world without alphabet: the strange printless place she was expected now to build her life in.

D I E R Y

1992

January in a cold year

I'VE GOT AN AMBITION TO GO.

Permanently, absolutely, I mean.

People tell me—the few people I've mentioned it to—that I should set my sights on something greater. With my looks and smarts, they say, I could really *do* something. You know, something important, something culturally key: an item that might get me profiled in *People*. Which, in their view, the simple self-exit won't do.

So as a concession to my well-wishers, I've decided to write this Diery and send it to all you people (whoever is out there). You'll notice that for the most part my spelling is accurate. It is just one short pun I can't avoid. I have a weakness for puns. It gives me a way to move through this world of too many words.

All right, I'm also writing this in order to leave some print in my wake. I think it's Woody Allen's line, "I don't want to be immortal through my work, I want to be immortal through not dying," but for me it's the opposite. I have a keen interest in mortality (my own, that is), but if I can leave this poetic little trace behind me I'll be—not happy, exactly, but at least with my ego satisfied. I'm an egotist on one level, I admit it. Ask my friends. They'll tell you. Better yet, ask my dog.

My dog and I cover a lot of ground together. My dog himself is partly responsible for keeping me in the neighborhood, breathing its air and treading its streets. He's called Minsk and I have a lot of fondness for him with his cute pert tail and his surprising intelligence. A small white poodle, but not clipped to look like a prostitute the way they like to with poodles. No, my man Minsk wears it long-haired, natural. He used to have a brother named Pinsk, who was the same shape and temperament but furred black rather than white. Tragically, Pinsk is no more. I used to say he was wiped out in a pogrom, but the prosaic truth is that he was run over by a car last year, and since then his brother has been orphaned purely to me.

One half of my family is Jewish. Let's clear that up right away. (You know you were wondering.) The other half, more's the pity, is not. I've found the Jewish side nicely tolerant of the sometime bleakness of my outlook. They understand anxiety and the abyss; or even if they don't they feel they should humor me, what with my being the only boy in the family. These are my miniature Jewish aunts and great-aunts I am thinking of, standing in a row like a gaggle of birds, clucking and chirping and fixing me dinner. I may be skinny and single, but I once held down a good job, so they think I'm cute. Of course, it's not like these aunts know how dire my moods are—if they did they'd send me straight to a shrink. They have enough ethnic solidarity to think Sigmund and his followers are on the right track. But in the meantime when my face is gloomy they don't try to jolly me out of it; they just give me hot food and assume it will pass.

It's the Wasp side of the family you've got to watch out for. They're well-meaning but deadly. They don't have that comedy that perches you on the edge of existence. For them problems are more like packages to be opened and then tossed—they consume them like candies. Having started out sympathetic to your wanderings, they then drink themselves into a corner and start muttering about past errors and the ill-advisedness of failing to find inner peace. They want you to live in the sun, the way they do. (They can't help that, actually: they live in California, most of them.) They're the ones who if they really knew what was going on with me would suggest medication. Half of them are on it themselves: that new drug, the wonderworker, the one that makes you happier than you have any right to be.

These generalizations are crude. I know. Here's hoping none of my relatives happen to read this. I'm trying to give you the basic set-up so you know how to place me. My friend Lili's always criticizing my habit of overgeneralization. She says that my mind has the hazy tendency to look at too big a picture. She blames it on the new technology, which she says has us thinking too grandly. She thinks I'd be better off if I kept with the particulars. That's another idea behind keeping this Diery.

Myself, I can't complain about the new technology. Technology can be your friend. It has definitely been mine. I mean, like any friend this one has occasionally kicked me in the teeth: the whole reason I have time to spare now for these frivolities is that I got FIRED from my job. Me and a million other people, I assume you've heard there's a recession on. What was my job? Being the human face on computers—yes me, my dark-haired, freckleless handsome-if-you-squint-at-it mug. My job was to go around offices—mostly of book publishers and magazines—telling people how to work the new systems their companies had installed with the aim of increasing productivity, which had all the employees stopped dead in their tracks. I was a kind of latter-day missionary, explaining the Way and the Word and what all those obscure symbols and letters meant. But then my company, my own little church, downsized itself to the point of not needing me, with the result that my days of zealousness have recently ended.

So I could be mad at technology and computers for letting me down. They promised so much: money, a permanent place in the employment chain, this pert, pleasant apartment on the ninth floor in a loud and yet hip neighborhood (that I'd go ahead and name, but for security worries). Also the bored disbelief of my artistic friends who thought I'd become a techno-freak, living on neon-colored soda and newfangled space wafers. Actually, I eat and drink perfectly normally, but you know how these people think.

My best buddy, David Krieger, has never seen the thrill. He thinks now I've been fired it's a great excuse to blow up my portable PC, which he enjoys calling my "schleptop"—and he's right, it's not as lightweight as they'd like you to think it is—and I don't know what, go back to the land or something. Become a Luddite. Though this is rich from a guy who thinks any town that doesn't sell *The New York Times* is unexplored and savage. I've tried to tell Krieger about the Internet and writing to people out in deepest Helsinki or Kansas; I would have thought the human drama element might catch his ear. But Krieger thinks I have fabricated the Internet. Doesn't believe a word of it. He refers to the people I write to—you folk, for instance, but don't take it personally—as my "imaginary friends." He says he's sure it's my vivid mind that makes these people seem real to me, and you can see it's on the tip of his sharp tongue to say to me, "JD—get a life."

On the other hand Krieger has a nagging suspicion that I may be onto something. This is why he never *does* tell me to get a life. I used to provoke him by saying, "You'll see, technology is going to sneak up on you. Just when you least expect it everyone's going to start sharing interpretations on-line, they'll have Shakespeare on CD-ROM and if you're not wired then you'll be in trouble."

In fact I'm sure this is already happening. And, you see, Krieger's a director: on the stage, of cutting-edge, up-to-the-minute obscurities. So this speech made him anxious; he doesn't want to get left behind. He has a hard time believing I could be at all right about this, because I haven't historically been right about much. But he keeps me around on the off chance, so if eventually it comes to pass as I say it will and the world as he knows it comes to a close, I'll be there to prepare him for the great day of reckoning—getting him an account and a password, teaching him what the different emoticons mean ; -), showing him how, when, and why to press *Return*.

I do know how self-indulgent this is, by the way. Writing and posting all this, treating the world on the Net like it's my therapist. But in my opinion Krieger does the same thing when he gets people to come see his plays; and so does my less good friend Phil, who is a performance artist and tends to dress up as a daisy on stage and talk about his childhood; and so do that pair I can't honestly describe as friends but could get away with calling acquaintances, you'll have heard of them, John and Jenny who do that late night comedy show. What I'm saying is, we all have something to *express*, man. This Diery happens to be my way of doing it. If I wanted to be pompous I would call it art. Luckily for you I won't. Still, you can call it whatever you want. That's your prerogative—you're the audience.

Tuesday

Now you may not know what it's like. You may be the kind of baffled person who thinks, what is *wrong* with these people, these leagues of the gloomy, the underclass of the underenthused. You may not get it. I've known plenty of people like this. I knew someone once who didn't believe in getting angry. (He played rugby instead; suffered a few dislocated shoulders and broken collarbones, which kept him perfectly happy.) I knew someone else, a girl with red hair and freckles if you can believe it, who genuinely believed that all was for the best in this—*this!*—the best of all possible worlds.

Of course, it's only a tiny slice of the population who will go that far in the spirit of what is popularly known as "denial." Most people, if pressed, will confirm that yes, they have had days where they can't get out of bed. They'll admit that they lost their appetite for a whole summer once, after a break-up, or else the opposite, put on forty pounds during a single month in August. Or that there are nights they can't sleep, when they stare black-eyed at the ceiling, wondering when it will get better, willing the dawn to show up with its clichéd but pretty promise of a new, brighter day. Or maybe they'll tell you they've had weeks when all they can *do* is sleep; dreams keep breaking over them like great waves or orgasms, and it's all they can do, after, to lift their eyelids to the light.

Plenty of people have had these spells. If you're a good, careful listener, you can get them to admit it. Which in turn will make you realize that you're not as alone as all that in having these spasms of pessimism. Because the darnedest thing, once you start asking around, is the number of folks who will confess to having had the occasional suicidal flutter—just images, they'll say, just idle thoughts that didn't qualify as intentions but merely mentions in the head, a subtle morbidity that lingered. Something along the lines of a purely hypothetical proposition. Here's a shortlist of people I've talked to who've told me they've thought about it, that the thought has crossed their minds: a young working mom of a two-year-old kid who's cute as a button and whom she loves to infinity; a skilled public defense lawyer, who does worthy things for humanity but was recently forced to move house; a college professor I had, who used to write seminal essays and books, earning himself the right to one of those terrible cartoons they draw in the intellectual press; an actor who had a decent part in a long-running soap. All kinds of people, you see. The rough with the smooth. The good the bad and the ugly. *And* the beautiful. That's the thing: it's even the beautiful.

So you see? None of us need feel so freakish for this. We are one of the many, one of the multitudes. And there is a reassurance in that fact, on the days when you're not overwhelmed by the desire to be somehow unique.

Wednesday

Ok, some local color for you.

So today, for instance, Gloria picked me up at my apartment. I used to work with Gloria frequently, back in the days when I used to work. She's in the accounting department of one of the glossy gals' magazines, the kind with names like *Lolita!* or *Babe Monthly*. Accounting constantly had problems with their system and called me for help. Me, by name, because I was known to have a good rapport with the secretaries. I enjoy the company of secretaries, and am of the opinion that it's time to come up with a new word for them, something that sounds less fifties and bouffant-ish. Anyway, I believe it was often Gloria who asked for me, largely because she enjoyed our conversations.

Now it's a different time. I see Gloria every other week now, when we drive out to a suburban hospital to visit her son. He's finally made it to the suburbs —Gloria says that always was his ambition. Not that it does him much good now, poor guy.

Our ride out there today was icy and quiet. In the summer the road is lined with things green and giant, but this winter there's been nothing but browns. It's a vicious season, a cold one, the kind that gets people muttering under their breath about moving to Florida.

Gloria's son Daniel doesn't always recognize her. He has departed with most of his mind. On a good day he'll look up, smile, call her "Mom," and ask for a Coke. On a bad day his eyes are wide clear spaces with car chases from the TV set zipping across them. His pulse is a butterfly wing. His hands have no veins.

Gloria's other son, Tony, won't visit Daniel. He's ashamed of the disease and ashamed of his brother, and he's chicken to look death in the face. It's a cruelty not worth explaining or fighting—you know how small and unworthy people can be, I'm sure you don't need me to tell you. Our way around this flaw in human nature, Gloria's and mine, is for me to pretend I'm him, that I'm the brother. I'm entirely the wrong shape and color for the role, but it's casting against type (which is big in the theater world now, Krieger tells me), and it seems to have worked. Daniel likes having me visit. At least I'm around the right age. So we have this innocent charade: Gloria calls me "Tony," and I say what seem to me brotherly things, occasionally inventing memories for the two of us since I'm pretty sure Daniel doesn't have any of his own left anymore.

I did it today. I had been sitting quietly with Daniel, watching the television—a not very restful news update on assorted brutalities and disasters. Gloria was off talking to the doctors, hoping they'd tell her something she'd want to hear. She spent a long time hashing it out with them, so finally to drive out the TV news I started to talk.

"Hey, Daniel," I said to him, touching my fleshy fingers to his fleshless ones. "I was just thinking about that time when we played football by the lake when we were kids. Remember that?"

He breathed in a slow, cluttered way. His lungs were not happy. But his dark eyes lit with a faint, fond light.

"You do remember! I thought you would. I was just thinking about that time.

Remember? Remember how I threw you the ball, but I overthrew it and it went into the lake, and how you went to get it back and for some reason it sank instead of floating?"

I looked out the hospital window at the end of the room. I imagined the lake. The day. "And then you dove down to try to get it back, and you were down there so long I wondered what had happened to you. I got worried about you! But then you finally came back up, and you said the reason you took so long was that there was a whole car, a whole sunken convertible, down there at the bottom of the lake and that it even still worked, and you had been driving around in it under there. Remember telling me that?"

Daniel's eyes were focused on my fiction. He seemed to be following me.

"Yeah." I shook my head; I still couldn't believe the mischief of it. "So whenever we went back there I always went swimming and dove down to find the convertible, pretty sure you were lying but not *totally* sure. I had to check it out for myself."

To my surprise, he smiled.

"Son of a gun!" I gave him a feather-light joke-punch on his non-existent arm, the way I figure brothers do with each other. The way I sometimes do with my sister, Cindy. "You're still laughing at me. You know that in my heart of hearts I'm still convinced that convertible's down there, somewhere. I'll find it, one day."

His thin smile suggested he believed I just might. But then his mother came back into the room, her eyes red. She couldn't look at me. She sat next to her son, electing not to say anything about her poisonous new information. Eventually Daniel's eyes wandered away from the lake, from his mother and me. He drifted back off to sleep. Gloria and I sat together watching his face, that face the color of a milky, milky cup of coffee.

And when I looked at this man, this plagued man whose footsteps somewhere took him on a collision course with that virus—well, it is strange for me to look at the rock-sharp cheeks of a man close to that end zone now, that zone I have thought about going to. I remember that there was a time when Daniel was awake enough and enough himself to know that he didn't want to go there. That he wasn't ready yet. Daniel was scared when I first met him, because he could feel the ground slowly being taken out from under him. It is better now; luckily for him and for his mother, who has her own terror and of course a grief that rips out her insides, he's past being afraid because he's past knowing what he'll lose. It is a relief to me that I, a well person, do not have to stare knowingly at an ill person and say, "Why, what a coincidence, I'm trying to get to that same place you're headed." It's like some skinny society woman going to a famine country, seeing the starving people, and saying, "You know, I'm trying to lose a few pounds myself."

Listen. I don't want you to think I'm heartless. That's not what it is. I cry for Daniel and for Gloria. Often. I even cry for stupid ignorant Tony who will wake up one morning when he's fifty and wonder why he's having nightmares and is too depressed to get out of bed. I sat there today with Gloria and thought about how backwards everything was—how handy it would be if sickness were a thing you could trade, like sweatshirts, if you wanted to be brotherly and help someone out. I swear to you that I'd trade places with Daniel if I could. For Gloria's sake if nothing else. It kills me to see her that way.

I thought, too, about the lake. That wide, deep water cupped at the foot of the tawny hills. God, I loved that lake. So blue when you looked at it from the hot, dry shore; so cool and brown once you were down inside it.

Friday

Now, I do have my own relatives, a family. I am not as alone as all that. Don't feel sorry for me. (Oh, all right, go ahead. Feel sorry for me.)

For example, let's take my mother. She is real. More than that, she is friendly and adorable, especially when sober, and wears brightly colored dresses that aren't quite flattering because she's never looked very hard for the line that suits her. She's short-waisted and busty, so something mid-length and loose might look good on her. Everyone's got a line—even I know that, though I come from the sex with limited clothes choice—but Mom hasn't yet gotten around to finding hers. I guess there's still time.

My mother, when she isn't juggling seventy-year-old boyfriends and her bitterness over my dad, makes paperwork her thing. Most of it relates to this environmental group she works for, and she certainly manages to generate a great deal of it—subscription forms, memos, newsletters, pamphlets. Some day the Environmental Protection Agency is going to go after this organization because of the amount of rain forest they are consuming via my mother, but it hasn't happened yet. She has her own computer that I taught her to do all kinds of fancy desktop publishing on. That released the true maniac in my mother. She has been cheerfully generating paperwork ever since.

My mother lives in that big yellow rich state, the one I left behind me, and I don't see her very often to our not mutual regret. We're down to the occasional secular holiday or fly-by-night visit. Thanks to the telephone, though, my mother's favorite item of technology after the laser printer, her voice lives on in my life. And she routinely sends me mementos of herself, something nicely fonted with justified margins. That or some new form to fill out. It's one of her ways of bonding with me—sending me forms. For instance, we're all, the three of us including my sister, Cindy, involved in some complicated life insurance program whereby if we all spend five thousand dollars every year on the policy then one day when Mom dies Cindy and I stand to make five hundred bucks and a free trip to Hawaii. Something like that. I don't claim to understand it, not being adept at the world of finance, but the women are on top of it. Given my future prospects, I figure it doesn't matter so much if I don't get the finer details.

My father is a non-topic in the family. We are all quietly obsessed with him, but no one admits this to anyone else. My mom is still in love with him after twenty-odd years of divorce and neglect; my sister claims scarily to have no feelings about him, which I take to mean she has nightmares about bludgeoning him; and my role is to pretend hopelessly he hasn't ruined my life.

My dad has gone down in history, mine anyway, as the wandering Joe. He started wandering when we weren't big at all, my sister and I, and at first we wandered with him from one apartment and job to another in and around the L.A. area, and then he just kept on wandering with new jobs and new lady companions, and the three of us stayed put where we were, a place in a bungalow court in an un-upmarket end of Pasadena which later self-gentrified. After that we didn't see a whole lot of him, though he left a Jewish clan in his wake (one branch in the West, another in the East) that was somehow meant to make up for the loss. And they did, in a way. The L.A. aunts fussed over us and promised us that Daddy would return. He made good on their promises, occasionally—popping back for the occasional group brunch or park outing—until the point came when you just realized by default that he had effectively pulled out of fathering.

These days the consensus among the family's chosen people is that he's gone to live in the hot small country for people of that faith and culture. That's what the aunts say. I don't know, maybe he *is* in Eretz Israel. It doesn't seem like the Joe I knew, who was not what you would have called in touch with his roots, but that Joe, in my memory, is a confused and self-absorbed guy who may have become anything after I last saw him, on a day in college when we'd managed to cross paths in this city I live in now. The last time I saw Joe he was moving away from me in a dusty green raincoat down a broad city avenue, hailing a cab, checking the money in his wallet, since in a weird moment of generosity he'd paid for my sandwich. Earlier I'd watched Joe order a ham and mustard on rye and then tell me I couldn't have the same because did I know it went against the Jewish faith? Of course I did, but when I asked him to explain why he was exempt, he said that I was only half Jewish, and through the wrong branch too, i.e., him, so I hardly even counted. That, according to our man Joe, meant I was always going to have to try harder in my life. That was just how it was.

"Try harder to do what exactly, Joe?" I asked the man with the slow guilty eyes and the remote, severe features. I was nineteen, and for a bunch of different reasons I felt about ready to kill him that year. Calling him "Joe" was one tiny act of revenge.

"Try, try." He waved his long hand, sipped his ice water, and then locked his fingers together in a large prayer-like fist and rested his chin on them as if he were a professor or a rabbi. "I mean, try to be what you are. Authentic. Different."

This seemed like junior-high material. I was doing Greek philosophy at the time and needed something more hardcore.

"What are you trying to say, Joe? What's your point?"

The thing that I might have liked to hear from him at this juncture was some great family revelation. That he wasn't really my father, for instance. That would have gone down well. Or maybe that my mother wasn't really my mother. Better yet, that I wasn't really *me*, there'd been some terrible mistake in my identity and I'd been switched at birth with a Kennedy or even a Nixon. (I would have settled for a Nixon.) The previous day I'd taken a nightmarish philosophy final on the pre-Socratics, the result of which I was none too optimistic about. The East Coast chilled me; I never dressed warmly enough. In general, my fancy college was giving me a headache, a continual wince of self-loathing and not even a girlfriend to make up for it. Altogether it was a time when such a dramatic piece of news would have really perked up my spirits.

No such luck. The guy never could come up with the goods.

"I'm just saying," he said, allowing his eyes to move vaguely off in the direction of more coffee, "you should stick to the diet. Order corned beef."

But I didn't. To defy him I had the tuna. Then I sat back to see how we'd fill the time before food with some pained urge towards talk.

Monday

I haven't entirely finished with the family background—for instance, I've told you next to nothing about my sister, Cindy, which is no reflection on her as she's a very nice person and additionally has a fantastic collection of shoes. (Her girlfriend, Jane, sometimes calls her "Imelda," after the shoe empress Ms. Marcos.) I will get to Cindy later. But earlier today I had a revelation, and in the order of things—sorry, Cin!—revelations come before sisters.

Now I am lying on my hard bed. The coffee's steaming, and Minsk is dozing because we had a good long walk. The traffic stops and starts down below like the call of the wild, like a movement of planets. And though my bedroom in this place is small, it seems big enough to hold everything about me and everything I might do.

Sometimes it seems like a great theatrical joke, my despair. Friends like Phil and Krieger always suspected I would have been happy on the stage. They think I say things for effect, make up stories just for the sake of it. So if you introduce hints into the conversation—your imminent departure, whether it should be off a tall building or under a train, who's going to get your books, how much to leave for charity and should it be an arts fund or some kind of pro–racial harmony group—it's not like people are going to pay attention. That's why you say it in a mutter. You expect them to ignore you.

I mean, it's not like you're going to resort to the only thing that would get people's attention in a city like this, that is grab someone like Krieger by the shoulders and say, "This is a cry for help, you idiot! D'you hear me? A cry for HELP!"

No. The point is you don't really *want* them to do anything. I don't. I realized this when I was walking earlier with Krieger and Minsk. We walked through the great park with our jackets pulled up against this insane cold, while our ears stiffened and my fingers drained to yellow because I have lousy circulation. Eventually, half-dead but with Minsk well-exercised, we went to eat in this dark café that Krieger likes, I think because it makes him feel European. We are all striving after different goals. Fair enough—being European is Krieger's. One day he'll move to Paris and just get it over with. Or Berlin, if they'll take him. Anyway it's true that even I, the original schmoe, feel European in this place because they let me bring Minsk in, which is definitely not an American thing to do. Krieger says if I held him in my lap and fed him scraps from the table, murmuring French nothings into his ear, it would complete the effect.

Krieger talked, once we sat down. I listened. I watched him smoke a European number of cigarettes as we awaited delivery of our elaborate coffee drinks. And Krieger, who has a permanent rotation directing at a little independent theater in an iffy neighborhood—that stays afloat I don't know how, on city grants and bake sales—told me about the new production of *Hamlet* that he's putting together. It's time in his career to do *Hamlet*, he tells me; everyone has a Hamlet moment and his, apparently, is now.

He has a radical interpretation. Krieger's idea is that all of the characters are figments of Hamlet's imagination, except for the ghost/father and Horatio. Everything else is the dreamworld that Hamlet, who really *is* going crazy, imagines around him. But Horatio is real, and Horatio is the only one who can touch Hamlet, who can really *talk* to him, because he understands Hamlet and so he can penetrate Hamlet's madness. Meanwhile Claudius, Hamlet's father, isn't really dead; it's just that Hamlet *thinks* he's dead because he has remarried, the father that is, to a woman Hamlet loathes (Gertrude, if you see what I mean), and so in his madness Hamlet has changed the whole story around and decided that his real father is dead and he talks to him as a ghost. It's a complicated idea. I can't totally do it justice the way Krieger did with ashes falling from his cigarette butt in a snow of enthusiasm. Obviously the thing is going to require detailed program notes and a number of line cuts. Purists will be none too happy. But if you could hear Krieger talk about it, you'd see that it might work, that it might really illuminate the play. Krieger can be very persuasive. He's large, which helps.

But here's the thing. While Krieger talked and I saw I would never get a chance to speak, that I wouldn't get a note in edgewise today because Hamlet was all we'd get to—I gave in. I gave in to Krieger's life and words and realized I wouldn't have wanted to talk anyway because what could I tell Krieger that he could do anything about, actually? Wasn't it better just to go over the details of his production? Nothing he could say to me would make it any better. If he'd tried to ask me, in a friendly way, what was wrong I probably would have gotten more depressed because I'd have had to explain that nothing was *wrong* in an objective sense in that I had an apartment and food and a dog and books and even friends, and that there was no legitimate source for complaint, except for getting fired, which story I'd already told him and it does not improve in the retelling. As I mumbled on Krieger might have tried to look sympathetic; I mean, he's my friend so there's obviously some affection there, but I also know Krieger is a *doer* and he would have looked at me with a clear expression on his face of, "Why doesn't JD just get off his couch and get out there?"

I would have found that expression hard to look into, beautiful as Krieger's face can be, particularly when it is lit with the excitement of a new play he's working on. It's less beautiful when he's chastising you on your penchant for whining.

So I kept quiet. I kept my own counsel.

But when fate is doing its job right, the way it does in the movies but rarely in my life, this is just the moment when something comes along to yank you out of your stupor.

When Krieger was talking about Hamlet and Horatio, his eyes, Krieger's oaky, often cynical eyes, became dark and sincere. Broken romance and passionate friendship jostled in his clear vision. He was drinking coffee—a tiny cappuccino moustache had formed over his full lip—and the coffee mixed with the deep brown of his eyes and the heat of his breath like the thick fumes of Elsinore— all of this made me fall into a desire, a hunger, not for my friend exactly but for what he saw as he spoke of Hamlet and Horatio.

"They have always had the closest relationship in the play," Krieger asserted with caffeinated urgency. "It's the only *real* connection: they are the only two who speak to each other, who are friends in a meaningful way. They love each other. Everything else, every other relation, is power, or duty, or lust, or contempt. Between Hamlet and Horatio there's real *sympathy*. They are like brothers, but they're more intimate than brothers can be; they're like lovers, but more trusting than lovers can be. They *know* each other. That's what it is. They know and are known to each other."

The cold of this winter, though we were sitting indoors now, gripped my whole body for a minute. I started coughing. I shivered in my loose-weave sweater, a cotton thing that looked good on the beefy men in the catalogue but turned out to have no warmth value whatsoever. My coughs got deeper and deeper, sounding like they came from someplace way back in there, from somewhere around the start of my childhood.

"Hey," Krieger said, reaching a big hand across to my shoulder. "Are you all right? You want some water?"

His hand felt good, I admit, but it was Hamlet I was thinking of. I was convulsed in coughs because Krieger had given me an idea of something to do with my time, something to busy the rest of my life, which as you are privileged to know may not last long.

I decided I'd look for Horatio. My lost brother. My soul mate.

It sounds fanciful, I know. A literary joke, even. But I'm serious. It's what I need—a small goal, a plan—and it makes me excited. Because just to die now,

to give up *now*, seems kind of feeble. Like being lazy about everything, including my own suicide.

But this, this gives me a project. It gives me a timetable. I look for Horatio
until the story's over and the money is spent. I look for this Horatio, for this
someone who knows me. I doubt whether I'll find him. If I do find him, I'll
do what? Shake his hand; buy him lunch; talk about life with him. Then go
on my way, proud that I didn't just leave without finding him. And if I don't
find Horatio? That's easy. When I come back, my search over, I'll return to my
small apartment, to the hole in the park that Minsk will help me dig. And then
I'll lie down in my hole, tired and at peace. Knowing I at least *looked*. That I
did make the effort.

Krieger doesn't know what he's given me. He kept on talking once I stopped
coughing. It wasn't until our food arrived that he finally raised his head and
took a good look at my face.

"JD," he scolded. "What's the matter? You look like death. Are you all right?"

I brightened under his questions.

"I'm feeling better. Thanks."

"Are you sure? Have some more water. Have something stronger. You want
a whiskey or something?"

But I'm trying not to drink so much anymore—the Wasp blood makes it
something of a health hazard, it can make me come across all sodden and
maudlin—so I accepted a Coke. I let him watch my face. For a couple of
minutes Krieger's eyes left his own drama and he noticed, with his directorial
perception, that I'd been distraught. But I'd already decided not to tell him
about it so I waved off his questioning. I smothered the inner screech of despair,
and instead I just grunted, smiling a little at him.

"I love the Hamlet idea," I told him. Truthfully. "It's great. It really—you
know, it changes the way I see things."

"You think so?"

It was the right thing for me to say. Krieger loves me, in his way, but he likes
to be allowed to get on with his work. He's also incredibly vain.

My old friend glowed that warm sepia color and put his concern for me to
one side. With his great mouth and his even greater ambition, he attacked the
gourmet sandwich he'd been brought, layers and layers of nice meat and rare
vegetables. In between bites he told me some of the ideas his designer had had
about the set.

MARTHA HAD DONE PUMPKINS AND PILGRIMS IN THE FALL AND WAS NOW DOING a month on Native Americans. She kept looking in the garden and anywhere outside for arrowheads and abalone shells. She informed Pi that abalone shells had been used by the Native Americans to draw borders around places and you could still find them buried in the ground and that people thought they were magic. Pi was impressed. When she was a Bay Area kid, as far as she could remember, they studied the Spanish explorers Cortés and Portolá; there wasn't a lot of mention made of the people who had first owned California without actually believing they did. Maybe her class had made fake feather headdresses once, but that was about it. On the whole it was the Spanish and of course the forty-niners who got the most publicity. Pi had always imagined the forty-niners in the red and gold costumes of the football team; it had taken her some time as a child to learn the difference between the two.

"Sometimes the arrowheads are just lying around like stones," Martha told Pi one cool afternoon as she rootled around by a poppy plant. "So people haven't noticed them. They have little pieces chipped off them. They're not smooth like they are when people make them now, with machines."

Sincerity seemed to work better with Martha than the overbright smile, so Pi decided for a while to try playing it straight. Though she was cold in the late air she made an effort to look, too. She kicked around vaguely in the dirt. This was just about the friendliest Martha had been to her so far and Pi couldn't afford to squander it. The modem had caught Martha's imagination, though they hadn't managed to get it up and running because, as Harry had pointed out, Pi didn't have the software. But Martha's interest in the gadget placed Pi more centrally on the girl's emotional map. It was important that Pi stay there.

Pi still felt she was in a trial period here with Martha and Abbie. Why not? They hardly knew her. And the unknowing was mutual: her patience was on trial as well as theirs. The connection was a remote if plausible one—Abbie was the aunt of Pi's old high-school pal Fran, who'd thought in a smart moment to match the two bereaved women: Pi, who'd lost the trappings of a life, and Abbie, who'd lost the trappings of a marriage. Abbie was in the bitter closing stretch of divorce from a lawyer, Abe, who lived still in San Francisco. She'd chosen to spend the year here, in their once summer home. "It will be great," Fran had promised Pi one dim November evening on a chilly Oakland street. "You can help each other. You can lick each other's wounds." "I'm not going to take that literally," Pi had answered.

Pi had been here about a month now. She'd come up after a depressing ninety-degree Christmas in San Diego with her mother and Richard. Their gifts to her? A couple of new shirts, borderline wearable; some nice organic creams and shampoos; hazelnut-flavored coffee beans; a new hardback novel and one bright self-help book, *Coping with Catastrophe*. Pi discreetly trashed the books —she wasn't anywhere near reading or book-owning again, particularly not *Coping with Catastrophe*—and piled the rest in the back of her Honda before making the eleven-hour drive up to Mendocino in one day.

She was living in Abe's old workroom. You could still see the shadows where he'd hung his tools. Pi had considered painting over them but decided she liked living with the grease-ghosts of someone else's hobby. There was a working counter the whole length of one wall that narrowed the room into the shape of an egg carton. Pi tried to fend off thoughts of the home she'd lost, but she was quietly pleased with the symmetry of moving from a converted garage into a former toolroom.

When Pi, exhausted from the drive, her head filled with too much radio and a queasiness from the few last winding miles of Highway 1, first met Abbie, her immediate thought had been:

This won't work.

Abbie was too pretty and nice and warm and normal. The combination was immediately stressful for Pi. Pi had imagined Fran's aunt to be Fran-like but forty: maybe not with dyed cherry-red hair but certainly with some kind of practical short crop and uneven teeth and a tough blunt view on the world, like Fran's. She might, being a Northern Californian, be the kind of woman adept with a chainsaw and happiest in a four-wheel drive, rollicking around dusty corners with her panting black Lab beside her. Instead here she was, alarmingly real and vivid and not a chainsaw woman of any kind. She was instead soft and purple-clothed, with smooth vanilla skin and simple, silky cottons that fell loosely over her curved, lithe body. Her face, creased more along laugh lines than anger lines, was old enough to contain fullnesses and stories. An early silver fell down her dark head in puppyish, uneven curls, and her lips were a carefully planted rose. She seemed to Pi the kind of woman who might volunteer in the children's section of the local library and you fell in love with her as a kid and wished she were your real mom; that, or like someone who worked in a crafts store called Earth Expressions and sat doodling all day to the waterfall serenities of New Age music.

"We're so glad you're here. Martha and I—and the house!—have been waiting for you," Abbie said in greeting, reducing Pi to a syncopated stutter.

"Yes, thanks—yes, thanks—good to see you, nice to see you."

It just wasn't what Pi had had in mind.

Martha, meanwhile, had been suspicious. She hung on to the handle of the screen door and occasionally pulled it back so the door slammed on its spring. When Pi tried to lure her into a standard adult-child exchange—"And how old are you? What grade are you in?"—Martha's eyes shifted and she looked bored. Abbie didn't appear worried about whether or not Martha replied; she didn't feed the child one of those maternal politenesses, "Honey? You're seven, aren't you? And tell the lady what grade you're in." This was the first thing Pi noticed in Abbie that put her at ease. She also liked the look exchanged between mother and daughter a few minutes later.

To Martha's deliberately wooden face, feigning a lack of interest in the whole new set-up, Abbie said calmly, "Marthamay? Do you want to come and help me light the lamps? It's getting dark."

For a second the kid in her Osh-Kosh b'Gosh overalls and blue sweatshirt maintained the scarily precocious expression of a sullen teenager. Then the child resurfaced and she came over, her feet sliding across the wood floor in skating movements. Abbie lit and held out for her a long match and watched as Martha lifted the high glass neck of the lamp and lit the thick, ropy wick inside. With small expert hands she replaced the glass neatly in its warm brass fitting so that the flame settled and steadied. When Martha was finished she climbed onto Abbie, winding up half on her lap and half leaning against her. From that vantage point she stared again at Pi with something less than friendship. Abbie pulled elegant fingers through Martha's hair and in a measured tone said, "There've been a lot of changes this year, haven't there, Martha? And now here's another one, someone new to live with us." Abbie looked up at Pi. "It hasn't been easy on her. She just started a new school here in the fall. We moved up from the city in August."

Pi nodded. In August she had been finishing the third and final rewrite of the Kant paper for the *Journal of Philosophy*. Thinking of it now that that career was behind her, sealed in melted plastic and grey dust, Pi realized that that paper on Kant was the only piece of her work that was still in the world. She hadn't thought about it since the fire: there *was* a single piece of her writing left out there. She had produced it not suspecting that that's what it would be, in a hot August garage apartment, while this woman was probably calling her lawyers on her soon-to-be ex-husband and sheltering her daughter (Pi hoped) from the worst of the couple's mutual abuse. And now the two stories had crossed paths, the prematurely retired scholar was sitting at a table with the mother and daughter and trying to think of something sympathetic to say on the subject of schooling.

"I had to change schools a couple of times when I was a kid. We moved around," Pi offered, addressing Martha. She did remember one thing about being young, which was how irritating it was when grown-ups talked to your parents, as if there were some problem in talking to you directly. "It's hard. People don't know your name or anything, and they all already have their friends. It takes a little while to fit in."

Martha looked at her for the first time with an approximation of curiosity. Then she buried her face in her mother's chest. Abbie rubbed her back lightly as if to comfort her daughter for being confronted with such an inadequate remark. Pi made an urgent mental note to dredge up Mary Poppins memories and cute appropriate kid jokes, then spoke in measured tones with Abbie about the practicalities of their arrangement.

When people found out you did philosophy—normal people, that is—they either made the standard joke about what a great money-earner that was, ha ha, or they said in awe, "That sounds so *hard*." It worried people, how hard philosophy must be.

It had never sounded hard to Pi. "Philosophy": the word itself was a softness, a breath. And that was how philosophy felt to her, a safe hushed place where people talked about what was important and how the world was made and they left behind the phone bills, the race wars, the love-making, the dishes—all of what cluttered your life, what actually did make your life hard. Next to having to choose between men and women as lovers, next to leaving behind people who looked at you with wounded brown eyes, next to having a mother who'd once claimed not to know you—how could philosophy be hard?

It was print and paper. It was voices from centuries ago welcoming you into their vision of the cosmos. It was a conversation without sound. Whether you were reading a book in your room or sitting in a classroom talking about Kant's categorical imperative, you were rationality, you were pure, your pale tall body was left to one side and for the duration of the class or book you didn't have to be aware of the breasts and hips and thighs of it. Philosophy was like religion—like the moment worshipping God when you lose your sense of individual self and give yourself over to whichever deity you worship. Self-consciousness was (so they said, the philosophers of mind) the mind's ability to represent itself to itself—the grid structure in the brain that gave human beings that blessed edge of abstraction and with it the ability to build bridges and write pop songs and boss around the planet's other species. But as any new student could tell you, it was also a responsibility and a burden, something to be fled in religion or sex or drink or the movies. In Pi's case, the escape was often philosophy. Ideas were for those intense philosophizing minutes all that she was, and that feeling was an exhilaration. Like skiing fast as wind speeds down a steep slope; or like the low panoramic flights of dreams; or like the perfect drive behind the perfect wheel, a late night on a long highway when the music inside matches the music outside of the moonless sky.

How could that be hard?

There was a night in college Pi would not forget. Raining, dark, black. A lot of college was like that for Pi. She'd left California to go East for college and had spent four years in a dim and heavy atmosphere surrounded by people whose names you recognized from soup cans or vacuum cleaners. (They were the children of the children of the captains of industry.) As far as she remembered, the sun only shone on a few occasions the entire time Pi was there. Still, she had learned a lot, and not only in the academic sense.

This night was a night on which she'd fought with the person who loved her. For the two years or so that their love held, Pi was a strong, bold soul. It was a love that gave her strength and humor and an ability at last to imagine herself embodied in the world. She had lacked that ability before. She had never known her body or the surprised pleasures that it harbored. The heart of this woman, Marie, opened straight into Pi and fed her everything—words (Toni Morrison, Walter Benjamin), songs, meals in diners, stories about Denver, jokes, Jack

Daniel's, corn chowder made on the tiny hotplate in Marie's one-room apartment. And love. Armloads of it.

But Marie, like most everyone Pi befriended in college, had a pain splintered under her skin, and there were times it made her red and angry and wall-punching and frightening. Given what Pi had come from, there was something intolerable to her about a muttering distracted person bruising her knuckles, untouchable by your cries. Marie loved Pi so thoroughly, and so *well*, but she couldn't always love her without sharing her private rage, which Pi was helpless to solve or drive away. Pi couldn't disperse the demons that sometimes came after Marie and got her talking late at night about things that she shouldn't have.

On this dark evening they made love on a narrow bed in a dirty yellow light over a coverlet that Marie's grandmother had sent from Baton Rouge, where she lived. The icons in Marie's life were few but careful: this blanket from her Louisiana "Tante," a Jewish star given to her by a former teacher, a beautiful young photograph of her brown-skinned mother, and a cassette tape made a few years before by her father that she kept but never played, which intoned against the unnaturalness of being a lesbian and promised that he had not brought her into the world for her to spoil her life with such sins.

Marie's body was deep, her hands deeper. Her limbs were strong and wise, her mouth adventurous. Their love-making was rich as usual, and afterwards Pi looked up at the cracks in the ceiling, tracing the path of a cockroach across one of them. She realized she needed to get home to study.

Battles start simply. It never takes much. Maybe the real battle was over Pi's dislike of cockroaches, her resistance to this small cheap apartment; or maybe it was over the fact that Pi was doing well at college then and Marie, shadowed not so much by nerves as by a kind of permanent dread, was failing her classes despite the sharpness of her mind and the rarity of her imagination. Maybe Pi had already started to retreat, for whatever reason, away from this love, and maybe the woman who would be abandoned felt it coming. Anyway, on this night, early still in the two-year course of things, they fought about Pi's wanting to spend the night alone back at her own home.

First Marie sulked. Her sulks were thick and intractable and often led shortly to the knuckle-bruised walls and the shouting. Pi, not even knowing why it was she hated the shouting so much, knew she had to stave it off. When Marie sulked, Pi wheedled. She reassured. She pleaded.

But pleading is oil on that kind of flame. Pi was not smart enough to have figured that out yet. The pleading in her voice turned Marie to stone and rolled Marie's fingers into a fist of resentment. They'd been so loving just a few minutes before, those fingers. Pi tried to kiss them and Marie snatched them away from her.

Soon she was shouting. Pi was crying. It had flung itself out of control, and you never know how that happens with a fight; everything is fine, then something falls out of place and a voice is raised and you're thinking, *Stop. Wait. Go back! How did we get here?*

"Go!" Marie was shouting. "I don't want you to stay here anyway. Just go, get out." She jumped off the bed in her T-shirt, found Pi's coat, flung it at her.

Normally Pi would have cried for a while longer, she wouldn't have moved, she would have waited for the rage to die down and said humbly, "No, I want to stay," and they'd have fought back and forth for a while, and eventually she'd stay and they'd reconcile. But that night for some reason the fight was breaking her heart. Pi didn't know why this night over other nights but she felt she *had* to leave; she had to free herself from this room. She might choke if she didn't. She took the jacket. She wasn't even angry at Marie; she just took the jacket and put it on over her shirt. She slipped on her jeans and sneakers. Marie watched, disbelieving, but she maintained her hardness and her pout for the sake of style and pride.

"I'll call you in the morning," Pi said through her tears. Without making a move to kiss Marie, she left.

She was pretty sure Marie would come after her. If she had, Pi might have stayed. She was always persuadable—she was too ambivalent to have the courage of any of her convictions. But Marie's apartment door remained shut as Pi made her way down the long corridor of the building, waiting for Marie's voice to call her back. When she got to the big mirror near the exit door, Pi saw her own figure in it, tall and thin and hunched and ugly, crumpled with upsetness.

Pi cried all the way home through the nasty rain. She was eighteen; she hadn't yet discovered dignity. By the time she got to her apartment she looked like a complete study in desolation, someone lost and torn and left outside to rot. Her roommate was home and opened the door to her, hearing Pi's keys struggle with the lock. Immediately on seeing Pi, tears came to Hannah's own dry eyes.

"Pi," she said, distraught, putting a hand on Pi's arm, "what's wrong? Sweetheart, what happened?"

Just then the phone rang. Hannah hesitated before she moved to answer it.

The household—the era—was just pre–answering machine. "I'll be right in to join you," Hannah said, gesturing towards their kitchen. "Go in and have some tea, I just put some water in the kettle, and I'll come in in a sec and we'll talk about it."

But the phone call took a while. It was Hannah's parents calling long distance, which she tried to mouth to Pi's back as she retreated. Pi wasn't aware of what they were talking about, though Hannah was only in the next room. A few minutes after she sat down in the kitchen, Pi had pulled out a book she was supposed to be reading, *Enquiries Concerning Human Understanding* by David Hume. Soon she was absorbed. The kettle boiled and she turned it off, but she forgot to pour the water into the waiting teapot.

Hume was discussing the difference between sense perceptions and perceptions of the mind: what he called *impressions* versus *thoughts*. It fascinated her. "And while the body is confined to one planet, along which it creeps with pain and difficulty; the thought can in an instant transport us into the most distant regions of the universe; or even beyond the universe, into the unbounded chaos, where nature is supposed to lie in total confusion. What never was seen, or heard of, may yet be conceived." Pi underlined the words. Wrote *The wonders of thought* in the margin.

Hannah came into the kitchen sometime later saying, "I am *so* sorry," in a stricken voice. "I couldn't get rid of them." Her face still wore the harried, self-important expression of a crisis. She came over to give Pi a hug, to bring her back to life, only to find that the face that looked up from the book was utterly altered.

Pi was quiet now. Her tears had dried on her face in pale streaks. Her eyes had settled into a steady, concentrated blue, the blue of an unmoved sea. Her hair was damp from the rain, but distracted fingers had combed it into order while she read.

Hannah fumbled, mid-hug. "Are you—What—" she stuttered.

"I'm OK now," Pi said, easing her body as subtly as she could away from Hannah's embrace. The last thing she wanted was sympathy. The idea of a warm hug, talking it all through over tea, spilling her guts to Hannah about a stupid argument, did not appeal.

"Really," Pi said, with a tight little smile. "I'm fine."

Hannah retreated. "Do you want to talk about it?"

"Actually, I should probably just go ahead and do this reading." Pi smoothed the pages of *Enquiries Concerning Human Understanding* with a flat palm, a calm hand that felt affection for the ideas it touched on the printed page. She stroked the book as if it were a cat or a blanket.

"It's Hume. The nature of the mind." Pi smiled, to show that Hannah's now useless gesture was appreciated. "I need to get through it by tomorrow."

What was this poor body like, that Pi heaped so much indifference on it? A perfectly nice one. Tall, thin, muscular when she swam, soft but not paunchy when she didn't. Friendly enough breasts. Elegant legs. And graced by a face that was not only intelligent but that could be pretty when she felt it to be: a plum quiet mouth, slate blue eyes, hair that was a shade you might tactfully call "ash." (Pi had been a bright blonde child, but mother traumas and the East Coast had faded her and there was no going back.) She'd worn her hair short in college, when she'd found convenient that shorthand of self-definition—independent, feminist, possibly gay. Since starting graduate school, Pi had let it grow, maybe because self-definition became much more complicated once you started to philosophize about it. Her hair now hung straight and bangsless to her shoulders, long enough to play with when she was reading if she wasn't stroking Zeno or chewing a pen end instead.

For her own dim reasons, Pi felt a distance from this form she'd been born with, that she'd watched develop into something apparently desirable. Her body could reel them in when she wanted it to, and there were times she took advantage of its pull, having brief fervent affairs in college or allowing friends or acquaintances to seduce her, later. In the so-called throes of passion, Pi was reminded of the goodness of bodies, even of the deep worth of her own, but she tended to forget the lesson soon after and so could seem cold, unfeminine, after sex. If it was all the same to her companion, she would creep off afterwards to the shower or a book, to restore her sense of balance and return her to the quieter workings of her mind.

Most recently, this body had been loved by Alan, a gentle soft-boned man with an eager face she'd met downing caffè lattes across from the Berkeley gym. Pi had spent long sweet Oakland nights with the divorcing young professor, watching with pleasure his warm eyes grow golder as they made love. The relationship lasted almost a year—until she discovered that Alan's separation from his wife was not exactly complete. He still spent nights with her, though he claimed they weren't amorous. Pi was not interested in this distinction. She left Alan on an evening when he was by turns angry and apologetic, pleading contradictions, corrections, promises. Pi drove back to La Vista, to a warm bath, a glass of wine, Zeno's serene stares, and music Pi had loved since her days with Marie. She hadn't returned his calls after that, though the touch of his kind hands lingered in her body's wistful memory. Pi learned from Oakland friends that Alan called them after the fire to find out how Pi was, what had happened to her. Pi asked them not to give Alan any phone number for her, but he was welcome to the catastrophic information about her burnt belongings. Maybe it would mean more to him than it yet did to her.

When Pi had talked to Abbie that first long night after the tired drive—after Martha had gone to bed—it was one of the first questions she faced from the would-be children's librarian.

"Fran told me that you're . . ." Abbie hesitated. "That you don't have anyone that you've left in the Bay Area?"

"I wouldn't say I don't have *anyone.*"

"I'm sorry, that didn't come out right. I just meant—that you're single?"

"Yes." Pi tried to keep her expression wry rather than bitter. "It sounds so solitary, doesn't it? But it's true. I'm a single. There's just the one of me."

Pi watched across the wine-dark table the woman asking her and searched Abbie's face with the habitual secretive stare of the sometimes gay. Pi looked in the moon-grey eyes for any of the telltale signs of awareness: embarrassment; overeager desire to establish sympathy and tolerance; thinly disguised horror and prurient interest. Pi wanted to know whether Fran had told her aunt. This Pi character, she's been with women, too, Abbie. Is that all right with you? Are you cool with that?

Pi couldn't read it in the face, though, either way. Couldn't tell if she knew.

The whole set-up was like a job interview, assessing each other over the kitchen table this way to determine whether the arrangement would really work. It reminded Pi of Jerry Berenson interviewing her for the teaching job years ago, in the post-college job frenzy. A drab egg-colored office, sports-jacketed potential boss, glassed-in eyes sizing her up, reading her soul, or trying to, but under time pressure necessarily skipping over some key chapters. As with Jerry Berenson, Pi was unsure whether to be open about her "sordid past," as she melodramatically referred to it—in other words, whether to come out. With Berenson, Pi had been panicked into a desperate desire to please the man and get the job, so she'd done the nice and easygoing but also intelligent pretty girl routine, which she could pull off even in spite of her then-short hair. She managed to hint, without ever actually saying anything specific, that her fondest hope was to get engaged to an upstanding liberal guy with whom she'd have several precocious children. This worked with Berenson. She got the job: teaching evening classes in a well-intentioned reading program which aimed to help business people and professionals realize their true reading potential and become better, smarter people. It involved the use of highlighter pens and booklets of xeroxed articles and none-too-lyrical catchphrases ("minimize the eye strain, maximize the mind gain"), in a series of classrooms of beige and grey fluorescence. Typically, once she had the job, Pi couldn't remember why she'd been so desperate to get it.

The same urge gripped Pi now. I *need* this position I'm going to make them like me, I'm right for this! Which produced in her the same decision to smother and obscure what parts of her might not fit into the program. Pi couldn't say she listened to New Age rainfall music—not least because she no longer owned any music of any kind—but she could pretend to this inquisitive woman that she was, in some sense, normal.

"I was seeing a guy named Alan until just before the fire," Pi volunteered. "But, you know. It didn't work out."

"Any reason?"

"Oh, the standard." Pi didn't want to go into it. "Mutual differences."

"I know all about those."

"I guess you do," Pi said, which she didn't necessarily mean as an invitation. She was tired, she had driven forever, her brain had run out of gas, all she wanted was to be judged worthy, fit, placeable for the minute at least, capable of doing some kind of child care, which she promised, promised, to develop a facility for. (She'd dredge up more of Mary Poppins. She *would*.) But Abbie took Pi's discreet "I guess you do" as just that—an invitation—and off she went on her story, the long, long way around.

It was the rehearsed, smooth-running version of the divorce event. It started out on a high road, from which she could admit that her husband Abe was a "bright, hard-working, fair-minded man," and if not necessarily the gentlest person you'd ever met still able to be warm, or at least pleasant. But somehow Abbie's direction wavered, and though Pi was too tired to follow the shift, she found them suddenly careening down towards sharp cliffs which threatened harshness, crash, disaster. "He's a man incapable of thinking of anyone but himself. When it comes right down to it, he's an egotist, he's selfish, he's disloyal—" She bit one of those rose lips. "He wants what he wants, and he isn't going to let anyone stop him from getting it."

What could you say to that?

"Sounds tough."

Pi wasn't holding up her end of the interview now, but the wave of exhaustion had just broken right over her, and her eyes, wine-heavied, were threatening to close.

"It *is* tough—it's tough for me, but of course it's Martha I'm more worried about. I didn't want her to have to watch this, every awful step of it. That's why I thought it could be good for us to move up here for a while, somewhere peaceful, while Abe and I . . . while we deal with the bureaucratic aspects of it all." Her lip spasmed on the word "Abe"; her mouth wasn't ready to mention him. "And, you know, I'm enjoying it here. There's so much more *time*. I'm going to start taking a ceramics class; I did ceramics years ago, in the seventies, and have been dying to get back into it. And I've managed to get work up here in a gallery. Four days a week—Monday through Thursday. Those are the afternoons I'd like you to pick Martha up from school."

"Sure. Of course."

"It's a blessing. To be able to work. It helps me get through it."

"And how do you find the library up here? Is it a good one?"

"What library?"

"I'm sorry, the gallery. I mean the gallery."

"Oh. It's fine."

"Crafts and things? That's what they mostly sell up here, right?"

"It's fine art. This gallery sells fine art."

"Of course."

Pi's approval rating was falling. She could feel the slide. She had to act fast to correct the trend. "There was a guy in Berkeley who lost his whole collection of landscape art in the fire," she managed—a fact Pi hadn't even known she knew. "Early century stuff. Very sad. I mean, irreplaceable, obviously."

Abbie shook her head. "It's terrible, what was lost in that fire. Just terrible. That awful story about the writer who lost the novel she was working on. I heard her interviewed."

"I know who you mean. I thought if I had been famous they could have interviewed me, too: I lost my entire dissertation. Five years' work."

Abbie leaned over the table—alarmingly close, suddenly. Close enough to cast off rosemary and lavender and other wistful, summery smells.

"Does it haunt you? Do you think about it all the time?"

Pi pulled back. Affronted, but wanting to hide it. "Oh, no! Gosh, no! I never think about it. Out of sight, out of mind. As they say." She could hear the sharp spice of sarcasm in her voice, though she hadn't meant it to be there. "No, I'm kidding. But, I try to remind myself, it's not like anyone I knew died. There are worse things."

"I'm asking you for a reason." Abbie cleared her throat. "This is actually the one thing I wanted to talk over with you about your staying here. I'm sure it will all work out fine. But I wanted to ask you one favor that has to do with Martha."

"Sure. Of course." Those final, crucial questions they sneak in at the end of the interview. *Do you know how to use our software? Do you have your own car and would you be willing to drive if necessary? Are you a team player?*

"I just wanted to ask you not to talk about the fire with her, if you don't mind. I don't want her to be scared. She knows you've had to move away from your home for a while, but I haven't told her why. And what with everything she's having to deal with with the divorce, I don't want her to have that to worry about too. I don't want her to have all that extra grief energy around the house."

Pi withdrew, stung by the phrase. Grief energy? But she reminded herself that this was charity she was getting here—charity. Pi couldn't kick this gift horse in the mouth. Not yet. Not so soon.

"Do you know what I mean?" Abbie leaned further in, her voice pressing.

Suddenly Pi was even more tired than before. Her whole system—of hope, of wakefulness—was beginning to shut down. *Grief energy.* How, she asked herself, why, had she thrown all her eggs—what very few eggs she had left—into this one perilous, unlikely basket?

"Oh, absolutely." The way to cope with the request, she decided, was to pretend Abbie had mentioned something simple and recognizable, like would you mind not taking showers at night or could you please buy your own tooth-paste. "Absolutely," Pi repeated.

"Oh *good.* I appreciate your being so understanding." Abbie gave Pi's hand a little squeeze, and her face became warm and worry-free, with a sweet sleepy smile spread across it.

"You know," she said, her eyes bright, her face taking on the vulnerable optimism of a girl from the seventies, "I have a good feeling about this. I really do."

Really? I have a hollow, sick sensation in the heart of my stomach.

Pi thought it, loud; but she decided on balance it would be best not to say it.

D I E R Y

Dripping girls

THERE WAS A GIRL DRIPPING OUTSIDE MY ROOM LAST NIGHT. IT WAS DISTURBING. She stood out in the corridor here and dripped and dripped, and there wasn't a damn thing I could do about it.

That's not true, of course. I could have invited her in. It's what she was expecting, and it's what any friendly person would have done. But I remembered what happened last time she came in here, which was precisely what I wanted to avoid take two of, which was also why she felt licensed to water the frayed red carpet out in the corridor, hoping I'd take pity on her, or maybe (more sinisterly) hoping her tears would cause fantastic trees to grow outside my apartment, eventually jungling me into my two small rooms and preventing me from ever getting out.

She didn't say any of that. I'm guessing. She wasn't being that spiteful, or for that matter so inventive. I'm putting words in her round "oh" mouth, the mouth that I did briefly remember, as we stood out in the corridor, causing me some pleasure as it moved across my body one unwise night a few weeks ago.

Mostly she was making an effort to get into a two-way conversation about what had happened between us and what it meant, and mostly I nodded and wore an inscrutable expression, the way you do in that kind of encounter. I was trying to weave a complicated route through averted eyes, mumbling and denial to arrive at a place where I would feel no guilt.

I shouldn't have buzzed her up, probably. But that small part of me that is not a jerk and would like to display some sort of honor was the part responsible for picking up the buzzer phone, hearing her voice, skipping a beat, and then saying with false bonhomie, "Sure! Come on up! I'm about to go out to the opera, but come up for a sec." This at least was not a lie. I wasn't due to leave for an hour, but I was truly going to the opera, and with my friend, with a legitimate friend, that is, Lili—who loves nothing so much as a roaring good opera.

Still, when she came through the elevator doors, not Lili but this woman, Marcie or Marcia her name is, my heart did experience the proverbial sinking feeling. I had opened the door to my apartment and was standing there to ward her off, making it clear from the beginning that she wasn't coming in. I tried to look square-shouldered and definite. The best defense is a good offense, I was thinking. Minsk was whining in the kitchen; I'd locked him in there so he wouldn't interfere in what really had to be a one-on-one encounter.

Her eyes were red even as she came out of the elevator. Her black hair streamed longly out from the powdery made-up face. I tried to remember viscerally the attraction that had gotten me into this situation. I tried to remember why I'd asked her up that night after we'd shared indifferent Japanese food and a Sapporo or two too many. What had we talked about? What was I thinking? Looking at her now, jangling and girlish, it was hard for me to re-create the motive.

"Jack Daniel's!" she said boldly, coquettishly, hoping to just bulldoze her way through this. She had realized at some cute moment during that short night that my initials and the Tennessee whiskey's were the same. Probably because there was a bottle of the stuff on the card table by the bed. Remind me to move it.

"Hey," I said in suave reply. "How're you doing?"

"I was in your neighborhood—at that great Japanese supermarket—so I figured I'd just stop by and say hi. Did you get my message?"

Possibly over dinner, since we were eating sushi, I made some remark about how I'd always wanted to live in Japan. Which isn't true, but it kept the conversation going, because she gushed back that she'd always wanted to too and wasn't that a coincidence. I have a bad habit, since I have no ambitions (except now to find Horatio), of inventing ambitions and trying them out on people to see how they sound. She put me to shame though by being able to toss off names like "Saipan" and "Kyoto" with ease, while it was all I could do to get my mouth around the word for the set dinner.

"Marcie—Marcia—I'd love to ask you in but I'm going to the opera very soon. Very soon. I'm about to get changed."

"How wonderful! Which opera?"

"*Eugene Onegin*."

"Wow! I've always wanted to go to the opera."

"Really."

"It sounds so emotional."

"Oh, it is."

"You know, I was—"

"Listen, I hate to say this, but I am kind of down to the wire here, I should probably—"

"You know, JD, I am the kind of person who feels things very deeply."

This was the prepared line. It had that rush of memorization. I sensed there was more, a whole paragraph maybe, and I tensed up as I leaned against the door frame. I figured I'd better let her go ahead and deliver it.

"That evening we spent together meant a lot to me. I really care about you, and I thought it was a very special time we had. I understand you're busy and looking for a new job and everything, but I was hoping you'd call so we could—you know—talk, at least. JD—"

She started to improvise. The tears were unscripted, I think.

"JD, I have strong feelings for you. I think I could really—you know—"

And here's what a jerk I am. Here's where I became not just callous but unforgivable. Here is where in retrospect you end up thinking, hey, if this person removes himself from the planet it will be a net gain, overall.

Because even though I wouldn't let her in, and even though Mr. Merkelson from across the hall emerged exactly then to run downstairs and get another pack of cigarettes—though last I heard he was trying to quit—I wasn't embarrassed or deterred. I took Marcie, I took Marcia in my arms and gave her a strong, friendly embrace. I couldn't bear to look at her smearing face anymore, with the tears of her great emotion causing the carefulness on it to slide. I couldn't bear either to witness the strange passion my own pessimistic self had inspired in someone else or the coldness that provoked in me. It seemed better to act warm and considerate in an effort to convince us both.

"Don't worry," I mumbled into her sticky hair. "We'll clear this up, OK? Listen, let's get together sometime next week, and we'll talk it over."

This brought scary sunshine to her face. *The reprieve.* The call back from death row. Like an executioner, like the judge on the end of the phone, I had the benevolence to give her a few more days of hope. I sent her off, back into the elevator, her face streaked but happy, her jangles in place.

The elevator dinged when it arrived. She got into it and from that yellow lit box, before the doors closed, gave me a little wave—a pink kid's flash of fingers, a heartbreak wave, a gesture of hope.

The doors closed and my heart was heavy. I returned to the apartment to liberate Minsk, who was indignant that he'd missed all the action. I calmed him with an absent-minded scratching of ears and reflected that the sooner I get the hell out of here, the better.

Tuesday

I had no business having dinner with her in the first place, I guess. She was someone I used to work with who'd been fired a month before I was, which gave us a bond. I figured we'd sit there and talk about what bastards they were and it would prove healthy and cathartic. If those damn Sapporos hadn't gotten in the way, that's probably all that would have happened. Alcohol—another fair-weather friend. When you're up, it's all sweetness and light; when you're down, it does you no favors at all.

I tried to talk to Lili about the situation. Lili came to the apartment a half hour later, dressed to the nines in something that made her look dark-eyed and ostrichy. I love Lili. She is loud and very funny, and pretends to take nothing seriously but in fact has a mind like a steel trap and can remember details from your pathetic personal history that even you had forgotten. She treats me like her slightly dumb younger brother—which is how my little sister treats me too so it's all very familiar. When I started telling Lili about the morose Marcie she said, while she fingered her lipstick lips in front of the bathroom mirror and I threw some sort of classical music outfit together in the bedroom, "You aren't careful enough about who you buzz up. Remember that Mormon?"

"What?" My brown shoes, I remembered as I put them on, had a dark sticky stain on them. It was maple syrup. How do you get maple syrup off your shoes? Why am I incapable of living an unstained life?

"That Mormon guy." Lili came out from the bathroom to see how I was getting along and to stare me into remembering. Her face was purplish and vivid with make-up, in a way similar to the way Marcia's had been, but with Lili the effect was deliberate/theatrical rather than desperate/overdone. Lili has a beautiful, strong-featured face: a long high brow and a firm, elegant nose. Sometimes you pass billboards or bus shelters and think you might have seen her modeling bras or fine brandy.

She sighed. "He stopped by to tell you about Jesus; he said his partner had just had a seizure and had to go to the hospital so he was finishing up the round by himself. And you buzzed him up, I think you thought he was a neighbor, and you offered him a cup of coffee, which naturally he had to refuse because they don't do coffee, and then you couldn't get *rid* of the guy, and you ended up arguing for hours about whether God could really be talked about in public or whether it—He, whatever—had to be a private experience. It was typical of you. Taking on God-talk with a perfect stranger."

"How do you remember all that? Can I wear these shoes?"

"We're late. You have to wear those shoes."

"I don't remember things like that about your life. It's unbalanced." Actually, this isn't strictly true. I could fill pages with what I know about Lili's family. It's all hysterical demanding mothers and ungrateful younger siblings. Unhappy phone calls. Rude visits.

"You're the only person I know who would try to argue with a Mormon. They're *very* convinced people. I should know."

"You dated one once," I half guessed.

"Willie Wilder, the record company executive. He wanted me to convert. He really didn't see the humor in it. Mostly he had a great sense of humor except when it came to his plans to convert me and the jokes I made about his name."

"Did you have sex? Isn't that against their philosophy?"

"Yes it is and we didn't. I think that's why he was in a hurry for me to convert. A certain amount of tension had started to build up."

By now we were out of the apartment—Minsk having let us go with a long regretful stare—and standing in front of the elevator, that fateful elevator, waiting for it to *ding*. I shuddered at the memory. There was a Stephen King moment before the doors opened when I became convinced that Marcie would be there in the elevator waiting for us with a butcher knife, her eyes reddened and wolf-like. It was enough to make my palms sweat.

"Lili," I said in a slight panic. The doors opened. Inside was little Miss Aerobia from the fourteenth floor, she who is generally kitted up and Walkman-ed and beyond the reach of human contact. There was no trace of Marcie.

"I've got to get out of here," I confided, slightly calmer.

"Where, the elevator? Your apartment?"

We started going down. I would have preferred privacy for this suddenly intimate conversation, but what can you do? I live in a city. You take your moments where you find them.

"This city," I said. "My life. *This life.*"

"Oh, please."

I had been pretty sure, I guess, that that would be her response.

"Don't be so melodramatic. You acted like a jerk. It's no big deal. People do it all the time."

"It's not just her—"

"She'll find some friend who will tell her what an asshole you are and what assholes all men are and then she'll feel much better and then she'll forget it."

I wanted to backtrack. I wanted to tell her, Wait, Lili, it isn't just Marcia. It's not even the job, or the pollution, or the fact that Minsk needs a new set of shots soon and I have a phobia about needles, even on other people's behalf. I wanted to stand on the street there and hug my ostrich friend and tell her, Lili, I'm serious now. We're standing here right now and I'm thinking of all the guns there are out there that could kill me. I'm really thinking that. You know how many guns there are in America? Something like two hundred million. I'm serious, it works out at nearly one per person. It's right up there with televisions—it's beyond televisions, in fact. It would only take *one* gun out there to do the job, it's only one life we're talking about, one little life, and you know American lives are squandered daily, so simply, mostly through guns, boom!, because it's such a quick, efficient way to do it.

You do see how ridiculous it would have been to say this to Lili. It wouldn't have been audible to her—it was in the wrong register. She *does* take things seriously, I mean on some level she does. On the level, last night, of the opera.

She urged me, before we went in, to allow the opera to pull me above my petty jerkiness—or maybe the phrase was jerky pettiness—and to experience the depths of a great art.

So, ever accommodating, I tried to.

Thursday

In the park where I am today, Minsk is catching up on his social life. It's cold, cold, cold, but not positively brutal.

Minsk has less complicated interactions than me and so is less likely to get into trouble than I am. There is no equivalent of a Marcie or Marcia in his life. Minsk is pretty straightforward with people. If they want to play, fine. If not, that's fine, too. He can't abide purposeless biting or petty yaps, but otherwise he takes you as you come.

I am sitting here allowing him to be carefree—admiring his very carefreedom—yet I'm also thinking of how, as with so many of us, his apparent joyfulness is entirely grounded on the denial of a crucial tragedy. I'm referring to the loss of his brother, Pinsk, at a tender age.

I relive the day periodically. I think it's important *never to forget*, though of course whenever I think of it I writhe around in guilt. Friends tell me there's nothing I could have done, but I find that hard to swallow.

It's tricky taking two dogs out together. Minsk and Pinsk were trained—basically. I mean, those Nazi-style dog owners whose animals walk, stop, and salute on command had the greatest contempt for all three of us. My dogs were willing to come when called, but only if there wasn't something else compelling at hand—say a bag of fried chicken remains or some pungent Doberman to sniff at. If so, they would take their sweet time getting back to me.

On this day I was in a ragged square near my apartment, one not wildly grassy but with a measure of space. I was trying to keep my eye on them while absorbing the inevitable compliments from the public. People constantly used to come up to me to press the flesh, tell me how cute were my boys. On this day an older troll-like woman came to tell me about the poodles she used to have, what wonderful dogs they were and how intelligent and so forth, your usual poodle-owner froth. While we chatted I kept a roving eye on the two. And then I saw Minsk, the white devil, edging dangerously close to the border of the park, so I shouted,

"Hey Minsk! Get away from there! Minsk!"

—with very little effect. He trotted purposefully towards the edge of the park, his brother tagging along behind. Minsk was the older brother, did I mention?, so he tended to take the lead. Anyway, I excused myself to the troll and jogged over. My jog turned to a sprint as he reached the sidewalk and seemed to consider heading into the street.

"Minsk!" I shouted. "No! Get back here! Minsk!"

The dogs, of course, treated the whole thing as a game. They were not sensitive to the note of panic in my voice—as kids generally aren't at that age. (They weren't yet two.) Minsk, as I got close, half pretended to make a dash for the road, though if he'd really been serious he probably could have gotten there. As it was, I lunged for his curly white body, shouting,

"Don't go out into the fucking *road!*"

The tragedy was Pinsk.

Pinsk—a little slower, the way younger brothers often are, though they make up for it in enthusiasm—wanted to be in on the game, so he came yapping along behind. And again, as you sometimes see the imitative younger sibling do, he took the game that bit further, just to prove he was bold, maybe even bolder. Pinsk dashed right out into the road while I crouched and watched hopelessly, clutching my Minsk.

A Buick nailed him in one quick tyre-screech, one brief alarmed bark. It was over in seconds. People cried out. You could hear the driver say "Shit!" loudly, over his tough whiteboy rap music. He half got out of his stopped car—a kid, a teenager like Minsk and Pinsk. We had two long seconds of looking into each other's eyes, sizing up each other's souls. In his I saw the dumb brutishness of a seventeen-year-old, some fear, and a thin trace (it evaporated before the seconds were up) of apology. In mine I guess he saw rage. Certainly the nascent desire for vengeance. It was enough to make him blink, half shrug, call out "Sorry, man" in a sluggish tone, and then climb back into his car before I could read him his rights and make a citizen's arrest. He backed up with a jerk, pulled around the bloodied soft body, and peeled away.

The passers-by clamored for blood.

"Bastard. Fucking *bastard!*"

"I got his license plate number."

"I'll go call animal 911. Do you want me to do that?"

Minsk and I were shivering together in a state of shock, so I can't now recall how everything proceeded. You do become numb in that kind of situation. Police come, vets come, you let someone remove the wrecked body and tell them no, you are not going to do a pet funeral so they can just cremate the body or whatever, thanks; then you go home, and that's when you finally wake up, later, back at home with just one dog and the TV on and you're sipping a small glass of vodka to help with the shock. And the dog that's left is lying at your feet, a morose white pile of curls, lost in his doggish attempt to cope with the catastrophe.

We both felt guilty, of course. The difference is that I've had a chance to talk my guilt through with friends and other dog-owners—who won't hesitate to tell you their raft of pet calamities from over the years. Rat poison, house fire, falling out of high-rises. One particularly tragic story involving a Chihuahua and a bowling ball that I'll tell you another time. They all tell you not to blame yourself, that you can't watch over them every minute. Except for the sadists who sniff, "You've got to expect that, if they're poorly trained and you let them off the leash."

For Minsk, though, it's more complicated, mostly because in some inescapable way he is at fault. I think he knows that. Minsk has survivor guilt. And like many survivors, he prefers not to deal with it—he's chosen to bury the event, like a bad bone, as if he never had a brother and the whole thing never happened.

I know Minsk hasn't forgotten Pinsk. That's just a front. When we go by that square—which if I had the hard cash I'd pay to have renamed after Pinsk—you can see a shudder pass through Minsk's frame. I can't speak for him, but in those moments I think memories of Pinsk are darting through his mind. He's remembering his opposite-shade brother who used to tag along behind him. The guy he could roll with, play-biting and barking. A dog who shared his same blood, and maybe something of his world-view. His brother. His partner in eating and sleeping, that creature whose smell he knew as well as his own.

Thursday

It's very suspicious that I haven't said anything to you yet about my sister Cindy.

Sigmund would have had a word or two to say on my silence, no doubt. Of course, Sigmund and his pals tend to have opinions on matters they know nothing about. Don't tell Lili I said that. She goes twice a week to a "Doctor O." She won't tell me what the O stands for, for reasons of her own. Doctor O has changed her life, so she keeps telling me.

So Cindy's big theory about me is that I should come out. I've tried to tell her, No, you don't get it, it's not *out* that I want to be, but further *in*. But you know how gay people can be—especially if coming out worked for them, they want everyone else to do the same thing. It's like people who've discovered new diets, or therapy for that matter—they won't be happy till you're doing it too.

My feeling is, if the shoe doesn't fit, don't wear it. You know? I mean, I'm sure you're all fabulous, but if I'd wanted to have sex with someone well-built and breastless, don't you think I would have done it by now? Not to boast or anything, but opportunities have presented themselves. Getting a couple of poodles certainly put me on a map I hadn't entirely meant to be on. I thought the poodles might enhance my image as a Sensitive Guy. (In truth, I fell in love with the puppies the second I saw them and was powerless to do anything but buy them on the spot.) But they seem to have acted more as a man-catching device. It gets awkward to keep making up tales about girlfriends I don't actually have, but I've found that the handiest way to fend off polite masculine invitations for coffee or the bushes.

Let's talk about this for one more minute. The careful reader, those hapless people who have sunk themselves into graduate school for instance, will detect the homoerotic content of e.g. any feelings about Krieger. Right? In some room somewhere a hip student could even now be giving me a Queer reading, the way they've learned to do with Dickens and Hemingway. That doesn't bother me. As far as I am concerned, there have been moments I've wanted to kiss men, men I've loved. But the sex act with them holds little appeal. I have too much fun having sex with women, especially on the extraordinarily rare occasions I'm not drunk while doing it.

I have explained this to Cindy. I think she believes me now, doesn't just think I'm mired in denial. She was most vocal on the "JD must come out" theory four or five years ago, when her own life was cataclysmically improved by meeting Jane and also when she couldn't figure out what the hell *else* could be the matter with me and why I didn't have a steady girlfriend.

Jane is great. I love Jane. She's blunt and smart and has a sly sense of humor. She has a better sense of humor than Cindy, in fact: Cindy plays the straight man, so to speak, to Jane's sarcastic riffs. She also sings in musicals. Jane, I mean. She's studying political theory, but then she also sings, she has a terrific deep voice like a steam engine and does dinner theater, if you can believe it, camp classics like *South Pacific* or *The Pajama Game*. This is in Baltimore, where they live. They met at a bowling alley, girls-only night. Is that cute or what?

OK, I'm supposed to be talking about Cindy, not Jane. Sigmund's tapping his cigar at me, squinting. But this is the whole problem with Cindy. What can you say about her? She is nice, very nice. Sensible. She has set up the Baltimore branch of a mildly intellectual bookstore/café chain. It's a huge success. We look quite a bit alike but she is prettier, doesn't have the jaw I got from some Lithuanian back there, has more of the Waspy pertness in her features. We have the same dark brow, though, if you want to get technical.

How did Cindy become so normal and stable? I have no idea. She's been sensible from day one. Sensible baby (didn't allow me to teach her how to walk; figured it out for herself). Always quiet and industrious. Gave up on Joe at an early age, claims an absence of bitterness about that. Watched me bend myself in contortions going to a fancy East Coast college and so stayed behind in L.A. for hers. Went to business school out East. Learned management. Moved to Baltimore, where real estate is cheap. Bowls. Watches baseball. Has a great girlfriend. What can I say? It all makes complete sense.

I can feel you're not getting her. My literary powers falter when it comes to describing my own flesh and blood. Let me give an approximate transcription of our conversation last night on the phone, see if that helps you. (She called me, as she has been doing frequently, of late.)

Cindy: Hey. What's up?

Me: Not much. Just relaxing in front of a replay of the Rodney King video.

Cindy: Ucch. What are you watching?

Me: I don't know. Some news show that thinks we haven't seen it in a few days so it's time to air it again.

Cindy: I think these news programs play it over and over again because secretly they *like* watching it, and they think their white viewers do, too. You know? They play it in the guise of "isn't this terrible?" but actually they're cheering along with every blow.

Me: Yeah.

Cindy: Did you hear they're moving the trial to Ventura County? Like it's going to be a fair trial out there. I'm sure everyone in the valley thinks the cops didn't go far *enough*.

Me: (getting vague. Cindy gets very blustery about politics. I often agree with her in principle, but I vague out at the intensity of her emotion) Mmmhmm.

Cindy: I was talking to Mom about it all earlier.

Me: Oh yeah? What did she say?

Cindy: She said, "Well, I'm just glad I don't have to be a policeman in Los Angeles."

Me: I'm glad she doesn't, too. She isn't cut out for it.

Cindy: Then she told me of about ten people she knows who have decided to leave L.A. Remember the Andersons? They've moved to Seattle. Everyone thinks L.A.'s gotten "overrun by crime." She says people can't get out of there fast enough.

Me: Does she plan to?

Cindy: Oh, no. She's going to be brave. Besides, she's too in love with SOE [Save Our Earth, Mom's organization]. She has a crush on one of the directors of the board, that philanthropist guy Walter Kirk.

Me: No relation to James T. Kirk by any chance?

Cindy: (not finding me funny) So what have you been doing, anyway? How's the job hunt going?

Me: Who told you I was job hunting?

Cindy: Mom.

Me: Did it occur to you your sources might have compromised information?

Cindy: What, you're not looking for a job?

Me: No, I'm kidding. I am. Of course I am.

Cindy: What are you looking at?

Me: Oh, you know, this and that. Computer related. Haven't started to look for bussing tables positions yet. That's next.

Cindy: How are you for money?

Me: (finding this an uncomfortable subject with my sister, who's fiscally sound, unlike myself) Fine. No problem. So how's Jane?

Cindy: She's fine, thanks. Are you sure it's no problem? I thought you said the severance pay was only going to last a few months.

Me: That's right. Listen, don't worry about it. I have enough to buy Minsk dog food, which is the main thing. He's still plump and healthy.

Cindy: JD, I'm worried about you. I wish you had a roommate.

Me: (bewildered) Why?

Cindy: Have you seen Aunt Frieda lately? You should go see her.

Me: What, are you worried I'm not getting home-cooked food or something? I'm fine, Cin. Really. Just today I had a hot, well-balanced fishwich. I promise I'll let you know before I waste away completely. Besides, if anything happens to me, you currently stand to inherit most of my worldly goods. You and Krieger.

Cindy: That's really hilarious. OK. Listen. I'm going to call the people at the JavaBooks near you and see if there's any kind of system support they need. It's a good company, you know. They've got great benefits. You'd like them.

Me: (knowing I won't do anything about it even if she does, and eager to get her off my back) OK. Great. Thanks a lot.

Cindy: JD—

Me: (bored, fidgety) Listen, I should go. Minsk is scratching a huge hole in the door to get out. Say hi to Jane—

Cindy: Listen, *call* me . . .

Me: I will. Definitely. Bye!

She had more to say, but I didn't think I had the heart to hear it. And that's it. The whole dynamic, in a nutshell.

Saturday

Today the thought is: *Stay alive.*

Which if you have an irreverent streak, as I do, and you're roughly my age, as I am, will produce the perverse image of three men with high-pitched voices and long flowing hair singing in dry ice clouds; a camera tracking wide-flared John Travolta as he once was down a meant-to-be-tough city street; and the sound of these voices, these spooky high voices, singing something not quite comprehensible but clearly urgent about *staying alive.* It was a hit disco song is what I'm trying to tell you, if you missed it or were somehow doing something better in the seventies. Maybe you were listening to *Eugene Onegin* and other timeless classics at the time. Or maybe you were into serious *funky* stuff. The rest of us were left listening to the Bee Gees, finding them ridiculous but somehow impressive in their capacity to make hits.

My point being this: sometimes, even when you're in a deep mood trough, as I am, you can't indulge it the right way because your mind, like Lili's, gets distracted and starts free-associating, and before you know it you're thinking about the seventies, and once you're on the seventies you can't take any spiritual crisis seriously because that is just not the mood seventies nostalgia puts you in. I'm sure what we all find comforting about the revival of interest in the seventies—and I'm probably quoting unknowingly from someone else's think piece—is that the seventies were so absurd in so many ways, and yet, for many of us, that's our home era, that's when we developed our sense of the world. The seventies were a flop, and yet that's where we're from. There's a certain deep comfort in coming from failure. So much less stressful than coming from success.

I used to think about this in college. I knew a guy there named Jake, a not very good-looking but clean-cut sort of guy. He was the son of a movie star. A major movie star. Not only that, he wanted to go into drama—he wanted to direct. What a terrible life Jake was having and was clearly going to go on having. People let him direct things, people wanted to work with him, because they loved his dad. I mean, people *loved* his father. They associated his father with their favorite Western or Hitchcock movie. To the extent that they could see Jake's father in his face—in his misshapen nose or the curve of an ear—

lobe—they loved him. Everyone—guys, girls, dogs, professors—whoever. They wanted to be near him. It mattered not at all what he was like. Actually he wasn't a bad guy, but the truth was he couldn't direct. Krieger tried to work with him on something like *Guys and Dolls* and ended up fleeing in terror, like he was trying to get out of a burning building.

Whereas my dad, Joe, was a failed writer. I mean *is*, I guess, if you believe he's out there somewhere having the Sabbath on Saturday and intoning against the Palestinians or whatever it is he's up to. When I was a kid, Joe had a novel he was writing for many years, the way people do. Depressingly, if you ever got him going on the subject—when he made those guest star appearances in your life, taking you out for waffles or enchiladas, once in a blue moon—he'd get a modest twinkle in his eye and mention the letters he'd exchanged with the Famous Writer about his work. Joe had lured some hapless hero of his into a brief correspondence, I think initially by writing a self-contained but fanatical fan letter to the guy. They'd written back and forth a couple of times, Joe had mentioned he was working on a novel, and FW told him to send it along if he wanted to, he'd be interested to read it. Poor old Joe. He did send it, too (though he changed subjects before he got to this part of the story, generally), and of course he never heard from FW again. Not a peep. Sad story. He never published the novel, obviously. I would have mentioned it if he had; I would have given him that much credit.

I still thought I wanted to be a writer when I was in college. In fact that's where the idea blossomed. I had some artsy and if I may say so self-important friends in college, each of whom had identified the mark of greatness on his or her person. I think in those surroundings it was good for me that I came, in what obscure way I did, from Joe—that is, from failure. Like coming from the seventies. There was no sense that I was born to greatness, or even that I would have it thrust upon me. But there was a sense among some people in that circle that gloomy, funny JD might be one of those ones to surprise you, might emerge from the darkness one day with a tortured literary masterpiece. The possibility flattered them: it would prove their discerning judgment in having me as a friend.

As you've gathered, it hasn't worked out that way.

The disappointed ones (we like to call them *shallow*), on not seeing my name in the *Times* within three years of graduation, succeeded in losing my phone number. A few have gone on to run the world as they always expected to—you see them setting the terms of the next cultural argument and writing books that show Astonishing Maturity and Insight. Krieger, as I've mentioned, is still a close friend. In fact, Krieger is the one who took me out for a drink several years ago and said straight to my face, "Leave the writing for now, JD. Do something simple. Get a job."

And he was right, that was the thing to do. I had gone around for a while telling everyone I was going to write and that I had something I was working on, and then it hit me belatedly one night when I happened to be drunk and following home some tough Waspy chick who worked in publishing—that here I was, a skinny, miserable, taller version of the wandering Joe. I even said something self-consciously asinine like, "Did I tell you I was working on a novel?"

She, being the hard-bitten type, said, "Oh. Is that why you want to fuck me?"

And it wasn't. I mean that desire had more to do with the fact that she looked great in her Levi's and had an elegant pale neck, and in some vampiric fantasy I'd had when I'd gone to the john in the bar earlier I'd imagined kissing or biting her neck while we were pressed together against her living room wall.

But because I was in a self-destructive phase, I said, "Yeah. As a matter of fact, I want to be honest with you. It is."

She had her wits together, though she'd drunk about as much as I had. She could hold it. It's one advantage of being a hundred percent Wasp: you can pull yourself together when you absolutely have to. She turned around and said, pushing her blonde hair behind her ears—it was her only nervous gesture— "Well, thanks for telling me. Maybe you should go home and jerk off over your manuscript, instead." She hailed a cab and left me.

That was the night I officially gave up writing. It was the night I realized, at home alone (there was no Minsk in my life then) and doing that absurdly melodramatic thing of staring at yourself in the mirror and talking to yourself, that the wandering fucking Joe was more in my veins than I would care to admit and that the only way to really get him out of my system, short of having my blood flushed—the way Keith Richards did when he was trying to get off heroin, so I read—would be to live some life that was crazily different from his, a life that looked regular and maybe even a little stiff-necked. That maybe I would find joy and fulfillment in that route, rather than in the squalor and humiliation that seemed otherwise likely to swallow me. Squalor is too romantic a word for it: *mess* is probably more accurate.

"You are not your father's keeper," I intoned to myself in the mirror that night in what I imagined to be a rabbinical voice. (Of course I've never had a rabbi. It's one of those items I've been meaning to get around to getting.) For a minute I think I honestly forgot that in the real quote it's brother. Naturally, I know next to nothing about the Bible either, having grown up in a kind of confused tipsy secularism. But as I said "You are not your father's keeper" to my stubbled, white, blurry face in the bathroom mirror—I gave my accent a heavy, Eastern European edge—I thought, And how very wise and apt that is. You know how those drunken revelations can be, especially mistaken drunken revelations that are based on having misremembered someone's name or gotten the quote wrong. Your dumb, sloshy brain sees its genius notion in a theatrical light, where it looks terribly dramatic, terribly *real*.

Yeah, I thought. It's not for me to worry about Joe. It's not for me to finish the fucking career he never did! Joe does his thing, and I do mine. I am not Joe's keeper.

Of course I didn't even know where the man was, at that time. Which is just as well. If I had, I would have been on the horn then and there, sharing my newfound biblical wisdom with him.

"Joe, man!" I would have told him. "There's something you should know. *I'm not your keeper!*"

As is the way with inebriated fantasies, I'm sure I imagined he'd be impressed but also wounded by this outburst. His son had seen and understood it all, and then moved beyond him. This would be painful for Joe. This would make him sit up straight. This would make him reflect, look back, reconsider. Had he been a good father? Had he been there for his son, ever?

I passed out in that floodlight of the bathroom and my revelation. My failed father stood over me in the dreams of my stupor, shaking his head and apologizing, dog-like, for everything he'd done wrong.

Sunday

These days the blood is too thin in my veins for me to drink with the determination I had then. That was an unusual time in my life, the post-college years, when I felt obliged to enact some of the scenes of excess and meaninglessness so popular in the fiction of the time. If I'd been on a corporate income I might have been doing lots of white drugs and going to nightclubs. As it was, I was living my own scaled-down version of same. Not with much panache, I might add. Mostly just going to bars with friends or dates and getting trashed enough to make bad judgments about my wit or my future.

Nowadays, in these truly grey days, I hardly drink at all. (If it leads to incidents like Marcie, frankly it's not worth it.) I am going back to my roots, the other ones. The situation in my family is so ethnically divided, it's ridiculous. The Lithuanian crew, Joe's tribe, who are stashed in various locations around this city and in Los Angeles, are mostly round, happy teetotallers whose pleasure consists in foodstuffs, not drink. Every now and then someone suggests wine with dinner to one of my aunts, and she'll raise her eyebrows in a loud silence, as if to announce that we've just gotten word that Beelzebub will be joining us for dinner if we wouldn't all mind making room for him.

Whereas Sally, my mother, is from sozzled Wasp stock. In her generation this no longer means three martinis before dinner, it's more like two bottles of wine with. She thinks that because she doesn't drink spirits it doesn't count. Spirits are for bad people, alcoholics. Wine is for nice people like us. She tends to keep a bottle or two of wine at her end of the table at dinnertime for her own private use, and she's often already put one away earlier in the day. Sometimes if you try to pour from one of her bottles, you can see a fierce battle going on within her: the hostess good manners that want to make sure everyone's provided for, and the MINE MINE MINE! of the greedy, childlike drinker.

Today she called me. My mother, that is. It is hard to predict when Sally will appear on the line from her home out on the Western seaboard. She lives within a mile and a half of Meryl Streep's house, something I think she'd like you to know. She's a great admirer of Meryl Streep. She loved that Alar testimony in Congress, don't know whether you caught it, toxic chemicals being sprayed on apples and Meryl was mad. My mother called me up specially to admire it.

Sometimes Sally keeps her own counsel for months at a time; I take it that's when she has a new boyfriend. She has had a series of boyfriends, often professors, the occasional realtor. None of them are as good-looking as my father or can kiss as well, she has the unfortunate habit of confessing when she's had a few too many, i.e. if she calls after five in the afternoon.

Today, though, she called me in the morning, always a good sign, and I have the weird impression that this is the third weekend in a row she's called, ostensibly to say hi and ask me about software. I think the real reason is that my sister has tipped her off that I've been in crisis. I don't know how Cindy picked this up, since I've tried to disguise it from her. Usually my sister isn't the world's most sensitive creature, but she is well-meaning, and in a well-meaning way she must have gossiped to Sally about her brother's self-destructive threats.

I was trying to do something very simple when my mother called. I was trying to make coffee in one of those geometrically shaped silvery coffeepot things. Italian. You know the ones. Lili, who has Good Taste—as she'll tell you herself—gave me one for my birthday last December because she thought it was pathetic and unseemly that I drink instant coffee. I did tell her that one of the joys of being in computers—Lili, have I mentioned?, is in music management, a sophisticated, alliterative career—is that you're under no compulsion to drink decent coffee, cook with olive oil of a high degree of virginity, or develop good muscle tone. I can drink, and have for years, instant. I find it so satisfying to watch those little granules turn into my favorite brown liquid. It's like some primitive magic. I used to feel the same way about Tang in my youth. I've never understood the thrill of coffee paraphernalia, unless it's leftover equipment envy from people who used to do drugs. To me the benefits of having coffee grounds everywhere—because you know they always spill over whatever surface you've just cleaned for them—for the sake of drinking marginally better coffee are far outweighed by the clean precision of the instant coffee technique. Clearly I am about ready to do a public service announcement on this subject.

I was just trying to figure out how high the burner should be so I didn't explode everything when the phone rang. Oops! No point in trying now. I'd have to make instant.

"JD? Is that you?"

My mother has a strange inability to recognize her children's voices on the phone. Cindy says she does it with her, too, though at least in that case there's some explanation since Cindy does live with another woman. I believe Sally knows that I live alone. I've certainly told her. She's never come out here to see for herself.

"Yeah. Hi."

"It's Mom."

"I know. Hi, Mom." She seems to think the problem is mutual. Somehow I recognize her every time.

"Listen, how are you?"

"Fine. Yourself?"

"Well, I'm not bad. Though, actually—I'm having that darn hip thing happening again."

"Did you fall?"

"No, dear, I've been keeping my balance well, you'll be happy to hear. Your ancient mother isn't so unstable as you think." When she's sober, it's always a laughable heresy to refer to the accidents she has when she's drunk. "No, and it's not arthritis, thank God. It's kind of a dull ache, right in my hip, you know, right in that joint there near the waist. What do you think it could be?"

"I don't know."

"Do you think it could be cancer?"

Minsk at this point gave an exaggerated sigh and went to take a nap on the couch. He doesn't have a lot of patience for the hypochondria that's endemic in our family.

"Cancer of the what? Hip cancer? Is there such a thing?"

"I thought you might know."

"I've no idea. I've never heard of it."

"But you know how all those bone cancer kinds of things, they always begin as little aches that no one takes seriously."

"If you're worried about it, you should get it checked out."

"I don't want to get it checked out. I hate that clinic, they make you wait and they don't know who you are and they talk at you as though you're already senile. I just want you to tell me it's not cancer."

"Well, I mean, it probably isn't. I've never heard of a kind of cancer that begins with an ache in the hip."

She sighed. I was useless, I know. "So how's the job search going? The new year should be a good time for things opening up."

I tried to fend off this line of questioning by muttering about résumés and phone calls and such. She asked me if I was getting out much. I explained that there wasn't a lot of appeal in the outer world when whenever you were out in it the wind ripped your face off. This led to minor talk about weather and some gloating at her end about how warm it had been there recently. Then, in the vague tone my mother adopts when she's about to tell you what to do, she said, "Maybe you should take a break from the city for a while. If it's so cold and miserable. Cindy said you were thinking of going down to visit her."

"She did?"

That was not true, as far as I knew, unless I was starting to have blackouts.

"Or maybe she said she was going to ask you down. I'm not sure. The point is she and I were both thinking it would be nice for you to get away. What I mean is—"

She realized she'd just blown her cover. You could hear her mind working —*you don't want him to think the women are plotting against him.*

So she tried to shift the subject back, but I beat her to it. I didn't care that much, in fact, that the women were plotting against me. Trying to keep me alive. It's a nice enough urge.

"I'll think about it," I said. "Listen, Mom, I do have one question to ask you, since you're on the line. It's going to sound strange, but it's important. OK?"

"Yes," she said, Momishly friendly, but you could hear the apprehension in her voice. She thought I was going to bring up her drinking.

"OK. This will sound strange. But I've been wondering—is there—was there—I mean, did you ever—"

"What? Did I what? Are you seeing a therapist or something now, JD?"

"No, no." I had to laugh. She's sharp as a tack, underneath all that paperwork. "I'm not wondering if you secretly tortured me with kitchen implements when I was an infant. No. What I was wondering is, did you—do I have a brother at all, somewhere, possibly? I mean, did you ever have another son besides me? Or did Dad? I mean, somewhere out there is there another, a half- . . . some-one . . ."

I trailed off into the long-distance silence. The line was full of nameless, airless quiet. It lasted for a minute, long enough to make my scalp itch, long enough for me to wonder if she'd had a heart attack at the other end of the line (we're hypochondriacs on each other's behalf, too). I thought she might have hung up, or maybe left the receiver in the living room and gone to get a drink, or out to the patio to take in some air.

"Mom?"

"Yeah, hi, I'm here." She sighed. "Are you sure you're not seeing a shrink?" There was a thin breeze, a faint laugh in her voice. She resumed her tone of vagueness.

"I really think you ought to think about getting away."

IT HAD BEEN HER ONLY TASK, TO FIGURE OUT WHERE TO GO AFTER THE FIRE.

Other people had complicated programs to get through: coping, claiming, recovering, rebuilding. They weren't going to leave their lives; they were going to remake them. Many had brought out the raw materials for a life before they'd fled. They'd had time to gather a small distillation of their past and future, whatever could fit into the back of a car. Photographs, insurance policies, computer disks, Bibles. A starter kit for the next phase of life. Like the bag they give you when you get out of prison—Here, take this little bit of your life back and the $24.29 you came in here with. Good luck! You're going to need it.

The steady if stifling obsession with insurance claims kept many people busy and quiet and alert. It was a relief to be able to throw yourself, in the wake of a disaster, at a great bureaucracy. There was no God, for a lot of these residents, to register a complaint with, so it was very satisfying to go through the same kind of pleading and appeasing with somebody closer than heaven, somebody here on the ground with an unromantic name like Prudential Life or Mutual of Omaha, who in the invisible fist of their computer bank held your fate and the financing of your future.

Pi was free of all that. Being uninsured had a stark simplicity that appealed to her philosophical mind. If you lost something, you lost something. That was it. It was gone. Of course material objects could be replaced—other objects could be found to fill the same function—and on that principle the denuded Berkeley crowds would eventually start running around town repurchasing stereos, computers, dishwashers, and televisions, in an ongoing effort to re-create their homes. But for Pi—even if she had been insured, even if she had been granted compensation money—the idea that she could restore what she'd lost would have been a fallacy. In fact, it would have harrowed her to have to spend hours writing lists of the books she'd lost in order to make her claim, as if a library were something as impersonal as a toaster oven. Pi's library had been something much closer to a friend: a character she had known and lived with since she first left home at seventeen. It was more than just the sum of its books. Though it revealed a suspect metaphysical dualism to say so, Pi had to admit to herself that it was the loss of the library's spirit that grieved her as deeply as the burning of each of its individual, physical volumes.

This consideration—what it was that defined her beloved library, beyond a simple string of its titles—reminded Pi of the "thought experiments" introductory philosophy classes were always posing in order to tease out your beliefs about matter or mind or the nature of identity. Were you a pure materialist or were you an idealist, or did you try to combine the two in some form of dualism? Where did you locate personal identity? Could you be trapped into confessing a view that mind was more than mere matter, that something ineffable moved beyond the firing of neurons? Related questions spilled out of those brain-in-a-vat problems: if your brain, with all your same thoughts and memories, were disconnected from your body and left floating in a vat, would you want to say that drifting brain was *you?* In which case, what would you call the body you'd left behind?

Pi's introduction to the pleasures of such problems was made forever memorable by the fact that at the same time she was first enjoying them—over coffee with friends or alone in her room—she simultaneously had a chilling example from her own life to test. It was her freshman year; Pi's mind had the life-widening hunger of the ambitious eighteen-year-old, which made her want to swallow philosophy problems whole. But there was one that she choked on. For this particular problem was embodied in Pi's own mother, who had a psychotic breakdown that spring. When Pi finally got away—reluctantly—to visit her mother in the hospital, she found the problem of identity staring her straight in the face.

Was this blank, wandering person still her mother? The notion stopped her heart. How could this be her mother when, separated from her reason, she stared at Pi shutter-eyed and from the whitewashed bed flatly denied having any idea who Pi was? She stared at Pi hard—her mad eyes clutching at something deep in Pi's own in a way that made Pi always suspect afterwards that her words were deliberate—and she said, succinctly: "No, no. You're not my daughter." Her thin lips were firm—her expression icily definite. "Believe me, I'd know you if you were. How could I forget her?" And from there followed a stream of terrible bitterness, a list of vivid disappointments in the small and dreadful person she had once given birth to—her real daughter, the one she remembered.

Pi never completely recovered from the shock of that denial. Doctors reassured, her stepfather sympathized, psychiatry books explained; but none of it helped, deeply. She returned to college significantly older than she had left it. The experience came to shape some of her basic philosophical views. *You are telling me that I don't exist.* After her mother stared straight at her and failed to recognize her, Pi felt the same lack of recognition, painfully, in response: *Then clearly you cannot be my mother.* Physically, the figure in front of her strongly resembled her mother—she had her bobbed blond-grey hair framing a weathered, delicate face; lips that looked very like the ones that used to confide in her with such life and warmth. But it just went to show that your sense perceptions could deceive you. This figure was an empty wrapping, and without the personality of her mother to inhabit it Pi had no belief in (let alone love for) the lying body. The disillusion helped hatch Pi's belief in the importance of the realm that existed beyond the material: for it was out there, outside this body in some unseeable place, that Pi knew her real, ideal mother must now be.

Eventually the doctors suggested shock treatment. Richard thought it worth trying, but he needed Pi's agreement to OK the decision. Pi, at a numb, furtive distance, agreed. The shock treatment worked. Her mother recovered.

And even years after the incident, when her mother had completely and cheerfully forgotten the terrors she'd issued from the hospital bed—the whole episode having been rinsed from her memory—Pi always felt she had lost her mother then, the one that mattered to her. The mother she still had was one she'd care for and respect, buy Christmas presents for, and telephone, but gone was the original one, the one who had cherished and raised her.

At least Pi had her library. It spoke to her and soothed her as she climbed into adulthood, in a way that stretched beyond the dimensions of the books themselves. With the eagerness of a precocious child, Pi poured into that book life all her own hope and intelligence. It became her oldest, best friend. How could such a creation ever be replaced? The library was gone now too—body and spirit—and Pi had no intention of chasing after its ghost.

Mendocino was a small place, easily crossed by curious feet. The heart of the town was a salty, gardened grid of no more than four streets criss-crossing five; its main street weighed lopsidedly along one edge of the grid, bordering the steep ragged cliffs that gave strolling shoppers their inspirational views. On a walk down Main Street, the Californian could have it all: on your left, the shocking blue of the blue Pacific, the beckoning sun of its wide horizon; on your right, a giddy range of pastel storefronts peddling earrings and chocolates, craft gifts and ethnic tokens. Along the way, there were places to stop for fine wine or strong coffee, the state's complementary specialties: the one for slowing you down, the other for quickening you.

Pi was using her hours of bookless time to learn the lay of this land.

Many of the town's buildings were a distinctive grey-mouse color—the storm-worn shade of long-dead redwood—and the streets were punctuated by the high, stilted dignity of several old water towers, the most visible landmarks in a town rigidly zoned against height and fast-food chains. Abbie had explained the logistics one night to Pi—what made Mendocino "such a special place," in her phrase, why it hadn't succumbed to the crass primary colors of other beachside resorts. It had taken determination and planning and a genuine fight to keep Mendocino pure, Abbie said. The place had worked hard to keep its character. And if that "character" seemed to Pi not so much bohemian ex–logging town as self-conscious Arts Community and Scenic Spot—surely taking Santa Fe, New Mexico, as its role model and rival—well, that was something Pi was just going to have to notice and shut up about. Abbie wasn't going to want to hear it.

So Pi ambled. There wasn't much else to do. She might as well learn how to see the place. Maybe she was missing something. Pi's eye was used to dreadlocks and shaved heads, streets clogged with dope paraphernalia and psychedelic candles and T-shirts bearing messages brash or inscrutable. Storefront after storefront advertising in yellow and blue the great university. She was used to a packed, multicultural consumer environment—Telegraph Avenue—still haunted by both the memories of its radical past and the realities of its tolerant vagrancy laws, which meant that every now and then she'd share the street with someone shouting *"Die yuppie scum!"* at her. That had happened one Berkeley morning before she was even awake, when she was heading to one of the various coffee shops for her privileged morning indulgence. A scrabble-headed, mis-clothed man walked behind her in angry, long strides, casting Pi in the role of wrecker of his world.

These Mendocino streets were altogether tidier and calmer. Such battles had no place on them. Mendocino spoke of mellow vacations and retreats from stressful jobs in the cities. The sandy sidewalks rustled with pockets full of disposable income; yellow cashmere and a serene, happy white of cloth and skin set the visual tone of most tourists, who on the whole were the quieter, richer kinds of Californians. Unlike Carmel or Santa Cruz, the place didn't seem to be a beacon to the non-natives. The whole town, Pi felt, glowed a Chardonnay color of self-content.

Elements caught her eye that seemed close to self-parody, but then the hippier places of California were always susceptible to such mockery, very much including Berkeley. It was a fine line to walk, as a native with a sense of irony: you didn't want to make so much fun of the place that you started to sound like some smug New Yorker. That was to be avoided. Pi collected a few phrases to store in her skeptical head, but she didn't plan to admit them to anybody. In the window of a store that sold bed linen and French crockery, potpourri, and quilt miniatures, a sign offered "Quilts—and so much more!" One shop sold "home accents, holiday treasures," and another, Pi's favorite, made the most optimistic promise: "A little magic—*a lot of style.*"

But smirking wore thin after a while. Pi wanted to find someplace she could take hold of, somewhere she could get a grip. Ordinarily, in a strange town the place she would go to regain her balance would have been the bookstore. And, in fact, one day early on she passed a high-ceilinged one that seemed full and friendly—nothing squeamish or apologetic about it. But Pi could not let herself go in. Not for books. Not yet. The idea, even just the idea of books, still made her skin crawl.

Pi found a storefront tucked away on Ukiah Street that seemed more interesting—mostly because its window was confused and had nothing woven or carved or airbrushed in it. The place was called Xander's Xerox, though its cluttered interior suggested more than just xeroxing. As Pi entered and her eyes adjusted to the pleasing dimness, she saw one wall flanked with comic books in their glistening insect colors of metallic green and beetle red; a table against another wall, on which yawned a computer's humming grey face and beside which a laser printer smoothly expelled freshly printed pages; and, in the back, a couple of well-used copiers, one of which was coughing up with a clattering noise a couple of sheets per second. Scattered around the room were a couple of card racks with *Far Side* items and random postcards. A sturdy counter bisected the room, where a cash register waited. In the corner, on a swivel chair facing away from the desk, sat a long-haired, sand-colored man poring over a comic book. Pi guessed that was Xander.

She stood waiting for him to look up, but he seemed completely absorbed. Finally she cleared her throat.

His eyes flickered up. "Hi," he said.

"Hi."

He waited for her to say something, but Pi couldn't figure out what to say.

"Do you need some help?" he asked finally.

"I don't know. What are you offering?"

"Xeroxing, greeting cards, comic books, stationery, desktop publishing, business card and ad design. Faxing." He looked at her more carefully. "Do you need any of those?"

"Not really." Pi was apologetic. "No, I don't. I don't know why I came in here—I was just curious. I'm new in town. Just moved here."

"For work?"

"No—just—I just moved in, with a friend and her kid."

"Oh."

Pi was peering at the machines behind the counter and, because she couldn't think what else to say, asked him: "I'm curious—does it bother you that you've called your store 'Xerox' when in fact it's Canons that you have there?"

"No." He sat up straighter. "If I was called Cameron or something, I would have used Canons in the store name—you know, 'Cameron's Canon.' But with Xander it just has a better ring to it. 'Xander's Xerox.' It's catchy. Wouldn't you say?"

"Yes, it is. It's catchy."

"Besides, one day Xerox is going to come up here and try to sue me for using their trademark anyway and then I'll have to change it. When that happens I'm going to go for another alliteration. Something completely irrelevant. I figure by then people will know the business and I'll be able to get away with it."

"What, like, 'Xander's Xylophones,' something like that?"

"Right. Or Xander's Xenophobes."

"Xander's Xenon."

"Xander's Zygotes."

"That's a Z, I think: Zygotes."

"Oh, you're right." But the game had cheered him up. "So who are you?"

"Pi."

" 'Pi'?"

"It's from my last name, Piper. My real name is Emily, but people call me Pi."

"Excellent! A name that can be typed as a single stroke of the keyboard." He looked pleased. "So, Pi as in Piper but no one calls you Emily: do you need a job?"

"A job?" Pi looked around the place, as if to discover where in the small room a job could possibly be hiding.

"It may not look like it, but business has really picked up lately. I've been getting a lot of design work. I'm doing the new logo for the art college, and word's spread up to Fort Bragg, so I have people coming down from there for my expert services. I need help running the store."

"That's great."

"Are you interested?"

"In a job? Well. Sure I am. But—I don't have a résumé or anything—"

"Give me a break. Can you work a cash register?"

"I'm sure I could learn."

"I'm sure you could." He stretched out a pale, friendly hand. "If you can spell 'zygote,' you can use a cash register. The one is just a short step away from the other."

Martha was sitting on Pi's narrow bed, making a cat's cradle with a piece of string. Pi had taught her how, after impressing herself with her own ability to remember it. Martha loved this new trick—she loved watching her clever fingers turn and twist to make the patterns appear in the string.

Pi was perched at the tool counter staring into the face of her computer, trying to install the modem software. Xander had been nice enough to lend her his disks. He told her to survive Mendocino she'd definitely need to get wired.

"Pi?" Martha asked over the whirr of the computer.

"Mmmm?"

"Where are all your things?"

"What things?"

"You know, your stuff. Where is it?"

"Well . . . It's not here." Pi didn't want to lie. "I didn't bring it with me."

"So where is it?"

"Can you hear the computer going?" Pi said brightly. "That's the machine loading it all up. We should be able to get it working pretty soon."

"Why didn't you bring any things with you?"

"Oh, Martha. Don't ask me. Your mom doesn't want me to talk about it. She doesn't want you to have to deal with my grief energy."

"What's grief energy?"

"I don't know, but you're not allowed to have any."

Pi clicked on OK and Continue and Proceed. The machine went through its hoops, performing its tasks. Martha's wide stubborn eyes were on her, and an odd rebellion persuaded Pi's mouth to open. How could it hurt to tell the girl just the bare facts? Pi told Martha in a few spare sentences: there had been a big fire where she lived, and she'd lost all her belongings—her things, her stuff—in the fire. That was all.

"But," she added, "don't tell your mother I told you about it. OK?"

"I won't." Martha's eyes glittered. Secrets were thrilling. "So what happened? Did you nearly get burned up?"

"I don't want to go into the details. That's it. That's all you need to know."

"No, tell me more! Tell me how it happened. Why didn't you get burned up?"

So Pi explained that she hadn't been home when the fire started; that, strictly speaking, she had not lost everything in the fire. At the time of the fire's beginning, elevenish on a Sunday morning, when a warm eerie wind blew across the hills, making people's skin shiver in an uneasy pessimism, Pi was in the Berkeley pool. She'd gone for a swim. She was doing smooth laps indoors while outside the sky became black and orange and the firestorm gathered and travelled and terrified. She noticed nothing when she got out dripping and headed for the changing room. She was probably in the shower washing chlorine out of her hair when the fire came into her apartment on La Vista, without even knocking, and hungrily ate all her books.

Pi didn't mention the terror or the firestorm. But she had already said enough that Martha understood it was not just Pi's house that had burned but many houses, that it was a big fire, a great one. She wanted to know—how big was it?

"Now, listen, that's enough. That's enough about the fire. Look! The computer's almost done."

"But where'd you go? Was there fire everywhere?"

"Martha, I'm serious now."

The girl sulked. Her face grew heavy and threatening.

"*Martha.*"

She wouldn't look up. Pi's fear of losing the fickle affection of the child returned. And they'd been doing so well lately . . .

"OK, look. If I tell you, I really mean it: I don't want you to tell your mother about it. Do you understand? Do you promise?"

"I *promise.*" The girl nearly jumped up in excitement. The smile returned to her little bird face, and her eyes were bright and lusty. Was *Schadenfreude* possible in a seven-year-old? "So where was the fire? Was it everywhere?"

"All right, all right. I'll tell you."

Sitting at the stool by the computer, Pi picked up the story from the point when she'd left the pool. And as she continued, the way it can go with disaster narration, Pi was suddenly there—she was back there in a way she hadn't been for months, because she'd been so busy fending off people's eager sympathy. Pi had an ash-dry explanation of what happened to her in the fire: it was more of a list, an accounting, and her voice didn't even quaver when she spoke it. This one, this voice that Martha had somehow coaxed out of Pi's throat, had a moisture in it that gave her story new life.

Pi had emerged from the gym into a town nervous now with the hot looming drama. She walked back to what would turn out to be everything she had left: her Honda, and strewn across its seats her hairbrush, a bottle of water, that day's newspaper, an apple; a few cassette tapes; and one book, Donald Davidson's *Essays on Actions and Events.* Pi had been intending to read it over coffee after her swim. Major caffeine was always necessary to make sense of Davidson.

But by the time Pi was tossing her gear into the back of the car it was clear from the sky's obscurity that things were going wrong. She was in a hurry to get home to see what was happening. And she was not the only one. When she drove over to the Elmwood neighborhood, cars clogged the streets; the roads above them were blocked to incoming traffic. People were being evacuated. Cars streamed down the hills while others, including Pi, parked and watched and waited for news. There was no way for her to get home. Pi stood on a street corner with gawkers and refugees for about an hour as the air grew grey and bitter and helicopters began to fly overhead like warplanes, depositing fire-killing chemicals over the untamed enemy. Punctuating the thick clouds were dim explosions like the eruptions of landmines—the sounds of fire hitting gaslines, also of the old immigrant eucalyptus trees going abruptly up in flames. Pi had the strange feeling of being on a film set, *Apocalypse Now,* or another Vietnam movie. She half expected movie stars to climb out of the haze, or at the very least for some important newscaster to come and interview her. Instead she watched, numb, surrounded by shock and chatter and the occasional flare of a radio. And then, suddenly, it seemed as if in one particular gust of heat she felt what was happening to her. The hairs on the back of her neck rose. Her tongue was thick in her mouth. Her eyes hurt. She couldn't watch any more of the slow suffocation of the hills she had lived in; she had to turn away from what was beginning to look like an ending to a long part of her life. She gathered her everything, and she left.

Pi paused for breath.

"But where did you go? What did you do?"

"I went to these friends' house, Mike and Debbie's, in Oakland. That was the first place I went. They didn't even have to ask me why I was there. They knew. They already had two other people there like me, people who couldn't get to their home."

"But how'd you know the fire wouldn't get you there?"

"It wasn't spreading down that way. It was like—the way the winds were, and the way firefighters work—pretty soon they just fix certain edges and decide the fire's got to stay *there*, within those edges, it's like a border of a country or something. So the fire knows, kind of, that it can have everything in those borders, but nothing outside it."

"But what about the people left inside?"

"There weren't any. That's what it means to *evacuate*. You get everybody out." The child certainly didn't need to know about the deaths.

Martha thought about this for a while, her hands working on the string.

"How long did it take them to put it out?"

"The fire was under control by the next morning. I think it was mostly under control that night, but I was trying to sleep. Though it was hard to because the other people at Mike and Debbie's kept talking about everything in their house, making these long lists of what they had probably lost—the wedding crystal, all that scuba gear, their college scrapbooks. It was driving me crazy, the way they kept listing everything. Anyway, it turned out in the morning that they hadn't lost a shred. They called their home first thing and got through to their answering machine, so see they knew their home must be OK."

Martha didn't say anything.

"Then when I tried the same thing, my line was dead. So I didn't know for sure, but there was a good chance my place hadn't made it. It was hard for Mike and Debbie. They didn't know what to do. Two people were celebrating, and one, me—I probably looked like I'd just been hit by a truck."

Pi stopped there. When she broke away from the vividness of that morning's stifled, uneasy Oakland living room, she found the wide worried eyes of a young child—looking suspiciously as though they might start to leak.

"Hey now. Hey now," Pi said awkwardly. Martha suddenly looked tiny and bereft. Pi panicked. What had she done?

She made a hesitant move over to the bed, where she sat down next to Martha. Tentatively, she put an arm around her. Wasn't this what nice grown-ups did in the movies, to comfort kids?

"Hey now." She looked for the right words. "Listen. You don't need to worry about it. I'm OK, right? See? I got here all right. Everything's OK now."

"But—*what if that happened to us?*"

"Oh no! It won't. It won't happen to you. There's no way."

"How do you know?"

"Well . . ." Pi held the girl tighter. She felt the young body in her arms, the thin heat of her fear. In feeling it, Pi experienced a strange, abrupt desire: a desire to keep this child from harm.

"I'll tell you how I know. Going through a fire gives you a special knowledge, kind of a second sight. And one thing that I know for *sure*—is that your home is safe. I know it."

Martha didn't say anything to that, and Pi didn't want to peer around to look at her face. She just kept holding on to her, and hoped the small girl would believe her.

At first Pi had gypsied around San Francisco, sampling different households. She stayed with college pals Renée and Jen; Ryan, who had once been her neighbor; and Mrs. Lerner, her old piano teacher, who lived with her husband in the Sunset District. Lastly, at the end of her tether, she'd gone to Fran's.

When Pi left Oakland the Monday after the fire, she hoped she might some-how wait a few days before having her gruesome fears confirmed. She wanted to pretend she was on vacation somewhere far away and the news couldn't be gotten through to her that her life had irrevocably changed. She wanted to dive underground, to hide, not to be told or reminded or made to accept. None of her friends understood this. How could you not want to see the wreckage for yourself, to understand that it was real?

"There's a technical term for what you're doing," Fran told Pi on the phone when she heard that Pi was avoiding Berkeley. "It's called 'postponing the in-evitable.' "

"If it's inevitable," Pi countered, "what's wrong with postponing it?"

Renée and Jen, her first hosts, told Pi her landlords, the Dixons, were probably desperate to contact her and let her know what was going on, not to mention find out what had happened to her. She couldn't just hide from them. Besides, didn't she want to make sure that they were all right?

Renée and Jen wore her down. They were both lawyers; they made their living wearing people down. Late Tuesday night Pi agreed to leave their telephone number at the history department where Jay Dixon taught. Wednesday morning, shortly after the women trundled off in crisp silk shirts to work, Pi was alone in spare high-tech lesbian domesticity with Martina, their neurotic spaniel. Pi was staring at Alcatraz floating on the cool wet bay when the telephone rang. The sound blistered her ears.

"Thank God I reached you," Jay Dixon said. His voice was dry. "We've been trying to figure out where you were. No one seemed to know. Mary was getting frantic, imagining terrible things."

Pi couldn't speak. Jay's tone seemed oddly optimistic—hearty, almost. Pi had a clear moment of certainty that her fears had been absurd. She had never been superstitious before and she shouldn't have been now. Everything was all right. Their two homes were still there, Zeno was unscathed, Kant and Kafka still nodded at each other from across the room.

"Oh, Pi." A sigh heaved itself across the bay, by phone. "Everything's gone. I'm sorry to tell you. We barely got out ourselves."

"OK. Sure. Yes—"

"We don't know what happened to the cat, either. I'm sorry, Pi. We tried to get him—we were pounding on the door of your apartment. Mary was worried that maybe you were asleep in there, until we realized your car was gone. This was all in about fifteen minutes: we'd gone from peering out the kitchen window calmly at the smoke in the distance to seeing the flames hit our side of the canyon and it was crazy, you know, everyone suddenly started packing up and getting away—so Mary tried to get your cat and I was throwing stuff in the car and then Bill Wood came up the street and just yelled to us, to anyone else left, 'Forget your cars, we're blocked in! Get out! Get out!' So finally, I mean Pi it was crazy, you know, half an hour before we were eating bagels and reading the *Times* and suddenly we were literally running for our *lives*."

He took a breath. He'd already told this story fifty times, Pi could tell. It was like the '89 earthquake. Everyone had had a story, including Pi. *I was standing there teaching a section about Hume and then I watched the Campanile sway back and forth and a wave in the ground ripple right towards us all in Dwinelle Hall. We didn't even have time to get under the desks.*

"I'm sorry," Jay said again. He seemed to be hoping Pi would speak. "Jesus. It's strange. I feel somehow responsible for it, like we should have *known*. Or we should have been able to stop it. We haven't slept. Every time you try to sleep, you see all the images over and over in your mind. We've been staying with friends in Albany. Where are you?"

"San Francisco."

"Right. And—was your stuff insured?"

"No."

"Oh. God." What could he say? "That's—that's a shame. That's—"

"Listen, thanks a lot for calling, Jay. Really. I'm still in shock, too. I guess everyone is." Pi turned away from the view of Alcatraz, turned her face to the wall. She didn't want to be faced with a horizon. "I figured this was what had happened. I watched the fire from Elmwood for a while. I looked out to see if I could see you or Mary coming down. But the whole area, everything around La Vista, was black. You could hardly see it. So I figured . . . Anyway, I'm glad you two are safe. That's the main thing. It's too bad about Zeno . . ."

Her calm broke. Tears wavered her voice.

"Yeah. Listen. About that—let me give you a phone number."

Jay always was a helpful guy. He was in his element coming in to help you wire your stereo right or fix a leak in the bathroom faucet. He'd just set up the timer on the VCR for Pi, about a week before the fire.

"OK, here it is. It's the number for lost and found pets in Oakland. They've got a special warehouse set up somewhere because this happened to a lot of people, their pets ran away before they could catch them. Have you got a pen? Here it is."

Pi took the number and also the number of the Dixons' friends in Albany. "Mary really wants to talk to you. She'll be so glad to hear you're OK. We were *worried*. You don't know what's happened to people. There's no way to find out. It's crazy. It's like a bomb dropped."

Pi thanked him and hung up. She spent the rest of the day watching movies from Renée and Jen's video collection while the dog tore newspapers into slobbery shreds. Pi watched *The Hunger, Manhattan, Julia*. A random selection. When Vanessa Redgrave wept to show Jane Fonda her amputated leg in *Julia*, Pi looked on dispassionately, thinking vaguely about the phenomenon of phantom limbs, which appeared with morbid regularity in philosophy discussions. Something to do with misleading sense perceptions—Pi couldn't quite get her brain to make the connection.

Periodically, Jay's words returned to her. It seemed true from the TV footage she couldn't help watching: it did look like a bomb had dropped. And Pi thought of green-eyed black-and-white Zeno, five years old, as old as her graduate study and as serious. Zeno had watched her all those hours she'd read difficult words, he'd warmed the stack of papers on her desk and kept her toes company at night and in the darkness seen shadows her human eyes could not read. She valued him for that. Pi wondered if this creature were in an Oakland warehouse now, calling her name. She should look for him. But in the corner of her eyes she saw the silver changes of the bay, and it seemed to her an unbridgeable ocean. She tried and failed to imagine herself having the heart or nerve ever to cross it again, to make her way back to the other side.

During those weeks of cloud and ash and post-tragedy analysis in the media, Pi still felt a little normal. Just a little. She was still eating. People fed her good meals; Ryan made a lobster ravioli with tarragon that kept her mouth soothed for days. People gave her things so she wouldn't feel empty-handed. Jen brought back jeans, socks, and a stack of plain T-shirts for her one night. Pi was glad the T-shirts were wordless, unlike all the ones she'd lost that bore letters from earlier places in her life (Boston, New Mexico, Santa Cruz . . .). Mrs. Lerner's husband, Sol, a writer, gave Pi his old computer. Just gave it to her, wouldn't accept any payment. He'd just sold the rights to his latest novel to someone in Hollywood "for a pornographic amount of money," and it would assuage his conscience, he said, if Pi accepted the gift.

Pi felt calm enough in that period to do a few dutiful things. Like calling around, the way you do after a death, to tell people the news you want to make sure they've heard. Of course, Pi's address book was gone so she could only call people whose numbers were stored in her strangely prodigious memory. She urged everyone she spoke to to pass on the information to anyone else they thought might be interested. *Pi's fine. But she lost everything.*

"So what are you going to do? Look for another place in Berkeley?"

This was her old roommate Hannah on the phone from Texas. Hannah had turned political since college and now did worthy, discouraging work in El Paso at a legal aid center that tried to explain to new immigrants their rights—which were dwindling with each mean new electoral year.

"No. Not Berkeley," Pi said. "I'm not sure where."

"What about school? Are you still teaching?"

"I'm going to take some time off."

"That's probably a good idea. Listen—if you need anything, Pi. Do you want to come out here for a while?"

"I don't think so. Thanks though."

"Well. Let me know. Maybe you should go down to L.A., see Lucy and the brood. You know the second one has learned to say *car* or something. That's the big news. I guess in L.A. that's a good word to start with."

It was like a death, the way people mumbled and changed the subject and you were relieved when they did since there wasn't much else to be said at your end, after all. There were offers of cakes and living rooms, suggestions of trips to ridiculous places like Thailand or Florida, fake optimism whipped up to hint that there was some hidden benefit to the catastrophe. Pi felt she was expected to say what so many people in Berkeley apparently were saying: "You know, something incredibly beautiful has come out of all this. I feel closer to my neighbors. My sense of community has been restored. I've been reminded of the transience of material objects and of what is truly important in life—love, friendship, joy in new beginnings." Pi couldn't honestly say any of this. She believed in nothing; she felt far away from everyone. Again as with a death you found yourself comforting the people who ostensibly were trying to comfort you. They were frightened because the news made them feel closer to disaster themselves. They needed to hear that you were OK, that it hadn't ruined your life; that you were able to go on.

But sometimes Pi became tired of being the human face of the Oakland fire for friends and acquaintances, and she longed to speak to other people who'd gone through it too. She knew there was a multiplicity of support groups out there, grief networks and interfaith healing circles and the like. It was Berkeley, after all. Like a reluctant alcoholic tempted to dip his toe into the icy waters of AA, Pi considered sidling along anonymously to try one of these groups. See if it helped. See if it was butter on the burn. But she couldn't do it. She couldn't bring herself to cross that bay. Not even for a support group—and not even for the university, which expected her.

It wasn't like Pi to let them down. She had a reputation for reliability in the department. So everyone, not just her friends Rob and Tamar but even the floating geniuses, expected Pi to come back.

She might have if the place had seemed real to her. It wasn't that Pi had lost her conscience. Nor was it that strange sense of shame that sometimes afflicts the afflicted. It was, appropriately, more of a metaphysical problem: Pi had lost her belief in the university's existence. Everything about UC Berkeley—its silver square buildings, its learned cement, its redwoods, what Rob called the "babbling brooks" of its bucolic campus—had become a fairy tale to Pi, a fiction that had ended dramatically, the way fairy tales do, with a dragon breathing a firestorm across the pretty picture and devouring its meaning.

The hopeful last-century men who'd founded this university—the "Athens of the Pacific," as they dreamed of it—had chosen to name their new institution after the British philosopher Bishop George Berkeley. It was a fact that delighted Pi, who had, as Rob said, "always had a lot of time for" Berkeley. The Bishop had been mocked once, which roused Pi's sympathy: Samuel Johnson had famously claimed to disprove Berkeley's theory—that things exist only insofar as they are perceived—by the simple act of kicking at a stone with his foot. But also Pi loved the idealistic philosophy that had earned poor Berkeley this simplistic scorn. His idea had a magic-trick appeal to it. If you cease looking at the chair, it ceases to exist, unless someone else is on hand to perceive it. Being perceived gives the world life. Luckily, to rationalize the order of things and make sure that chairs don't disappear the minute you turn your back on them, you've got God all-perceiving all the time. God keeps everything in order—organized, present, and correct.

On this model, God must have stopped looking over in this direction, to allow everything to have disappeared so fast. Pi was fairly certain she didn't believe in God—or in Berkeley's idealism, for that matter—but she wished that she did, because it made such sense of the situation. Not just her own loss but the loss of the whole place, including the venerable Athens of the Pacific itself. God had simply turned his back on the entire geography and—poof!—it was gone. Not a single stone left for Samuel Johnson, or any other skeptic, to kick.

She didn't actually tell anyone these ideas. By gypsying, Pi could avoid explaining her new cosmology of the gone university. The people Pi stayed with in San Francisco simply assumed Pi had explained to friends and faculty what had happened and made her movements known to them.

In reality she hadn't. No one knew where she was. Rob must have done some detective work to find the number of Pi's mother in San Diego. He left a message there with Pi's stepfather that he and others wanted to find out how Pi was doing. He, Rob, was handling the section Pi had been teaching, and Tamar was running their dissertation group for the next month. People in the department were being uncharacteristically nice about her predicament. Pi should see it. Offers of help for her were pouring in. Rob was organizing the campaign and taking only a small cut, as was his due . . .

Pi could hear the Philadelphia twang of Rob's voice in her mind when Richard faithfully relayed the message to her. Internally, at her mind's desk, she sat down and wrote Rob a free and full letter telling him how she felt, thanking him, telling him she was going to go away for a while to figure things out. To come up with a (small p) philosophy for how to manage after the fire, with her thoughts and books and writings all ash.

If she'd had an actual, perceivable desk, she might have done it. As it was, Pi didn't get in touch with Rob at all. He was left without a trace, though he learned from Richard that Pi was physically all right and was somewhere in San Francisco. Rob was left to wonder in turn if Pi had ever really existed—or whether she had been collectively hallucinated by a department eager to produce a smart female metaphysician.

The only place the university continued to exist, for Pi, was in her dreams. There were times at night when, through the chemicals and charcoal smoke and bright lights the fire had traced against the lids of her memory, Pi saw the university looming up like the great stern of a ship in a storm. There it sailed still, with its Nobel Prize winners and its multicultural politics, its greying paunchy professors and its fitter, younger faculty who looked like models for jeans ads.

Yet in her dreams the place had become ancient. European, even. It was an old, old place. Pi had lived in Europe for a couple of years as a child—a difficult, itinerant spell when her freshly divorced mother was trying to make it as a painter—and the place haunted her still with its ageing walled faces of ruin and condescension. Sometimes Europe was beautiful and sometimes it mocked her again for being American. In these dreams of Berkeley, Pi was most emphatically an American and it, the university, had become a noble old European village. Italian, probably. The buildings took on that warm Mediterranean ochre, the roofs sensibly turned to brick-colored fireproof tile, and the Campanile struck a solemn tune for Catholic sensibilities. In this old village of Berkeley lived a quiet, humble people who were weavers and potters and shepherds and wives. People who lived close to the land. Who harvested carefully; who took care of their resources. They made a sweet, robust wine in the hills around this village, and once a week they gathered to drink it, growing drunk and cheerful on a moony long night, singing songs that had existed for centuries before she was born. Together the people of the village slept late into the clear light of the following morning. They woke confident of the approaching seasons, knowing that the sun would remain a blessing and the clouds a comfort and that the rains would come, every year, to keep their land moist and green and unfriendly to the hellfire that lurked in angry heavens.

They lived quietly now, Pi's mother and stepfather. Pi didn't see them very often. Everyone got along fine when she did, but they got along even better when she didn't. From time to time Richard promised Pi—in a low, embarrassed tone as if the problem were really Pi's and not theirs—that her mother was fine now. Fully recovered. Pi had no need to worry.

Her mother seemed recovered. She had had years to rebuild an ordinary coping self, and she'd succeeded. To do it she had edited out distractions from her earlier life. She was no longer the kind of person who would adventure husbandless to Europe; she no longer threw open-ended parties for blue-jeaned, long-scarved people; she would, Pi guessed, no longer call herself a feminist. Since the breakdown she had downgraded her painting from what had once been—Pi remembered the tearful confession—"the only thing that gives my life meaning," to a modest sideline on a par with tennis or gardening—"something I enjoy doing." She wore clothes in hushed colors. Her hair was tidy and consistently blonder than Pi's. She often wore a sunhat to protect herself from the San Diego sun and sunglasses so that her eyes did not have to be responsible for sliding away or turning reclusive.

Not that she wasn't involved with the world. She told Pi about volunteering at a local charity that helped the homeless—not directly, but by raising money at theatrical fundraisers. And Pi's mother had, belatedly, developed a wifely interest in the politics and personalities of Richard's department. She seemed to enjoy gossiping to Pi about them on the phone. Richard liked San Diego so much better than Stanford, she told Pi. The people were more genuine. Not so snobbish. San Diego suited them both: sunny all the time, clean, colorful, friendly. It rained just two or three days a year.

"Every time we see a piece in a magazine about how great San Diego is, we just shudder. Our great dread, Emily, is that other people will move here and ruin it."

Her mother was now the only person besides academics at conferences who used Pi's given name. When Pi was a child, her mother had called her Emster, Femily, Empkin, Emmie. Since college and the arrival of the nickname, even Richard had taken to calling her Pi. "Emily" unnerved Pi now and heightened her sense that this woman on the phone was not someone she knew well but some later, necessary acquaintance.

Pi couldn't face calling them. She knew she ought to. They would have seen the news of the fire on TV and would be worried, of course they would be. They'd be trying to call her. Pi just wished there were a way of telling them other than by telephone—something voiceless, less personal, that would get the news across without going into the emotion of it. She was tempted to send a telegram: AM ALL RIGHT. LOST EVERYTHING INCLUDING CAT AND DISS. WILL CALL WHEN I HAVE NEW NUMBER. DON'T WORRY. Or she could have embarked on an elaborate deception, keeping the whole catastrophe a secret from them, claiming her apartment had been saved. She could have lived a parallel, reassuring life for years afterwards in her parents' minds—a life in which she completed her dissertation, received her doctorate, and was awarded a fine job at an upstanding institution far away, lecturing young people on the perennial problem of the existence of chairs.

Pi never had the chance to try this fiction on them. They found her first. Wednesday morning, about an hour after Pi spoke with Jay Dixon, the phone rang in Renée and Jen's living room, and after a brief hesitation she answered it.

"Pi! My God. Are you all right?" The voice was curt and pained.

"Richard, hi."

"We've been *so* worried. Why didn't you call us? We just reached Jay and he gave us this number."

"I'm sorry. I'm sorry. I just—I needed a few days for it to sink in. I'm—"

"Where are you?"

"I'm staying with friends in San Francisco."

"Are you OK?"

"I'm fine. I mean, I'm OK. Physically everything's fine—I was down on campus when it happened."

"Emily, honey? Are you really all right? Who's taking care of you?"

Pi's mother's voice joined in, a warm maternal character from a different era. The steadiness of her mother's voice drew out Pi's own grief, brought it up, with the urge of anti-gravity, to the surface. This was why she hadn't wanted to talk to them. She wanted to keep the grief *down*, submerged. For a minute she wished the old, nutty Mom the painter would come back. The painter would have said something eccentric that might have kept Pi company in her new surrealism. *Well, honey, you must feel a lot lighter now! It's a Zen state, think of it that way.*

"I'm staying with my friends Jen and Renée. They're being very good to me."

"How bad was the damage? Do you know yet? Have they let you go back?"

"Oh." Pi cleared her throat. "I thought Jay told you. I lost everything."

"Oh *honey.*"

"Are you sure? Everything? Have you gone back?"

"Yes, I'm sure. It's gone. Everything's gone."

There was a gasp and a gap, awkward.

"Listen, sweetheart. Do you want to come down here for a while? It's lovely right now, warm . . . There's room for you. You can stay in Richard's study, and just relax. Right?"

"Absolutely. Of course. Pi—come whenever you want. Come tomorrow."

Pi, polite, refused the offer. She told them she'd call in a few days to let them know where she was. To appease them she said she was thinking of staying with the Lerners, old family friends from Bay Area days.

"Oh, that's perfect," her mother said. "What a good idea. Irene will love to have you there. You can stay in Josh's old room. Has his wife had the baby yet?"

They talked in this way for a little longer about rooms and vacancies, other local friends. Richard had to be discouraged from immediately calling his old Stanford colleague Phil Lennox, who would want to help out however he could. Richard himself was safely in physics, but Phil bridged the gap, teaching physics and some philosophy, and Pi had to refuse assistance from any philosophical direction. Her stepfather then relayed to Pi Rob's friendly, worried message, which she absorbed in silence. He started to ask Pi about the philosophy department, but she let his sentence flounder, airless. He was wise enough not to pursue it.

Her mother, who'd been quiet for a minute, chose that moment to pipe up.

"It's so strange, isn't it, to think about what it means." Her voice was high and drifting. "Here I am, working to help the homeless, and yet you don't always realize what it means. And suddenly here's my own daughter made homeless. It's strange, isn't it?"

"Well, that's not necessarily the way Pi might want to—"

"Actually, Mom, I'd better get off the phone—I have to take their dog out."

"I know. We'll let you go. It was just making me think, that's all."

"Listen, Pi. Are you sure you don't want one of us to come up there?"

"No, thanks. Really. There's not much to help me with, you know. It's just—"

"Honey, *call* us wherever you go next. Keep us posted on your movements. And—I'm so sorry. I'm so sorry, honey."

"Thanks. I will. I'll call you."

"I'll tell you one thing they always say about these situations, Emmie." Her mother became kind and counselorish. She wanted to leave her with something helpful.

"What's that?"

"They say that maintaining your dignity is important."

Richard, who underneath his thinning red hair was sensitive and quiet with it, sent Pi a check for two thousand dollars. Included was a short note:

> I hope this helps tide you over for a while. Your mother and I are thinking of you. Let us know if there's anything else we can do.
>
> —R.

Pi folded the check and kept it in her back pocket, wondering when and where she was going to deposit it. She didn't want it in her Berkeley account. In fact, Pi decided early on to close that account. By phone. They wanted her to come in and do it in person, but she said she had been badly injured in the fire and was calling from the Alta Bates Burn Unit. That shut them up. They agreed to wire the remaining cash directly into her credit card account. The sums were not vast enough to raise suspicions.

By mid-November, when Pi was moving over to stay with Fran, the folded check from Richard had worn into a smooth curve the shape of her buttock. A bundle of cash, various people's offerings, sat at the bottom of her toiletries bag smelling of smeared toothpaste and a sweet coy body spray. Like everything else she owned now except the car and that one Sunday set of clothes—jeans, tank top, cream-colored denim jacket, tennis shoes—the body spray was new. Pi didn't recognize the smell of herself when she wore it.

Pi began to gather her resources. She knew she'd be leaving soon. Her spirit would shatter if she didn't. San Francisco, it turned out, wasn't far enough away. Initially, she had stayed calm: shocked, heart-stopped, numb; but calm. Now the calm was leaking out of her, a slow puncture, and if she didn't move soon to a new quantity of air, she would be left flat and lifeless like an old tyre. Pi had to go. Fran, the last stop on her itinerary, had to help her figure out where.

Pi had known Fran since they were fifteen. They had gotten high together, they'd cut school, they'd drunk fiercely strong coffee at the highbrow bookstore or else sat by Fran's tiny back-yard pool talking about boys and sipping martinis Fran made in a cocktail shaker she picked up for a quarter at the Salvation Army. With other high-school renegades—at a school where most kids were either jocks or wore cowboy boots and listened to country music—Pi and Fran had driven up on weekends to San Francisco to hear punk bands. Fran's hair was leopard-spotted then; she sang covers of ska songs in an all-girl band called the Second Sex. Fran had been getting into Simone de Beauvoir at the time. She had always been precocious. She and Pi were precocious together, taking a philosophy class at the local community college in their senior year, when they were bored with their high-school classes and thought it would be fun to sit around the quad discussing *The Republic*.

Now Fran divided her time between working at a drug rehab clinic, getting an M.A. in classics, and windsurfing or rollerblading, depending on the season. She'd made the transition from punk to punk jock. Her apartment was filled with the subversive colors of her surf and skate gear—pumpkin orange, nuclear green, acid blue—that weirdly comforted Pi by inducing in her a painless futuristic frame of mind. Just now Fran was still smarting over a boyfriend who'd left her. She sizzled with fury as she stood in the kitchen at night cooking too-hot Thai curries for her and Pi that were edible only when washed down with lots of cold cheap beer. She was going to write a novel about him, she told Pi. *Death Comes for the Arch Sexist.*

Fran had always been a clear thinker. Even high. Even drunk. Even on quaaludes. When she sat down and applied herself to the question of Pi's future, she got straight to the point.

"OK. First of all. What are your responsibilities now, if any? Like, where's Zeno?"

"Didn't I tell you? Zeno was lost in the fire, too."

"Lost how? Killed, or lost?"

"Well—we don't know."

" 'We' who?"

" 'We' the Dixons. I wasn't there. The Dixons were there. They couldn't get him out."

"So you don't know if he was actually killed or not? Did you go back to look?"

"No—I told you. I haven't been able to go back over there since."

"But, Pi." Fran frowned. "What about Zeno? Come on. You can't leave until you've checked whether he made it. Maybe someone found him. You've got to at least *look.*"

"But that would mean going over there."

"Well, I'm sorry, but that's what we're going to have to do."

"Fran. You don't understand—I can't."

Fran picked up her purse and keys. She got a Coke out of the fridge. It was six-fifteen. She'd been home less than half an hour. But tonight was the night they'd designated to solve Pi's future, and she was onto it.

"You don't understand—"

"Of course you can." She pulled Pi's arm. She'd known her too long to care whether she hurt her a little. She had never been a wildly patient person. "Come on. We're going."

Pi liked the nights here. She liked the breathing of the ocean; she hadn't known the sound before, not to live near, not the smell and steadiness of it. It cooled her mind.

She heard a sound on the stairs and assumed it was Abbie. Pi's toolroom was downstairs near the kitchen. Abbie had been having insomnia-long nights of late and might be coming down to warm up some milk for herself.

But it was Pi's door that swung open. A pale uneasy face stood at her door.

Pi sat up, alarmed. She waited for Martha to speak, to make sure the girl wasn't sleepwalking.

Martha came in and sat on the bed looking mournful, before she finally admitted to the question that had been keeping her awake.

She wanted to know what had happened to the animals.

Had they burned? Who had saved them?

Oh, Pi said. She had worried this poor child so. She had to make it all seem less worrying. Even now, even in the middle of the night. (Especially in the middle of the night.) She patted the bed so Martha sat close, where Pi could speak to her in a whisper.

Lots of the animals had managed to run away, she said. Animals are fast when they're scared, like people are. The birds flew up and over the flames. The beasts that could go underground, tunnelled. The dogs ran. The cats ran, too, or hitched rides with people taking their cars downhill.

Many, many animals were saved. A whole great warehouse opened in Oakland to store them all until people could come and claim them. It was a huge place—like an old gymnasium. Inside it there was raucous animal noise echoing all the way up to the ceiling. Even a month after the fire, when Pi finally went there, the barks and caws and meows clamored the air.

There were many reunions, Pi told her. You read about them in the papers: a woman united with her precious Madagascar finches; a cat who'd had kittens in the animal shelter so when her owners found her there were six more of her than there had been before; a long-haired Afghan whose face was singed but who managed to make it through all right. Pi had gone over there with Fran, and together they'd seen one of these emotional meetings themselves. They watched a couple with two girls about Martha's age going into the shelter, looking so sad and worried. (Fran and Pi had been sitting in the truck: Fran was persuading Pi that she had to get out. Pi, lockjawed and nauseated after having had to face the blind, blackened hills of that once-loved landscape, was trying to refuse.)

And when they came back *out*! It was something to see. Fifteen minutes after they'd gone in, the same family returned, but this time smiles and excitement jumped over their faces; they left the building backlit by a goldenness from inside. (It was pure Hollywood, and Fran and Pi were embarrassed by how susceptible they were to it. Tears choked their eyes.) And all around their feet, twisting himself on the leash held in the dad's strong hand, a tiny brown thrill of disbelief—their little dachshund. They'd found him, waiting for them, in the shelter.

Martha smiled at this story. It made her happy. But what had Pi been doing there that day? Was she looking for someone?

Well. Not all the animals made it to the shelter. Some of them might have found their way into other homes. Some of them might just have run away. Pi had been looking for her cat, Zeno. A black-and-white cat. She'd gone with Fran just to check, just to see if Zeno was there. But he wasn't. A lot of other animals were there and had been saved. But not Zeno.

"But poor Zeno!" said Martha.

"I know." The darkness and the ocean swelled. Pi made her voice light. "Zeno was a good cat. You would have liked him. But you know, we don't know for sure. Maybe he found some other people to take care of him. He might have. He was smart. He might just have found himself another home."

She and Martha looked at each other in the scarce light: two human faces thinking about the death of cats.

"You better go back to bed," Pi said. "But before you go, we can play one game on the computer. It's working now. Do you want to?"

Martha nodded, and they both went to sit on the work stools at the tool counter, turning the machine on to cast its eerie blue light into their night.

Pi thought of that evening with Fran. She remembered the taste of ash on her tongue from Oakland's lifeless grey air. She remembered her lack of surprise at not seeing Zeno among the remaining tabbies, calicos, Siamese. She'd known he was gone. Then, in an effort to distract Pi, Fran had relayed her new, brilliant idea: that Pi could go up to live with her just-divorcing aunt and her kid, who had recently moved up to Mendocino. Her aunt, Abbie, was making a great life change, too. They would be well suited. Her aunt—out of pity, maybe, or out of the need for child care—would be happy to take Pi in. Fran was sure it would work.

Fran was a good friend. She was trying to help Pi. When it was clear that they weren't going to find Zeno, Fran made a move to hug Pi. At least put an arm around her shoulders. But Pi had pulled away from her. Not in anger; in shame. She felt apart from everyone else. She could not be touched. For reasons Pi had no words for she could not accept the kisses or caresses of the people around her, who wanted to draw her back into her life. The hopes of her body had burned right out of her on that recent Sunday, along with all the materials that had given that body challenge and comfort.

D I E R Y

Leap season

THE CONSENSUS IS BUILDING. IT'S TIME FOR ME TO *GET OUT OF TOWN.*

On the one hand people are well disposed towards me and want to suggest a kindly solution to my mental health problems. On the other hand I'm sure they will just be glad to get rid of me. I'm talking about the local, short-term departure, the one where I go see my sister and whoever else may be out there, including Horatio. I'm not so inflatedly pessimistic that I think my friends would be happy to see me go on the longer, permanent departure—the one they don't know I'm planning. I think I have a fairly level head about all that. I know they'll be sad, a couple of them really pretty sad for a while. That's the hardest part to think about, because my dark urge isn't one of those "I'll show *them!*" adolescent fantasies. I don't even feel that about my ex-boss who fired me (you may also refer to him as "Evil Incarnate").

Still, I also don't think everyone will spend years wailing and beating their breasts over it. Most people in my life, especially the women (Cindy, Lili, even my mother), are copers, when you get right down to it. They'll do the appropriate amount of grieving, in late-twentieth-century American fashion—having coffee with friends and being honest about their anger—and then they'll put it behind them, one more of life's misfortunes to be processed, transcended, and then banished. Maybe if one of them is especially lucky they'll get to go on a talk show with a theme like "Relatives of Suicides." That could be a healing experience. You have to believe me that I'm not trying to be overly flip here. It's clear-sightedness I'm aiming at, and if anything a wishful optimism about how sensible they all are. And here's one honest prediction: Krieger, a few years down the line, will produce some fabulously powerful piece of theater based on my premature exit. I know this is an egotistical thought, but I find it a strange source of comfort. For some reason, I trust him with the material.

Anyway, like I say the consensus is building that some sort of movement is in order. I had more confirmation earlier today when I went downtown to meet Gloria for lunch. It was a timed affair—she was on her lunch hour—and she spent the first twenty minutes grilling me about jobs. This becomes very tiring after a while. There's only so much lying and evading you can do before you start feeling bad about it. I always mumble vaguely about positions whose closing dates are a month from now, in the hope that by a month from now she'll have forgotten about it and won't ask. Gloria, bless her heart, still can't believe the company fired me. According to her I was one of their stellar employees. Actually, she always tells me not to say I was "fired," power of positive thinking, and strictly speaking she's right that I was "let go," which is supposed to sound much more honorable. It doesn't feel any better, though.

"They're crazy," she said again today. "You're the best one they had at explaining things to people. Sheila didn't ever used to do envelopes until you came and showed her how. She always got someone else to do it. They should ask me, I'll tell them."

"They will ask you, if I ever get an interview anywhere. You're on my list of references to call."

Gloria thinks it's very bad for me that I don't have a job right now. She's worried about my self-esteem, which for some reason she pronounces *self-esteen* like it's some kind of decongestant. Her worries are similar to my mother's, but in her case she's less concerned my staying at home jobless will make me introverted and anxious; Gloria's worry is the money. If I had longer-term visions for myself, I would probably share this worry. I might sit around thinking, what if I have to give up my apartment? What if my electricity is shut off? What if I'm reduced to eating Minsk's dog chow along with him?

As it is, I figure I've got the financial situation wired. I'm still working out the finer details, but I think with the money I've saved I can swing a short trip to Baltimore, land of the cheap, while also still having enough to fund a few spontaneous excursions to other prospects, Elsinorean or otherwise. "Saved" is a euphemism, of course. It's really the severance pay. I love that term, *severance pay*, it sounds so dramatic—it makes me feel I've lost a limb or something. Which is how it feels. Yes, the least you fuckers could do for me if you're going to rip my limbs off is give me money to make the separation bearable. Help fund my purchase of a nice plastic prosthesis.

Sorry. That was a digression from the story at hand which is my lunch with Gloria. I just didn't want you to be able to forget the basic source of my disasterhood for longer than a couple of minutes. Anyway, I didn't go into the financial business with Gloria over lunch. We don't speak the same language in that respect. I probably speak a middle-class "there's a margin for error if I fuck up" language and she speaks a "second generation my father was a janitor and I want my kids to have more security than I've had" language. So I changed the subject. When you have an hour lunch for conversation, you have to stay focused. It's not like when you're working in an office with someone and can carry out the conversation in dribs and drabs throughout the day; or on e-mail, when you have hours between messages to think through your response. A face-to-face hour is very different: it forces you to be efficient, parceling out your news in succinct two-minute presentations.

I decided to use the time we had left to tell her my dream. Gloria is great with dreams because she doesn't go all Freudian on you, referring everything back to the damn family. I get very tired of that. Lili does it all the time because of Doctor O. I hear so much about her analysis I might as well be in there with her. I feel I know Doctor O better than I know my own father: I could tell you the kind of sweaters he likes to wear, what his laugh sounds like (Lili does a great impression of his abrupt, overdramatic roar), and how he interprets Lili's dreams—which is to point out that underneath the surface they're all actually about him. I find Gloria much more creative about dreams. She reads them as portents of what's coming up for you. It's like checking your horoscope.

So I mentioned I'd had another one of my celebrity dreams. We've decided that my celebrity dreams signify that something important is about to happen to me. (Less than three days after I had an excellent dream about going ice-skating with Oprah Winfrey, I came across young Minsk and Pinsk.) These dreams of mine are not, as you might be imagining, dreams where I'm making love to some sexy blonde sex symbol. I never have those dreams, more's the pity. Mine are very friendly, pals-ish dreams about people I would never even guess I was thinking about—ageing rock stars or the President's brother. They're often men, first of all. My favorite one ever, from years ago, was when William Shatner was counseling me on where to go to college. We were walking by some river, one of those fake *Star Trek* rivers they would discover on other planets, and he was acting warm and fatherly. I found his advice intelligent and useful, though sadly I couldn't remember it in the morning.

So this one was about Jack Nicholson. Jack! When was the last time I saw a movie with him in it, I couldn't tell you. The main gist of this dream, again, was just that I *knew* Jack, we were friendly in a manly sort of way, and I happened to be on the street and saw him in a pickup truck. Maybe he was pulled up at a red light and he saw me. I don't even think we exchanged words, we just each raised a hand in a simple, regular guy salute, and smiled—you know, Jack with his famous wily Jack grin, me with the long-mouthed version that is my own. Then Jack drove on.

That was it. That was the whole dream.

But Gloria is great—she's the best. "He's going somewhere," she said immediately. "Right?"

"I think it was in the city. Actually I don't know where we were."

"But he was going somewhere, right? In his truck. And he's Jack Nicholson, so you know that wherever he's going is somewhere important, somewhere sexy."

I let her chew on that for a minute, along with her bagel.

"Are you planning to go someplace?" she asked me finally.

I raised my eyebrows. "Nowhere sexy and important," I said. Not meaning any disrespect to my sister, obviously.

"Yes, but are you planning to go away someplace?"

So I told her about my wondering whether to go along with the conspiracy of women by taking a quote unquote vacation (not that I've yet gone so far as to mention this to Cindy), and Gloria—she's so cute, sometimes, for an accountant—actually clapped her hands together in excitement. She loves to be right. I wonder if she claps her hands down in the windowless accounting department of *Lolita!* every time she's right.

"You see! It's about your trip! Something will happen on your trip."

"Not something sexy," I insisted.

"You don't know, JD. You don't know. I think it's a good idea for you to go. I think this dream is telling you it's a good idea. Maybe you'll meet someone, on your trip!" She was so excited for me, it was kind of heartbreaking. "I mean, Jack *Nicholson.* That's got to be what he's saying."

"I'm not trying to meet anyone," I lied to my good friend Gloria, figuring it wasn't worth going into the whole Horatio scenario. She and I are close, but I've tried to shield her from my more extreme eccentricities.

"JD, of course you are." She put a hand on mine, without thinking about it. We were having lunch in this bagel shop that was beautifully warm, suffused with one of the most comforting smells known to man, the aroma of hot yeasty things in the oven. Around us, suited people were wolfing bagels without much grace, dripping bits of smoked salmon or slippery tomatoes down their hurrying chins.

We both felt her hand there and reacted to it. Gloria's got to be at least ten years older than me. I've never wanted to ask, and she's very coy and feminine about that kind of thing. But she has a son, two sons still, in their twenties. I was thinking about that as I felt her hot caramel hand on mine and realized that there was something in that touch, that there was actually a current of attraction switched on by her small, elegant unringed hand.

I found this more depressing than anything else. Flat-out depressing. How could attraction happen here and now, between us? We were just two ordinary people trying to have a conversation. Was it Jack's fault, God damn him? Was his spirit hovering over this encounter and cackling?

But I didn't want to upset her, or be rude, or act freaked out, or anything. I love Gloria. That's the whole point. She is like my guardian angel. So I decided, since it seems to work well in awkward situations, to put on my rabbi persona. I put my free, slightly cream cheese–smeared hand over hers in a gesture of friendly consolation, and I asked her the question that was genuinely on my mind. I have to admit, though, to knowing that we had about three minutes left to our lunch.

"Listen, Gloria," I said in the hushed tone of the Sabbath. It was Friday, after all. "We've talked enough about me. I know you have to go soon, and I wanted to ask you: How's Daniel doing?"

I did genuinely want to know—it had been a couple of weeks since I'd seen him. Still, you can judge whether my asking this was in fact evil and expedient or sensitive and caring. Whichever it was, the eyes that were watching me altered in every way: shape, color, hoodedness, age. The moment changed. She should have been angry at me, she could have been, but her eyes didn't mention it. Instead they became infinite, black swallows of grief.

She didn't say anything to me—she couldn't, thinking about her son. She couldn't get the words out. She just gripped my hand harder, and I figured he had to be worse.

Thursday

I am beginning to pull things together. I am beginning to narrow my life.

Before you go on a big trip, you have to get matters under some control. It's only if you never travel that you can really let things slide. If you don't travel, the stacks can just stack on up and you can refuse to look at them, act like they're not there. Travelling forces you to pay the stacks some attention.

This reminds me of when we were kids in L.A. My sister used to have a best friend named Harriet, who was English. Harriet had this great phrase—"Sending you to Coventry," which meant that she was going to stop talking to you, ignore you. It must be the kind of thing that comes up frequently between girls. (It's not much of a boy's weapon, ignoring someone. Too subtle.) Anyway, she once said it to me like its meaning was utterly self-evident: "I'm going to send you to Coventry, JD!" and then she *and* Cindy stopped talking to me, pretended I didn't exist, all because I wouldn't let them play Monopoly with me and my friends. Which can I just say was a reasonable decision, because Cindy had a terrible habit of buying up the best real estate and then just sitting on it, never selling it or anything, which made her a very irritating Monopoly player. Though I'm sure this relates to her later excellent business acumen. Anyway, I had no idea what Harriet meant when she said she was going to send me to Coventry—it sounded so physical, and she was such a scrawny kid. I kept waiting for her to try to hit me. It was a phrase whose definition I finally worked out from context, the way they teach you to do with new vocabulary: if you were sent to Coventry, no one talked to you. Coventry, I came to think, must be a very quiet, quiet place. The phrase comes back to me now whenever I'm thinking about the many things in my life—bills, taxes, ex-girlfriends—that I spend a lot of time ignoring. I always figure I'm sending them to Coventry, which sounds more active and responsible than the slackerish "blowing them off."

The point being that I can no longer send my stacks of papers to Coventry because I am sending myself to Baltimore instead, and Lili's going to stay here while I'm gone. Her roommate's driving her crazy, she's obsessed with Seattle grunge bands that offend Lili's refined musical sensibilities. But I can't let Lili rummage through all this mess and find ample evidence of my disasters, financial and otherwise. Before she gets here I have to sort and confront. I have to get a grip.

I realize that travelling can work the other way, too. Sometimes people just split, leaving behind bad debts and laundry checks and thank-you notes still to be written. That is travel as flight, as denial. Joe is who I'm thinking of here. Joe's wandering feet meant that nothing ever stacked up for him anywhere, because he wasn't in one place long enough for it to stack. I wonder if he's still as mobile that way as he used to be. Who knows. Maybe he lives a stable, cluttered life in Haifa or somewhere, gathering magazine subscriptions and bills and paying them like any normal person. Maybe this Horatio I'm after, maybe he really exists and he's a dark-headed boy who speaks only Hebrew. That would be tragic—as a heathen, I don't know any Hebrew—but also somehow lyrical and moving. I could see it being the subject of an opera. Are there any Jewish operas? Not set in Haifa, I'll bet you.

You can see what I'm doing. I'm sitting in a corner writing about how responsible I could in theory be, rather than getting over to that *other* corner, over there, where all that organization lurks, waiting to happen. It's still minus a large number of degrees outside with the wind chill factor, and at this moment what I am putting off even more than pulling my life together is taking Minsk out to the big park. Today's our day for it. I've already promised. He is sitting not too far from me watching me type, his face shaded in expectation, as if all I can possibly be doing on the computer at this point is drawing up an itinerary for us on our imminent travels. In fact, Minsk old boy, I am going to complete this particular set of thoughts while my blood is still warm and fluid enough for me to think at all. By the time we come back my heart and brain will be frozen in place—which will probably be the right transcendental state to be in to go through all those desk papers.

I don't know what it is with me and that aspect of adulthood. It used to be called, back in my college days, "being a fuckup." I had this roommate in college for a couple of years, Lars, who was incredibly anal. He had a terrible tragedy in his background, his father had died in a car accident when he was ten and so his mother appointed him, as eldest boy, the new head of household. From then on he organized the mortgage payments and balanced the checkbook and kept all the family's domestic accounts in order. He was a genius at it. Various groups in college, singing groups, theater groups, all appointed Lars their treasurer, he was so good with the books. When he told me his story, I had to think, What's my excuse? I was the eldest boy too, and nothing like that ever wore off on me.

Lars was a godsend as a roommate, even if he did aggravate me with his neuroses and make me live an unnaturally clean life. But it was worth it, because he told me how and when to do things—"Write a rent check now"—and I would. It was that simple. This is criminal to admit, but I have no reputation to protect anymore: Lars also balanced my checkbook for me, after one time when I wrote a rent check that bounced and our landlord threatened to evict us. I knew the landlord was bluffing, but Lars was alarmed. I think he thought that his impeccable credit rating, which made up about three-quarters of his identity, might be tarnished. So from then on he thought it would be better if he just did my checkbook for me. It was something that embarrassed us both, and we never really talked about it except when he would come up to me slightly formally and say, "JD, I think you should know that until your loan check comes in you have twenty-eight dollars in your account."

It's been downhill ever since Lars and I parted company after college. He got a job as the business manager for a dance company—presumably an organization which, like me, was worthy and creative but fiscally irresponsible. I was probably great training for him. It was good news for the dance company but terrible news for me, since it dashed my hopes that we might be forever roommates and I would never be in financial hot water again.

I can't describe the hollow, sick feeling I get in my stomach when a piece of money or business news comes in the mail. It doesn't even much matter whether the news is good or bad—check or bill, innocent bank statement or threatening letter from creditors. If you get it too, you don't need me to describe it; if you don't get it, you're just sitting there thinking, Why doesn't this kid grow up? Or else, if he was forced to balance a budget, he'd damn well have to learn how to do it.

There's something to this last point. Something unfortunate happened to me two years after I graduated. Those first couple of years I was doing respectable things—a badly paid slave job at a trendy weekly, where I was surrounded by (fellow) hipsters, including the above-mentioned diva, Miss Lilian Hofmeister. I was living at that point within my means, just about. (Basically. I was running scared from my student loans, but then so was everyone else.) Then, just as the job was entering the "be promoted or die" phase, tragedy struck. My grandmother died—Sally's mother. Nice lady. Knew Eleanor Roosevelt. I'll tell you about her sometime. The tragedy was not so much that she died—it was merciful really, she was in terrible pain at the end and I happen to know the doctor slipped her some extra morphine to help her go quicker—but that she left me (and Cindy, and my mother) a wad of money. I am not at liberty to disclose how much, but let's just say it was a handsome amount. My grandfather had been a financial adviser who'd done very well for himself, also in L.A., and so there were stocks and shares to spread around after they died.

Cindy and Mom have a good grasp of this material. Cindy especially. Mind like a steel trap. She's got the financial adviser blood in her—hence the book-store/café management—and so she did something very effective with her money, didn't touch it for a bunch of years, let it grow, then finally used it to buy a house in Baltimore, where houses are dirt cheap. She was pretty young at the time, but she's always been smart and organized. Developmentally she's running roughly eight years ahead of me—I worked it out once.

I'm mentioning Cindy to avoid talking about me. Minsk, at this point, is climbing the walls to get out of here, but I have to finish this. You can imagine what I did with my wad. Yep. Blew it all, basically. This is where we go into the romantic/disheveled/unsuccessful writing phase of my life I mentioned before. I quit the slave job and became one of the idle not-so-very rich. I was livin' large, as they say. In fact, I was livin' pretty modestly, but if you live in this city off nothing but a wad and you go so far as to eat red meat and have the occasional alcoholic drink, the money drains away like water from a tub. It didn't *all* drain away—I woke up just before it got that bad—but, typically, when I could see after several years that the hemorrhaging had been severe, I resorted to extreme methods. I should have asked Cindy for something intelligent to do with it. But that would have meant confessing how much I'd managed to get through, much too galling a prospect. So instead I called a financial helpline: I saw the ad on the subway, "Has your spending gotten out of control?" written in about ten different languages, and I figured they were the agency for me. I asked them desperately what you could do with money if you wanted to put it somewhere where you literally *couldn't touch it* for ten years or so. They recommended a savings bond, so like a crazy person I took all the rest of the money, except for about two thousand bucks, and bought a "you touch it, you die" bond. One of the things I have to do before I leave on this trip—because I've never done it, of course—is put these damn bonds in a safety deposit box in a bank somewhere. What happens now is that I find them when I'm in the middle of going through some other kind of stack looking for keys or vet certificates or job listings or whatever, and then I get anxious and toss them in the back of a drawer and pretend I don't know what they are.

Needless to say the savings bond idea now seems ludicrous because I don't plan on being around till then to cash them in. I may have to write a will before I go. But who should I leave my savings bonds to? To Minsk, to support him in the lifestyle to which he has become accustomed? Or maybe to set up some small trust. "The JD Levin Memorial Checkbook Balancing Fund," to help wayward souls get a grip on such important worldly matters, before they're embarrassingly old and find out it's too late.

Friday

And then suddenly, for no apparent reason, the pit opens up again in front of your feet.

And it's so tempting, it's tempting in an immediate way, *now*; it wants you now and there doesn't seem to be any reason to wait. Everything suddenly seems like a postponement of the inevitable. Every scheme and fantasy takes on the pale shadow of untruth.

Forget the local journey. Why not go on the Big One? You've organized everything. Why not make the big departure now, now that you're ready?

The window is right there. And it's open.

It's a strange sensation. Like being on a cold and muddy hillside, alone, your feet chilled and firmly stuck in the mud. There doesn't seem to be any way to move. You lift your head and "Horatio" is an unconvincing bleat from a faraway hillside. You can't remember how you planned to get there and what you expected this Horatio to say or do if you found him.

On a closer path but still inaccessible because she's beyond the place you're in, the place where the wind freezes your feet into the mud, your sister stands, shaking out her pleasant-colored hair, hair that in a previous era might have earned her the name *brunette*. She's looking into a brighter sky than the one that hangs over you, and she wants you to visit her colorful territory. It's impossible to explain to her that you can't move your feet.

Far ahead of you, deep in some unseeable valley, are the friends who want to take you out from where you've gotten stuck. They're shouting instructions to you about how to get out of there. They promise that in the valley where they are there are people and movies and good food and life-purposes—those useful little scraps of paper that remind you why you should stay alive, all the bright items still left on your "to do" list. But you know that valley they're talking about. Of course you do—you've been there yourself. It is fun but it's not what you want. Even if you could move these feet now, you wouldn't choose to go to the valley with your friends. It's past the point where you'd want to.

And I hate to say it, but the window is still open.

Oh and look! Look who's right here, waving frantically to get your attention. It's your mother, that lively not entirely sober individual who made the brave effort years ago, with mixed success, to give you life. She widened her legs and broke open her womb for you, and yet there's the tragedy now that you want to give her her gift back. Thanks, Mom. I appreciate it. I really do! But the life you gave me doesn't fit anymore. Can you return it at all? Get some kind of refund?

She's trying to talk to you. She hopes her talk will perk you up, or at least keep you standing.

"Now, son," she starts telling you, and before you know it your heart is full of stories of the father who left you. She's telling you about that man who gave you half the blood in your veins, one portion of your eye color, a great slice of your body height. She's telling you how kind he once was. That he's not the demon you imagine him to be. She lists his good qualities and his intelligence, and as if her script were penned by a Hollywood hack she comes up with some story that's supposedly of your childhood which involved you swimming in a lake with him, a time when you and he were out in the cool water and caught up with someone's retriever that was swimming there, too. You bobbed around, the two of you, playing with the retriever for half an hour, then you started to get cold and numb and your father swam back with you. On the shore you and your father made up a story about the magic swimming dog, a story which ended with some great line, which in Disney-ish fashion sums up the triumph of love and the strength of the human heart and the father-son bond. Fortunately for you, this last line is inaudible.

Your mother has told you all this to lead up to her point, which is that your father, bless him in spite of his absence, would in no way approve of what you're doing now. Thinking about ending it—why, that's ridiculous! He would never stand it, not for one minute. And yes, your father had feet that moved too far and too fast, but that is no reason for you to allow yours to freeze into place now and give up. You think that's smart, to react against him by doing the obvious? You think suicide is such a new idea? You think just because your father lives carelessly that's reason to empty your own life with a smart person's care and precision? Come on now, do something original. I didn't bring you up to be the kind of dope who'd fall for such melodrama.

On and on these words came, from the little grey mother with her voice like a second-grade teacher. After some time, much as you love her, your brain no longer absorbs the words she says. A ghost in you, a fill-in, keeps listening to her, sympathizes with her even. Wants to help her, certainly doesn't want to let her down. Meanwhile your unhearing heart is a tight fist of unnamed deadness and the undesire for a future—and there's nothing your dear mother can do about that.

There comes a point where you're alone from all of it. Your listening ghost has left you. It's your own private hilltop, after all. It's your building to jump off of, your bus to dive under, it's you perched over the shouting traffic nine floors below. It's your window. You're alone here. You cannot really hear their language anymore, even your mother's, because it happens not to be the one of the sea and the fall, the one you're speaking now. You can do what you want. Nothing that they say, ultimately, is loud enough to pull you back.

Except. *Except*. Except you are not entirely alone. Two fathomless eyes look up from beside your cold, terrified shoes. They're the eyes of another creature. They're eyes yours can look into when they can't meet anyone else's. You hear a bark. And because these eyes and this bark don't speak in words—they have neither letters nor phrases, there's none of that English to clog up the airwaves—they succeed in getting through to you. There's not even sympathy in these eyes, which is good because when a certain kind of bleakness courses through the bloodlines sympathy (the sympathy that's being shouted at you by your friends, for instance) can strangely set you off.

It is simpler and more selfish than sympathy, what this creature is saying. It's a demand for affection. It's a plea for food and for exercise. It's an offer of friendship. It is, most plainly, a flat white-grey statement of your connection to each other, of the fact that you've each entered into a promise to look after the other.

With Minsk watching you like that, you can't end it. Not right now, anyway. Minsk is too small to be left at this brink on his own. He couldn't manage it. He isn't ready for it yet. He doesn't expect it. What he expects, what he deserves, is a walk in the park.

You glance over at the leash, an ordinary object, by the door. Minsk sees your glance—he's watching you very carefully, because he's not stupid and he's sensed you're in trouble—and starts wagging his tail, a delicate thump on the ground.

And now you really can't end it. Not now that you've looked at the leash. A leash-look is as good as a nod to a small dog. You must move your feet. You've made a promise to keep living to this white furry creature, and you're the kind of person who honors your promises—for the next hour at least.

(Some damn time. Four a.m. or so)

I picked up the phone, not sure whether I'd be able to speak. I don't know how she knew to call right then.

"JD?"

Her voice was kind. Matter-of-fact, and kind.

"Yeah."

"Are you OK?"

I paused, tilting on the hilltop again. But I didn't want to get caught. I didn't want her to know that's where I was. "Mmmhmm."

"You don't sound good."

"Well, you know."

"Are you really OK? Is anyone there with you?"

It was hard for me to talk. I was sober, obviously, sober in the literal sense. I patted my dog. "Minsk," I articulated.

"I'm glad Minsk is there. But I mean is there any other person there, like Krieger or anybody?"

"No."

You could hear a shiver of panic over the line; you could hear a sweet strain of love. You could hear somebody not calm, wanting to sound calm on the phone. There was a pause before she formed her next sentence.

"You know what I was thinking about the other day?" When it arrived, the voice came out clear as a bell. Sensible as a shoe. Nice as a rose garden.

"No."

"I was thinking it would be fun if you came down here for a visit. Mom said she was talking to you about it. I mean, you might as well take advantage of not having a job yet. You're bound to get one soon, and then you won't be able to do fun spontaneous things like this anymore. And I know Jane would love to see you."

"Mmm."

"And not to exploit you or anything, but if you were here you could teach me how to use this new software we have at work, maybe, that I'm not getting the hang of."

"Yeah." This was an effort, saying this. I think she knew it was, but I wanted to pretend that it really wasn't, that it was coming out easily.

"I'm serious, JD. It's a good time for you to come. Just hop on the train. It's so close, even if any journey away from your precious city seems exponentially huge. It's hardly any distance really."

"But—Minsk."

"Oh, right. Well couldn't someone take him for a little while? Couldn't Krieger, or Lili—"

But we're related, and if you're related you can hear things at a pitch that no

one else can hear them at. She heard, at the mention of my leaving Minsk
behind, she heard the grief coming down the wires, the squeal that meant for
me this separation wouldn't be possible. It came to her at a high, unbearable
frequency, the fact that I couldn't make it out of my bed without Minsk, let
alone all the way to Baltimore, that without that other species of fur I might
not have moved in days . . .

"Actually, you know what? I have a better idea." She said this quickly, though
she was trying to strain the hysteria out of her voice. "You know what, JD? This
is a good idea. Why don't you just rent a car? Their weekly rates aren't so bad.
I can help you out, if you need—"

"No."

"Doesn't that seem like a good idea, though?" She really tried, she tried not
to sound desperate. "If you don't say yes soon, I'll start guilt-tripping you, which
will be worse."

I sat there patting Minsk. I tried to picture some ordinary part of life, like
renting a car. Many, many miles away from where I sat there were people
renting cars. It happened every day. It was normal. It was part of what went on
at this point in the century. People rented cars; it wasn't a big deal. But for me,
these transactions seemed to take place somewhere way far out there. Another
planet, maybe. A different century.

"Come on. Road trip. What do you think?"

There was another pause, which I tried not to let get too long. I had to get
out of this conversation. I couldn't sustain it. It was making me too sad. It was
making me sad to realize how sad it was making *her.*

"Cin," I said definitely. I tried to make my voice sound alert and authoritative.
I doubt I pulled it off. "I've got to go."

"Why? Where are you going?"

"I've just got to go."

I didn't want to break down on the phone. I wanted to be firm and clear, so
I could go on to do whatever I had to do by myself.

"Hold on a second. Talk to—"

"Cin—"

"Wait. Jane wants to say something. Hold on."

So then I had Jane on the phone. I wanted to hang up on her. I was exhausted. But it did seem that it would be too rude to do that, and I didn't want
to feel bad about being rude, on top of everything else. She told some long
rambling story that she thought I'd find funny and that I might have if I'd been
able to listen. It was about being in line at the post office. Some woman had

come in there trying to mail something crazy—eggs, or a barbell, or something. The details weren't important. The art of it was in the telling, was in Jane's voice that was full of a quiet, ironic hilarity that when I can absorb it I've always really liked. Every now and then as she told this story she'd go, ". . . right?" or "You know?" so I'd have to say, "Mmmhmm," to prove I was still there. I could manage this. However, I started to wonder what the hell had happened to Cindy.

Finally she came back on. She sounded breathless.

"JD? Hi. You're still there. Glad Rambling Rose here entertained you." She was much more cheerful for some reason. "Listen, I went rummaging around and I found some coupons for a car rental company. OK? So you have no excuse. I'll send them to you first thing tomorrow morning. It will knock the price right down. And once you're here, of course, you're our guest. And so is Minsk. We'll get that fancy chow made of goose livers or whatever it is you feed him."

She stayed on the line for a while longer, yammering about which freeway was the best one to use getting there and how Minsk would love this big reservoir near them. I still wanted to get off the phone, but I was numb by now. I was accepting my fate of having to stay chained to my sister's voice until she saw fit to let me go. It wasn't hurting quite so much anymore to listen to her, maybe because she did have this surreal perkiness lighting up her end of the line. I almost wondered if she'd taken some drug while she was off the phone.

"So will you call them? Cars book up fast, so you should call pretty soon."

I told her I'd think it over.

"What's to think? Think yes. Think now. Think next weekend."

"I can't—"

"OK, OK." She tried to calm down. "Come as soon as you can. Really, I'm serious, next weekend would be good because Jane's going away the weekend after."

This sounded like a lie.

"And next weekend, you'll get a kick out of this, Franklin Hayes is reading at the bookstore."

Franklin Hayes was a name from some impossible, tiny past of mine. Once, I knew, I had read Franklin Hayes and admired him—he had a story about two brothers hunting in the snow that I liked—but now I could barely remember who he was or where he came from. Some strange place, a place that had books and publishers and a reading public and coffee.

"Well—" I said.

Then the buzzer went. Which was strange. It's not the kind of city where your buzzer goes often with a casual visitor. I did think briefly of bread-knife Marcie, and the thought wearied me. I was tired of rings and buzzes in my life. City life is full of the indignity of all these fucking noises. I was tempted to send the buzzer to Coventry. And after that, the telephone.

"Was that your doorbell?"

I grunted.

"I'll hold on. Go ahead and answer. Are you expecting someone?" She remembered to add the last part. I was finally figuring out what was going on. It had been obvious for a while I guess, but my brain was gelled in aspic and I hadn't been sharp enough to get the situation on a conscious level. Now I got it. I felt like one of those lions or giraffes you used to see on that wildlife show (the show sponsored by Mutual of Omaha, I'll never forget it—you never knew what "Mutual of Omaha" *was* as a kid, but you were grateful to them for sponsoring the show). You remember how the animals would get hit by a sleeping dart? You watched them running and running, then they got shot with the dart, then they had about half a minute before they stumbled and fell down— usually in slow motion—and finally slipped into a drug-induced stupor. How humiliating. You could just imagine the lion as his lids were closing and the world was turning black, thinking, *God damn it.* I've been shot. Now they're going to round me up in their nets and throw me in the fucking jeep, and the whole damn thing is going to be on camera. How humiliating.

"Wait a second," I told Cindy. Resigned to my fate. The dart was in.

I almost hoped it would be bread-knife Marcia, but in fact I heard the familiar tan voice over the intercom.

"JD?"

More extra friendliness. From Krieger, also sounding very, very perky. It was getting kind of funny. I was almost ready to find the whole thing funny, though I guess my captors probably weren't. They were still sweating, wondering if I could get away. I felt like making them sweat a little longer.

"It depends," I told Krieger. "Who's this?"

"Krieger—it's Krieger."

"Oh."

"Can I come up?"

I wanted to torture him. I felt it was my right to enjoy one small sadism before they loaded me in the jeep. My last moment in the wilderness.

"What for, exactly?"

He laughed. Or tried to.

"What for? Well—I was in the neighborhood, and—it's fucking cold out here, you know."

I saw the whole thing lucidly. Like someone was playing an old eight millimeter for me in a darkened room in my head—you know, with everyone's movements coming out edgy, and the film sort of grainy. I saw Cindy running out of her house. I saw her running to a pay phone. I saw her shouting, gesticulating into the phone. I couldn't hear the words, but I imagine they were something like *Now. Now. However the fuck you can get there. You've got to just get there. Get there, Krieger.*

"Are you selling something?" I asked Krieger.

His nervousness clinched it. I knew I was right about what had happened. It must be a crisis, because Krieger had successfully forgotten that I had a sense of humor.

"JD, come on. It's me, Krieger," he said. He tried to sound calm. "Can you let me up please?"

"Well—"

"I'm not kidding. It's cold as hell out here."

"Hell isn't cold," I said, but without much conviction.

I pressed the buzzer and heard him come in. Then, because I didn't want to go through the whole rigmarole all over again when he got to the door, and before I could change my mind, I unlocked and unlatched the door so he could just come in when he got to the ninth floor.

I went back to the phone. Cindy was still there. You have to know that she's brutally conscious about her phone bills, so this took real devotion for her to stay on the line during all of that dead air.

"Who was that?"

"You're a bad actor. So is Krieger. You I can understand, but Krieger's in the theater and should be able to do better."

Krieger came through the door. I stayed on the phone but said to him, "Did you hear what I just said? I said as a director you really ought to be able to act better."

Krieger looked at me and shrugged. His face was a scared yellow. Minsk came over to greet him. At least somebody was glad to see him.

"It's freezing in here," Krieger said, and without asking went over to shut the window. He locked it. I focused on the phone again to have a last minute of privacy with my sister.

"JD—" she said.

"I know. I know." My voice was dull.

"JD." You could hear tears running through her voice now. "You're my brother. I can't let . . . I mean I can't let—" She was trying to hold it together but she couldn't. She was about to lose it completely. I can't say I felt a lot of sympathy.

"I know." My voice was winter cool and bitter. I was in the Land Rover now. The struggle was over. I'd been cheated out of my wilderness. Tricked off my hilltop. She'd had good reason for doing it, maybe, but I wasn't ready to forgive her.

"I know," I repeated. "I appreciate it."

And though some distant part of me wanted to be sincere in saying that, my heart was rigid with disappointment and anger as I placed the dirty white instrument of rescue back into its receiver.

Part 2

"I DON'T SEE WHAT THE BIG DEAL IS."

"You don't?"

"No. I don't. I thought once I tapped in my secret code that, you know, the world would multiply in front of my eyes. I'd suddenly transport myself to virtual China or somewhere. It didn't happen. It's just numbers, words, addresses. It doesn't seem that big a deal."

Pi was talking to Xander at the store. She worked there now, mornings. Pi had become mistress of the two beat-up coughing Canons, while Xander did the important, manly work on the computer. They shared the gender joke—it was fitting, they agreed, that Pi's job was reproducing. In her case, not the human race but various stacks: of the familiar Twelve Steps for several different recovery groups; of posters explaining How to Identify Poison Oak, a Dangerous Tick, or Mountain Lion Tracks for the alarmist parks department; or drafts of the outraged exposé of the logging industry brought in by a guy who wrote under the name "Sequoia Sam" and called his manuscript "The Silence of the Trees—The Serial Killing of Our National Forests." He didn't have a publisher yet because, as he bitterly explained, "Corporate America isn't ready to hear this."

"So where'd you go?" Xander asked.

"Where? What do you mean? I figured out how to send a letter to Fran at her job. And I sent a note to my friend Hannah in Texas."

"Pi, that's so primitive. It's cute. Did you even look up any bulletin boards?"

"I don't know. What are they?"

So far this great invention, this ethereal being the Internet, this conglomeration of technology that well-informed people were calling the most significant change to human communication since the printing press, had achieved the fine distinction of making Pi feel stupid. She didn't like to feel stupid. Studying philosophy had meant she rarely had to be stupid. Now the Internet, the first item to engage her intellect in months, was making her feel something Hegel or Wittgenstein never could—like an ignorant child.

"*Bulletin* boards. BBSs," said Xander, slowly, the way you give instructions to a tourist. "People set them up on a subject, any subject, and then like-minded people come along and post notices on them. Have conversations. You must have heard about this."

"Conversations about what?"

"Anything. Blues singers. Astrophysics. Health. I often go to one about fasting, I've gotten some great tips on fruit fasts that way. I'm thinking seriously of running an on-line fasting workshop. You could do philosophy, if you want. See what people are saying about Kant. I bet there's one on Kant."

"Oh my God." Pi turned cold, in spite of the heat from the busy machine she was leaning against. "You're kidding. Why would I want to do that?"

Xander spun his chair back to face his screen. He was testing ideas for a new logo for *Astral Plane*, freelance music teacher—stars, moons, notes. "Now don't get upset," he said. "I'm just trying to tell you, if you wanted, you could check it out."

"The whole reason I came up here, so far away, was so I could *stop* thinking about Kant." Caffeine—a double latte—frenzied Pi's voice. "I have to *forget* about Kant. I have to pretend Kant doesn't exist anymore. Now you're telling me Kant's followed me up here and is lurking in my computer, lots of little Kantians all lined up with their messages about the categorical imperative. This is horrific. I don't want to know about this."

Xander swung his long thin hair over his shoulder with a toss of his head, a girlish motion. "That's what it means to be on the Internet. It means you get connected."

"But maybe I don't want to be connected. Maybe I just want to be isolated up here, listening to the waves and getting back to nature and occasionally window-shopping for CDs I miss that I used to have. Just talking to you and to Martha and Abbie. To people who live *here*, not people who live in Omaha or wherever."

"Then unplug."

"I don't want to unplug *yet*. I've only just started. I mean, I want to see if Fran or Hannah writes me back."

"Then stay plugged in."

Pi kicked her feet back against the humming Canon in protest. "It's like a monster or something. If I stay plugged in, what if people start talking to me about Kant? What if people at the philosophy department get my e-mail address? How can I stop it?"

"Look, Pi. Relax. It's—like—it's selective. If you don't want to talk about Kant, you don't have to. It's like a bookstore. You know, there may be books about Kant in Mary's bookstore—"

"I doubt it. Outside of college towns most bookstores' 'philosophy' sections have Carlos Castaneda and the *Tao of Pooh* and that's about it."

"Whatever. The point is, maybe there would be a Kant book in there which might be very disturbing to you because of your history, but you don't have to look at it if you don't want to. You go in and browse something else. It's your choice."

"But I can't go into bookstores. That's a bad analogy. For that very reason, I still can't go into bookstores."

"Really?" He spun back around to her. "What, you don't read anymore? How about libraries?"

"Can't do libraries either," Pi said. "But I do read still. A little. I'm reading poetry right now. It's thin—I can read things that are thin. I've been raiding Abbie's bookshelves. I'm on to Sylvia Plath's *Ariel*. It's frightening, but weirdly enjoyable."

"Look, all I'm saying is, it's about *choice*. You can choose who to talk to. People in your department will only e-mail you if you give them your address. It's like normal mail that way. It's not like they're going to come and invade you. It's your choice. That's what the whole thing is about. You decide."

"Can I decide not to do anything?"

"If you want to."

"I'm not very good at decisions right now. I'm not together enough yet to make choices. It's like being in junior high school and suddenly having electives forced on you. Having to choose your classes. I wasn't ready for electives either, as I remember."

"Come on. This can't be such a shock. You elected to borrow my software, to install it, to get an account, to send e-mail. You elected to have some interest in what it was all about."

"Mmm. Maybe," Pi conceded. In fact, his argument was unassailable. Her only counter was—again, embarrassingly—to plead ignorance. "But I had no idea what I was getting in to."

When Pi picked Martha up from school that afternoon, it was obvious that something was wrong. Martha's shoulders were curved in a slump. Her eyes were dull. She looked like a cold grounded sparrow, nursing a broken bone.

"Hey," Pi said after Martha had strapped herself in silently. "Don't I get a hello today?"

There was no answer.

"Martha?" she tried again. "Is something the matter?"

She wouldn't say. Pi tried a few more times to squeeze some words out of her without success, and then drove the rest of the way home in a silence she tried from her end to make companionable, though Martha's remained so loud and brick-wall-like that by the time they got home Pi was worried and discouraged.

Pi's first concern was that her fire story had somehow scarred the girl. It was a few weeks since that long blue night that began with whispers of Zeno's disappearance and ended with the soothing, metallic tune of a computer game. But Pi didn't know children. She knew nothing about them. Who knew what traumatized them? Maybe there really was such a thing as grief energy that was cooling now in Martha's veins and making her stiff and unapproachable. What if Pi had wrecked everything? Up until recently, Pi might have been able to cope with getting fired from this non-job of hers, being asked to leave her tenuous position in this small, private firm, Abbie's Mendocino household. But now—what with Xander, her tiny actual job, a room that included a computer and a view of the neighbors' garage, the prospect of teaching Martha more cat's cradle tricks—Pi didn't want to leave. She wanted to stay.

It had been years since Pi had cohered in any way to a household. In the first years of grad school, Pi had pooled with other philosophy students: Tamar and a smart woman who did ethics, Leah, who was so smart in fact that she dropped out and went to law school instead after her second year. The three had shared two floors of a rattly North Berkeley house, but it never seemed so much like a household as like three separate lives overlapping in shared space/time. The shelves of the refrigerator were divided into their three personalities: Tamar—health; Leah—junk; and Pi—bread and cheese; a list pinned up by the door kept track of who owed what to whom on bills. Boyfriends or occasional girlfriends spent the night and departed nameless in the morning, unless they'd stayed often enough to qualify for an introduction. But for several years Pi and Zeno had been co-habiting, just the two of them, at the Dixons' place. It was a good deal—the rent was low because of the murky legalities of the converted garage. By now Pi had gotten thoroughly used to the silences and rhythms and selfishnesses of life alone. She had eaten and slept, showered, stereoed, and read in any order she chose—loudly or softly, for hours or minutes, indulging un- mentionable private habits and depositing crumbs and papers and yogurt pots at will. Only Zeno was on hand to reprimand Pi or keep her schedule remotely regular, his jade eyes watching her in the morning to demand his breakfast, his body sneaking around her calves in the evening to remind her to give him dinner.

But this, this Mendocino life was regular. This was life as "three squares," as her mother put it before sending Pi off to college. ("The important way to stay healthy is to stick with three squares a day—I don't care what any of your friends say.") Pi hadn't lived that way for years. Outside, life might be New Age shop- ping and cosmic seaside revelations, but inside this house Abbie and Martha had an old-fashioned timetable, and if Pi had initially imagined she'd exist outside it, she soon found herself three-squaring it with the rest of them, in spirit if not always in body. She sat with them morning and evening at the table, though her appetite was still a mysterious and often absent companion.

Pi had worried she'd be an awkward shape in the lives of the mother-daughter pair. When she first met them, with Abbie in her purple librarian outfit, Pi had imagined herself colliding with them clumsily around the oak table, trying to make herself a hasty sandwich on a side counter while Abbie and Martha carried on with sprouts and pulses and plenty of whole grains, center stage. It wasn't like that. Abbie was an easy presence in the kitchen, who without making any obvious fuss produced spaghettis and casseroles, omelettes and soups and big, colorful salads with scatterings of surprising ingredients like fresh flowers or bright fruit. Her food was inclusive. She made a warm kitchen and a comfort- able one, one in which Pi found a role for herself doing the tasks that fell somewhere between those of the helpful adolescent and the eager boyfriend: she loaded and unloaded the dishwasher, set the table, made the salad dressing; she sliced the bread and found the butter and poured the apple juice, or opened the wine. She tried, in an unpracticed way, to make herself useful.

And if she was still shy with her benefactors, nonetheless Pi listened with fascination to Abbie and Martha's talk—about school and projects and all the information that lay stored in the world for Martha to discover. Pi watched

Abbie field a bewildering spread of questions, about stars or animals or movies or school buses, or what exactly was the meaning of California and was it or was it not its own country. Pi enjoyed these how and why sessions, and sometimes even joined in. ("Some states are more like countries than others," was her contribution to the California conversation. "On the East Coast, there are states hardly bigger than shopping malls—you can drive across them in half an hour.") Then, in the post-book-at-bedtime evenings, over fruit-fragranced teas or sometimes more wine, Pi and Abbie began a little to get to know each other.

They stayed away at first from the bruising source of their acquaintance—the separate new realities that kept them both awake at night, fighting the good fight against loss with the fearsome energy of their separate brains. They kept their talk to the basics of biography. Pi learned that Abbie was a native Californian, born and educated and duly hippied there, in the seventies. Abbie's sister Lucy, Fran's mother, ten years older than Abbie, had fled to Oregon for an early disastrous marriage, followed by the birth of her just-legitimate child (Fran) and her ravaged death from lung cancer. Abbie, the quiet child, stayed behind: for college, art school, a teaching job, and drugs, though few more exotic than what you could grow in the back yard. She'd had a spell in an ashram, an experience memorable, she said, mostly for the fact that she learned to make ceramics there and came to loathe white clothes. She'd been removed finally from hippiedom in the early eighties by Abe, who was leftish but always very straight at heart. And there followed the unspoken-about years of marriage, nine of them, to Abe, on whose name Abbie's lips still bit with pain. Pi did the math to solve her own curiosity: Abbie must be around forty, which her alive and travelled face suggested to be about right.

Pi was waiting for the return of that face later that afternoon, as Martha sat upstairs sulking and intractable and Pi drafted in her mind a confession to Abbie that her indiscreet tales of the fire had driven Abbie's child into some nightmare of distress. When Abbie came back, she found Pi stiff and gloom-weary, hoping she was not about to be banished.

"What's the matter?" Abbie asked, her voice rising in alarm.

"It's Martha."

"What is it?"

"She's upset. She won't tell me what's wrong. She didn't want me to make her any food or anything. She won't talk to me, and I'm worried—"

"Damn. I'll go talk to her," Abbie said. "I was afraid this might happen. Thanks, Pi."

"I'm worried I might have upset her. I told her—"

"No, no." Abbie shook her head. "I think I know what it is. Don't worry. I'll talk to her."

Abbie put a careless palm of gratitude on Pi's shoulder as she left to go upstairs; and for a few happy instants Pi felt she was part of something, after all, and that she had done something good.

As the evening settled into an indigo dusk, Pi moved to light the kerosene lamps. They had long elegant chimneys like glassy swans' necks, and when you replaced the chimneys over the flame the light swelled and settled in its clear captivity. Abbie had chosen these lamps. All around the old water-tower house Abbie had placed small and careful lights, so that no one had to face overbright revelations before they were ready for them, and also so that no one need succumb to darkness in any of its corners. At night there were porcelain-crafted nightlights in strategic locations so that the path to exit, as on a burning plane, was illuminated. It was the kind of touch Pi would never have noticed before, since her light and furniture priorities had always been organized around reading and writing rather than living and perceiving. Pi was getting to be grateful to Abbie for what she subtly knew about living.

After a while Abbie came down, made an obscure face at Pi—part worry, part eye-roll—and fixed up a tray with peanut butter and jelly sandwiches, some corn chips, grapes, and a glass of milk. After she left Pi threw together some adult food, bread toasted with goat cheese, a plate of sliced tomatoes, a dish of olives. Picnic food. Fine food for salt lovers.

When later the mother returned, her tray empty but for jelly-smeared crusts and a grape skeleton, weariness creased her face; but when she saw the readied table, the creases disappeared in a fondness.

"Oh, Pi, that's great. I couldn't face cooking tonight." She sighed and rubbed her eyes. "I need a glass of wine. Would you like one?"

"Thanks."

Abbie uncorked, poured, and then sat leaning back at the table, inhaling the reassurance of the sea-dark wine. She sighed. "It's what I expected. She wants to come with me to the city this weekend."

Abbie was going to San Francisco the next day. She had planned to meet Abe for dinner. It was her last attempt, she said, to figure out an arrangement between them that wasn't clogged with lawyers and courts. She wanted, if possible, to deal with the problem in a human way, without ugliness and accusations. The words she spoke were calm and rational, but Abbie was plainly apprehensive about the meeting—her olive skin had turned slowly paler and tauter as the weekend approached, and now she was nervously twisting the rings around her fingers.

"And you don't think it would work to have Martha come with you?"

"Absolutely not."

Pi sipped her wine.

"I just don't want Martha there, at all. It would only confuse the issue." Abbie's voice tightened. "Given that she *is* one of the issues. How much Abe will see her—and where. Whether his household is one that I feel is appropriate for her to visit."

Pi had heard about the paralegal from Fran. There was a paralegal, twenty-something, at the pale heart of this marital collapse. The story was that Martha had come home one afternoon to find the paralegal making coffee—*in nothing but a T-shirt*—in the kitchen, Abe and Abbie's own kitchen. It was hard evidence of a kind that was a blunt weapon in the hands of a wronged wife. To discover whether her ex-husband's new household did or did not harbor the paralegal must, Pi figured, be one of the hidden missions of Abbie's trip.

"Martha will let it go, eventually. I've explained it to her." Abbie took another slab of toasted bread. "You've hardly eaten any of this, Pi. Aren't you hungry?"

"Not really."

"You know, Pi, you're awfully thin."

"Oh, thanks. It's not deliberate, it's just—"

"I didn't mean it as a compliment. You seem too thin. You don't eat enough." Abbie looked at her with a sudden clarity. "You still look like you're in trauma. You know, I hope you don't mind my asking this, but—did you ever talk to anyone after the fire?"

"What do you mean?" Pi gulped some wine. "Sure I talked to people. Back in the Bay Area. To my friends."

"I meant a counselor, or a therapist."

"Oh, no. No, I didn't." Pi folded her arms. Sat up straighter.

"Did you think it might be a good idea?"

Pi didn't like this spotlight on herself. It made her squirm. But the wine, on her empty stomach, threatened to loosen her tongue. "No, I didn't. I suppose I figured that what I need is philosophy, rather than psychology, to deal with what happened. Do you know what I mean?"

"Mmm. Not necessarily."

So Pi tried to explain her non-traditional view that a good philosophical perspective on the loss would help her more than one which covered family history, emotions, all the details of what Pi dismissed with a taut little wave as her "personal life." What was there to psychologize? She'd lost everything; any idiot could explain why that was upsetting. What she needed was a description of the world that would include fire loss in it in a way that she'd recognize. Pi wanted a philosophy of loss: a view of what it meant, why it existed. It was the kind of question religion would formerly have handled (or would still, if she had one). Any great trauma, Pi claimed, her voice suddenly emboldened by dogma and wine, was bound to be better handled by contemplation than by theory.

"Including divorce?"

"Sure. Divorce too."

Abbie's expression had evolved into one of bemusement as Pi talked, but she was curious. "So what's your philosophy of divorce, then, if you have one?"

"Oh, it's simple." Pi shrugged, modestly. "That it's inevitable. And that the best thing to do, before you ever get involved with anyone, is to play the entire story out in your mind, including the ending, so you know how you'll manage when the end inevitably shows up."

"But Pi! That's so pessimistic."

"I know. But look at the statistics."

Abbie was beginning to look positively pitying. "And is there a matching philosophy for the children?" she asked, but skepticism by now brittled her voice.

"For the children it's hideous," Pi said promptly. "That's a given. But—I guess I think it's better, on the whole, not to shut them out of it completely. Not to stop them seeing both parents. My mother did that with me and my father, with not good results . . ."

"But was he having an affair with someone half your mother's age? In front of you? Did you ever come home and find him in bed with someone else?"

"No—"

"Did he try to explain himself by insisting they were doing *work* together?"

"No, I know, it's—"

Abbie slapped the table with a surprisingly firm palm. "Everyone has something to say about how forgiving women are supposed to be to their husbands in these situations. Well, I'm sorry, but how can I trust Abe with her now? How can I! I talked to Faith about this earlier today, I told her I'm trying, I want to try to be fair to Abe but as far as I'm concerned he's forfeited his rights—and I don't want Martha to have to get in the *middle* of it, and be exposed. It's bound to be a difficult meeting, of course, and—and Faith agreed with me, that the kindest thing is just to keep Martha here."

Pi retreated. "Listen, I'm sure you're right. You know what's right. I just thought she wouldn't have to be right there, with you, that she could stay with Fran or someone—"

"Yeah! I could go to Fran's!"

It was a seven-year-old's error: trying secretly to listen in on a grown-up conversation and accidentally giving the game away by joining in. Pi could hear the child's gasp of regret at her misjudgment.

"*Martha!*"

Abbie stood up, clattering the chair over as she did. Martha scampered back upstairs for cover.

"Martha, it is *not nice* to go sneaking around like that. I don't like it. It's sneaky. It's not what nice people do!" She moved after her daughter, her face red and agitated, her heels slapping angrily against the wooden steps in syncopation with Martha's. She was about to chase her upstairs, but paused briefly to complete her conversation with Pi.

"We'll figure this out, don't worry," she said, trying to sound calm, but her voice was shivering. "But listen. If you change your mind about therapy, I see someone who's very good, locally. Faith Kuralt. She could give me some other names for you. If—for some reason—your philosophy turns out not to be enough."

Pi absorbed what sounded to her like sarcasm from the benign librarian.

"Thanks. I appreciate it," Pi said, drily. She finished her wine, then watched as Abbie and Martha disappeared into an early low cloud of mother-daughter conflict.

Martha won. She was allowed to go with Abbie. They left Friday, braced for traffic, and Pi was left to guard the fort alone, for the first time in more than two months of living there.

After they left, Pi sat for a while at the broad oak table, counting long minutes of salty light breaking in late waves through the grey window. On stormy nights the downstairs windows rattled, and Pi had the feeling she was sleeping in a narrow cabin close to the elements. She'd never felt so close to the edge before. Always in her life—East Coast or West—a land spit or foothill had blocked her path to the sea, reaching an arm out to hold her back from falling in. The edge was out there, reminding you of infinity and of foreign horizons, but you didn't often look at it directly. Here in Mendocino the sea was your neighbor, and if you were restless in your sleep, as Pi often was, you wondered if sometime you might not thrash your way out of your dreams and slide by mistake right into its wet embrace. End up like Ophelia, all drowned.

The sea was everywhere around you in this house. Mostly it met you in a scent on the air, or in sound, speaking to you at night about its troubles and yours, urging you up on a long wild night to share a brandy with its midnight howlings. You felt the sea in the sharp salt at the corners of your eyes. And you tasted it in everything—as a thin film on the wine or an added bite in the salsa. The sea in this house was a friendly, constant ghost, an unseen lodger. But there was only one room in the house, Abbie's, from which you could actually see it.

Pi decided to explore. She went upstairs to the second floor—Martha's spacious bedroom, the bathroom, a small hexagonal hallway on which a New Mexican rug stretched its sunset colors. From there she ventured up the narrow staircase to Abbie's room at the top.

Abbie's room was full of light. Not much space, but plenty of light. It was surely Abbie's choice when she and her daughter moved back up here to divide the rooms this way. When Abe and Abbie were here together, Pi guessed, they'd had Martha's second-floor room, which would have been big enough for a real double bed. Now Martha's room had it all—television, bookcases, built-in closet, even a desk. This attic-like room at the top, with a slanting skylight along one part of the roof, was big enough just for Abbie's simple futon and a dresser and one bookcase. She had a single painting on the wall, a textured Californian hillscape. Otherwise the room was bare of anything but light. Abbie must have felt that light was what she'd need to live on to get through the divorce.

From one window, through which sea-light poured, there was a view of the water. Pi stood at the window and looked. The house was a long road away from the sharp drop of the coast itself, which waited past the winter-brown headlands and rock-steep paths. Pi allowed her blue eyes that were still more used to text than beauty to roam out to the unsketched horizon.

On a clear evening like tonight, late winter, early spring, the Pacific's turquoise had subsided into a heart-lit cobalt, purpled in streaks that suggested seals or kelp and stung by unlikely jewels at its crests as the disappearing sun scattered its brightness along random moments. The waves murmured. They didn't have much to say. The jutting arches and creatures—strange rock formations common to this part of the coast—took the break of the waves calmly on this evening. When wind and sea kicked up their stormy fuss, these same rocks inspired great cymbal-crashing wave breaks, and the air close to the edge was hectic with sea foam and a salt excitement.

A great good thing, this Pacific. Pi was an idiot never to have paid much attention before. She'd spent so many years so close to it—it was the place of picnics and boardwalks in her childhood, bodysurfing and shell-combing and sunburn-cooling along the splashy edge. But now as she stood closer to its watery language, hearing its hidden infinity of fishes and speeches, she realized how sheltered she'd been all along. It began to seem brave to Pi, all these people living so close to the sea. Yes, beach living was a luxury; it was what people with money in California always hankered after. But it must too be a worry—living with the chance that the sea would rise in impatience to swallow you. In California, that did happen in the wet season; every February or March, houses slid down cliffs to their murky ends. California was like a god that way: homes were given and homes were taken away. It wasn't only earthquakes. It wasn't only the constant threat of fire.

Pi's legs wavered. Her head felt thin. She couldn't watch anymore. She sat down abruptly on Abbie's bed, aware of an uneasiness that hollowed her stomach, a wariness that pinched at her eyes. Some dislocation was going on within her. Would she pass out? Would her heart seize up? Or was it simpler. Was it something she'd forgotten: the basic, urgent clutch of grief.

She began to cry.

Just crying—the deep and ugly kind, the kind you lose yourself in, thanking God no one has to see how rubbed and blotched your face becomes, though some detached part of you also wishes there *were* someone to see you now, to see and understand how sad you are, at heart. They don't see it, of course; you'd never show them.

It was a funny line that kept returning to Pi to trigger her sobs. When you're deep in weeping it just goes on with its own momentum—the snowball effect produced by the fact that the louder you hear yourself cry, the sorrier you feel for yourself and the louder your peals become. But there are phases when your mucussy hiccups slow down and the grief might end, and that is when some sentence or image returns to remind you of your misery and set you off again. For Pi, the sentence she heard in her mind's ear was Abbie's blunt appraisal, her non-compliment: "You're too thin. Look at you."

For some reason this small, accurate judgment undid her. Pi knew perfectly well she was too thin, and though she felt a morbid satisfaction in it, she knew there was now something cadaverous in the sharp jut of her hips. The thinness, her own obvious unhappy bones, reminded her of how untouched she was. Maybe the appetite loss was a strange protest against the lack of touch. But thinking of touch made Pi think of Alan, who last had touched her, and this sent her thoughts spiraling backwards, a giddy time-travel through lost loves and murky mistakes, the dead minefield of her string of secular, non-legal divorces.

For instance. What business had she had dating Alan in the first place? He was married, for God's sake. What did she expect? "You are beautiful," he had told her with his honey-gold eyes. He'd stroked her face, all gentleness and murmur. "Being with you makes me feel alive." Maybe so, but was that supposed to be love? The man was still married! He was still sleeping with his *wife*—as husbands are supposed to. Why had she trusted him? Then again, why had she left him? Wasn't Alan, in his kindness and generosity—Pi remembered him dashing around his Oakland kitchen fixing rice and raisins and chutneys for an Indian dinner he'd made her—wasn't he better than the years with that woman named Babe? Pi travelled back to before graduate school, when she was still on the other coast teaching "minimize the eye strain, maximize the mind gain" to unhopeful adults under after-work fluorescence. In that strange stretch of her life, the dumb early twenties, Pi had poured her intellectual fervor into an obsession with Babe, a cute punky redhead, a brain-twister, a girl who blew hot then cold then passionate then crazy, whose antics strung Pi along for years, through travels, betrayals, separations, and reunions and all along the wearing down of Pi's slender set of personal resources. Thank God she'd escaped Babe when she came to graduate school. It had been Kant, Pi sometimes felt, who'd finally cured her of that debilitating involvement. Yet another reason to revere the German rationalist.

But how, she teased her memory, had she gotten into the Babe trap in the first place? She was led there! By none other than the New York poet of erotica, the handsome, muscled Buddhist who'd made love to her amply, slowly, with the not-so-hidden thrill of a man seducing a self-described lesbian. Pi had let him. Why not? She'd enjoyed it. He was a good lover. "I think I could really get to care about you," he'd told her obscurely one morning over Polish food in a dim-lit diner, when maybe half an hour before she'd held him in her mouth, tasting his excitement. As opposed to what? Pi had wanted to ask him. The indifference you feel now? His long warm arms had not held Pi, and in their openness they'd sent her straight to Babe. He'd introduced her to Babe, in fact, though it was months before she and Babe figured out they'd been having affairs with him simultaneously.

Those East Coast years seemed poisonous to Pi. She should never have left California in the first place. The only important thing she would have missed if she hadn't was Marie. Pi would always love Marie, deep in her body and her imagination. Furthermore, if she'd stayed with Marie, Pi might be famous by now. Marie was. Marie had transcended her college troubles to become a successful movie maker. She had attained a *People* magazine level of fame, giving interviews in which she was invariably described as "the female Spike Lee." Pi, unfamous, unconnected, did not always have her phone calls to Marie returned these days. The last time she'd caught up with her was a year before, when Marie was briefly home between locations and film festivals and trips to the Caribbean with glamorous young girlfriends. Pi had had the childish thought that Marie might hear about, or perhaps even intuit, Pi's disaster in the fire and try to call her. But the lines had been silent. The connection remained unmade.

And now, of course, Pi had neither work nor cat nor books nor room to sustain her through this particular season of aloneness.

The sobs subsided. Pi felt herself emptied. Her mind grew exhausted with its own grief and unimpressed with it, and the sadness receded to be replaced with an ordinary, coping thought.

It's good for you to cry.

The banality of the thought awoke her humor. Pi had a wry thought that she ought to issue a little bulletin to all those concerned folk back in the Bay Area. Memo: CCs to Mary Dixon, Ryan, Renée and Jen, Sol and Irene Lerner: Guess what, everybody! I finally did it. I let myself *grieve.* I broke down and cried, just like you said I should.

Now, with night breaking over the breaking sea, having leaked tears and spit and gunk into Abbie's pretty, embroidered quilt cover, Pi found it easier to consider what had happened to her in the fire. A line of Fran's came back to her. It was when they were talking about whether Pi should travel as a way of putting the disaster behind her. Jen and Renée had been urging Pi to spend a month in Thailand, as they had the summer before. They said it would be "healthy" for her to have an adventure somewhere so different. The Dixons suggested Europe—they invited her to spend Christmas vacation in their small apartment in Paris.

"Vacation?" Fran said when she heard this idea. "No, no. That's a bad idea.

You don't need a vacation. The thing about vacations is that you have a great time, and then at the end of them you get all excited and ready to go back to your old life. But that wouldn't work for you. That's the whole point here—you don't have an old life to go back to."

Even Fran realized as she said it that this was a little too harsh to actually say to someone in Pi's position, even if it were true. As soon as she'd issued the sentence Fran tried to paper it over with other, cheerfuller sentences. But the phrase in its simplicity had clung to Pi's memory, and now, dried out of all her salt and water, she lay facedown on Abbie's bed and sounded the monosyllables out in her mind, testing the taste of them. *You don't have an old life to go back to.*

It wasn't the same as having nothing to go back *for*. Pi might, she knew, still decide to return to the Bay Area. Not to philosophy—never, she was fairly certain, to philosophy—but to her friends, her past, its history, those comforts. To packed, chattering cafés. To good movies. To clean, well-lit places for books.

What she didn't have anymore, though, was an old life. She was going to have to understand this—get it through her deaf, flat heart. The world had changed, and it was not possible to stop a changing world by leaving it. This was something she had to remember. Of course, stupid though it was, she'd indulged the thought that by leaving Berkeley and not going back there she had cleverly managed to preserve it as it was before the fire. Yes. That was the recent idiocy that lurked in her brain. It was a shameful metaphysics of optimism that she'd concocted, keeping the room she'd lived in cosmically alive by not going back to where it no longer was.

No, Pi. She told herself the truth now. There is no parallel universe. There is no life you should have lived, no life you could somehow be living now. There is no ring on your finger from the oaths you and Marie swore to each other to stay together. There is no child living with you out East, as there might have been if the Buddhist poet had gotten you pregnant (as you once feared he had). There is no teaching position you already occupy because you went to graduate school three years earlier. There is no Californian Pi who never left in the first place. There are no more books, Pi. There is no thought. There's nothing.

No, not true. The last part wasn't true. Thinking wasn't over for her. If she couldn't think she couldn't live, and she did, definitely, intend to go on living.

Pi got up. The room was just about dark now. A few stars appeared through the skylight—big, bright, fairy tale–ish. Pi would have to come back here in the morning, straighten Abbie's poor drenched quilt. Grief energy: was it something you could get out in a hot wash?

She wound her way down the two sets of stairs back to her room and the kitchen. Her footsteps creaked like nightbirds waking up for the hunt. She thought of the present. Of Xander and Martha. Her little job. The Pacific. She had plenty of things still to learn. She had Sylvia Plath's dawns in her ear, the inverse of the dusky hour she'd just spent. "The window square/Whitens and swallows its dull stars." There were still words and people left, after all.

By the bottom of the staircase, her feet flat on the floorboards, Pi felt a strange, unruly seizure of enthusiasm. She thought about turning on the computer, seeing if what Xander said was true. BBSs. She'd have to find out what it meant. But first she was thirsty. All that crying had drained her. She moved into the lamplit kitchen to scare food from its cupboards, something for dinner, something to moisten her tired throat.

```
Re: Liftoff
  Welcome to 1992, Pi. The rest of us have been here
for two months already but hey--better late than never.
Glad you got the software.
  Self-evident answer: yes I got your message. Yes we
have liftoff. Are you excited? Do you feel modern?
You're very modern now. All of us here in the twentieth
century are very proud of you.
  Write back so I know you got this and that I'm not
being too obnoxious,
LOVE Fran
```

And one from Hannah.

```
Re: Hello!


Dear Pi,
  I don't even check my e-mail that often because of
this nightmare situation--there's some guy who keeps
pestering me on it. So it was a treat to open it up
today and find lovely *you* on it. I'm not sure how to
get rid of this guy, I've started just deleting his
```

messages without reading them but that doesn't seem necessarily the most forceful approach.

This guy, can you believe this? is on *Border Patrol,* he was at a conference in San Antonio called "Beyond Borders" that was supposed to be a new look at improving communications between Mexican border towns and Texan border towns to try to decrease illegal immigration. Why am I telling you this? Because Officer Ed was at this conference for some reason, and he took a shine to me. Yikes! What am I doing wrong, Pi? Is it my hair? Was it the cut of my jacket? Anyway he came up after my paltry little presentation and said he'd enjoyed it every much, that it was very interesting and would I send him some information about our organization? I couldn't even tell if he was just spying or what, I was half convinced he was a member of some militia group. But I did send him some info, god knows why, which happened to have my e-mail address on it and now he's my most faithful correspondent.

The worst part of it is, he had a kind of big man with guns sort of sexiness about him, which is truly frightening.

Now did you really want to know all that? This is what e-mail opens you up to, Pi, long accounts of your friends' dreary lack-of-love lives. Talk about opening up the borders! There's something very metafictional about my border story I think. Did I tell you I'm taking an evening writing class once a week? I might just have to turn Ed into Material. I hope he wouldn't mind.

Better get back to work. Clearly this could become a real time drain. But it's fun to have you reachable again. I hope you're OK in Mendocino, wherever that is. Tell me more about it--
lots of love,
Hannah

Pi still shivered when she sat down at the computer. This was one of the main reasons she hadn't, as Xander put it, "gone anywhere" in her first encounter with the life-changing technology. Even typing short letters to Fran and Hannah had been traumatic. Pi's fingers knew the keyboard better than she knew the back of her own hands: for her fingers the letters of the keyboard were the frequent entryway into philosophy, into the words of her thought. Sometimes she typed words in the air when she heard them without knowing she did it; she'd hear a phrase and her fingers would silently twitch out the words in simultaneous translation. Putting her fingers back on **ASDFJKL;** was like opening her old door on La Vista, hearing the windchimes jumble mountain music as the door swung open and her eyes moved to her answering machine to count the number of flashing lights that listed the voices there.

What saved Pi now, what allowed her to go on and type e-notes to Fran and to Hannah, was that no paper was involved. The thought of printing out her own words still raised the ghost of pages past, and horrified her. But typing something and then watching it disappear under a cheerful heading "Message Sent Successfully" was, as it happened, bearable. She typed the message and watched it go, the way your words went out of the air once you'd spoken them, to live on only in the memory of anyone who heard them. (And found them memorable.)

Pi hadn't wanted to stay in touch with anyone, she'd said. That was the starkness she'd imposed on herself when she moved up here. The decision had come partly from Pi's natural asceticism and partly from her judgment that it would be easier not to talk to any of her friends for a while. Till she'd reached some unspecified point of cure. Till she could ask and answer normal questions without feeling weak. It wasn't masochism so much as a feeling that what was simplest would best match her new complexity.

But Pi's asceticism didn't know what to make of e-mail. E-mail seemed permissible to her. It was quiet; it didn't require immediate response, as a voice on the telephone did; it was in her familiar medium, print, so it emerged through the loved language of her fingertips. But it didn't require a physical body of print on paper. Ontologically, e-mail was not in any recognizable category: neither voice nor paper, neither pure mind nor pure matter. And uncategorizable items often make it past regulations that don't know how to understand them. Pi's edict might have been to stay out of touch, but when she read her two pieces of e-mail she replied to them instantly.

Re: Modernity

Hey Fran,

Modern. I'll tell you about modern. In the modern
world children are allowed to interrupt the divorce
schedules of their parents. It didn't happen in my day,
let me tell you!

Martha and Abbie are en route to your town as I write
this. Martha persuaded Abbie to take her with her. (For
persuaded, read: emotionally blackmailed.) But maybe you
know this already. Maybe Martha's asking to borrow your
skateboard even as you read this message . . .

So, yes. It's exciting to be doing this. Are you really there? Do you read me? It does feel like being an
astronaut and contacting Houston. If I run out of oxygen, I'll have to come parachuting down in something
more conventional like a phone call or a letter.

This is the first time I've been alone in this house.
It's spooky. The walls may start to talk, and what if I
listen? I don't really have anyone to hang out with up
here, except for the guy at the xeroxing place/comic book
store/desktop publishing biz I work at. Xander--have
I told you about him? He does fasting workshops on the
side. He makes me feel like an outcast because I refuse
to drink carrot juice. But he's designing a business
card for me with the logo for pi on it. Of course neither of us can figure out what to list for my job on
the card, since all I do at the moment is reproduce.
(On the copier, I mean.) Any suggestions are welcome.

Xander tells me I should look into bulletin boards on
the Internet. So I might do that. If I do will I immediately become a weird loser computer freak? I'm nervous about this, Fran. You have to help me. As you know
my life isn't exactly stable right now so I might get
led astray. I am probably also very vulnerable to cult
leaders right now. I have to hope none pass through
Mendocino any time soon--or that I don't get stuck onto

some guru's bulletin board and not know how to get off
it. (I'm not sure I have the bulletin board concept
down yet.)

All I'm saying is: keep an eye on me. So to speak.
Let me know if I start to sound like I'm possessed.

That's it for now.
love 3.14159 (pi)

Re: Hello!

Dear Hannah,

Ed sounds like an axe-murderer. Stay away from him.
It's that kind of story that makes this Internet thing
scary. Don't feel guilty about turning him into Mate-
rial--it's better than he deserves.

So what's the writing class? What kind of writing are
you doing? The word "metafictional" bears an uncanny
resemblance to the word "metaphysical" so my eye did a
small jump when I got to it. I'm trying to get over
metaphysics still. Trying to move on. I'm favoring poetry these days, also the books on young Martha's
shelf. My two current favorites are Bedtime for Frances
and Plath's Ariel. I somehow graduated from college
without having read either. Kids' books and poetry, it
turns out, are much more useful than vacations in Thailand would be for Coping with Catastrophe.

Anyway. Thanks for writing me back. It was good to
see your name on my screen. I hope Ed won't stop you
from tuning in. I've got that beginner's thrill with it
all still. Maybe next time you hear from me I'll have
figured out what a bulletin board is.
Wish me luck--

love Pi

Outside the room, night had fallen thick. Pi had long since lost even the non-view out her bedroom window of the side of the neighbors' garage. She was alone in her lighted cell, sheltering against a real night. Elsewhere in the world—actually not so far away from where she was—Friday night had significance for people. It marked a place in the week. Even graduate students, whose work was of the endless Möbius strip kind that wound on and on, twisting back over itself and over and back again—even graduate students tended to take Friday night off. Pi and Rob and Tamar had in the past year drifted into a Friday night film lottery together; they got together every Friday for whatever movie the Pacific Film Archives in Berkeley happened to be showing. It was a genuine lottery. Some nights you got lucky—a restored print of *My Fair Lady* or a hard-to-see Cassavetes movie. Other nights you just felt worthy and broad-minded, struggling with badly printed subtitles.

Pi wondered whether Rob and Tamar were carrying on with the lottery. Maybe they'd signed some new people on, like that charmer Helmut. Maybe Tamar had a boyfriend by now, or Rob a girlfriend closer to hand than the one he had in Seattle who always seemed more theoretic and telephonic than actual. For all she knew Rob was married by now. Pi could find out. Rob had made sure Pi had his e-mail address, in case she broke down and got in touch.

There were few hiding places in Pi's new existence. Her old existence had been full of them. Books make, among other things, excellent places to stash forgotten reminders. Pi could open a book—Calvino's *Invisible Cities*, say—and out would flutter a brittle old love letter from Marie, written in Marie's sweet blue insect writing a decade before.

The city I'm in has diamond walls and cobblestones made of jazz. The trees move not to the wind but to the look in your limbs. There are no streetlamps here, and the light is always that thin mauve that means sunrise or dusk, the kind of light in which new possibilities flutter and swoop overhead like the boldest birds. This city I'm in is the city of my love for you, a city I've looked for, that I always knew I'd find.

Not that all bookmarks were so charming; not too long ago Pi had found the New York poet's erotica folded inside a volume by Richard Rorty.

Your juices
mine

the salted thrust
of our sweet recipe . . .

Perversely, she'd left it in there.

But here in the toolroom, in the computer chamber, in her downstairs maid's quarters—there was hardly any place for such written items to get squirreled. The affectionate postcard Rob had sent her with the modem was meaningful to Pi, but she wanted to keep it out of her sight, and therefore out of her mind. She had hidden it underneath the computer where she couldn't see it.

But she could find it, use it, send him e-mail. "Dear Rob. I'm sorry . . ." And then she'd have to list all the things she was sorry about. She'd have to explain, at least briefly, the scorching chronology of events. She'd *have to*, to be friendly, ask him how his work was going, make at least some reference to her former department.

Pi left the card hidden where it was. Possibly right now in that Berkeley screening room, possibly even now titles were rolling up the screen and a group of people—graduate students, undergrads, film nerds of all ages, Europeans and Asians impressed by this rare outlet of foreign culture—were getting ready to watch some great Jimmy Stewart flick. *It's a Wonderful Life*, maybe, even.

Pi cleared the image from her mind, focussed on her screen here. What the hell. She might as well explore. Poetry. Why not?

By clicking her way through various broader categories, she figured out how to arrive at a place called Poetry Lab. Once inside Poetry Lab, she finally had the sensation of stepping across a border—into an abstract country where you could read the sentences of strangers, where people you didn't know were suddenly typing their words right into your house.

Conversations to choose from. This was what Xander had warned her about. She had to make choices! And would people know what she was choosing? Pi didn't really understand this about the Internet. Now that she was on, and in, could people see what she was calling up? Was it like being in one of those rooms with one-way glass—behind it, people you couldn't see were watching you, clocking your every move?

No need to work up a sweat, Pi. She took a sip of water. Conversation topics! Choose one.

She chose "Pulitzer Prize." People were sharing views on the guy who'd just won the Pulitzer for a volume called *Some Forgotten Moon Country*. Pi had never heard of him, but she read through anyway. People had strong opinions, but to Pi's relief the overall tone was verbose/cranky rather than frothing/lunatic. It was the kind of conversation you might overhear in a café on Telegraph. These folks didn't seem like social outcasts: they weren't writing in some baffling geek language. They were writing things like "It just bothers me that he wins for this volume when 'Flight from Saigon' was so much bolder" and "He isn't doing anything Levertov hasn't done, a hundred times better." Harmless academic chat, stuff Pi was used to.

She sampled a few other topics—love poetry, Pablo Neruda—that were amiable but equally specialized. After all, Pi knew next to nothing about poetry. She'd taken one feminist poetry class in college and had somehow sailed right past all the Chaucers, Spensers, Eliots, and Audens. Pi began to realize that Poetry Lab was, not too shockingly, for poetry people. Specialization was the thing in today's world, right? How else could she have been a neo-Kantian? It was probably equally the case, as Xander had suggested, that in philosophy sections people were getting all hardline and technical, rather than sitting around discussing the general virtue of posing philosophical questions.

Discouraged, she was about to go, when her eye hooked on a subject that looked intriguing. It was called "Dickinson 536." Pi clicked on the name and read through a series of messages.

```
>>Any people looking for Dickinson 536, we've moved to
the Literature chat room for technical reasons that
have to do with the Diery. Please look for us there,
anyone who's interested. --Janet, SysOp


>>PMFJI, but what's Dickinson 536? --Risa


>>Risa:
   Dickinson 536 started out as a kind of quirky topic.
It's a Dickinson poem about suicide somebody liked and
copied out, and then gradually it turned from a discus-
sion of the poem into a general discussion on the sub-
ject (of suicide, I mean).
   So it's mutated into a discussion group, which sounds
sinister because the people in the group take on nick-
names of famous suicides . . . But actually it's just a
literary discussion group with a streak of black humor.
```

You're welcome to take a look at it, it's in the Lit section now.

> Best,
>
> --Janet

>>Janet, is the Dierist back? --Will S.

>>Yes, that's the reason we've moved. He's posted a whole new section of the Diery. You can open it up under "Diery."

>>So, not to be a huge pain, but who's the Dierist? --Risa

>>Risa, why don't I save Janet the trouble of explaining. It's easiest to understand if you go look it up, the past installments of the Diery should all be there still.

About 2 months ago someone who calls himself "JD" started posting his "Diery" in Dickinson 536. It reads like a real diary, but the guy knows enough about computers to have scrambled his address so no one can trace him back, or reply to his postings. It's not even possible to be sure it's all written by the same person. Though it reads like it is.

So a lot of the discussion in Dickinson 536 at this point is about the Diery. If you read it, you'll be able to keep up with the conversation. Hardly anyone talks about Dickinson anymore!

Hope that helps -

Will S (BTW, in the group my handle is "Hemingway")

PS, here's the original poem for you:

The Heart asks Pleasure - first -
And then - Excuse from Pain -
And then - those little Anodynes
That deaden suffering -

And then - to go to sleep -
And then - if it should be
The will of its Inquisitor
The privilege to die -

>>Janet, I'm relieved he's back. The last entry had me
worried. Is it the same old JD? --Will S.

>>Thanks for doing the summary. Yep. It's vintage JD.
About to go off on his big trip. I'll let you read the
new section, called "From the departure lounge." Check
you later! I'll see you in 536.

                                        --Janet (/Anne Sexton)

Pi took another sip of water. She decided to get out of Poetry Lab, but not
before jotting down a note or two.

She stood up. She stretched. She moved to the window. Outside all she could
see was the Rubins' garage light. The sea sounded in her ear. All of it was still
out there. If she wanted to, she could wrap herself up, put on her shoes, and
stumble out into the air. She could take a solitary nightwalk along the headlands. Not that it would be safe; Mendocino was a small town, but not so small
that it was different from most towns. Abbie had warned her—in the summer,
someone was raped on the headlands at dusk.

But it wasn't only rape or danger that stopped Pi now. There were nights she
had gone anyway, keeping her city alertness about her. There were nights she'd
felt reckless, boundless, when fear for her safety was nowhere within her.

Something besides fear pulled Pi back in now. Her mind was itching in a
way it hadn't for months. *This was a good feeling.* It was the lack of this feeling,
curiosity, that had made her feel so different from herself since October. She
hadn't felt curious for months. That was the familiar itch that made her reluctant now to leave the house.

Was she about to get weird? Was she going to turn inexorably into a greasy
computer junkie? Was it like those movies they showed you in high school with
titles like *No Turning Back* or *Just One Hit*, where some kid took heroin once
and six months later wound up in a Dumpster with a rat running over her body
and a needle sticking out of her arm? "She only wanted to try it," a girl says
tearfully about her best friend as she sobs into the camera. Was this the same?

If she followed her curiosity here, would it take her beyond the safe comforts she'd known into a place that would transform her into someone incomprehensible and alien?

Pi had never in her life experienced such doubt about an object of her curiosity. That had been the whole joy of inhabiting her mind; of living surrounded by her beautiful library. Her library housed so many potential questions. It promised endless paths, infinite pursuits; it promised the paper-bound affirmation that curiosity was a good, crucial, human quality. She had centuries backing her up in what she did. All those silent voices egging her on.

But this? How was Pi supposed to know whether this new curiosity had anything like the same kind of worth? Oh sure, there were people in magazines predicting a grand importance for this form of communication—this unaesthetic, unbeautiful method of exchanging ideas, this invisible shopping mall, this frantic quiet freeway, this private campus, this infinity of digits: this Internet. Smart people who ran rich companies said in a hundred years this would be all that would matter. Books, of course, would become obsolete.

It's too late, Pi. You're here. You're plugged in. You're curious. Why not explore? Who's going to bother you? How could it hurt?

The wide sky wouldn't answer her questions. It was busy. It had Milky Ways and black holes to worry about.

Pi left the window, returned to the computer. She cracked her knuckles. She sat down in front of it and looked at her notes. It took her a minute to figure out how to do it, but soon she had gone into Dickinson 536. The Diery was easy to find. She saw it was in four sections, "January in a cold year" through to the most recent, "From the departure lounge."

Pi took a sip of water, and she started to read.

D I E R Y

From the departure lounge—

THERE'S AN INGREDIENT IN MY LUNCH TODAY THAT TASTES LIKE TURPENTINE.
Could it be? In this nice, fancy deli where people think carefully about what sort of mustard to order on their sandwiches, and the degree of Frenchness of their bread? Normally this would not be my choice of deli, I prefer your "Would you like coleslaw or potato salad with that?" kind of place, but this one is close to Lili's job, and when you're unemployed you travel to the other person's lunch spot of preference. That's the etiquette.

I am, in the medical lingo they'd use on a television drama, "out of danger" now. I have temporarily regained my taste for living. I've regained my taste for pasta salad in a balsamic vinaigrette with a hint of turpentine.

More accurately, I'm now in danger of getting sick of having Krieger around all the time. It has made me eager to set out on my Sentimental Journey. I leave in three days. Krieger has been shacking up with me ever since the night of the abyss, almost three weeks ago now, which has caused eyebrows to be raised by friends who know us both. Partly because they can't believe we wouldn't be at each other's throats—Krieger's notorious for snoring, talking, pestering, being generally intrusive, while I'm a "carefully guards his privacy" person, in case you hadn't guessed. Partly also people wonder, you know, if there's any kind of *subtext* to all this. I'm here to tell you there isn't. It's all been perfectly innocent. It's been a friendly, medical-supervision type of relationship. (Ask Minsk if you don't believe me.) If anything, Krieger is eager for me to go, too, so he can revert to his ordinary schedule of seducing beautiful actresses in his own trendier apartment, which he has tactfully refrained from doing while staying *chez* me and Minsk.

Krieger and I have talked a lot about Hamlet and Horatio. The play, and his

concept; but also my life, and my concept. It was one of the first things I told
him, after that night when he came over and I'd ranted and sulked and he'd
been kind of ugly and demanded I take some Valium of his; after I refused;
after he sweet-talked me into it finally and I agreed to take the Valium sometime
around dawn in exchange for his allowing me half an hour to type that last
account on the computer, which inspired him to dark incoherences again about
my imaginary friends; after I then conked out for about ten hours, only to wake
up to Krieger bright-eyed and entirely too bushy-tailed, sitting in an armchair,
keeping an eye on me even as he read through the *Times* and made tsking
noises over some theater review he disagreed with; after he then made me go
out with him for coffee and a bagel in an effort to normalize in some way
though I sincerely found it hard to keep anything down; after eventually he
broke down a little and told me not to fucking scare everyone like this, and
what did I want to do, get hospitalized or what; and after I said it wasn't a ploy,
and it might not be aesthetically appealing but I couldn't help it if I'd just
stopped wanting to *live*, damn it. Well, anyway, after all that, and more, but I
don't have the time to go through the whole thing right now—Lili's arrival is,
we assume, imminent—one of the first things I said to Krieger that was coherent,
a few nights later over boxed, cold, salty kungpao chicken, was—

"I'm going to try to find Horatio."

We were both eating straight out of the box. Krieger had the beef in black
bean sauce, over which his fast chopsticks paused for a millisecond.

"What?"

"I'm going to try to find Horatio."

"Oh, thanks." He waved his chopsticks at me, before they went back into
action. "But we've already got him."

"Who?"

"He's a guy named Russell Jamison. He's got walrus lips and an ego the size
of Alaska, but he has a great voice. I think he'll be good. He does a very nice
'Good night, sweet prince,' which is all anyone remembers anyway."

"That's marvellous. But that's not what I meant. I'm going to find a real
Horatio. In a metaphorical sort of way."

"What the hell are you talking about?" He re-assumed his worried, clinical
stare.

By now I was speeding on all the protein, which was getting my blood and
organs busy and excited. They'd had so little sustenance to go on lately that
they'd just about given up hope of ever getting any. Also Krieger thought I
should stay away from alcohol, so he asked the take-out guys to bring us a couple

of Cokes. As I'm sure you know, under certain conditions Coke is a stronger drug than beer. I don't know what Krieger was thinking. On Coke I tend to start connecting everything very rapidly, speaking in my own local dialect, becoming convinced that I have direct access to a unique kind of truth.

So I frothed to Krieger about the trip I was going to take to see my sister and maybe my mother and any other relatives who surfaced *en route*. I explained that it was not merely a mental health excursion or even some crude attempt to save on my food bills, but that I was also going to use it to look for Horatio. The metaphorical aspect was that this character was no doubt not actually *called* Horatio. But I emphasized to Krieger that the search itself wasn't metaphorical, a search for lost innocence or the inner child or any of those other modern intangibles, but that I was genuinely looking for a brother I believe may have been lost. Not that *I* lost him, you understand, but that one of my parents had, lost or hidden him, and then kept the memory or record out of sight thereafter. I told Krieger that I thought I had memories of this Horatio. Some blank space in my deep memory where he had once lived. Of course he assumed I was getting confused and was thinking of Cindy, but I told him no, it's not that, I remember Cindy vividly, I was already three when Cindy showed up with her big noise and no hair and I remember all of that vividly—the excitement, the irritation, the relief when she turned from looking like a drowned red rat into looking more normal, like a genuine baby.

I could see how this would sound to someone with an analytical mind, like Krieger, who given that both of his parents are shrinks more or less drank in Freud with his mother's milk. Krieger thought this whole crazed fantasy of mine was some twisting of my feelings about Cindy, maybe even some wounded sort of reaction to the not very new news that Cindy is gay. He trotted out some theories about how rejected I would have felt by Cindy's choice, how that in turn would have made me want to reject her, turning her into a boy, a brother, whom I'd somehow lost. The sexually unattainable sister becomes the physically and emotionally unattainable brother, blah blah blah. He spelled it all out for me in words of multitudinous syllables.

"That makes a lot of sense," I told him. "That really works as an explanation."

He shrugged modestly.

"It would make a good play. Don't you think? Maybe you could turn it into your next interpretation of *Hamlet*, where Hamlet and Ophelia are really brother and sister, and Hamlet is actually Laertes' shadow self, his darker self, and there's a crazy incest thing going on . . ."

That in turn offended Krieger, so we spent a while trading barbs, having one of those pro- and anti-analysis fights which no one ever wins because each side always says the other is resisting; and then this turned into a general tussling between the two of us as we tried to establish which territory was ours that the other guy should just stay *off* of. I may be mentally ill but I'm not crazy, I told Krieger. There is a specific quality that my memories and feelings about Cindy have. I remember her learning to walk, for instance—I remember waking up my parents at six in the morning to tell them, and it turned out they already knew because she'd walked the night before. I remember the goodness of that discovery, my thrill that my little sister Cindy at last was *on the move*. Separate from that entirely is a cool melancholy that has run through all my years, that I am now tracing to this absent Horatio. It's this damned emptiness I feel all the time. It's the sense of someone who has been left behind.

He's got his interpretation, I've got mine. I could see behind Krieger's dark eyes that he thought the only place I should be going right now was into a well-paid professional's office and not off into the grits-eating wilderness. But he polished off the black beans and beef and refrained from comment. Citing artistic differences, we agreed to change the subject.

Tuesday

Lili said something unexpected at lunch.

She said, after she'd gotten over her irritation that I'd started on my turpentine salad without her, which I'd only done because she was *late* because she had been in the middle of an important *phone call* which she couldn't interrupt because she has an important *life*, unlike some of the rest of us—

"I want to come with you."

This is what she said to me.

At first I thought she meant to the vet's to deal with Minsk's shots, because she knows I am very squeamish about needles. Or possibly she meant back with me to my apartment—have I mentioned Lili's borrowing it while I'm away? To escape her evil roommate who plays Seattle grunge rock, which hurts Lili's delicate shell-like ears. I thought maybe Lili wanted to come back with me after lunch and check out the appliances, pick up the keys.

It turns out she meant on the *whole trip*.

Lili's going through a sad unrequited phase currently. There's some opera singer who was flirting with her, then cooled off inexplicably. I have tried to cheer her up by telling her all men are assholes, but that remark doesn't seem to help, coming from me. Her real problem, I think, and she agrees, is that she hasn't gotten over this mercilessly short fling she had with a woman about six months ago who picked her up at a concert I was supposed to go to with Lili but couldn't due to the fact that I was soon to be fired but didn't know it yet so I'd been working late to ingratiate myself with my boss. Anyway, this glamorous six-foot-tall woman came on very strong to Lili, "turning her head," as Lili put it and causing her to go against her typical attractions to fat men with big voices. Two weeks later this woman dumped her. I think it was a conquest-of-straight-women thing with her. You know: introduce a novice to the delights of sapphic love, then move on. The woman has since become prominent in the public eye by taking over the reins at a major fashion magazine, so you can't help reading about her all over town, which doesn't make life easier if you're trying to forget her. "All women are assholes," I want to tell Lili to comfort her, which I half believe, but I figure that remark would sound even worse coming from me, so I just try to be sympathetic.

But Lili said if I can just give up on everything and leave it all behind, why can't she?

"Because you have a job," I reminded her. "That's the difference."

"Yeah, but explain this to me. Having a job is supposed to be good, right? You are supposed to envy me—"

"I do envy you."

"—Because I have a job, and full benefits, and a guaranteed Christmas party to go to each year, at least one. So why is it I feel trapped and bored and you get to go off like Jack Kerouac and find yourself?"

"It's not going to be anything like Jack Kerouac. They're going to put me in some hideous Ford Taurus or something. Besides, I'm going to *Baltimore*."

"Baltimore's very in, these days. It has character. Everywhere you go you read about Baltimore having character."

I tried to explain to Lili what travel writers mean by *character* (old-fashioned pedestrian crossing lights, crab houses, people calling you "Hon") and what my experiences of the city have actually been like (a thousand-degree humidity in the summer, and very large people on the street, black or white, accurately spotting me as one who doesn't belong there). I admitted that it was possible to see the director John Waters at the local bars, but I said that was one of the place's only true cultural advantages.

"I don't care how snobby you try to get on me about it," Lili said. "I want to go with you. It's not fair. You get to go, and I don't."

So then I tried to explain that the only reason I "get" to go somewhere as characterful as Baltimore was that I a) have no life, and b) am considered mentally unhinged by members of my family who will probably commit me as soon as I get there—hopefully in the same ward Zelda Fitzgerald had when she lost it back in the twenties or whenever.

"Don't be ridiculous," Lili said. I hadn't filled Lili in on the finer details of my Night on the Edge, and I think she was vague about why Krieger was staying with me exactly. "You're blowing this whole depression thing out of proportion. I'm depressed, too. We're all depressed. You're not such an exceptional case, JD. Depression is the norm, at least among anyone we're friends with."

"If you said that to my sister she'd commit you, too."

"Then we could be committed together, in separate wings. That would be so cute. We could meet at lunchtimes, just like we do now."

"But you're a productive member of society! We can't have you committed. Who'd be left to keep the arts alive?"

Lili sighed, and eyed her watch. She had about eight minutes of her lunch left. The Diet Coke was making her frazzled and melancholy all at the same time.

"You know what I feel like?" she said. "The kid sister. I bet Cindy used to feel this way all the time. Did you used to exclude her from all the things you did?"

"No! She used to play Monopoly with me. Sometimes. And basketball. And touch football—even tackle. She was a vicious little tackler. She'd come charging right at you. Fearless."

"Well." Lili looked at her watch again. "Lunch is up. Great talking to you. Gotta go." She had started to put on her real face, her grown-up face—her working face. I wonder if I used to have a working face. I don't remember it. I certainly don't have one now. Lili was snapping everything shut and smoothing everything down—it's scary, how fast it happens.

"So I'm meeting you at your place tomorrow night, for the guided tour of the appliances?"

"Yes. Eight o'clock. Don't be late. I have an appointment immediately following yours," I said to her, but she was too up and running to get my Doctor O joke.

Friday

Minsk and I are all packed up and ready to go. Unlike myself, Minsk is travelling light—bringing only a very old sweatshirt of mine that has become his security blanket. I'm glad he's taking it. He's not going to like the Taurus—it's got that acid smell of chemical air freshener veiling the smell of the last person in it having smoked an emphysemic quantity of cigarettes. I don't get this whole air-freshener idea. After a point you have to wonder: which makes my lungs un-happier, really, secondhand cigarette smoke, or firsthand air freshener?

What happened to travel, is what I want to know. When did it get so technical and uninteresting? I mean, flying has always been technical, it probably was even for the Wright brothers. Flying has always been about rules and restrictions and taking out the card in the seat pocket in front of you so you can follow along as we go through the safety features of this aircraft. Taking a moment to locate the exit nearest you, bearing in mind it may be behind you.

The sad thing is, even cars and trains have lost their glamour. If trains were glamorous—if they allowed dogs on them, the way I bet they do in Europe—that would be my preferred route to Baltimore. But I think when I agreed to this scheme of Cindy's, a small part of me, like Lili, thrilled to the idea of hitting the Road. It was impossible not to imagine a Mustang, or a pickup, or even, you know, Dustin Hoffman's Spyder in *The Graduate*. Something con-vertible with a cinematic quality, that would have my dark locks flapping in the breeze, in time with the flapping white curls of Minsk.

You only had to talk to the car rental people to have that idea blown out of your head. On the phone it was all Waivers and Subcompacts and Coupon Values and Reservation Numbers, and it wasn't so much like renting a chunk of American mythology as it was underimpressing a booking agent by not be-longing to some complex frequent flyer/conference goer/long distance tele-phone points program. When I hung up I was humbled and drained. I felt like I'd just failed a very simple job interview, like they took one look at me and said, "Thank you for taking the time to apply, Mr. Levin, and good luck in your future endeavors. Next!"

The fact is, it is not easy to slip into that casual dream we peddle so effectively to our traffic-clogged friends in Europe and Japan—that dream of the wide open car on the wide open road. For one thing, if you want to put yourself in that picture you really should live in the West. (Preferably, assuming you want beach scenes and not the iconic rock formations of Utah and Wyoming, you should live in California.) Driving in big East Coast cities is neither cool nor fun. It's only cool if you're a cabbie and have intriguing opinions about peace in the Middle East ("They should get the Irish in there to help figure it out," e.g.), or harbor homicidal fantasies like Travis Bickle. Otherwise, it's all about red lights and aggression, neither of which I happen to excel at.

I am biased. I learned to drive in California, where if you can't drive by the time you're sixteen you might as well commit suicide then and there because your whole life is shot. Specifically, I learned to drive in Los Angeles, which is a living hell to drive in because of the freeways but is nonetheless the manufacturing epicenter of the aforementioned dreams we peddle in our movies. But once you get out of L.A.'s metropolitan sprawl the freeways turn into the images you recognize, you're out on a six-lane highway between bare groaning brown hills, and your whole life is before you. When I was in high school, aimless and lonely, before I got to college, where I became aimless and befriended, I used to take long drives for just that kind of mind-clearing exercise.

I can't help wishing those were the roads I was getting onto later today. I wish that was the car—my Mom's old crumbling Volvo—a car that had, in spite of being a Volvo, its own particular cool.

As it is, post-park, Minsk and I will descend into the ninth circle of some demonic garage which has never seen natural light. My guess is we'll spend a good hour climbing up and out of this city's chaos and clutter—allowing time for me to get turned around a couple of times, because I don't know the place by car, and to get stuck behind a delivery truck which is generally my driving karma. After all that, by which point I'll be sweating like a pig and Minsk will be whining in fear that my distress will cause me to rear-end someone, and as Minsk well knows we only took out the cheapest insurance—after all *that*, we'll hit the freeway. The great American freeway.

But in this part of the country the freeway doesn't mean freedom and glory. In this part of the country it means potholes and tollbooths, long dark tunnels and, when you get out of them, a low yellow sky of unease and pollution; that doesn't so much welcome you to your adventure as fill your spirit with a sour doubt about the wisdom of movement, and about what is ever accomplished by trying to leave your troubles behind.

That night Pi slept a long, travelling sleep, a deep one.

Martha, who was spending the night at Fran's place, stayed awake. She couldn't sleep. Her mother had never come back to get her that night, so she was camped out on the couch in Fran's cluttered living room. Fran's surf gear hung around the walls. Its neon strips and symbols glowed brightly, the colored constellations in Martha's long night-sky.

To make the time pass, she decided to write a letter.

Dear Pi, she patterned the words out in her mind.

I miss you. I wish I didn't come here. We had a long drive. My mom let us stop at McDonald's, that was fun, she doesn't usually let me but on car trips she doesn't mind.

My dad was nice to me but didn't say much. He hates my mom, you can tell. His face changes when he sees her. We were only there a few minutes. Patricia was there and she tried to be nice. I met her over Christmas. She's not so terrible, but my mom won't look at her.

Mom took me over to Fran's and then promised she'd come back and get me after dinner unless it got too late. If it was really late she'd pick me up in the morning, and then maybe take me over to Dad's so I'd see Dad, by myself. I asked Mom where she was going and she said Well honey if it gets late I'll stay at Rod and Janet's. It'll be easier than coming back here, and then I'll see you in the morning. I remember Rod and Janet. They have a black dog named Groucho.

How are you Pi. I wish you'd come with us. You and me and Fran could've gone rollerblading. Fran keeps a special pair of rollerskates for when I visit.

I skated with her in Golden Gate Park. I hardly ever fall over anymore. Then we had Kentucky Fried Chicken, which Mom doesn't let me have either. Fran says you shouldn't eat KFC all the time but that it is healthy to eat it once a month. She says your body needs junk food once a month to stay in balance.

I am not going to be able to sleep tonight I don't think. But I'm going to stop writing this letter since it's only in my head and you're never going to get it anyway. I'm going to try counting Fran's surfboards. Counting's supposed to help.

Yours sincerely,
Martha

Pi, asleep, found herself reading a book on the beach, reading it avidly, when a dark-haired guy came up to her. A white dog trotted along beside him.

"That's so weird!" Pi said. "I'm just reading about you. Right here!" She pointed at the book. It was his.

"Oh, you can stop reading that," he said. "It's just me complaining. It's just me making a lot of mountains out of a lot of tiny molehills."

"No it isn't. I like it. I want to keep reading. I want to find out what happens."

"I could tell you what happens—"

"No, no! Don't spoil it. OK? I hate knowing the ending beforehand. I'll just keep reading. I'd rather find out for myself."

"Did you want to at least put it down for a minute, and take a walk with me along the beach?"

"Actually, I don't want to be rude, but . . . I'd sort of rather just sit here and read right now. Some other time, though, I'd love to."

"That's all right." He shrugged. "I don't mind. Come on, Minsk, let's go."

"Oh, is that Minsk?" She stopped him for a minute to scratch the dog's ears. "He's so cute," she said.

"I know."

He made a move to walk off again, but she touched his pants leg to stop him. For some reason he was wearing long pants, even though they were on the beach and it was a dry, sultry day. She noticed now how pale his skin was. How sweet his mouth.

"I want to tell you something, before you go," she said to him.

"What?" His face was neutral. Not unkind. His dark eyes hid something that embarrassed him—the fact that he had a good soul, maybe.

"Yours is the first book I've ever bought," she told him. "Ever. In my whole life."

He squinted at her skeptically. She looked so much like a reader.

"Really?" He shrugged, smiling a little. "Well, that's nice. I hope you like it."

"I'd really love to come with you," she said to him. "But I just have to stay here and find out how it ends."

Pi woke up on Saturday morning feeling hung-over, and with the strange sensation that she'd had a one-night stand.

Her head hurt and her eyes itched, and her mouth felt thick and dry and gummy. Even her limbs strangely ached, the way they do after the odd night of passion, when you are reminded that sex requires a special kind of fitness, of body not just of mind. Pi almost expected to find a male or female shoulder next to hers this morning. Slow patterned breathing. An unfamiliar smell. The shivering of her own skin as it brushed against someone else's.

It had been a while since she'd had random sex. Alan hadn't counted as random; they'd spent a decent amount of time getting to know each other first. Random sex was something perhaps from her past: like that intimate week she'd spent in college with the goat-faced woman who owned a friendly curly-haired terrier—the terrier who watched from the corner of the woman's well-appointed apartment as Pi and its mistress became a flailing tangle of arms, sheets, and glasses. Or the wintry night Pi had shared a bed with her cute boy roommate, allowing him in the small hours to touch her back in unroommate-ish ways, to do unroommate-ish things with his mouth to her. They'd stayed pals after. (They'd even stayed roommates.) Then there was the chain-smoking Korean woman who persuaded Pi to show her the ins and outs of sex between girls; and an old friend, one of her oldest, that long-destined night in a Washington motel the week before his divorce became final. Random nights in Pi's life. Nights she'd woken up from stiffly, her mind slow to remember the new depth of her that had been touched in the night, her whole self moving and adjusting to cover over again whatever hiddenness had been revealed.

But she was alone here. Pi felt the empty bed surround and embrace her, and she knew this bed was a private place that no one had come into with her, ever. Ever in the two and a half months since she'd moved in. Her sleeps had been solitary. Her dreams all her own.

Still, if her body was untouched, Pi woke to the recognition that her spirit was not. Something had moved her last night. Some new character had crept into her mind. It was the feeling she used to have reading a great novel—*Anna Karenina*, for instance, which she'd read a few years back when she was feeling ignorant, not suspecting how much she'd actually enjoy it. Sometimes Pi had gone to sleep then with those characters too deeply lodged to leave her; she'd dreamed of them; she'd walked around for bright California days, accompanied by Anna and Vronsky and Levin, talking on in their snowy seriousness, in her listening inner ear.

You don't read novels anymore. Remember? Your novels are gone. So who came to see you last night? Who's on your mind?

He was dark, she knew that about him. "JD." That was his name. A man or a figment of a man, a guy or a character. Which was he? Had she made him up? Had he made himself up? How was she supposed to tell? If he were from a book, the idea was you just flipped to the back of it to see if it was called Fiction or Non, in order to tell the truthfulness content. If it were a movie, you might fall in love with the actress (Meryl Streep, let's say), but you did realize that she was not the same as whatever accented person she played.

But JD. What category was he in? She wanted to believe in him, she wanted to think he was real. Could she allow herself to? Pi didn't know who she could ask about this.

Outside the house the day wheeled on. It was a sunny ten o'clock on an early spring weekend, passers-through would be in town already, parking and brunching and shopping and saying loudly, "Ted? Come over here for a second. Take a look at this. Wouldn't it be fun to have one of these?"

Pi fixed herself some coffee, and, though the day beckoned, she knew she'd have to go back to the only place that might give her more information about this person who swam through her head.

She turned on the computer.

She climbed back through the brief maze and into Dickinson 536. Rather than go into the Diery, she went into Discussion.

```
Is Romance the Answer?
>>I'm curious at this point. How many people think JD
would be happier if he just had a girlfriend?
                                        --Anne Sexton
>>Anne, I'm sorry to say the question seems a very fe-
male one to me. Women have been raised to think if they
have love they have everything, which is a mistake--to
```

put it mildly. Love in itself can't be enough to give
your life purpose (besides, if that's what you're
counting on, it's going to be a pretty sick relationship). I don't think JD would feel much better if he
had a girlfriend. But also--I don't know that he's in a
state right now where he *could* have a girlfriend.
                                         --Virginia Woolf
>>Or boyfriend, Virginia. Let's keep an open mind on
that question. On Anne S's point though: it's a valid
question. I'm sure statistics would show that people
not in love are x times more likely to jump off a
bridge than people who are in love. Let x equal,
what? A thousand? A million? A kazillion?
                                         --Madam Butterfly
>>Let's not forget the people who jump off bridges pre-
cisely because they're in love. That happens too.
                                         --Hemingway
>>Being in love is a specific, euphoric state. Obvi-
ously--it's produced some of the world's great poetry.
(This is Poetry Lab don't forget.) Anyone should feel
lucky who's experienced this state. But I would argue
that being in a relationship isn't necessarily the same
thing. You may live with someone happily for years and
still be able to get into the kind of depression JD has
been fighting off. Love is not the *complete* answer.
                                         --Van Gogh
>>*Prozac* is the complete answer. I thought everyone
knew that by now. If you'd had Prozac, Vince, that ear
would never have come off.   --Young Werther
>>Love is not the answer. Love is the question.
  (Or is Prozac the question?)
  But seriously. I'm sure people might say JD is just
lonely, that he should get a girlfriend. Or they
might put it more bluntly and say he should have sex.
But in a country where divorce is twice as common as
marriage (or whatever that stat is), who's to say that
tying the knot wouldn't turn out to be tying the end of
JD's noose?

Incidentally, I should know. I'm the one who offed
myself on my own honeymoon, remember. Not to get gloomy
on you, but for those of you who haven't read your Sal-
inger lately.   --Seymour Glass
>>Seymour, I wasn't trying to suggest he get married.
Just date a little. ;-)

It sounds like you have your own particular views on
marriage? Besides the fact that it drove you to suicide, I mean?!   --Anne S.
>>Anne--

No *particular* views.

No, in truth I feel lousy (as Seymour Glass might
say) because an old friend of mine got married recently, sort of out of the blue but everyone was very
happy, and there was champagne, bridesmaids, lots of
pictures, dumb speeches, the whole nine yards. A year
later this couple is divorcing! It quote didn't work
out unquote. One of them got a job in Arizona and the
other refused to follow. It just seemed like a lot of
trouble to put people to for something that didn't work
out.

And furthermore I blew $400 I didn't have on the
ticket to get there! And now I'm wondering why.

                                              --Seymour
>>So you can guilt-trip them into coming to your wed-
ding one day.:-)   --Anne S.
>>I don't really think I'll be getting married anytime
soon! Can't you tell?   --Seymour
Is Therapy the Answer?
>>What do people think?   --Anna Karenina
>>I think Krieger's views sounded reasonable, to tell
you the truth, and I also thought his analysis of the
Horatio business made sense.   --Hemingway
>>But is there any point if it's not something he's in-
terested in?   --Anna K.
>>If it's behavior modification you're looking for:
Therapy is the answer. If it's a cure for soul-sickness

```
you're after: You're going to need something deeper.
The benefits of therapy are skin-deep, at best.
                                          --Abbie Hoffman
```

Pi stopped reading. These formless exchanges were taking her away from the subject she wanted to explore, into a disembodied chatter she wasn't ready to participate in. She wanted to ask someone about JD. What she wanted, really, was to try to write to him. But all these messages seemed to take for granted that you couldn't write to JD directly. It was as though they were all using JD and his writing as a spur for their own ideas and problems. Was Pi being naive to be worried about the guy himself?

```
>>Getting in touch
I'm sorry if this is a very stupid question, but is
there any way of responding directly to JD?
```

Pi paused for a long minute. She had to assign herself a name. She had to come up with an identity for herself, even just to ask a question. Pi ran through the list of participants in Dickinson 536 and couldn't find the obvious name that came to mind. How could there not be somebody who had taken her on? But there didn't seem to be. So, with an uncomfortable twinge about the melo-drama and immodesty of it, she signed her question --Sylvia Plath.

It felt a bold move. As she did it Pi's heart started beating faster. Her fingertips sweated. This, she felt, must be some irrevocable turning of a corner into com-puter nerddom, into a strange underworld of people pale and lifeless, bug-eyed, stale-breathed, green around the edges. That was it. Pi was going to become one of those. It would be like one of those *Star Trek* episodes, where on arriving on a foreign planet the *Enterprise* crew—all but the stars—gradually succumb to the foreign planet's insidious infection.

Off! Off. She exited, left, split, quit, closed down, turned off, stood up. Watched the screen and all its black on grey promises zap down to a dull dark green. It would take some time before anyone got around to answering her, she knew. She'd leave it for a while. Become a real person. Even if that man, JD, wouldn't leave her mind, she could take him with her out into the world of sky and beach and water. And air.

The telephone rang, sending Pi into a jitter of alarm. The morning, she'd hardly noticed, had been so quiet till now.

"Pi? At last. Thank God. I've been trying to get through to you for over an *hour.*"

Pi flushed, invisibly. It seemed so shameful. She felt as though someone had caught her holding a porn magazine. She wanted to say—I have no idea how I got hold of this! Someone just put it in my hands!

"I'm sorry. I've been—I've been on the line."

"Obviously." Abbie's voice was tart. Sweetless. "Listen. I'm calling because—has Fran called you?"

"Fran? No."

"You haven't heard from her?"

"Well—no."

"Shit." Clearly Abbie had no wish to explain what was going on. She breathed a short sigh of impatience. "Let me give you a phone number where I can be reached in case Fran calls. You see—Fran took Martha last night so I could try to work things out with, with Abe. But when I went over to Fran's this morning, they weren't there. Obviously I'm worried. I thought Fran might have tried you, to let you know where she—where they—were going."

"Well—"

"Of course, she might have tried you but the line was busy."

"I guess so. I'm sorry. I didn't realize—"

"That's fine," she said sharply. "Look. Let me give you the number I'm at, in case she calls you. If she does, please call me right away to let me know, will you? Obviously I've left a message on her machine too, but I mean in case she reaches you first."

Pi's head spun for a moment with numbers, messages, answering machines, absences. She took down the phone number of Abbie's friends, apologized again for being on the phone so long, and, both of them nervous and twitchy and irked, they hung up.

Pi took a cold sip of coffee. It was black and acrid. The telephone rang again. "Hello?"

"Is that—ah—Ms. Pye?"

A man's voice. Her heart thudded again. Why did so many people suddenly need to talk to her? She'd hardly received a single phone call in this house since she'd moved in, except from her mother and stepfather. Was the FBI onto her? She should never have logged on that morning. She'd been sure there were all kinds of sinister ramifications to it, it couldn't be as simple as Xander had made it sound.

"Ye-es. This is Pi . . . Emily Piper."

"Oh, sorry, Miss Piper. Listen—I've got someone here who wants to talk to you."

There was a pause. Who could it be? JD? The ghost of Sylvia Plath? Meryl Streep?

"Hello?" a little brown voice said.

"Martha!"

Pi's mouth grew moist and sweet with relief.

"Pi? Is that you?"

For a nasty instant Pi had a new terror. *Kidnapped!* Someone had kidnapped Martha! Pi's heart went stone still with fear, a deeper fear even than her irrational fear of the FBI.

"Martha, are you OK? Are you all right? Where are you?"

"I'm at my dad's."

That wasn't kidnapping, then. Probably.

"Does your mother know you're there?"

"Nope."

"Well, Martles, we should tell her. She's worried about you. OK? Is Fran—"

"Fran dropped me off here. My mom never came to get me last night."

"Listen, sweetheart—" Pi swallowed on the word. She hadn't called anyone *sweetheart* for some very long amount of time. No one in this new life. No one post-fire. "I'm sorry that happened. But we've got to let your mother know where you are."

"My dad says Mom is trying to stop me from seeing him."

"Hello?"

"Martha?"

"Hi, Miss Piper, this is Abe Kaplan speaking. Listen, I'm sorry to drag you into this. Martha came over here this morning, we're supposed to have the day together here, but she said she needed to talk to you first."

"Oh—hi. I should just let you know that Abbie's wondering where Martha is. She called here a minute ago to see if Fran had called—so I guess someone should let her know where Martha is. She sounded pretty worried."

"If dear Abbie was so worried about her daughter's well-being, it's not entirely clear why she didn't go back to Fran's last night to pick her up."

"Yeah. I don't—I don't know—"

"No, listen. This isn't your problem, I realize. This is one of those unfortunate situations where several people are getting involved in what is essentially a two-person problem. My concern is I don't want Martha caught up in it. Do you understand what I mean?"

"Yes . . ."

"So can I ask you to call Abbie back? Tell her we're fine, we're going out for the day, she doesn't need to get hysterical. I'll meet her back here at five o'clock, and she can pick Martha up then. I'd call her myself, but—frankly—our communication is not very effective right now, and I'm concerned that Martha will just be exposed to more unpleasantness. I don't want that for her. So if you would be good enough to call Abbie and give her that message, I'd be grateful to you. Could you do that?"

"Sure. Sure I could."

"I'd be very grateful. Five o'clock. Tell her we'll be back here by five o'clock."

"And she knows where you are?"

"It's her old house. Yes. She knows."

Pi's face got hot again with embarrassment. At least he couldn't see it.

"I'm going to put Martha on again. Thank you very much for your help. Perhaps we'll meet sometime. Here you go."

"Pi?"

"Hi there." Pi tried to sound normal. She didn't want Martha to be upset. But she couldn't think of anything to say.

"What did you do yesterday?" Martha asked.

"What did I do?" Pi laughed. "Nothing. Nothing really. I—I fooled around on the computer. That was about it. It's quiet here without you, you know. What did you do?"

"Went rollerblading with Fran."

"That sounds fun."

"It was." There was a pause. "I'm going to ask my dad if we can go again today."

"Oh. Does he rollerblade?"

"I don't know." A little laugh sneaked out over the phone line.

"Well, I hope you have a great time. Are you going to Golden Gate Park?"

"Yup."

"Oh." For some reason she said spontaneously, "I wish I could go with you."

"Me too. OK. Dad says we should go. OK, Pi. Bye. Goodbye."

"I'll see you soon, Martles—"

But she had already hung up. Pi was left holding a dead receiver, the way people do in movies. In movies they always say, "Hello? Hello?" and try that not-so-smart trick of clicking the button down to see if that brings the person back. It never does. Pi replaced the receiver.

Instantly the phone rang again, before she'd even taken her hand off it. Pi's heart did another little back flip. Abbie? Abe? Deep Throat?

"Hello?"

"Jesus *Christ*. What a fiasco."

"Fran!"

"My God. Did you get a call, too?"

"From who?"

"From the fire-breathing monster. Jesus. Hell hath no fury—they weren't *kidding*. That's the last time I try to help my blood relatives."

"What happened?"

"It's a miracle I'm not calling you from police custody. She was about to haul me in on charges of child molestation, abduction of a minor, satanic rituals, the whole bit."

"Wait—tell me what happened."

"What would you have done? I mean, she dumps the kid with me, she goes off on this assignation with Abe, being *very* secretive about what they're doing exactly and where they're going, she's very noncommittal about whether she's going to come and get Martha that night or in the morning, which is fine, I mean I *like* having Martha here, she's a great kid and everything; OK, so she has also told me Martha's spending the next day with her father, so I get up in the morning, the poor kid hasn't slept a wink, her eyes are all red and pathetic, she tells me she wants me to take her to her dad's, i.e. her old home, I haven't heard from Abbie by eight-thirty . . . I mean, what would you do? Is that supposed to be a crime, to take the kid to see her own father?"

"I don't see why."

"So I take her over there, fine, it's early, and Abe is a little surprised but he's perfectly polite, there's no sign of Bambi or Lolita or whatever the she-bitch paralegal is supposed to be called, Abe's very nice, no problem, thanks me, says yes this was the arrangement with Abbie, so I'm feeling kind of Samaritan-like, kind of like a social worker easing the transitions, you know, providing a safe haven for the poor *kid* in all this . . . And the second I get home the phone rings and there's this *screeching* down the phone, What have you done with my daughter, how could you be so irresponsible, do you have any idea how worried I was, I was going to take Martha over to Abe myself screech screech screech and this is the last time I'll ask you to help out because you obviously don't have any tact, and on and on and *on*! I mean, can you believe it?"

"She called me, too."

"I'm sure she did! I'm sure she called to see if you were part of this satanic conspiracy ring with me and Abe and Bambi and God knows who else. My mother, from beyond the grave. They never did get along."

"I'm supposed to call her, Abe asked me to, to let her know when to pick Martha up."

"Hold the phone a couple of inches away from your head when you do it." There was a snort down the phone. "Jesus. I know she's my aunt, but really. It's too much. I was going to quit smoking today. Forget it. I've already gone through half a pack. If I get lung cancer I'm going to sue her for damages, I swear to God."

"Is this typical of her?" Pi ventured.

"No! My God, Pi, I wouldn't have sent you to live with a lunatic. I was trying to *help* you! No, you remember how I used to talk about Abbie. She was the mellow one. She was the Cool Aunt I could get high with. God knows what's happened to her. It's the divorce. It's Abe. He makes her crazy."

"He sounded pretty calm on the phone with me, but he did say something about communication not being good between him and Abbie right now."

"Right!" Fran laughed. "I.e., 'She's hiring a hit man to come after me as we speak.' He should be careful. He should move. I'd move if I were him. You know what I think?"

"What?"

"I think they had sex last night. I'm sure of it. It was such a set-up. I'm sure that's what happened. You can picture the whole thing. She goes over, she gets all dolled up and then she goes over to the house, *their old home together*. They have some wine, she says something like 'I'm so tired of fighting, it's so unconstructive, let's just talk to each other like human beings,' so they do, and he puts some nice music on, and he's sort of smart enough to know what's happening but he's tired of fighting too and he decides to just go with it, and so eventually she makes a move, he lets her make the first move because he's a lawyer and he knows he has to be able to say, 'You started it! I wasn't going to touch you!' OK so they make love, low lights, pretty music, not too sparkly sex but it's nice enough, she's happy, she got what she wanted, she's proved that it's not only the she-bitch paralegal who's sexy and desirable but she is too, and she knows Abe, she knows what he likes, OK so then in the aftermath of it all, when she's still sort of glowing, he says to her he doesn't think it's a good idea for her to stay, it will only confuse everything, then she has a *fit*, what are you talking about, everything's already confused!, she goes ballistic and starts screaming at him, throws shoes, glasses, wine bottles, etc., and he tells her she has to leave, seriously, could she please stop making such a disturbance, she's outraged, she's a little drunk too of course, and he starts getting aggressive also, he says she's totally out of control, she's always had this hysterical side, it makes her impossible to talk to, he says he's calling her a cab to take her back to my place, she screams that she's not coming back to my place tonight it's on the other side of town she'll just go down to Rod and Janet's and by the way has she ever told him what a terrible father he is and how Martha's never forgiven him for not visiting her in the hospital when she had her tonsils out, she wants that to be her exit line but she throws a few more things around and says she's not taking a fucking cab and then gets into her own car, drives away even if she is drunk, because a cab really would be too humiliating, she makes it to Rod and Janet's place, not a great parking job but she manages it, she gets there in one piece and then tiptoes in, crashes on their sofa, oversleeps, wakes up in the morning with a hideous hangover and a foul temper so she leaves the house without even talking to her friends in order to come straight over here, where of course Martha and I no longer are."

"Fran. Take a breath."

"Then of course when she finally gets *me* on the phone she lets out a pure stream of unadulterated mid-divorce hung-over bitterness bile, right into my sensitive ears." Fran did finally breathe. "That's what happened. I'd bet on it."

"You sound so sure. Was there just a TV movie on with the same plot?"

"I can see the whole thing. I can just see it."

"Are you still writing that novel about you and Neil?"

"Yeah. Sometimes. When I'm not working on my song cycle about the *Aeneid*."

"You should slip this scene into your book."

"Neil and I didn't have a kid together. The kid is crucial to the whole dynamic, because they both keep appealing to the kid in their competition to prove which one is the most responsible, the most successful in rising above these petty disagreements."

"Poor old Martha."

"No kidding! They should both be arrested. Anyway, listen, the good part of all this is it's gotten me on the phone with you. So how are you? How's it going up there? Tell me before the police vans come to take you away."

"Oh, fine. Everything's fine."

"Really? Fine?"

"Well, it's quiet, you know, but—that's all right."

"Gives you time to mull things over?"

Pi was quiet. This was why she didn't like the phone. It was entirely too direct. "I'm enjoying e-mail. It's new and different, as we used to say."

"I'm glad you got it finally. It's fun."

"Yeah. Crazy stuff. I'll tell you more about my secret Internet life by e-mail."

Fran got the hint. One thing fifteen years of friendship is good for—people read well between your lines.

"I should get going, too. I've got to stop by work later, once I get through the rest of these cigarettes. Listen, tell me one thing: is it really working out between you and Abbie? Are you co-habiting all right? I feel so responsible."

"We're getting along fine," Pi said. "And I really like Martha. She's a sweet kid. I like Abbie too, it's just—I mean, we're different, obviously, but that's all right. And it's a hard time for her, and I guess the situation makes her a little . . ."

"Psychotic?"

"That wasn't the word I was going to use."

"That's OK. I'll use it. I'm allowed to. I'm family."

"But she's calmer up here. I haven't heard her as upset as she sounded this morning."

"Yeah." Fran's voice turned thoughtful, finally. "I'm sure she's much better off up there. It's the best place for her. She can just sell her crafts and take in the lovely views and get all spiritual, while pretending little Martha was born by immaculate conception and had nothing to do with the sperm or otherwise of the evil Abe Kaplan."

After a few more such thoughts, Pi hung up the phone with her friend. She was surprised after all the ringing and shouting how deep the good silence of the morning still was.

By Sunday, Pi had developed a strangely physical guilt in all her limbs. She felt too attached to machines and devices. Her muscles complained about their lack of use. Her heart struggled under the weight of too much caffeine. Her spirit mumbled an admonition: if Pi's life didn't include anything in the way of churchgoing or meditation, the least she could do was go admire the splendors of the planet. Climb into the world, revive her internal breathing.

It was funny what you spent money on, when you essentially needed to buy everything but had limited funds. Every single day Pi missed her music, in all of its incarnations. Her college music, the sad soulful women singers; her high-school music, two-toned dance tunes; her grown-up music, piano mostly, Beethoven and Schubert, those nice men in dark suits on the covers. Then there were dozens of tapes friends and lovers had made for her over the years, all those lost gifts—cassettes inscribed in careful handwriting, boy friends urging on her rare reggae, Chicago Art Ensemble and other jazz geniuses, or classic Johnny Cash and Woody Guthrie; girl friends compiling the soaring poems of Joni Mitchell or scatty Rickie Lee Jones. And all that Franmusic, ancient Second Sex demos, or tapes Fran had crafted for Pi over the years because she knew Pi would never get around to finding these people herself: punky tough chicks who spat, strummed, and hollered; their songs intercut, because this was Fran, with unrelated geniuses like Billie or Ella or James Brown or Ray Charles.

So much music was gone that it was impossible to know where to begin again. Pi didn't have the same feeling about her music that she had about the library. She would have replaced it, if she could. The tapes made especially for her were lost to all but memory, of course; but otherwise it was a simple question of money. If someone had given Pi a credit card and set her loose in Tower Records, she would have had no problem at all getting through a thousand dollars in an effort to reform her collection. She would have been happy to do it. But it would cost that much to get started, and it seemed somehow depressing to start buying tapes again in ones and twos. Instead, her days here were radio-filled: newschat and popfuzz and odd bursts of classical.

So when Pi had moved up to Mendocino and finally deposited Richard's well-worn crisis check into a new seaside account, the first thing she spent any sort of money on was something totally different. Something she'd been meaning to buy for years but hadn't felt she had the cash for. There had always been books or music she'd wanted to buy first. With her parents' compensation money Pi bought herself a beautiful, sturdy, strong pair of boots.

Pi cherished these boots. She loved them. She loved them like they were pets, or people. She loved them more than any other item of bodywear she owned, and kept them in a sacred corner of her room like a pair of religious icons. Not that she wasn't smart enough to see the dumb symbolism in it. Aha, the new pair of boots with which you will rediscover the world in the post-fire apocalypse! The boots in which you will learn the new shape of the earth beneath your feet! Pi almost wished, for this symbolic reason, that her first serious purchase had been something completely pragmatic—an electric blanket, for instance. (The nights were cold up here.) But she reasoned with herself that in her profoundly objectless state anything could seem symbolic. Of course—an electric blanket to bring you in from your numb shocked cold! Or maybe a sleeping bag, because you no longer have a home and you want to be able to sleep wherever you may be! Or a camera, because now you want to observe a world you used to be too busy reading about to notice!—There would be a meaning trap in any purchase.

So Pi went ahead and bought the boots. She wore them all the time. The great thing about living up here was you could and no one would bother you. It was hearty enough country, even with the boutiques and ceramics classes, the cappuccinos and garlic-stuffed olives, that nobody cared if you constantly looked ready to go on a five-hour hike. This was a shift from the Bay Area that Pi welcomed. In the Bay Area it was all about gear. Everyone had gear for whatever their leisure activity of preference was, whether it was Fran's surfing and skating gadgets or Renée and Jen's endless closets of skis and down jackets, or even Ryan who had recently become obsessed with sea kayaking and had whole hunks of equipment suspended from his ceiling. In Berkeley, Pi had felt that boots were pretentious, that people bought them to show off their purchasing power and discernment. Up here she got them for that old-fashioned, Russian-seeming reason: she wanted her feet to feel *safe*.

With her boots on that Sunday, and taking a small backpack of figbars and a bottle of fruit fizz, Pi drove on up to one of the state parks. She stopped her car in a cool flickering shadow. She smiled at a young family getting ready to head off towards the beach. It was cold for a beach day, but they looked determined, like tourists. Then Pi launched herself onto one of the long paths. She walked. And walked.

It was one of her new great pleasures. Pi found that her feet and body working rhythmically together provided a similar kind of engine for her thought that reading had before. Pi had always walked some, with friends; she'd once had a very tough, good conversation with Rob on a hike in the Berkeley Hills in which she tried to explain to them both the ideas behind her dissertation. But walking here, in Russian Gulch, she had to make her thoughts dwell in some new, different territory.

Pi was trying to open her eyes more now. There was no point in being in one of the world's glorious places and not. Before, for instance that day in Tilden with Rob, she hadn't much noticed the land around her. Even when Pi was a girl and playing in the yellow grasses and apricot orchards of the peninsula's mild foothills, though she loved the land and it was her home, she mostly used it as a rich, great backdrop to her thoughts and fantasies. She was grateful, in a dimly realized but openhearted way, for the clean air, the brush, the greens, the space of California. The high, built darkness of the East Coast felt claustrophobic by comparison. Pi found the infinity of these Western hills reassuring, maybe because it imitated the wishful grandeur of her philosophy. Especially when she was older and her thoughts roamed over the giant, Kant: when she was trying deeply to understand what it meant for there to be a world of forms beyond our senses, a world that governed the lines along which we think and perceive.

Pi could not seriously pretend her interest in the nature of the world had died with the fire. That would have been to deny her own head. *Si non cogito, non sum,* she reformulated to herself in fake Latin, in response to Descartes. As a philosopher you were supposed to believe in universal truths, not relativism (unless you followed Richard Rorty's elegant pragmatism). Pi did believe in truth with a capital T, but she also believed that people sought the truths that suited them. A curious part of Pi—the part that could be detached not just about lovers and bodies but also about philosophy and her own endeavors—noticed with bemusement that fact about people's minds: they're susceptible to different kinds of ideas. Some minds were ample, supple; some butterfly-ish, aphoristic; some plodding, methodical. Some were strong and searching and hungry for resolutions. It was, she thought, an idiosyncrasy like any other—favorite color, preferred flavor of pizza topping. Rob's mind, for instance, was essentially mathematic. It worked in speedy languages on high clean planes. Rob cherished Frege's early logic because it was beautiful to him, it fit into his own mind. He didn't, Pi knew, understand the mystical streak in Pi that drew her to Kant. Everyone thought to study Kant you had to be hyper-rational, but Pi didn't find this. She found an order in Kant that actually freed her. He took you into a new ether of possibility. For Pi, Kant was a romantic.

But here she was, walking, and her mind now couldn't work on Kant. Pi took the wide path, a path cut for bikes and families and dogs, that wound along a jungly, shadowed canyon bordered by moss-frosted pines and blood-colored redwoods. She needed a new place for her thinking to go. The redwoods might pose a new challenge for her; they were as high, straight, and difficult as Kant's first *Critique.*

She climbed farther into them. Into a grand silence, a place where the human form became humble and buglike, where the moist scent of the hushed needle-covered ground dampened the darkness of the branchless shade. As she walked, Pi became more and more puzzled. What *were* these trees? What did they mean? She'd have to work hard to make them yield their truths. People walked in these woods, lost people like her, hoping the redwoods in their noble silence would offer them solace or answers. But that was not their job, surely—to solve the small and very human problems people brought to them?

The line put Pi in mind of her favorite thin book of the moment, *Bedtime for Frances*. She'd taken it from Martha's shelf; Martha gave it willingly, saying she'd outgrown it. Pi couldn't imagine how anyone could ever outgrow the story, so busy it seemed with intriguing wisdoms. The one she thought of now was the exchange between Frances and her father:

Father said, "Listen, Frances, do you want to know why the curtains are moving?"

"Why?" said Frances.

"That is the wind's job," said Father. "Every night the wind has to go around and blow all the curtains."

"How can the wind have a job?" said Frances.

"*Everybody* has a job," said Father. "I have to go to my office every morning at nine o'clock. That is my job. You have to go to sleep so you can be wide awake for school tomorrow. That is *your* job . . . If the wind does not blow the curtains, he will be out of a job."

Pi had read this section back to Martha and said, "Don't you think that's true? I find it so comforting." "No. It's silly," Martha had said. "Why?" "Because. The wind doesn't have a job, it just . . . *is*." Pi considered that for a minute. "That's deep," she said finally. "You think that's true of everything, even people?" Martha looked confused. "I mean," Pi clarified, "maybe people are like that too, they don't have jobs, they just *are*. I like that idea. It works for me." "No, people do have jobs. *People* have jobs." "Oh," Pi said. Her face fell. "Well, then I guess I'm back to square one."

But there was something in Frances's father's point, Pi was sure of it. The redwoods did have a job: not solving the petty crises of human beings, maybe, but setting their own kind of example by remaining straight and tall for all those hundreds of years, showing what was possible if you kept still and determined. So far they'd beaten out wars and conquests, one people's history being torn up and replaced with a different one. The trees had stood still for all of it. And meanwhile, they, unlike all the other trees, had learned a great secret of survival: how to survive the great fires.

```
>>Getting in touch
I'm sorry if this is a very stupid question, but is
there any way of responding directly to JD?
                                    --Sylvia Plath
>>Is this a new Sylvia Plath or the old one?
                                      --Hemingway
>>JD's unattainable, that's what's so fascinating about
the whole thing. He writes us, we can't respond. It's
like narcissism gone haywire. And we love it! It's
sick, really.                      --Madam Butterfly
>>Hi Sylvia, welcome to the weird and wonderful world
of ED 536! Not to alarm you on your first posting here
but I did run a check on your normal ID, because we had
a Sylvia Plath in here previously--as you'd expect,
she's a popular figure--and, without going into the de-
tails of it all, Sylvia turned out to be unpleasant and
abusive, so there was an involved process of getting
that person removed from the discussion group. (Sylvia
eventually turned out to be a man, incidentally. It's a
crazy gender-bending world out there!) Hope this
doesn't discourage you . . . :-)
To answer your question: JD knows his way around a few
tricks. We can't trace his postings. And there's no ob-
vious sign that he reads the discussions here. After
the first posting a lot of people wrote things like,
Are you serious? Where do you live? Do you want the
name of a good shrink? What's your name? etc. and he
never replied to any of them.
But you'll see there's a general heading we've created
called "Right to Reply" where people put thoughts to
him, in case he ever stops by. Feel free to use it if
you want to.                      --Janet/Anne Sexton
>>The last S Plath, just to let you know, used to post
long, rabid defenses of Ted Hughes and eventually these
```

```
*very* long "poetic" pornographic love letters to Ted,
from "Sylvia." Yikes. But Sylvia, we're sure you're a
different kettle of fish altogether! Welcome aboard.
                                          --Hemingway
>>Sylvia, is it true that you quote eat men like air
unquote, as you once wrote? And if so, how does that
work exactly? I've always wondered.        --Van Gogh
```

Pi was trying to figure out how and whether to answer this when she heard the sound of a key in the door. She jumped as though it were the sound of a previous universe, before she recognized the familiar fall of people's footsteps coming into the house.

D I E R Y

The eyes of March

Tuesday

WELL, FOR GOSH SAKES. I'VE BEEN OUT OF TOUCH. I'VE BEEN SHIRKING, I ADMIT it. For all you all know I've died and gone to heaven by now, and if anyone has been harboring that concern, I apologize. But it's not true. Not yet. So far I've only gotten as far as Baltimore, not heaven. Not having been to the latter I can't make a definitive comparison, but my guess is: with Baltimore heaven might have in common long lines of blossoming abalone-pink magnolias; but in contrast to Baltimore, heaven would almost certainly lack extensive roadwork and steamy, bad air.

Time has passed. You'll have noticed that it is now March. So that's happened since I wrote. And we made it here, obviously. In the event all was uneventful and we made it to Baltimore without further ado.

I'll tell you one reason I haven't written since I got here. I'm hardly ever left alone. I'm still on suicide watch, weeks now after the projected leap. The eyes of March are upon me. I feel like Charlotte Perkins Gilman in *The Yellow Wallpaper*, no one's letting me write because they think it only encourages my hysteria and madness. In this case I think it's got an extra technological fillip: they put some of my insanity down to the computer, specifically. So now it's no e-mail for JD! No Net! It's bad for you. Little do they know it's actually been one of the thin wires that's held me together. They never take the patient's word for these things, though.

I don't want to seem ungrateful. The gals have been good to me. Cindy couldn't do a whole lot at first because JavaBooks had some massive inventory extravaganza going on and she had to be responsible and managerial and *there*, but Jane was saintly and took a couple of days off her work so she could entertain me.

It's not easy to be entertained in Baltimore, outside of strip joints and shopping malls, but Jane has done her best. Basically Baltimore is a town that was left to rot in hell for years and years and then someone got that very nineteen-eighties bright idea—I know! Let's fix the city by making the train station look nice and developing a whole new *shopping* area, in this case down by the harbor. That was supposed to make everyone happier. Shopping malls: the crux of eighties urban renewal. Not parks or libraries or schools. Just malls.

If I sound more politicized and Cindyesque than usual, it's because I got a lot of this from her. She has a long rap on Baltimore and how it has suffered and is a showcase for some of the country's worst problems, poverty class divisions gun violence infant mortality crumbling infrastructure et cetera—but her rap ends on an upbeat note because she's very pro the city's black mayor and one of its congressmen, hers in fact, who changed his name from something like Joe Blow to the much more resonant though unpronounceable Kweisi Mfume. (I admit I couldn't just type that one in off the top of my head—I had to run around for a minute to find the refrigerator magnet the girls have that bears his name.)

It might be relevant in all this, and I can't remember if I mentioned it before, that Jane is black, or African-American as Cindy now says dutifully. Jane herself doesn't like "African-American"—she says she feels about as African as apple pie and that they might as well just call themselves the "Brought-Here-in-Chains-Americans" if that's the idea they're trying to get across. I told you Jane has a sharp sense of humor. Jane also says if she could pick a name for her "people" she'd choose "Rethas" or possibly "Stevies," after her two favorite black music icons. So you get into these comical conversations in this home in which Cindy holds earnestly forth with something like, "If the Democratic Party thinks African-Americans are just going to vote by *rote* for them, they'd better think again," and Jane sits it out for a minute before saying, "If the Democrats want the Rethas to vote for them, they ought to put Jesse on the ticket, but they're scared if they do that they're going to lose all the Mr. and Mrs. Cleavers." One more interesting biographical fact about Jane: she is mixed race by birth, with a white mother, but was adopted by two black parents, lawyers who live in Silver Spring who have slowly come around to accepting her Lifestyle and now invite Cin and Jane over together to their Fourth of July barbecues along with their other (black, adopted) son and his Puerto Rican wife and their kid, Louis. Just one more crazy melting pot story from this great nation of ours!

Moving right along. In spite of the aforementioned, Jane and I did go down to visit the harbor one day soon after I arrived. I've never been allowed to go there before. Generally I'm escorted to one of the town's famous open markets that are all pig's toes and cow knuckles and other unthinkable farm animal body parts; truckloads of shrimp and the inevitable crab; and stalls selling hot deep-fried items to go—pretty well anything you can stick into batter and fry, they'll do it. It's all very colorful. On a good day in the summer Cindy might take me to a baseball game—we both have a genetic predisposition for baseball fandom. Cin's one good word on Joe is that he used to take us to games when we were kids, which I remember happening precisely once, when the Dodgers lost, but never mind. (Sally's mother was also a great Dodgers fan. She had a baseball signed by all the Dodgers' team members that she was, I swear to God, buried with.)

Anyway, I finally got to explore the town's number-one tourist attraction. And Cindy's pieties to one side, I can't see what is the big deal about the harbor. I always had the impression that it was going to be so gleaming and blue and maritime and *special*. Like San Francisco, is what I was picturing. I remember people, like my old co-workers at Incompetence Incorporated, who if you said you were going to Baltimore would always say, "Oh I *love* that harbor. They've made it terrific." And they'd tell you about all the fun microbrewery beer they drank there and how they listened to some sort of funky-for-white-people jazz band.

So. Cut to action. Jane and I take a bus down there, and we find—what? Some shops by the water. A bunch of restaurants by the water. Some guy selling balloons by the water. You can eat hamburgers or pizza or, yes, more *crabs*—expensively, after shopping for unisex denim jackets, by the water. That's the whole thing. Is the water poetic and beautiful? Not especially. Mostly it's grey and fumey, and suspiciously slick-looking.

Jane and I did have a good time nonetheless. I had thought I was going to have to pretend, look like I was enjoying it for the sake of the effort Jane was clearly putting into beefing up my state of mind. But there can be something oddly soothing about malls, even if you're broke and desireless. Probably exactly when they *are* soothing is when you're in that state. We cruised up and down escalators in the "Galleria" (so L.A., that name!) marvelling at a thousand brand-name products that I don't need to list for you because you have the exact same mall near you, wherever you are. Suffice it to say there's one of those snazzy gadget shops—the kind put together around the concept "for the professional who has everything"—where you can get inflatable typewriters, sunglasses that double as calculators, cameras hidden inside toothbrushes. Useful stuff. I found myself tempted by a laptop bag covered in fake zebra fur. The item appealed to me. Maybe it was a subtle moment harking back to my capture by the men in jeeps experience, that night several weeks ago. In any case, I refrained.

We ambled along the harborside after that. It had turned into a freakish early spring day, warm enough for strolling. And that's when we happened on a splendid harborside sight. Three white chicks, one with a guitar, crooning in harmony. Forgive "chicks"—it's what Jane called them, saying they reminded her of Charlie's Angels. (While we're at it, you also have to forgive me calling Cin and Jane "girls": I have to tell you it's what they call themselves, and I have written permission to use the term myself in spite of my inherently oppressive gender.) There was even a Farrah Fawcett candidate among them, doing the lead singing, shaking big locks of frosted hair away from her mouth to get all the words out.

I don't know where these people came from. Baltimore is like that—it has people there who make you wonder: Do they know that this is 1992 now? Have they been lost in time? Have we all wandered into an episode of *The Twilight Zone* by mistake, one set in the fifties, in which Baltimore is the special guest star?

This singing group made you laugh, they made you cry. They made you laugh because at first you assumed these three were being deeply ironic. Baltimore may be a dump, but it is often precisely in dumps that you get people being peculiarly, preternaturally, hip. I've sometimes suspected that Baltimore is secretly hipper than my city that's so deeply convinced of its own hipness that it doesn't actually bother producing anything especially hip anymore. (With apologies to Krieger as I write this.) Cindy has taken me to some great wacky stuff here in the past. One brilliant surreal band, for example, called Lambs Eat Ivy. The lead singer of that group is the only woman I've ever wanted to marry—she projected this remarkable combination of satire and a sense of sacredness that stirred my prune-like heart into something like passion. Had I had the opportunity, I might have tried stalking her. Sadly I never found out where she lived.

But the frightening thing about Charlie's Angels was that you slowly realized they *weren't* being ironic. They were like Charlie's Angels, they were like the Partridge Family, but they seemed unaware that those were their sources of inspiration, so they failed to make postmodern hay out of it. Basically, these were girls in jeans, with long hair and nice teeth—and they wanted to SING.

The tragedy was, they started singing "Respect." And even then they did not appear to glimpse the humor in it. We saw them launch into a chirpy, good-natured version of "Respect" that had clusters of black shoppers looking on in disbelief and got Jane's eyes big as a dinosaur's. "I can't believe it," she murmured. It did seem shocking. But by the time they were singing, "R-E-S-P-E-C-T, Find out what it means to me—" you had to start believing it. Once they got to "Sock it to me, sock it to me, sock it to me, sock it to me," to which the two chicks on the outside did a mock-boxing dance move that made your scalp crawl with embarrassment, Jane said, "This is really happening. Isn't it? This is really happening." I couldn't lie to her. I had to tell her it was. The girls wrapped it up, still cheerful and determined and not apparently incredibly attuned to their audience's deep dismay. They finished on a triumphant note. Hardly anybody clapped, though plenty were still staring. There was a silence, which grew, until Jane gallantly broke it.

"I'd like to make a request," she said, totally deadpan. I held my breath. What could she possibly say to such people?

"Can you do 'We Shall Overcome'?"

Thursday. Car due: Today.

All right. I admit it. That day in the mall I did make a purchase. I bought a new pair of shoes, to make myself feel respectable. And I see now as I look down at my feet that I have succeeded already in staining them. What skill, what timing it took, to mark my new shoes so soon after purchasing them. It is these small achievements that keep you going in life.

It was not maple syrup but red wine on this occasion, spilled in nervousness. I blame my sister, which may seem unfair. After all, is she my keeper? No. But I blame her for organizing a situation which produced hand-juddering nervousness in me.

It's all part of the rehabilitation program. Cindy was trying to be nice, as usual. I've made clear, I hope, how unfailingly nice Cindy is. She wouldn't have me down here, with fresh dog food bought for Minsk and helpful self-help books placed in strategic spots around the house like brightly colored Easter eggs, if she weren't so damn *nice*. I may be doltish for finding self-help books (called things like *Suicide: Not a Way Out*) unhelpful, but I'm good enough to appreciate the effort. When the girls aren't here I pick up the books and move them to different locations in the house so they can imagine I've been reading them.

But this event—this was a step beyond the self-help books. This was being kind only to be cruel, in an inversion of the line from that eighties pop song which is, I realized, something Hamlet says to his mother in the bedroom scene after he has just rhetorically ripped her guts out and left her sobbing hysterically—shortly after he's offed poor old Polonius. "I must be cruel," the young Turk says, "only to be kind." Do you suppose the writers of that pop song were big readers of Shakespeare?

So: Cindy had a dinner party. That's all. I know, it's no big deal, right? Dinner parties—people were having them in the sixties, they're having them today, life goes on as it always has. Especially in Baltimore. In my city I'm not sure people have dinner parties as such anymore, I think they went the way of conference calls and lava lamps. They were fun for a particular cultural moment, but now people have moved on, getting together to watch TV shows or try out new restaurants together instead. Even Lili, who has Good Taste, doesn't have dinner parties, though she has been known to have people over for cocktails, which is anyway a sort of retro-kitsch thing and is mostly to show off her set of gold fifties highball glasses.

In Baltimore apparently it's still happening, though. Baltimore has great bars, but Cindy boycotts them out of some logic about our mother's habits, so her preferred way to socialize is to have people over for fancily cooked dinners. Which is what Mom does anyway and hasn't been proven to keep you from drinking, but whatever. It makes Cindy happy. When in Rome, if they throw dinner parties you go to them, and you try to be a good sport about it.

Quite apart from the company and what eventually happened, I have to say it was very weird for me to watch Cindy turn *into* our mother, circa 1969. Cindy was just a pup when Mom was doing her hostess number—she got into it in the late sixties and early seventies, in spite of the new absence of the wandering Joe, or possibly because of it. We were usually tucked away in a corner while Sally produced tray after tray of cheese puffs and mushroom caps; elegant soups, juicy roasts, chocolate soufflés. This was in the Craig Claiborne era of cooking, you know, *New York Times* guru to homemakers all over, back in the era when herbs were dried and french and the word "virgin" did not show up in super-markets. Her entertaining urge fizzled out eventually, around the time Jimmy Carter came into office. The Nixon years were my mother's big dinner party years. I think once Carter got in dinner parties started to seem frivolous. Mom started dating an environmentalist, which led to the SOE job, and somehow things changed.

So here was Cindy yesterday, lesbian feminista, bursting through her door with bags full of red snappers and peppers and lots of Baltimorean green things, a yuppie-ish cookbook out on the counter. Jane and I made mumbly offers to help, but Cindy dismissed us with early season ice teas to the living room. Minsk considered watching Cindy for household hints, but she shooed him away too so he pottered out to join us. He, of the four of us, seemed the most relaxed about the impending arrival of Company.

While we were out there, with MTV soothingly on in the background, Jane just came right out and asked me about my love life. No hedging. So that was the first stress item, because I had to tell her I don't have one. She said, what not at all, no one you've even got your eye on? Come on, fess up. And I said, no really, I'm not looking, I don't have any secrets in my heart. There was a pause. I was considering telling Jane about my hunt for Horatio. I haven't forgotten about him, you know. He's still on my mind. I go to sleep and I dream of him. His face is an unfilled-in hope in my inner eye. But as I tried to assess how flexible Jane's spirit might be on this notion, she leaned towards me and said, Well I want you to know we've got both options covered here tonight. Which wasn't a sentence that made a lot of sense to me. I said, What are you talking about? and she said, You know, your sister still thinks maybe you could find Mr. Right, and I promise you I have been *telling* her, He's not looking for a Mister, fool! He's looking for a *Miss*! So we compromised and invited two friends over, both single, both eligible, a man and a woman, both nice people and both easy on the eye. You'll like them. I mean, we think you'll like them, no matter what, but if the extreme cuteness of either of them moves you too, so much the better.

This was something of a bombshell. As Jane realized right after she said it.

What? she asked. What's the matter? Come on, James Dean, don't take this too seriously. All I'm saying is—

And I just said quietly, so quietly that it woke Minsk up, he could hear the unnerved vibrations in my voice:

I'm not *looking*.

I think my voice probably sounded somewhat strangled as I said it.

So much for telling her about Horatio! It's not like I want to keep that quest to myself, I'd like to be able to explain it to people, but sometimes everyone's minds are so contracted around the shape of the done thing there's no way to get them to see anything different.

Poor Jane. How could she know? She's not without tact, so she deftly moved the conversation onto neutral ground, something about the video playing just then on TV, neon-clothed people playing guitars in the Grand Canyon or some such, and Minsk went back to sleep and there was peace in our time again. But I could see a story running across Jane's curious eyes. *JD, she was thinking, clearly went through some terrible break-up or disappointment recently and that's what made him so depressed, and he doesn't want to talk about it.*

What can I say? People prefer crises to be domestic rather than existential. They just do. Hamlet had the same problem, don't forget. Polonius was sure it was heartbreak over Ophelia that pushed Hamlet over the edge. Corruption in the court, the likely murder of his father, a deep suspicion that the world and especially Denmark were not such rosy places, plus the guy's doubt that he could do anything about any of it—all of that was too complicated a cluster of ideas for someone like Polonius to grasp. He thought Hamlet was just reacting to being jilted. Now I know how he felt. (Hamlet, man, I've been there. I know.) I thought about correcting Jane's idea but decided it wasn't worth the effort.

The upshot was I was a nervous wreck by the time they arrived. Susie and Paul. Susie: small, rodentish, bob-haired, very rapid speech and an irksome habit of sucking her teeth. Paul: big, curly blond, Jewish Aryan type if you know what I mean. Walked with a bit of a stoop; high, unpleasant snorting laughter. And the first thing I did in my graciousness—I mean the *very* first thing I did, before I'd even shaken hands with them, as I was pouring Susie a glass of wine—was to tilt the bottle over with my shaky hand and spill wine all over my new shoes. This is the kind of clumsiness that in a movie is incredibly endearing and makes everyone fall in love with everyone else, as they stoop to the ground to clean it up and their eyes meet and they know—bing!—that this is The One. In real life it is just embarrassing and bothersome, your sister has to run around getting a sponge and the guests look away and someone like me ends up saying FUCK! with, possibly, too much feeling. Susie recoiled a step in reaction; Paul did the first of his many high laughter snorts of the evening.

It wasn't a good start.

And what did Susie turn out to be? A Shakespeare scholar. How perfect. Paul was even loftier, doing exalted Queer things with Spenser or somebody—one of those poets where you go, "Oh yes, Spenser," while thinking, "Who's Spenser again? What century is he? Is he the guy who did *Paradise Lost* or no that's the other one, which one's Spenser again?" Anyway it was Susie and Paul who were really on the same wavelength. Within minutes they were gossiping wildly about some gay professor of theirs who's in a complicated three-way relationship with two medievalists in Houston, they take turns visiting and sometimes do leather vacations all together in Florida or God knows what, I stopped following the particulars. Cindy was hiding safely behind her char-grilled vegetable preparations so she wasn't much help, and Jane could see I wasn't entirely with the program but didn't know how to intervene. Finally, after Paul had reduced Suze to a cascade of squeaky giggles about some ornate breach of conference etiquette that one of this threesome had committed, and its likely sexual implications—there was a brief pause, and Jane said, "JD has a friend who's directed a lot of Shakespeare. Right? Didn't you say he's doing *Hamlet* right now?"

Two pairs of "I'd sort of forgotten this guy was here" eyes turned to me, so I felt obliged to do more than just go, "Yup. That's right. He sure is." I told them about Krieger's novel interpretation, the inversion, the madness, the relationship between Hamlet and Horatio. Since I'd had a glass of wine by now, I got pretty lathered up about it. Krieger should pay me for this.

"Hmm. That's interesting. That's *interesting*," said Susie. She paused for a minute, in honor of how very interesting it was. Then she said intently to me, "Do you know the Puffendorf *Hamlet*?" Puffendorf, Schlessendorf, I can't exactly remember. I of course don't know who Puffendorf is so she explained, he's a crucial avant-garde German director from the early part of the century, *very* radical, *very* ahead of his time, and then she told me all about his 1912 silent movie version of *Hamlet*, which does some very daring thing, makes Gertrude a man or Claudius a tree or something, something suitably German. Paul murmured reverently, "I *love* Puffendorf" while she was describing it, and even Jane said, "I've always meant to see more Puffendorf." I've clearly missed something major. Still, I couldn't see how the movie related to what Krieger was doing except on the general level of, Don't people do the darnedest things with *Hamlet*? So I just took a page out of Susie's etiquette book and said solemnly, "That's interesting. That's *interesting*," when she had finished. It seemed to placate her. Thus ended our Shakespeare bonding.

We struggled on. The Puffendorf business was before we even sat down at the table, so there was a lot more conversation to be waded through before the evening was over. But then Paul turned out to have a decent sense of humor, i.e. he finally decided I was funny, which made me like him. Then after some more wine and a general movie roundup—it turns out these poor, hardworking graduate students have seen every single movie under mainstream release—we got ready to dig in to (I'm not kidding!) the *chocolate soufflé* Cindy had made for dessert. And Susie started telling me about her last horrific boyfriend, Jimbob or Jimboy she seemed to call him, so we got very intense about that at our end of the table while the other three were engaging in spirited "We're here, we're queer, we're fabulous!" chit-chat. Theirs sounded more fun than ours, but I was sympathetic to poor Susie, who as I've mentioned had a face not unlike that of a mole and who did seem to have been manhandled by this Jimbob character. And we got to a point where I could work up my key line:

"All men are assholes!"

—which she seemed to agree with. Eventually she looked at me with her beady eyes and said, "What about you? What's your situation?" and I just said, "I have nightmares about someone named Marcie coming out of the elevator on my floor, brandishing a bread knife," which she thought was funny enough that she didn't ask me any more about it. So that conversation topic was pretty trouble-free in the end, thankfully. Because God knows squeaky Susie, Shakespeare scholar and lay expert on Puffendorf's early *oeuvre*, was not the person to talk to about Horatio either. I can just imagine her small dark eyes blinking at me if I told her, as if I were an overbright sunlamp, before she scurried back down into her safe black hole of conference gossip and scholarship. Someone who takes Shakespeare literally, she'd think: Help! Someone who's moved by the actual character! How naive! How scary!

Cindy, I have to say in closing, is a very good cook. I'd like to credit her, in spite of her cruel kindness, with making a delicious meal. It's just one of a thousand arenas in which my little sister has surpassed me.

Friday. Car due + one

Jane's back in the library, Cin's done inventory, and I'm still here, feeling too guilty to call the car people to ask for an extension.

C & J don't mind my staying here—so they claim—and Minsk and I try to make ourselves useful around the house, putting all the mail order catalogues together in neat piles on the coffee table (after sitting for long hours on the couch going through them, me wishing for the winter-chiselled looks of the men in the pictures and Minsk feeling the shots should feature more dogs). Today I did the decent thing and did the girls' laundry. I felt it was the least I could do to earn my keep. The only thing Cindy tends to ask me is, "So the car people were cool with you having it an extra week?" and I, craven coward, have claimed, "They said it's fine," when in reality they've said no such thing. How could they? I haven't asked them.

It's another college throwback. You might have spotted it. In college, I used to know early on when I wasn't going to be able to do the paper on time. I really *knew* it and I planned to talk to the professor, or the bearded twenty-four-year-old teaching assistant, generously ahead of time—to let them know how sincere I was, how I wasn't taking advantage of them or just being an ordinary, late, student fuckup. I used to feel if you got your bid for procrastination in early, that proved how responsible you were, basically. But then what would happen, somehow, as in a nightmare, is that the days would slip away from me. Where did they go? It was never clear. It was just that I'd wake up and think, Oh shit, that paper's due *tomorrow* for Christ's sake, I've got to find that guy today and get the extension. Then the day would pass. It would just pass—serenely, simply, like any other day. Then I'd wake up and think *Fuck!* that fucking paper's due *today*. God damn it! (By this point I'd have some ideas, some notes for it scribbled together, but no paper.) And I wouldn't do it. I just wouldn't do it. Then, from then on, the paper was of course officially late, and I'd have to start that bobbing and weaving routine—avoiding the bearded TA in the courtyards, slipping into obscure aisles in the library when I saw him headed my way. Finally, ignominiously, days or weeks late, I'd slip the paper by their office, after hours so they wouldn't see me, and I wouldn't even put any excuse on the cover at all because I was so mortified about how late it was.

Which is why I didn't always get good grades, in case you were wondering.

Look, I'm not trying to relive my whole past for you, I'm just introducing some background material relevant to my apparent inability now to call the car rental people to ask them if I can keep the car for an extra week. I figure—well, I guess I figure they'll work it out for themselves. You know:

Bud: Hey, Bob, is that guy back with the Ford Taurus, that tall dark hunched guy who came in here a couple of weeks ago?

Bob: Nope.

Bud: When was it due?

Bob: It was due Thursday. Two weeks. Due Thursday, but we haven't heard from him.

Bud: Whelp. Guess that probably means he wants to keep it for another week, huh?

Bob: That's about how it looks, Bud.

Bud: OK then. I'll write him down for another week with the Taurus.
Bob: Good idea, Bud.
I'm assuming the conversation went something like that.

Monday. Car due some little while ago now.

There are other amusing stories I could tell you. I could describe the crop-haired academic I met, friend of Jane's, swathed entirely in clinging floral Lycra, who lectured me on Wilkie Collins's ghost stories. Or I could, more simply, try to replicate Jane's comic monologue on the Charlie's Angels trio, which had Cindy crying painfully with laughter.

But I'd like to break off for a minute instead to give you a depression update. That's the reason we're gathered here in the first place, isn't it? It's all very well my telling you jolly anecdotes about Puffendorf and shopping malls and wan-nabe Rethas, but that is not why we keep meeting like this. We keep meeting because some of us are susceptible to attacks of hopelessness, and rather than take pep pills to defeat it we submit to the organic biochemistry that got us where we are today. Or, even if we do take pep pills, we also indulge in this, the "writing cure," as Sigmund didn't call it, as a way to express our troubles.

I'd like to tell you what the silent majority thinks of these depressions. "Silent majority": it's a great phrase, even if we do owe it to Richard Nixon. Somewhere underneath it all Richard Nixon must not have been such a bad guy, to be associated with such an evocative phrase. That is a huge heresy for me to say. In my childhood, Richard Nixon was the number one figure of evil in our mother's cosmology. The wandering Joe was a distant second, next to Nixon. (The foulest language I've ever heard out of Sally's mostly kind lips was on the day she heard the news of Ford's pardon.)

The silent majority, in a nutshell, thinks depression is dumb. How do I know this? Because I was sitting here today in Cindy and Jane's lovely house and the mood suddenly hit me again, like a brown cloud of pollution. It made my lungs hurt, my eyes dip, my fingers turn yellow. Like I said, I have lousy circulation. I tried to raise the depression issue with Minsk, but if we weren't going to talk about park-walking opportunities, he frankly wasn't interested. You try to tell a dog, "Parks? In Baltimore? Not unless we're looking for crack cocaine, or a bullet in the eye"—but he won't believe you.

The fact was I needed to talk to someone. Suddenly it was overwhelming. I started to think, what the fuck am I doing? Sponging off my sister, who has a job providing a worthy service for people who need it—getting them the books they deserve. Mooching too off her girlfriend, who will one day turn lots of bright young minds on to the meanings of Haitian political culture, which is what she is disserting on, if I haven't mentioned it. Off in another city people I know are keeping themselves and other people busy—*busy*, God damn it!—performing the bard or singing the blues or singing *Aïda* or even, you know, adding up the figures on *Lolita!* magazine's latest sales. They all, what I'm trying to say is, they all have a *job*. And I don't. I have no job. And a human jobless life, involving a guy, a living room, his dog, the day's silence, the inability to concentrate, the clear feeling in a town like Baltimore that somewhere right beyond your reach people are suffering in the most basic ways with bad food in their stomachs, rage in their heads, guns in the air, sickness and worry and no money, no money, no money—well, all of this makes it very difficult for you to look at your own face in the mirror and not spit.

So. I called Lili. She was at work, of course.

"JD! Hi!"

That was touching. Very touching. She still remembered me.

"How's it going? How are you? How are Flopsy and Mopsy?"

"Oh, fine. Everyone's fine. They're off earning a living, you know. As people do."

"I have to admit—I'm doing it myself."

"I know. How are they, the preemies?" Lili's mother is an obstetric nurse who works in the ward for premature babies, affectionately but sort of creepily known as *preemies*. So we have borrowed the phrase for Lili's charges who tend to be—get it?—preemie donnas. Opera singers. (In-jokes: they take so long to explain.)

"Acting up, as usual. Lawrence Vogler says he can't go to Houston so soon after the BAM *Tosca*, even though Houston's been booked since about 1912 and if he pulls out of it Houston will never want to work with us again. Same old story. I'm going to have to spend the next week massaging his fat ego and then he'll probably break down and do it."

I sighed.

"What was that? Was that a sigh?"

"Yes."

"What are you sighing about, you ninny?"

"It's just that that's so *real*. It may be a pain in the ass, but at least it's real, what you do. It has people and deadlines and responsibilities and phone calls. It's real life."

"JD. What are you talking about? Since when is taking an opera singer out for a flattering expense-paid fancy dinner real life? Has your sister been getting at you? She can browbeat you, you know, I've noticed it. You always say Cindy's such an angel, but I've heard her talk you down."

"Cindy's being an angel. So's Jane. They're treating me like their foster child. They couldn't be nicer."

"Sounds patronizing. You should come back here."

"How's the apartment? Are you enjoying life on the ninth floor?"

"Beautiful. I don't want to give it up. I'm so happy to have Kurt Cobain out of my life. On second thought, maybe you shouldn't leave Baltimore just yet."

"Has there been any exciting mail for me? Or messages?"

"Actually, yes, I should have called you. Then I'd better go. Sharon Weinstein's supposed to be calling in a minute to talk about Raul Valenzuela. Oh my God, JD. You've got to see this man. I'll tell you about him later."

"Who? Who called? Did a guy from—from Interlect call?"

"Yes." Her voice got all kind. "Yes, he did. He said thank you for applying but they filled the position. But they were *really* impressed by the interview. You didn't tell me you had an interview."

"Well. It doesn't matter, now."

"But they were very impressed, he emphasized that." She allowed that to sink in for an instant. "I'm sorry, hon. But, if it's any consolation—'Interlect' is a dumb name. You would have been embarrassed to work there."

I hadn't told anyone I was applying for it. It was just a weird, one-shot deal, right before I left. It wasn't at all right for me. They wanted a systems consultant, for clients in the financial world. We all know how comfortable I am with *that*. Still, I sent in my résumé and an application, and yes, they interviewed me. Ten minutes. I can't tell you if it was a day on which I was coherent, or if I mumbled into my tie, but either way it obviously didn't wash. It was like my goodbye note, that application. Lili wasn't supposed to find out about it, unless I got the job.

"Anyone else call?"

"Yeah, the Zippy Car Rental people. They'd like to hear from you. They're eager to get an update on their Taurus. Do you want their number?"

"I've got it. Thanks."

You could hear her holding back her censure. She wanted to scold me, but she was feeling too sorry for me.

"So, listen. When are you coming back? And then I've got to go."

"Oh, you know. Probably not for another week or so. Or more. I might keep going. I might just drive myself right on into oblivion, somewhere. I'll keep you posted."

"*JD!*" Lili hissed. I jumped. I'd never heard her *hiss* before. It's startling when people do it.

"What?"

"Would you cut that out?" Now she was speaking in a mad, hissing whisper. She scared me. "I mean it. You've got to stop *saying* things like that. It's not funny. It's not charming. It just gets people worried for you and then eventually it gets them—me—fed up. You're a lovely, intelligent person, you're going through a bad patch, it will end, you'll get a job, for Christ's sake! It'll happen."

"OK. Sorry."

"Don't be sorry, you idiot. That's not the point. The point is it's not the world's most hilarious throwaway line, 'I might just sink into oblivion.' It's not something you just *say.*"

" 'Drive.' I said 'drive.' "

"*Whatever.* Suicide references are in bad taste, JD. All right? I love you as much as the next guy, you know I do. But drop the Madam Butterfly routine, would you? I get enough of the melodrama around here."

"You're right. It is in bad taste."

"Anyway, not to get clinical on you, but you know what they say. People who talk about it aren't the ones who actually do it. It's the weird insurance agents who never breathe a word; they're the ones that get found with a paper bag over their head."

"Well, that's helpful information." So on top of everything else, I'm not up to standard on my despair, either. It figures.

"Oh, don't get all touchy." Lili's voice finally, again, became kind. "Look, I've got to go. Sharon Weinstein's going to be having a conniption. She's not a patient woman. But I'm glad you called, hon. I miss you. Don't stay in Baltimore too long. Don't let them hoard you. I've got symphony tickets in a few weeks, and I'm counting on you to be my date."

"You should take a real date, Lili. Take Raul Buenas Noches or whoever."

"Listen to you! That's ridiculous. I love you. You are my real date. I'll tell you about Raul Valenzuela another time. He's all brawn and voice, I haven't found out yet if he has room for a personality. But I think he's been flirting with me. Anyway, have fun with Mops and Flops. My last question: How's Minsk?"

"Thriving. Doesn't miss the ninth floor one bit. He sends his regards."

"Excellent. Give him a kiss for me. Bye, Chotchka. I'll talk to you soon."

"Bye."

And I hung up the phone warmer and colder than when I started. Warmer, because. Well, because. Because it's nice to have people telling you they love you. All right? I admit it. It's nice. It cheers a person up.

Colder, because. Because. Because it didn't help, really, talking to Lili. It didn't fix anything. Besides, she told me about Interfuck. It's true, I had thought it was a dumb name when I was sending in the forms. But it was one of those weird things, like gambling on a horse, something I've never done in my life— the name just jumped out from the paper and I thought, That's it. That's the one. They'll hire me.

Which, as it turns out, was a false premonition.

But worse, finally, than Interfuck even was the voice behind the voice, the message behind the words. What Lili said to me. What she really meant.

I may have misled you earlier with that favorite Nixon reference. I might have mentioned it just to bring Nixon's name into the conversation. He's been on my mind lately, God knows why, maybe because it's an election year.

Lili may not really represent the silent majority. She's a little loud for the role, to be frank. But she is the majority, in some important ways. And what she was saying to me was perfectly clear. And perfectly understandable. God knows I've said it often enough to myself.

Shut up, JD, is what she was saying. Shut up.

Just shut *up*.

"SHAKESPEARE."

"You're kidding."

"Why should I be kidding?" said Pi. "What's funny about Shakespeare?"

"It's not that he's funny. It's that he's fat."

"Who's fat?"

Claudia entered the store's chattery dimness in time to ask the last question. Claudia had been coming into the store frequently of late, Pi noticed, more than she really needed to to run off her few educational bulletins. The pretty yellow-headed girl clearly had a crush on Xander, but Xander wouldn't come close to admitting it. Claudia, early twenties, clothed in batik dresses that came from someone's idea of India, was the librarian at the art center, where she also taught afternoon classes to under-fives.

"Hey Claudia." Xander waved from the fax machine, where he was feeding a many-paged message to San Diego. "Shakespeare, that's who. Don't you think that's fair?"

"I've never seen a picture of him." She shook her wispy head, a ponyish gesture. "I mean, not of his body. Only his balding head, you know, and shoulders. It's hard to tell from that if he's fat."

"I meant the books. Pi has been claiming that because of her recent Loss she can't read anymore or go into bookstores. She can only read things that are thin, like poetry or kids' books. Then today she announces she's been reading Shakespeare. I don't believe anybody would call him 'thin.'"

"You'd be surprised," Pi said. "You can get these handy little paperbacks, so compact they practically fit into the palm of your hand." She took the sheet Claudia offered over the counter—"What your child should bring to class." Pi had run off twenty of these already last week. "How many do you need?"

"Twenty. I made a mistake on the last one. I left out potatoes, for potato-printing." She smiled in apology and simultaneously cast a look of lemony longing at distant Xander, faxing. "I haven't read any Shakespeare since high school—*Romeo and Juliet.*"

"Have you ever been up to Ashland for the festival?" Xander asked.

"No. I've always wanted to."

"It's cool. The randomest combination—all this wild rugged land and forests and Shakespeare. It's wild. You can go salmon fishing in between plays. You should go. In fact, sometime we could get some friends together and all drive up there . . ."

"I'd love that," she cooed.

Pi hovered by the counter with Claudia's stack of copies, waiting for the flirtation to flutter down. Xander started to mumble that the fax machine wasn't feeding the pages through correctly and turned his back to them; Claudia's arrival had made him lose his place.

"Thanks," Claudia said politely to Pi. "So which Shakespeare are you reading?"

"*Hamlet.*"

"That's supposed to be a good one, isn't it?"

"It beats *Romeo and Juliet.* Here—see? You couldn't call this fat, could you?"

"Hey, wait a second, wait a second!" Xander finally abandoned his fax. "How did you get this? It looks suspiciously *new.* Where's it from? Is it Abbie's?"

"In fact, no."

"Aha! You purchased it!"

"I didn't say that."

"Why shouldn't she?"

"You're over it! You're cured."

"No, I'm not. I didn't go into the bookstore myself."

"What do you mean? You stood outside and got someone else to do it? Like getting someone to buy beer when you're underage?"

"It was pretty much like that."

"What are you guys talking about?"

"So who'd you ask? Did they get a commission?" Xander laughed. "Pi, you are so weird."

"I know I am. I can't help it. I asked Martha. She went in and got it for me."

"Martha! That's insane." Xander leaned in closer to Claudia—close enough to smell her girlish apple-y scent. "Pi has this phobia about bookstores. She can't go into them. So now she gets someone else to do her dirty work for her. A youth! A minor!"

"It's not that dirty," Pi protested. "Shakespeare isn't fat, and he isn't dirty, either."

"Don't let him tease you, Pi—"

"I still think it's twisted."

"Hey, this reminds me. I knew there was something I wanted to tell you two. A couple of friends of mine and me, we're starting a reading group. I got the idea from a radio show. Lots of people are doing it. You pick a different book each month and get together to discuss it. Are you guys interested?"

"Sounds cool," Xander said. "Sure."

"Thanks for asking," Pi said. "But I don't think I can."

"See, if Pi did it, all the books would have to be thin. There'd be a weight limit on them, otherwise she couldn't participate."

Pi narrowed her eyes at the comic-book man, her boss. "I'll give you a list of titles I'd recommend, though. The first one is *Why Bad Things Happen to Obnoxious People*. It's a sort of self-help book, and is very informative."

Claudia laughed, somewhat unsurely. "Well, listen," she said, leaning in towards Xander. The air was definitely stirring now between them. Claudia's smile was a pretty plum, her skin a warmed-up peach. "You can always change your mind. Besides—who knows? Maybe *Hamlet* will be the book we kick off with."

Abbie and Martha returned from San Francisco subdued. The first night back Abbie pleaded fatigue and retired after dinner; the next she announced she was in the mood for a movie, so the three of them drove to Fort Bragg for dinner out and a "family" offering in a multiplex which was all sun-faced kids and grinning dolphins. Pi couldn't bring herself to find it enchanting. It wasn't until Tuesday that Abbie's body finally uncoiled and she seemed readier to face Pi; which made Pi feel badly for having become someone who had to be *faced*.

Seeing the liveliness in Abbie's features again that evening as she cooked, Pi wondered what had changed her landlady's perspective. She finally got it: Abbie must have seen Faith that day. Pi understood the rhythm of Abbie's week now, how she must need those sympathetic hushed-room hours. They seemed squarely to improve her ability to cope. Faith was the prism through which Abbie understood the rearrangements that were going on within her as the marriage drew to its dry, shuddering end. Maybe Pi did shelter a tiny envy of

Abbie for this consolation. Not that Pi wanted a Faith for herself; she'd take her own kind of comfort in her digital adventures. But she saw the opening and warming of Abbie's eyes and felt an odd, almost wistful gladness for her.

That night, post book-at-bedtime, it was a sober peppermint-infused atmosphere in which Abbie said firmly to Pi, "Listen, Pi. I owe you an apology."

"For what?" Pi asked disingenuously.

"For the phone conversations over the weekend. I'm sorry. I'm sure I was curt with you, and you hadn't done anything to deserve it."

"Oh, don't worry about it. I understand, it was a difficult situation—"

"But it was wrong to put you in the position of negotiator like that, and I'm sorry." Abbie remained firm. She spoke as if there were a checklist of points she had to get through. "It wasn't right for Abe to engage you that way either, but I have to take equal responsibility for it. I was very upset. I'd thought that being up here away from Abe was going to make it simpler, but it really hasn't. There's still all of that work to do, distancing, adjusting. Still the same work to do. When I go back to the city, I realize that. And it—it upsets me. It's not a situation I can control completely, obviously. And when I feel things getting out of control I get angry." Abbie smiled a tight grimace of regret. "I don't like to think of myself as an angry person, but as Faith keeps pointing out to me, these days I just am. I have to accept that."

Hell hath no fury, thought Pi. Fran could have told you the same thing, free of charge.

"I know you're skeptical," Abbie said abruptly, with a surprising sharpness. "About Faith—about therapy. But you'd be surprised at how she smooths some of the pain away. Like a good masseuse. She knows where the tough, tight places are, and she presses them until they begin to loosen and give up their secrets. It's the same process, really, but working on the mind rather than the body. You know what I mean?"

"I guess. I've never been to a masseuse."

"Oh, Pi, you're not serious." At this Abbie had to laugh, and the low wall that had built up between them was washed partly away. "Never? What do they do to you people in grad school? Lock you up? I would have thought grad students—philosophers especially—could do with a good massage once a semester. It should be a requirement."

"You're probably right. But, you know—" Pi's brow darted up, "—we're all too busy working on the mind-body problem to take a break."

For Pi this was a leap of trust: to share a joke at philosophy's expense with an outsider. Like any marginal group, philosophers felt safe among themselves making fun of who they were and what they did—"I sometimes think philosophers are like another species, creatures from Mars," an eminent female philosopher once said to Pi—but they bristled and scowled at the mockery of the uninitiated. Pi was, she felt, betraying her people even in making this one small gibe.

"I'll tell you something." Abbie lowered her voice confidentially. "I had a massage Sunday morning. God, did I need it. But guess where I had it?"

"Where?"

"At the Fairmont Hotel!" She looked wickedly pleased. "We stayed there, Martha and I, Saturday night. Can you believe it? I know it was self-indulgent, and I'm sure I'll regret it when the credit card bill shows up, but you know what? It was worth it. Every penny. Only—don't tell Fran, will you? She'll think I'm crazy."

And Abbie started relating, with cute girlishness, the pleasures of the Fairmont Hotel: the views, the masseuse in the ninth-floor spa area, the fact that her own grandparents used to stay there when they came to San Francisco and there was still a doddery old fellow at the reception desk who remembered them from thirty years before. A memory of her big sister taking her to the Venetian Room once. The Venetian Room! What a treat. Her sister drank some fabulous cocktail and Abbie had to make do with a "Shirley Temple"—some brightly colored fruit concoction for children. It was a different world, she said. The band played clean, swinging music and a tall man had asked her sister to dance, and while she watched her sister dance the waiter had come up to her and brought her another Shirley Temple "on the house," he said, winking at her, and she'd kept the little wooden cocktail stirrer for years afterwards as a memento of the occasion and that waiter, her first true love . . . Abbie shed years as she told these stories, which led right up—accidentally, somehow—to the detail that she had spent the start of her own honeymoon at the Fairmont, with Abe, before they'd taken their flight to Hawaii for a week exploring one of the remoter islands.

And then, as ever, she had to stop, as the inevitable name—that simple syllable—caused Abbie's face to withdraw again. The joy left her eyes, her features unanimated themselves. Pi wanted to say something—do something!—to help those eyes, to change them back; but her uncertain words were too slow, and Abbie corrected herself first.

"And you, Pi," she said in a soft voice. "What did you get up to while we were gone? Did you throw any wild parties in our absence?"

"Just the naked fondue orgy, that's all." Pi smiled. "Otherwise, not much. Except take a long hike in Russian Gulch. The redwoods there—they're magnificent."

"If you think those are great, you should go over to Hendy Woods sometime. Some truly ancient, giant redwoods are there. It's fantastic. I have a picture of Martha there when she was three or four, we took a picture of her in the burnt-out center of one of them and it's so funny—you can hardly see her, she's the size of a mushroom against the great bulk of the tree."

Pi cleared her throat. Now really. It wasn't like it was a crime. Why act guilty? She had a confidence to share with Abbie, in exchange for hers. "I did do one other new thing this weekend," she ventured, scratching at an invisible mark on the table.

"What's that?"

"I did some experimenting on the computer. You know—on the Internet. Xander's been telling me how to get on it. That's why the line was busy when you called. It's going to be the next big thing, everyone says, so I thought I ought to give it a try."

"Ah."

Abbie nodded soberly, and to Pi's distress she was faced again with the charitable look, the look of concern, the look that wanted to send Pi to a therapist to cure her various mental ills. *Sad. She thinks I'm sad. She thinks I don't know how to make real friends—*

"It's really interesting," Pi said, defiantly. "More fun than I was expecting. Very smart, interesting people are on it. I've written to Fran on it. And my friend Hannah in Texas. It's a good way to keep in touch with people."

"But you can talk to Fran on the phone."

"I know, but it's not the same." Pi felt impatient. She wanted Abbie to understand, to get it, not to judge. How could she explain the new thrill in the unseen possibilities?

"I'm sure it is interesting," Abbie said kindly. Her voice was vague and had already gone somewhere else. She got up to follow it. "As you say, it will probably turn out to be the next big thing."

Martha had been especially quiet since the San Francisco weekend. She'd taken to playing a new kind of game, which she thought was very funny and entertaining, though the adults had a hard time agreeing with her. She pretended to be mute. Sometimes she'd turn completely voiceless and wouldn't utter a sound; sometimes she'd pretend to speak in real sentences but she wouldn't open her mouth, so she'd end up humming conversationally—

"Mm mm mm mm *mm* mm mm mm-mm?"

—And then wait for you to guess what she'd said.

"Can you go to Mary's house today?" Pi might, if she was very lucky, guess on the fourth or fifth try.

"*Mmm!*" Martha would hum triumphantly, if you'd gotten it right.

The game quickly palled.

But you couldn't make her stop playing it. There was no way to get her to speak. If you said, "Martha, I'm not going to talk to you anymore until you speak in real words," she'd shrug, sulk, and go upstairs to her room. If you ignored her, she ignored you. Worse, if you tried pleading—"Martha, sweetie, I don't know what you're trying to say. What is it? Come on, Martles, say it in real words"—the girl would look at you wide-eyed and shake her head, as if she would help you if she possibly could; or she'd whine back at you, "*Mmmmmmm,*" like a dog apologizing for something it has inadvertently done wrong.

Abbie felt the best thing was just to ride it out. She was sure her daughter would snap out of it when she was ready to. She'd get bored with it. In the meantime, Abbie had a clever idea: she bought a mini chalkboard and chalk for Martha to write on when she wanted to, not that her writing was so accomplished yet but, as Abbie pointed out to Pi (with a hint of defensiveness), it wasn't a bad way to get her to practice. Besides, one of Martha's favorite characters of all time was Louis the mute trumpeter swan from the book by E. B. White, and that was how Louis communicated—by chalkboard and chalk. It was probably Louis who'd encouraged Martha to go mute in the first place, Pi pointed out. The hazards of reading!

So Martha wrote MILK on the chalkboard when she wanted a glass or HOLE IN SHOOS to show how her sneakers had been pierced by a thumb tack. And one night after dinner she wrote PIE READ ME?

"You want Pi to read to you tonight?" Martha nodded, and Abbie raised her eyebrows to Pi. "Would you mind?"

"Not at all!" Pi was flattered. Her irritation fell swiftly away. "I'd love to. Sure. What are you reading these days?"

"Mm mm-mm mm-mm."

"*The Starlight Barking,*" Abbie translated. "By Dodie Smith. It's the sequel to *The Hundred and One Dalmatians.* We just started it."

"I didn't know there was a sequel."

"That's because Disney never immortalized it. A friend from New York sent it to us for Christmas, a beautiful first edition."

Martha grabbed Pi's hand. "Mm mm mm mm-mm?"

"Yes, you may be excused," Abbie said, rolling her eyes, and the child pulled Pi eagerly up to the mystical land of the evening book, leaving Abbie to fend for herself in the real world of chalk dust and dirty dishes.

Martha led Pi upstairs, thumping her triangle-shaped feet against the blue painted boards as she climbed. In Martha's big, messy, toy-happy bedroom, Pi felt nervous again, the way she had around the child when she first moved in. Martha managed her routine by herself, changing into her pj's and brushing her teeth, while Pi stood awkwardly in the bedroom, half-babysitter, half-interloper. She plucked *The Starlight Barking* from the shelf and paged through it, feeling as though she were about to take part in an audition.

"Mm!" Martha said when she came back, and wriggled herself into the short flannelly bed. She looked at Pi expectantly.

The page was clearly marked where they had left off the night before, and Pi was just getting ready to get going on it, when her eye did a wild skid across the contents page and screeched to a terrible, shocked halt.

Metaphysical.

The word "Metaphysical" was in one of the chapter headings. "Chapter Three: The Meaning of Metaphysical." Was it a set-up? Had Abbie laid a trap for Pi to test her—like putting someone back on the horse right after they've dropped heavy-boned to the hard unfriendly ground? Get back on, that's the only way to get over the trauma!

Pi's breaths were coming quickly, and the blood in her veins was running too hot. Indignation tensed her jaw. Then she looked at Martha, who was staring at her quizzically.

"Mm mm?" she asked softly, in concern.

Pi made herself breathe. She quieted her brain enough to realize her paranoia was absurd. It was an accident. Who would know that the shape of a simple word—*metaphysical*—might cause her such trouble? At some point she'd look at the book, see what the story was. But for tonight she'd leave it. Pi tried to compose her face and thoughts. This was still an audition that she did not want to fail.

"I'll tell you what, Martles." She put the book back on the shelf. Martha waited, wide awake and curious. "I'll tell you what," Pi repeated. "This book is

some kind of metaphysical—some kind of magical story about dogs. Right?"
Martha nodded.

"Well, it's given me an idea. Yes, it's—it's given me an idea to tell you a different story, instead. Would that be all right? A different metaphysical story about dogs. How does that sound?"

"Mm!" she said, with enthusiasm.

"OK, then. Here we go," Pi said, her mouth nervous, her heart philosophy-jittery. Outside in the night the sea growled its lively, inkdark approval. A million fishes swam about there, while rock was turned to sand and sand to rock again: such movements were part of the sea's job. And Pi's job, for this minute at least, was to tell a story. Sitting on the soft edge of Martha's small bed, Pi the untried storyteller cleared her throat to begin.

"This is the story of a dog named Pinsk."

She paused. She was just going to have to start, and see what happened.

"He was a small black dog, a poodle with curly hair. And this dog, Pinsk, lived a different kind of life from a normal dog, because he was—well, he was what we'd call a 'ghost.' We'd call him a ghost because he didn't live where we live, but in this other place called—called—the 'Other Side.' It has lots of names, but that's one of them. The Other Side is an incredible, magical place, with amazing mountains and valleys, but where Pinsk lived was on a beach, a sandy, stormy beautiful beach—kind of like Mendocino, coincidentally.

"As I say, we'd call him a ghost because we don't know any better, but that's not how he thought of himself. He enjoyed his life on the beach, playing and exploring. Sometimes he missed people from the old world, this world that you and I know—because he had lived here once, you see. He'd left behind a brother, Minsk, also a poodle, a white one, and his old owner, JD, who lived in a city. Pinsk missed them, but when he tried to send them messages from the Other Side—you know, by making the wind blow in the trees around them or by making them hear some funny song unexpectedly—unfortunately they didn't realize those were messages from him. That's one of the only drawbacks about having to live on the Other Side: nobody from here can hear what you say there. That's why when anyone from there tries to communicate with us they have to do it in unusual ways like sending a shiver down your spine or making the dishes rattle in the kitchen.

"So, unfortunately, Minsk and JD didn't realize when the wind was blowing that that was actually Pinsk trying to say Hi. If only they'd been a little more alert!"

Pi paused. Keep it simple, she reminded herself. But she did have Martha's attention.

"One thing you have to know right off the bat about the Other Side is that it's more fun than our world because there are fewer rules about how to behave. So here, for instance, you have to look and talk a particular way or people will think you're crazy, but there you can be as eccentric as you want and nobody will bother you. In fact, they *prefer* it if you're eccentric."

"Mm mm-mm-mm?"

"What's 'eccentric'?"

Martha nodded.

"Oh. *Eccentric.* It's a fancy word for being strange. So, for instance, I'm eccentric because I won't go into bookstores to buy books. I'm eccentric because I spent money I barely have on a pair of hiking boots. There are various other eccentricities I have, but I don't need to go into them all here."

Martha pointed at herself.

"Oh, you! Yes, you're eccentric, too. Absolutely. Well, for one thing, your preferring cereal without any milk on it, that's eccentric. Or not talking! That certainly counts. In *our* world, where people ordinarily do talk, that's extremely eccentric."

Martha gave her a pained frown.

"OK. Back to Pinsk. I'm just trying to explain that you and I would both benefit from these loose rules they have on the Other Side, because people wouldn't bother us so much about what we do.

"Anyway. Pinsk was eccentric in all kinds of ways. He liked to drink milk-shakes rather than water. He liked to play Frisbee, which isn't that unusual in dogs, especially on the beach, except that Pinsk liked to throw the Frisbee as well as catch it. He had a very effective flick-of-the-neck action. And while some dogs wear kerchiefs around their necks, Pinsk's preferred item of clothing was a—a scarf, instead, a long wool purple scarf to keep his neck warm. Kind of like the one you have, coincidentally.

"Anyway, as I've mentioned—have I mentioned this?—the other thing about people on the Other Side is that they are invisible. Which is awkward for them in one way, but in another way it means they can coexist with our world quite comfortably; since we can't see them or hear them, they don't bug us or get in our way. So in fact they're all around us, all the time."

Pi looked around the room suggestively, narrowing her eyes to see through the obscuring atmosphere. Martha carefully tracked her gaze as though, if she looked where Pi looked, she might see whatever secrets Pi saw.

"Most of us never see them though, because our eyes are very weak and can only see the incredibly obvious things around us. Someday someone will make a pair of glasses that will be so strong that humans will finally be able to see new things, like creatures we'd now call ghosts, or atoms, or the words going through the cable wires as people speak them on the phone. Or things hidden underground, maybe, like those arrowheads you were looking for. Things that are buried. Who knows? Maybe when you grow up you'll invent the kind of glasses that will enable people to see stuff like that.

"And that's it for tonight! I can't think of any more, and it's getting late."

"*Mmm!*" Martha was indignant. She pulled on Pi's sleeve.

"What, more?"

"Mmm!"

"Oh, all right. Just a tiny bit. But there's only one more thing to fill you in on tonight, anyway, and that is—that is, what these folks on the Other Side do with themselves all day. Because they have jobs, too, you know. Their main job is . . ."

Pi looked out the window for inspiration.

". . . the weather. The weather! It's the perfect job for people who are invisible, you see? Because *we* can't see them making the wind blow or the sun come out. They have all the controls. They can switch the air from hot to cold or dry to rainy. That's their job. And when they get into arguments with each other about it, that's when the weather is very unsettled.

"So Pinsk, specifically, has a job, in—in the rain department. Yes! The rain department." Pi was suddenly very pleased, as she realized the secret symmetry lurking in her tale. "And that's why people say 'It's raining cats and dogs.' That's where the expression comes from!

"And *that's* enough for tonight. I'm not going to get a better ending than that."

"Mm!" Martha said. Her face was bright, awake, and alive.

"Did you like that?"

"Mm! Mm-mm!"

"What? You want more?" Pi said. "Tomorrow night, maybe. That's it for tonight."

Martha shook her head with great emphasis. She made inscrutable gestures with her hands. She was sitting up now, excited, trying to communicate some very pressing idea.

"*Mmmm!*"

"Martles, I'm sorry, I don't know what you're saying. Come on, now, let's tuck you back in. That's enough for tonight."

"ZENO!" The voice finally blurted. The shock of the sound made Pi jump. "Zeno?" she asked.

Now that Martha had started, she might as well go on. She had plenty to say.

"Maybe Pinx is friends with your cat, Zeno, maybe they met over there on the Other Side, and maybe they do the rain together, like a team, because you said, 'It's raining cats and dogs,' so the cat has to be *Zeno!*"

The girl was immensely pleased with herself. She didn't even mind having temporarily sacrificed her muteness. It was worth it. The idea was too good to pass up.

Pi had to agree. It was a deep, important breakthrough.

"You're right, Martles! I'm sure you're right." Her satisfaction was complete: not only had she passed her audition; she had, inadvertently, lured the child back into speech. "We'll have to figure more out about that tomorrow. But now! Bedtime."

She turned off the lamp next to Martha's bed. Lion-tamers and jugglers were stenciled in warm paper tones on the lampshade. It was another of Abbie's craft items, one that Pi imagined must prompt colorful dreams.

"Goodnight," said Martha, turning her cheek for Pi's kiss. "You know what? I'm going to look for them in the sky next time it rains."

No one had written back any information about JD. No one had any. People had gone into discussions about antidepressants and whether depression runs in families. There was also a side discussion on Baltimore started by Abbie Hoffman, who lived there, it transpired.

But the only thing you could do if it was JD you were interested in rather than the talk he generated was to sit around waiting for him to post more of his Diery. It was like watching for important news to come in the mail. It reminded Pi of waiting to hear back from graduate schools a few years back; or, worse, from colleges when you were seventeen and desperate to get away from home, and those envelopes—the fat ones, of course, not the bitter, thin anorexic ones—were the salvation you waited for. They were your ticket to ride. Pi was beginning to feel the same way about Dickinson 536: it was a kind of escape route. But day after day she'd checked it with nothing new appearing from the guy himself.

Then one day, a couple of weeks since the San Francisco weekend and Pi's first encountering JD, since he'd crept into her mind and changed her point of view—when by now she was beginning to wonder if she had come to discover this character just in time for him, like so many things in her life, to disappear—a new installment of the Diery appeared in Dickinson 536. It was him! It was JD. He had made it to Baltimore. And he'd written a whole new section, called "The eyes of March."

It was after that that Pi had asked Martha to buy *Hamlet.*

She started the play in a state of distraction. She was reading it for clues not story, as if it were a map to some place she urgently needed to get to. She quickly got lost reading it that way. That wasn't the right way to read. If Pi weren't so out of practice, she might have remembered this. You had to go slowly, slowly—especially with *Hamlet*—almost as if it were a philosophical tract. If you, for your part, took all of it in, the world would eventually draw you into itself. That was the deal, in reading. Eventually, after keeping up her side of the bargain, Pi was absorbed into the play: she began to breathe those clouds of suspicion and artifice and ambition. Pi began to feel sorry for and puzzled by this man who pulled out his insides in front of everyone else, who seemed so eager to make a performance out of his despair and rage. There were others she felt sorry for too: confused Gertrude, enfeebled Ophelia. Even old bumbly Polonius. Even guilty Claudius, trying in a dark corner to find the heart for prayer.

"So," Abbie asked her. "What's gotten you reading *Hamlet?*" All Pi had to do was say the word, and Abbie would find her a therapist. She was ready to do it.

Pi tried to look nonchalant. "Someone I know was talking about it, so I thought maybe I would read it again. I haven't read it since high school."

"Someone you know?" Abbie, mother-sharp, picked up on the careful vagueness. "What kind of 'someone'?"

Pi wanted to tell someone about this someone, but Abbie didn't seem the right person. She'd thought about telling Xander and Claudia. Xander was an obvious choice. But then she'd had to realize that they might start reading the Diery, too. After all, it was *there*, on the Net, for anybody to read who wanted to. That was the whole point of the Net—universal access. It was democratic that way. But Pi didn't feel democratic about JD or his Diery. She didn't want anyone else reading it. She wanted JD to herself. She didn't like the messages on ED 536 for that very reason: all those insensitive people, chattering on, winking their too-cute emoticons ;-) when there was a guy there, a real person, someone she felt she understood from what he wrote, whom she felt she *knew*. "The eyes of March" had only confirmed it. JD's brush with graduate students had had her in tears, followed shortly by a worry about the pit JD was edging towards again. The notes on ED 536 afterwards frustrated her more than ever. Other people were worried, too, but expressed their concern in syrupy helpful-isms, in perky pick-him-ups, or in boyish dark jokes. They reminded Pi of the sentences she'd met herself, after the fire.

So Pi told Martha.

She hadn't meant to. It came up a few nights later when Pi was tucking Martha in, getting ready to tell her more stories about Pinsk. There was an understanding now that Martha might talk during these bedtime sessions—if only because she had so many of her own thoughts to offer on the world of the Other Side. The stories had become a collaboration between them.

That night Martha had a specific question in mind.

"I want to know more about Pinx before he was a ghost. Where did he live before? Around here, near Zeno?"

"Well . . ."

Pi had never been good at resisting temptation. "Do you want to know a secret?"

Martha nodded. Of course.

"Well, Martles, the truth is—where he lived before—he lived on the East Coast. Really. I didn't make up Minsk and JD, or even Pinsk. Minsk and JD, they really exist."

Martha sat up straight in surprise. "Do you know them?"

"Not exactly."

Pi explained how they were like a story. How she'd read about them—sort of like how you read about people in the newspaper—and how every couple of weeks you could find out more about them, because more of the story appeared. So it was also sort of like a TV series with episodes every week, but (and this was hard to explain) it was *real*. It was almost definitely real. Because it was in print. On the computer.

Martha was skeptical.

"But where are they? Where do they live really?"

"According to the story, they're in Baltimore now, a city on the other side of the country. But no one knows where they really live. It sounds like New York."

"But who are they? I don't get it."

So Pi tried to explain what she didn't well understand herself. It was like those times TAing when the class was reading someone like Davidson, and her own comprehension was maybe half a step ahead of her students'. She reminded Martha of the letter they'd sent Fran on the computer—how they'd jointly written her about the movie they'd seen, and then how Fran had written back about rollerblading in the park. Martha nodded. She liked Fran's letter, which Pi had let her read for herself off the screen. Martha understood that part, that it was like getting a letter in the mailbox but instead you got it on your computer. So Minx and Pinx was like that? Sort of. So JD was writing letters about Minx and Pinx? Yeah, in a way, except not about Pinsk anymore because Pinsk really wasn't around anymore, that part was true.

So do you write them back?

"That's exactly what I'd like to do," said Pi. "I want to write a letter to JD. But, see, I'm not sure he'll get it, because I don't have his address. People try to write him letters, but he doesn't write back. It's like—praying, sort of." She laughed to herself. "That is, Martles, it's like Santa Claus. You know how people write Santa Claus letters? 'Dear Santa, This is what I want for Christmas . . .' —but then he doesn't necessarily write them back, so you can never be sure whether he got the letter or not."

"But Santa Claus doesn't exist."

"Don't you think so?"

Martha frowned. "*You* know he doesn't, Pi."

"Well." Pi grimaced. "I wasn't absolutely sure till you said that."

"I don't think these people exist if they never write back." Martha shook her head.

"But maybe, you see, no one's written the right thing yet. That's what gets me excited. Maybe if someone wrote JD something really interesting, or funny, or strange, he *would* write back. Maybe. You see?"

"Maybe you can figure out something that will make him write back!"

"That's what I'm hoping. That's what I want to do. I'm going to write *something*. I have to try. I just can't think of what to say. What do you think I should say to him?"

Martha sat for a few minutes, thinking it over. Her nut-colored face creased in concentration, and her arms were folded to help her think better.

Finally, she said, "I know. It's easy."

"It is?"

Her brown eyes twitched with their own cleverness, her small sparrow mouth skipped into a smile.

"Tell him your stories about Pinx."

```
Re: March. Something.
Dear Fran,
    Weirdness continues.
    I'm becoming a poetic Shakespeare Internet geek.
Thought you should know. Sending messages to people who
don't exist, and the like.
    I'm glad to hear you've found someone suitably cute
to date. I like the sound of Peter. Anyone who can make
a living out of their voice has got to be OK. I'm sure
that's the direction I should move in. Away from the
written tradition, back to the oral. Maybe one day I'll
become an oral philosopher, ha ha, instead of a moral
one. But SERIOUSLY. Is there any way I can get his sta-
tion up here? It would be fun to be able to listen to
the voice that is now whispering sweet nothings into
your ear . . .
    The oral tradition between Abbie and me, incidentally,
is slowly evolving, i.e. we are talking more than for-
merly. I like your aunt. I've seen more and more why
she was dubbed the Cool Aunt in times gone by. I've
been hearing lots about the past, in fact. Tales of Ab-
bie's ashram days. I guess that predated your meeting
up with her again? Or did you ever go see her there?
Sounds wild. Tell all.
    So, you see, personal history. I'm finally getting
into it. I think if Personal Space was the item when we
were in high school, maybe Personal History will turn
out to be the thing in the nineties.
    Abbie's been trying to get me to talk about mine,
too. My family. My past Loves. She's been asking
```

Pi paused, her fingers over the keyboard.

There was a light knock on the door.

"Pi? Can I come in?"

Pi hurriedly closed the letter, tossed it into a place ready to send. "Sure!" She checked the computer's clock; her room didn't have a normal one. 10:51 p.m. Pi sat on her stool at the computer counter and gestured politely at the narrow Indian-blanketed bed.

"What's up?" she said, as if pre-midnight visits from the proprietor were a regular occurrence.

Abbie sank into the bed. She was dressed, Pi could hardly help noticing, in one of her long natural-dyed garments and wore over it a creamy brushed-cotton bathrobe. From its loose hem stretched rich brown calves, tidy nail-painted toes. Pi realized that the triangular feet were, not surprisingly, a grown-up, tended-to version of Martha's. The thought made her pull her own sweatshirted arms more closely around herself.

"I can't sleep. I've been trying. That herbal drink, the valerian—it isn't working anymore. My body's built up an immunity to it."

Pi pushed her hair behind her ears, tried to think of something bright to say.

"What are you up to?" Abbie nodded at the computer. "Am I disturbing you?"

"Oh, no. No. I was just writing a letter."

"Ah."

Abbie's eyes were gull grey in the dim light; her damp, curled hair nested closely around her face. The face, which had once seemed so open and readable to Pi, now sheltered ambiguities and unsaid thoughts; a slyness that was either real or imagined on the part of the younger woman, whose mind had been changed by fire and might not any longer have reliable perceptions about this kind of thing.

"I can turn it off. Here, I'll turn it off." Pi touched a key to bring the screen back to life. There was something too absurd about her planetary screen saver to allow it to flicker its light on this unusual encounter.

"No." Abbie sat up, gathering her robe. "No, don't do that." She got up and moved to stand next to Pi at the computer. Close. She stood close enough that her hip touched—just feather-touched, lightly brushed—Pi's waiting waist.

"Can you show me something on it? I feel so left out. You know all about it, Martha seems to know everything about it, and here am I, still completely ignorant."

"Are you serious?" Pi hesitated. "I thought you thought this whole thing was only for troubled, backwards people."

"Of course not. It's just that I don't know anything about it."

"Well." Pi swung back to face the screen, feeling as she spun the curved, strong hip mentioning its shape again against her waist. "What can I show you?" Pi's left hand moved instinctively to her own neck. She often loosened her neck while she sat in front of the screen, waiting to figure out what to write, trying to loosen the words from her body and mind.

"Is your neck sore? Here."

Abbie put a hand on Pi's neck, a daring thing to do and, Pi thought, not necessarily such a good plan.

"I don't know," Abbie said. "Show me—show me what you do here. What is it you do? Send letters? Meet people?" Her strong fingers worked more effectively than Pi's ever could on the tough area around her shoulders. "Pi, my God. You're so knotted."

This was college material, wasn't it? Back rubs? It was what you did when you were eighteen, when you could get away with being girls giving and receiving back rubs, pretending it was all perfectly innocent, when your excitable adolescent thighs knew otherwise and lit themselves into quiet fires of expectation.

"That feels great," Pi said matter-of-factly. "Here. I know what I'll show you."

She opened a letter from Fran, an old one, one Pi knew wouldn't have any references to Abbie in it. Pi had saved it for sentimental reasons.

```
Re: Love for sale


Hi Pi.
    Quick note. Thought you'd like to know Marie's latest
masterpiece, title as above as I'm sure you know, has
just opened here. It's showing down at the Kabuki. The
posters for it are insane: all black girls with wild
hair and guns. Attention-getting! It's getting great
reviews, though.
    So, what do you say? Should I see it, or not? Is
there a Piper boycott on, is what I want to know. Also
I want to know if there's any way you'd be in the
credits. Did she base any of the characters on you?!
The one with the big hair, I'm thinking.
```

"What's all that about?" Abbie leaned forward to read the screen. Her supple fingers briefly stopped their massaging.

"It's a note from Fran about a movie made by a friend of mine. Marie Jackson—you know, the filmmaker? I knew her in college. She was a friend of mine."

"Oh yes, I know about Marie. Fran told me all about you and Marie."

Now this was a tidy little bombshell. But it was too awkward for Pi to arch her neck back around to look at Abbie and read her expression. Pi wondered with what face Abbie mentioned, touching Pi's shoulders, that she knew Pi had loved women in her life. Was she smug? Pleased to catch Pi off guard, to point up the pointlessness of her months of secrecy? Maybe this was Pi's punishment for not telling Abbie those stories herself—to be mock-seduced by a languorous creature in a creamy bathrobe, with long brown legs and a persistent hip, and a hand that was communicating something hot and important to Pi's tired back.

The machine blipped.

"What's that?"

Pi shifted her body slightly closer to Abbie's. She moved her shoulders under those hands. It was beginning to happen—that sensation. That sliding sensation. When a hungry body tells an active mind: You can't worry about this anymore. This may be a bad idea, but you can't worry about it. *This time is mine.*

"What did that noise mean?"

"It means," Pi said, "that I just got some mail. Someone just sent me some mail."

" 'Someone'?"

Abbie straightened, millimetered her way away from Pi. There was a laugh in her voice, a question. For all that she was playing with something dangerous here, and knew it, she could slip back into a jokey tease whenever she wanted.

"Which someone?" she said. "Why don't you find out?"

"Abbie—"

"Come on, Pi, let's just see." She pressed her shoulder. Then she laughed again, this time with embarrassment. "No, I'm sorry. It's probably private. I'm sorry, I'm prying."

"No, you're not prying . . ." Pi breathed. "Here—I'll show you. It's nothing. It'll be from Fran. Or Hannah."

Her fingers did a small jig over the keys to call up the sender. Her brain and body were split; her heart was in her stomach. She felt bashful about this computer charade, but at least it gave her an extra minute to figure out what to do about whatever the hell was going on in this room.

When she read the name, Pi couldn't help yelping.

"Oh my God."

"What? What is it?"

The name of the person sending her a letter was a new one to her. It was Hamlet.

··► Part 3

Re: The Ghost of Pinsk

A friend writes:
Everyone thinks it's such a big deal, being a ghost.
What's it like? they ask you. How is it? Will I like
it? Is it awfully cold?
  It is really not so hard to get used to. The first
thing you notice is that nothing is what it seems. It's
like trying to live on a photographic negative: what's
white is black, what's black is white, only what's
bland and grey stays the same. And it doesn't stop at
color. It applies to other categories too: what's up is
frequently down, what's night may turn out to be day, a
joke you might have made in life becomes serious while
here the serious stuff--life and death, Shakespeare,
the waging of Presidential elections--will always be
treated as the best kind of joke.
  Not that I'm complaining. I like it here! I wouldn't
want to go back now, even if I could. I was a little
disoriented in the beginning--who wouldn't be? down was
up, for God's sake!--but now I've gotten my bearings,
and I've got my pals, people I can talk to when I stop
by the cafe on the beach. (The cafe is where you go in
the evenings to get drunk and cheerful, and start confessing a few personal details. The bar is better for

morning, to get you waked up and wired, help you focus
on your jobs for the day.)

Plus, the scenery's spectacular.

I'll run a biographical fact or two by you so you
know where I'm coming from. I'm a dog--a poodle I'd
have been called in the old world, but here I'm a mutt.
Which is more relaxing, because you don't constantly
knock up against people's dumb preconceptions about
blood and breeding. There's no set line about mutts,
you know "Mutts are so intelligent" or "Mutts are cute
to look at, but they have a tendency to yap." You know
the crazy ideas people get about breeds. They think it
gives them some kind of handle on you--it's a way of
trying to make other creatures easier to read. (And
isn't learning to read each other one of the main
tasks?) Here there's more room for individuality since
we're all mutts--all different, hence all the same. I
imagine I don't have to spell that paradox out for you.

But I don't want to lecture you. I'm just trying to
get across what it's like. Let me give you an example.
I have a good friend here, name of Zeno. (As in the
paradox. That's how that word sneaked into my vocabulary. I'm always teasing Zeno about it--the flight of
the arrows, the mad divisibility of time.) In his old
life Zeno was a black and white cat. Owned by a philosopher, hence the pretentious name. And you know as well
as I do what I'd have had to do, in the other life, if
I'd seen a cat. Chase it. That's the order of things.
Not to say there can't be the occasional humorous re-
versal--it's always a good gag for the cat to fight
back, scratch the dog's nose. That gets a laugh out of
folks because it changes the roles around. Ha ha. So
funny I forgot to laugh, as my old owner might have
said.

The point being, in this set-up, we don't have to go
through any of that nonsense. Zeno happens to be a nice
guy, smart and friendly, so we can sit around the cafe

of an evening shooting the breeze together, and no one
has to chase anyone or scratch anyone's nose. See what
I mean? It's so much more civilized.

And the scenery. Like I said--spectacular! I don't
know how I got posted out here, to this particular
job--I have a post in the rain department, making up a
small part of that weather--but in the course of moving
to the Other Side (as you call this place) I got trans-
ferred to some place western, beachy and free. I'm here
with the redwoods; close to the water where once-
extinct creatures swim underwater, and once-extinct
birds make prehistoric arcs in the sky.

In the old language, this would be called California.
Hardly an adequate name for such a great collection of
wilds and wanderers, but at least it has a poetic ring
to it. California was Zeno's home state so he fills me
in on the local customs, the flora and fauna. The
cliffs here are sheer as the sword of a giant. The
trees--great, ancient trees--are tall as that dead ship
the Titanic. Each one contains a miniature map of its
own history, secretly written in the tale of its bark;
the inner rings build up a gospel of life up to now.
The sky is full of the birdcalls of millions; sunlight
that knows things, and bright loud storms for percus-
sion. I'll tell you one fact about the grandeur of this
place: it makes someone like myself, a humble mutt,
feel really quite small. It's not necessarily a great
place for the ego. That's why I'm glad to have Zeno--
like I say, we keep each other company. We engage in
ordinary chit-chat when the sheer dimensions of life
here threaten to silence us.

It's a beautiful life here, out with the others you
might choose to call ghosts. And in case you were wondering about that other point: we actually find the
temperature here pleasantly warm.

Re: The Ghost of Pinsk

To Whom It May Concern,
   What eloquence. Is it possible for you to explain how you got hold of the story of that dear pooch? I would be intrigued to hear more of it. It's a relief to imagine him as part of the California climate, with some new (not entirely clear) relation to rainstorms.
   Something of the fellow's spirit obviously weathered its way over to you, wherever and whoever you are.

Yours sincerely,

Hamlet

PS I'm writing you back directly, privately: I hope you don't mind.

Re: Your inquiry

Dear Hamlet,
   No I don't mind. If privacy is possible over the Net waves (a fact I'm unclear about) I think it's a fine idea.
   The story of how we made contact with the ghost of Pinsk is somewhat elaborate: it has to do with metaphysical tales and, in an unlikely twist, the sequel to the story of the Hundred and One Dalmatians.
   While not wanting to burden you with too many details, I can also say that a girl named Martha had a lot of input into the discovery of Pinsk's story, and in all fairness she should be credited here.
Best wishes,
Whom It Concerned

Re: My inquiry

Dear Whom,
So who's Martha?
  And I'm curious: how did dalmatians, in whatever
quantity, get into the picture?
  Lastly, I couldn't help noticing you're called Sylvia
Plath. May I address you as Sylvia?

Sincerely,
Hamlet

Re: Who's Whom

Dear Hamlet,
1. Martha will probably be the first of any of us to
see Pinsk--and Zeno the cat--flying across the sky, in
our next big rainstorm. She is a very observant young
person. If it weren't for Martha, the Ghost of Pinsk
might have kept himself to himself.
2. I happen to share living quarters with Martha. Also
with the Dalmatian sequel. It's called The Starlight
Barking, and it prompted speculations on dogs' lives on
the part of Martha and me.
3. Yes, it's true and you may. Don't let it alarm you,
though: I'm milder than the original.
Best,
Sylvia

Re: No alarm taken

Dear Sylvia,
  I like the sound of Martha.
  And I don't see why you should apologize for Ms.
Plath. Anybody who can put "ich, ich, ich, I could
hardly speak" into a poem has my greatest respect. (Are

we supposed to pronounce it "spich" is what I always wanted to know.)

So, for the ignorant among us who never knew there was a sequel, can you give a quick overview of The Starlight B?

Yours awaiting enlightenment,
Hamlet

Re: Enlightenment

OK, Hamlet, here goes, but only because you insist.

In brief, The Starlight B is a story of a day in which dogs are the only creatures awake--all the people and other animals are asleep (except for two cats who are honorary dogs). Other magical differences this day: dogs can get around very quickly by a kind of flying motion called "Swooshing." It's very cool. I myself would like to be able to swoosh. Eventually the dogs all show up in Trafalgar Square in London to find out what's going on, and I won't give away any more because that would spoil it for you, but I can reveal that Sirius the Dog Star has a cameo role.

The best and truest line from the book, which I found poignant for my own reasons--is when Missus, the Mom Dalmatian, is trying to figure out what "metaphysical" means, because they all agree the day's changes are metaphysical in nature. This is at the beginning, when they're trying to figure out what's going on. And Missus says: "I think metaphysical means magic--a kind of magic that comes from our own mind."

How true that is (as Dan Quayle might say).

Best,
Sylvia

Re: The Starlight Barking

Dear Sylvia,
  Sounds very cool. I may have to read it. I happen to
have a good bookstore connection so maybe I can come up
with a copy.
  So why did Disney never get his animated hands on it?

Yours,
Hamlet

Re: Disneyfication

H--
  Well, see, Disney couldn't do anything with it, be-
cause it doesn't feature Cruella de Vil. She's asleep,
too. And Cruella was really the star of the show. Don't
you think? Without Cruella you end up with Lady and the
Tramp, basically, which was never as compelling.
Best,
S.

Re: The world was such a wholesome place until . . .
  (For some unexplained reason, I have a great modern
recording of the Cruella de Vil theme song.)
  I agree. Without Cruella, her great black and white
hair, the laugh, that trail of cigarette smoke--the
whole thing might fall apart. The cuteness of the puppies has to be offset by the dastardliness of Cruella.
I'm sure this says something deep about our need for
evil in narrative to give us direction in an amoral
culture--but I don't know what.

H.

Re: Something deep
  If I might add to this depth, Hamlet. Just to note
something I have discovered recently, largely through

reading aloud to Martha, or by sneaking in and reading her books behind her back: Many of the world's best truths are hidden in children's books. Were you aware of this? It's something of a shock to me, because you aren't necessarily able to appreciate it at that age (youth is wasted on the young: THAT'S what they meant when they said that) but it turns out that that's where everyone's stashed much of the good stuff, the stuff you need to make sense of the world.

This happens to be of special interest to me in my life because of my odd and tormented relation to the adult book world, which I'll explain another time. Suffice it to say that the best of the kids' books also say something deep about our need for evil in an amoral et cetera.

Thought you should know.

S.

Re: Youth is wasted

Re: This. I quite agree. Why can't we all have it back, now that we'd know what to do with it better? Mine without the divorce trauma and that terrible third-grade teacher, though, please.

Re: the wit and wisdom of kids' books: I've always suspected that kids get the best deal in many aspects of life, so it doesn't surprise me that their literature is quietly superior to ours in peddling the answers to life's problems.

There are times in the ritzier areas of the great park in my city, when I see these kids and think: Now there's the life. These are rich kids I'm talking about, obviously, and I'm sure half of them actually have miserable mothers who are quietly addicted to Valium or coke and probably fathers--or again mothers, for that matter--off vacationing with their secretaries in the Bahamas. My point simply being:

These kids do look great in their clothes.

You take your standard adult outfit--tennis shoes, leather jacket, jeans--and you make it tiny and perfect, and suddenly it's adorable. What is that about? Everything looks better on kids--baseball caps, tennis shoes, goofy T-shirts. I have fashion envy I guess. I want to be able to put on ordinary schleppy clothing and look adorable, like they do.

This is not impressive, is it? Kids' clothing envy.

Sorry to be so damn shallow.

Hamlet

Re: Hidden depths

No, no, I know what you mean. Martha has a pair of pyjamas with little constellations all over them that I completely covet. I'm aware that I would not be able to wear them with the panache she has, but still I'd like a pair.

Equally shallowly,
Sylvia

Re: Shallow waters

Hey, you can't be that shallow. I mean, think of your poetry! Specifically, you did write some pretty nifty suicide poems. Plus, no offense, but you're dead, aren't you? Right there that guarantees you some depth.

Hamlet

Re: Dead Poets Society

It's true that dead is possibly the only way to be if you're a poet--it makes people much more likely to read you. Do you think everyone would know "Ariel" as well as they do if it weren't for my stunt with the gas oven?

But enough about me. Let's talk about you. How is life in Denmark, anyway? Still rotten?
Sylvia

Re: Rottenness
  What can I tell you about Denmark? Denmark is a state
of mind--like every other place, I guess. Right at this
minute it is seeming more floral and breezy than rotten, but that could change at any time.   Hamlet

Re: The state of the state
  (Do they have magnolia trees in Denmark?) Here's a
question.--If Denmark is a state of mind, what does
that make California?
S.

Re: California
  A state of denial? That's my best effort.
  So may I assume that you, like the g. of P., reside
in California? I happen to know a thing or two about
that state myself. I mean, of Calif., though also of
denial.   Hamlet

Re: state of Calif.
  Yes, California, but an unfamiliar northern edge of it
where the living is easy and the people long-haired.
I'm newish to town and it hasn't yet altogether grown
on me. Though it is a place, if I may quote from a
storefront I passed not too long ago here, with "a
little magic--and a lot of style."
  It's important to know that "a lot of style" is in
italics.
Sylvia

Re: a little magic
  That's so touching, as a description. I wish someone
would say the same thing about me.
  So I know that poets guard their privacy, which I can
certainly respect, and Lord knows you Sylvia Plath have
already had about 10 salacious biographies published

about you which is a lot for someone who's only been
dead 30 years or whatever it is.

  But I'm curious. Why the unfamiliar edge? Or is that
getting too personal? I don't want to pry.

Hamlet

Re: and a lot of style
  No, no, pry away. I was a confessional poet, don't
forget. I laid it all on the line for people. I haven't
been in this particular (small h) hamlet long--just
long enough to begin to figure out my way around. I
came up here to deal with a major Life Change.
Yours clearly fishing for more curiosity on your part
but not wanting to assume you want to hear the whole
damn thing, Sylvia

Re: Fishing
  OK, I'm biting, I'm biting.
  Re: The whole damn thing. Do it, tell it. I'm guessing, as a careful reader, it may have to do with the
dark reference you made earlier? I think "odd and tormented" was the phrase you used, as in an "o. and t.
relation to the adult book world."   Hamlet

Re: Tormented relations
  Well spotted.
  I won't belabor the tale. Doubtless I should hold off
altogether and write more nifty poetry out of it. (If
only I could.) Basically, I used to live and work with
many dead philosophers--more than you could shake a
stick at, as my fifth-grade teacher used to say--and
they all died in a fire. A second death, a permanent,
existential one, if you see what I mean. Stacks and
stacks of them. A career's worth. I had been planning
to become one myself, and had been trundling along for
years in grad student ignominy to that end.
  And along with Kant, Hume, and the other guys, the

fire took everything else too: furniture, photographs, sanity, cat--Zeno, my black and white cat who went the same way as the philosophers. I was left with a whole lot of nothing. (Was that a pop song?) So I have been Coping with Catastrophe, as my mother's ohsohelpful self-help book would have it. These days I live with no dead philosophers but instead with young Martha and her nice alive mother, who is part employer, part charity officer. Also, of course, the g.s of Pinsk and of Zeno.

And that's the story, in a nutshell.

Sylvia

Re: Whole lotta nothin

Dear Sylvia,

Yes it was a pop song. Written as above, in the original.

But listen:

Re: The fire. The philosophers. Zeno. I'm so sorry.

I don't even know you, and I'm sorry.

Which isn't that unusual, in a sense, because I was raised on a healthy diet of guilt (Wasp and Jewish both, as was once pointed out to me) and am liable to feel sorry about almost anything, if given half a chance, whether or not I bear any responsibility for it. But I really am sorry. What does that make you, a recovering ex-philosopher? A philosopher from scratch?

I was a philosopher once too, of course. Though I had my disillusionments with it. I'm sure you're familiar with the old saw, "There are more things on heaven and earth, Horatio, than are dreamt of in your philosophy."

But back to the main point. What a very dramatic and sad nutshell that was, Sylvia.

In sympathy,

Hamlet

Re: The nutshell

I know. It's an attention grabber, that fire. But thanks for the sympathy. We try to keep very tough and

resilient about it all, me and the ghosts, but a little
sympathy every now and then helps the tragedy go down,
as Mary Poppins might have said but didn't. Mary Poppins, help. I'm regressing. Must have been my inner
child interrupting the flow. Don't you hate it when
that happens?
Sylvia

Re: inner children should be seen and not heard
  They're pesky little devils, aren't they? In my experience it's best to be firm with them. I know when mine
is acting up I send it upstairs without any dinner.
That or thrash it within an inch of its life. Whichever
proves more effective.
  But, HEY. There's no need to start knocking Mary Poppins! After all, we have already canvassed Cruella de
Vil, to whom Mary P is superior in several ways. I
mean, let's just say it: Julie Andrews, sex goddess
manque. Am I right? I think when I was a kid I knew
Julie had that special star quality; Dick Van Dyke
couldn't hold a candle to her, though he was more convincing (as I recall) in Chitty Chitty Bang Bang, without the dire fake cockney accent.
  If you stop to think about there being a car, a song,
a movie named "Chitty Chitty Bang Bang" it seems sort
of surreal, doesn't it? It makes you wonder. What will
the extraterrestrials think of us when they find out
that that's what we spent 2 million years of civiliza-
tion working our way up to? And speaking of surreal,
was it not more than a little when J. Andrews resurfaced years later to be the transvestite in Victor/
Victoria? Wasn't that something of a paradigm shift
there, or am I just a cultural conservative?
  Yours hoping this isn't too obviously a screen for
not knowing what else to say about your terrible fire,
Hamlet

Re: C.C.B.B.

Realizing your proneness to guilt I don't want to
place too much emphasis on this, especially since I realize you meant NO HARM. Nonetheless, it is a harsh
fact that since your last message I have been unable to
get the tune of "Chitty Chitty Bang Bang" out of my
head. I didn't even know I still knew the damn tune.
Very scarily, I can even remember the words. (Chitty
Chitty Bang Bang, Chitty Chitty Bang Bang, Chitty
Chitty Bang Bang, we love you. And so forth.)

Power of the printed word, eh? And they say we're becoming a purely visual culture. They say that not knowing what effect reading the words "Chitty Chitty Bang
Bang" can have on a person's brain.

I think I can see some connection between Ophelia and
Julie Andrews as objects of desire--the soft feminine
touch, the flowers of the mountainside, etc. Myself,
I'm more drawn towards your Audrey Hepburn sort of gal,
but that is probably due to my mother parking me in
front of My Fair Lady at an impressionable age. And I
may as well admit to you that I found Professor Higgins
just as seductive as Eliza--which must say something
sinister about my later attraction to the academic
world and my tolerance of crotchety old professors
telling me what to do. I probably kept hoping one of
them would turn into Rex Harrison.
Sylvia
PS Don't worry about the fire. No one knows what to say
about it, including me, so it's easier to change the
subject. Consider it changed.

Re: Rex appeal

It's probably just as well that none of your professors did. (Turn into Rex Harrison, I mean.) Were you
aware, by the way, in keeping with our otherworldly
themes, that Rex Harrison himself becomes a ghost at
the end of one of his movies, Blithe Spirit? Maybe he's

out playing with Pinsk on the beach, even as we speak.
   Not that we're speaking, of course. I meant metaphor-
ically.
   I do know what you mean about Rex appeal. He has that
old English-accented avuncular routine down to a T.
Though putting marbles in Eliza's mouth before getting
her to talk about the rain in Spain was a little kinky,
if you ask me.

                                                    H

Re: Marble mouth
   I don't know. It seemed to be an effective teaching
tool. Maybe if I'd stayed in my profession I could have
pioneered the use of it myself: "Here, children, put
these marbles in your mouth and try saying 'the categorical imperative.'"
   Your use of the word "avuncular" brings us to an interesting point, however. Something I've been wondering
about lately. We have the word "avuncular" to mean
acting uncle-like--not quite paternal, not fraternal,
but somehow in between. Rex Harrison-ish, in short.
   My question is, why isn't there a word for acting
aunt-like? I happen to know someone (all right, my
landlady/charity officer) who sometimes acts precisely
that way--not maternal, not sisterly--and I'd like to
be able to name it. Is there such a word? If so, why?
If not, why not? (That was always my favorite format of
exam question. I liked the way it covered all the options.)
Semantically yours,
Sylvia

Re: The new semantics
   I don't know why not. It's weird. If I had more Latin
I'd try to coin something for you--"auntuncular" or
whatever. "Auntly" does not seem the word you're look-

ing for. It sounds too much like the small industrious
black guys who live in dirt hills.

Sorry not to be of more help.

                                                            H

Re: Thanks anyway
Thanks anyway
S.

Re: Re
A random thought.
Don't you kind of love "Re"? And how e-mail gives you
Re? It's so handy. It helps focus you on the issue at
hand. Plus it gives you the discipline of titling your
thoughts.
It's a shame we can't use it in our day-to-day inter-
actions, you know? I feel it would cut down on unneces-
sary blather. You could just call someone up and say:
"Hi, Bob. So, listen, re: the movie. Let's go to the
9 o'clock show. Re: the baseball game. The Orioles
lost." Or you know, "Hi, Marcia. Re: our relationship.
It's over. Don't call me again." Or whatever.
Wouldn't that be kind of cool?
Or not?

                                                            H

Re: Re: Re
I sense the possibility of an infinite regression
here.
I know what you mean. On the other hand, you could
say Re cuts down on non sequiturs. For instance, I'm
trying to figure out how to change the subject to
whales, and I can't really think how to do it because
it has nothing to do re: re.
Sylvia

Re: Charles
Dear Sylvia,

Sorry. We needed a new Re: and for some reason he was
the one that came to mind.

Hey, if you want to talk about whales, you go right
ahead. I certainly wouldn't want to sacrifice non sequiturs on the altar of Re. Non sequiturs are beautiful. Ask my mother--they're her specialty. ("But enough
about the election. What size shoe do you wear?")

                                                    Hamlet

Re: A word about whales

Thank you for giving me the green light here. I feel
I have to get this off my (virtual) chest.

I'm guessing that whales don't come up a lot in conversations where you are. This is assuming that you're
somewhere east of Eden. Let me tell you something.
Whales come up all the time here. You can't walk a yard
without someone talking about whales. Particularly now,
because March is whaling season as I can now confirm.
Not in the Moby Dick-Let's harpoon the bastard!-
tradition; rather in the Honey, could you get out of
the way of my zoom lens, you're blocking my shot-
tradition. People come flocking up here, loaded to the
gills with equipment (Block that Metaphor!), in order
to capture the giant beasts as they go spouting their
way down the coastline.

So everyone is very excited here right now. People
are wired. It's like some great primitive ritual--ex-
cept, as I say, for all the technology in the air, all
sleek and black and whirring and digital.

Now my own stance vis-a-vis the whales is not clear.
This is what I wanted to write about. And let me state
unequivocally that I have never gotten through the
great white whale of American literature, so don't expect anything else in the way of cunning references to
that icon from me.

I'm trying to work out what I feel about the whales
themselves, whales qua whales. For instance the mistress of the house, the auntuncular one, thinks whales
are incredible, she's ecstatic that she and Martha
could be up here this March so they could see some together. (Have I explained she's in mid-divorce from her
husband? That's her big Life Change.) She has taken M
on a whale-watching boat--for an exorbitant fee they
take people out early in the morning to watch for w.'s,
throwing in a free breakfast of instant coffee and nonfat blueberry muffins. The two of them are out there
right now, even as we speak, not that we're speaking.
They invited me to go too and I refused. Ungracious or
what? So out they went to marvel at God's creatures
while surrounded by cameras and naturalists.

Why do the whales leave me cold? That's what I want
to know. What's wrong with me? I'm relatively eco-
friendly--against seal-clubbing and killing poor Flipper
dolphins in tuna-nets and the wholesale destruction of
the environment and all that--and I'm practically a
tree-hugger (quite a literal phrase in these parts) in
my new reverence for redwoods. Who knows, maybe if you
gave me coffee and a blueberry muffin and sent me out
to the spoutings, I'd have the kind of epiphany everyone else seems to experience. But from here on shore,
while I'm happy as a clam that the whales are enjoying
themselves out there, I can't bring myself deeply to
care.
Yours well aware that the above nearly qualifies as a
heresy, Sylvia

Re: Your virtual chest
Your phrase. I couldn't resist it.
Hey, it's never safe to make assumptions. You don't
know when whales are going to come up in conversation,
even here, east of Eden. Just yesterday I found myself
chatting on the phone with a friend on the subject of

whales. Though I have to admit it was after I got your heresy, I mean note. I introduced the subject.

He, my friend, had seen a bumper sticker that said, "*!@!& the whales--let's save the plankton." We both acknowledged that this was a juvenile joke and that bumper sticker humor is a very low form of humor. Nonetheless we thought it was kind of funny. (Being overgrown juveniles ourselves.) It got funnier as we talked because my friend started free-associating about plankton. "It's so typical, you hear all about the big guys, the whales, they're like the poster children for the marine world, them and the seals, but the little guys, the ones you actually couldn't live without because they happen to be a key link in the food chain--they never even get a mention, they get no press at all, no celebrities are lining up to make public service announcements and entreat you to give big bucks to ensure their survival. It's a great metaphor for how the world works. Next time I have some spare time, I might write a play, or a screenplay, called 'Revenge of the Plankton.' Isn't that a great idea for an absurdist drama, with a secretly radical message?"

My friend is involved in theater, which is why his thoughts moved in this direction. When he gets onto an idea, he gets very energized and excited about it. This is a great part of his charm--his enthusiasm. Less charming is his tendency to see me as his lieutenant (his gofer, less flatteringly). In this instance he carelessly said to me, "Hey, you have a lot of time on your hands, why don't you use it? Why don't you write a play called 'Revenge of the Plankton'? Funny. Make it funny. And then I could direct it!"

This suggestion I found not so endearing. I am not about to direct my literary efforts, however humble, towards plankton. I wouldn't even turn them (the efforts) towards whales. As you rightly point out, to be an American writing about whales is to enter a mine-

field of our literary canon (Block that Military Metaphor!). Better for a writer to pick a whole new beast
to mythologize--the chicken, say, or the mountain lion.
Even the pine marten.

I'm not entirely sure you were asking me about the
literary value of whales. I suspect I have veered
widely from the point you were making. On the question
of real whales, and your guilt or indifference in regard to them, I would just say:

Why feel bad?

So you have no feeling for whales. Is that so terrible? Can everyone be expected to have fellow feeling
for all of the creatures out there? Surely you have to
make choices at some point. And let's be frank--whales
are not cute, the way seals indisputably are. And unfair though it is, I'm afraid looks do matter in this
world.

I say, don't worry about it. If you're feeling bad,
put a bumper sticker--a serious, earnest one I mean--on
your car. And have the nonfat blueberry muffins in the
comfort of your own home, where you can really enjoy
them.

                                        Yours,
                                        Hamlet

Re: Fellow feelings

I'm sure your literary efforts are not humble, even
if you are, and I agree that they shouldn't go towards
plankton. Don't let the theatrical guy strong-arm you
into anything. Even over the phone.

But thank you, you made me feel much better. It turns
out they didn't actually see any whales on their whale-
watching excursion after all that. The auntuncular one
insists they had a great time anyway, but young Martha
was less enthusiastic. She was a little green around
the gills when they got back.

Still, it helped to be able to confess my irrational whale hatred (the technical term is Mobyphobia) to you. As if bibliophobia weren't bad enough.
Gratefully,
Sylvia

Re: Mobyphobia
Feel free to confess such feelings to me anytime you want. I don't mind a bit. Besides, the computer in this day and age takes the place of the confessional--a place you can sit down with a faceless listener, telling them your own private all.
Did I just make up that intelligent point all by myself? Or is that something I read somewhere? It's so hard to tell in this postmodern age. We're all trying so hard to be original, damn it, but plagiarism sneaks up on you without your even noticing it.
You can tell me more about your bibliophobia, too, if you want. I'm all ears. A phrase that seems inaccurate in this context; I guess I should say I'm all eyes.

Hamlet

Re: Bibliophobia
Dear Eyes and Ears,
In fact I've been thinking about the book question lately. Ongoingly I should say. All this print is bound to bring it to mind. So I'm going to take you up on your offer of ears. And eyes.
I told you about using kids' books as a cure for my bibliophobia. (The most recent one I've read is Dr. Seuss's "The Lorax," and I must interrupt this broadcast to bring you a special message, courtesy of the Lorax: "I am the Lorax, I speak for the trees. I speak for the trees, for the trees have no tongues." Is that lyrical or what?) Truly, some of my philosophy books could have learned a thing or two from kid-book design and presentation; they might have benefited from being

written in rhyme and accompanied by bright, enlivening
illustrations.

This is how I am trying to reconcile myself to the
ongoing existence of print. Plus I have been dabbling
in poetry (hence the Plath handle). I never read much
poetry in college so I am coming to it full of brand-
new observations. Like--poetry: Gosh, it's just so darn
. . . poetic!

Also I recently began my new "library" with one
small, new book. I don't plan to get any more, neces-
sarily--this particular book is an icon as much as it
is a book, I guess you could say--but it's a signal to
some sort of metaphysical authority that I do still believe in books, even if I live largely without them.

Sorry to get heavy-handed on you. It is, I admit, not
a subject I am able yet to be especially light about.
Sylvia

Re: Unbearable lightness of being
Sylvia--
Love that Lorax quote.

What kind of philosophy did you do, anyway? Myself, I
only ever got to the pre-Socratics. Never got past Zeno's paradox, ha ha. But seriously--do you philosophize
still, just sort of off the record? I take it the urge
isn't totally out of your system?

I'm also tempted to ask you what's the one book, but
a) that too seems like prying, and b) it's more fun, in
a way, for me to imagine which would be a person's one
Iconic book. The Bible? The Book of Lists? Ulysses?
101 Favorite Balloon Animals?

I do, genuinely, know some small thing about loss of
employment. It's a soulcrusher. So however hamfisted
this Hamlet missive may be, the empathy is genuine.

                                    Your obedient servant,
                                            Hamlet

Re: The urge
Dear servant:
  The urge, the urge.
  Do I still have it? That was the question.
  But what is the urge to philosophize? If philosophizing were simply holding forth about the world and
what's in it, one could imagine impromptu notes on
whale-watching or re: re, for instance, qualifying as
philosophizing. It might then be possible to say: This
person who calls (him or) herself Sylvia, still clearly
has the "urge." Still notes down responses to the
world.
  But if philosophy is reading a sentence like "The
only thing that is good absolutely is a good will"--I'm
quoting from memory from Kant's Metaphysics of Morals,
I don't have the text anymore obviously but its main
thoughts are etched in my mind, right up there with the
words to Chitty Chitty Bang Bang--and wanting to know
what Kant means by a "good will," and what it would
mean for a good will to be the only absolutely good
thing, over and above love or life or whales or the
ocean . . .
  Well, if that wanting is what philosophy is, then--
yes. I mean, yes I still have that, I can't help it.
But I don't know what will happen to that part of my
mind now. Because on the other hand if philosophy, as
practiced in late millennial North America, is deriva-
tive, i.e., thinking re: other people's thoughts and
about other people's thoughts re: other people's
thoughts, that's an activity I can live without. I've
managed life without it happily enough. I have had no
one else's thoughts up here (until recently) to think
about. And I realize that's probably why I chose to
come here, to get away from those other people's
thoughts for a while.
  You asked me. All right? I haven't talked philosophy
with anyone for a long while, so it feels illicit--ill-

advised, maybe even. But you asked me, so I'm telling
you. I haven't told anyone else all this. So yes it is
true: you are my invisible confessor.

I had been working for two years on a thesis when the
fire showed up. (A straight fact: this was the big
Berkeley fire, last October.) I was developing my response to Kant's ideas on how reality is shaped by our
ability to perceive it--to put it at its crudest. But
for the purposes of the academy, I had to canvass 50
other people's readings of Kant, so I could make clear
my own reading, my own small private path through the
forests of Kant, because these days if you want to get
ahead in academia you have to--like Julie Andrews in
Victor/Victoria--shift a few paradigms.

The truth is (and Kant was a stickler for truth) I
would rather have produced my own meditation about
Kant, perception, and reality; with some reference to
new work in biology, to what we are beginning to know
about how animals perceive. I might have thrown in a
little Berkeley, just because Berkeley is a nut and
you've gotta love him. But I wasn't that fascinated by
other people's opinions about Kant. Or no--I liked
reading Kant scholars, I just didn't feel like writing
about them.

Anyway, now I don't have to read any scholars at all.
Now I'm left--I mean, it is sort of a poetic irony,
when you allow yourself to think about it--with the
ghosts of Kant's ideas in my head. I'm left with some
pure distillation; the point I first took from Kant
when I read him as a college kid, that beyond this phe-
nomenal world we know there is a noumenal realm that
shapes what we can know. I was always tempted by the
idea that there was some realm of the unknowable that
our brains weren't equipped to understand. (To put a
contemporary spin on it.) I think scientists are beginning to get to that knowledge now, and we're beginning
to find that our brains--truly--are underequipped to
deal with what we are beginning to know. Einstein: God

knows how he fitted relativity into his mind, it hardly fits into anyone else's.

You asked me, Hamlet. I worry that this horrible long, earnest reply will put you deeply OFF. I won't be too shocked if so . . . People can find philosophy daunting. It's not what you'd call a growth industry, unlike literary criticism, or balloon animal research for that matter.

Sylvia

Re: Oh what a putting off was there
Dear Sylvia:

So pessimistic! Why should I be so off-put just be-cause you happen to have written a spontaneous treatise on what is dreamt of in your philosophy? What do you think I'm tuning in here for--sex scenes and car chases? I can go to the multiplex for that. I come here for--conversation. Of this particular kind, about the meaning of life and the unexplored depths of Julie An-drews; or, if it comes up, of Kant. I admit I'm more familiar with the former than the latter, but that didn't stop me from being interested in hearing what you had to say about Immanuel K.

Whether I understood what you were talking about--the noumenal realm and all that--is another matter en-tirely. I will try to take it in slowly and then, when you least expect it, come up with some great profundity on the subject.

In the meantime, on the subject of Ks generally, I recently came across some Kafka aphorisms--little things, just scraps, genius scraps of Kafka. And here for you my friend is one I liked a lot. I thought you might, too. It seemed to be possibly even connected to what you wrote about the other K:

"It is a question of the following. One day many years ago I was sitting, sorrowfully enough to be sure, on the slopes of the Laurenzburg. I was examining the wishes that I had for my life. What emerged as the most

important or most attractive was the wish to gain a
view of life (and--this was certainly a necessary part
of it--to be able to convince others of it in writing),
in which life, while still retaining its natural, full-
bodied rise and fall, would simultaneously be recognized no less clearly as a nothing, as a dream, as a
hovering. A beautiful wish perhaps, if I had wished it
rightly."

And now, dear Sylvia, because I have the sense that
it worried you to write about Kant and reality, a confession for a confession. Having quoted Kafka--and who
knows? maybe he's your one iconic writer, I imagine
he'd be mine if I had to pick one--I am now moved to
tell you something I've never told a living soul. For
obvious reasons: it's deeply humiliating. For a nice,
marginally "normal" person like myself to admit this is
humiliating. But somehow I feel like telling you.

I once placed a personal ad. OK? I did. I was lonely,
I live in a city, for reasons I don't need to go into
I wasn't meeting anyone new, friends of mine had the
appropriate boyfriends or girlfriends but I didn't and
I just felt like going on a date, for Christ's sake. So
sue me. I placed a personal.

It's not a simple thing to do, however. It immediately raises huge daunting questions about your identity, what you do, what you love--the very questions
you'd hoped to escape.

Because the first question you confront once you've
decided to do it is, how to describe yourself? With a
sheaf of appealing adjectives, that may or may not be
true? "Funny, intelligent, quiet, thoughtful . . ."
--thereby making yourself sound like a scheming axe-
murderer? Or do you ironize the whole process because
we all know how idiotic it is, and call yourself "Neurotic, sentimental, with a tendency towards depression
. . ." which may be true but people will think you're
kidding? Or do you flat-out lie and see what happens--
"Blond, philanthropic neurosurgeon seeks woman to bear

him lots of beautiful children"? And how about interests? They sound so ludicrous, in a list. "Books, movies, people, parks, balloon animals . . ." I mean, so what? Same goes for half the city. You know? So, before I had a complete personality collapse in the wake of the task, I decided to pick just one description, one essential name-tag, to see what would happen. I kept it short. "Tall, decent-looking Kafka reader seeks similar." I figured that would separate out the sheep from the goats, if that's the phrase I want. Who would respond to an ad like that, except someone marginally interesting? And I didn't feel I'd promised anything I couldn't live up to.

So here's what's heartbreaking. I was FLOODED with responses. Really. For weeks I got envelopes full of letters. People quoting The Trial and The Penal Colony, The Hunger Artist and of course The Metamorphosis; people who apologized for not having read Kafka for years but who said they really loved him when they first had; one woman who sent in a Kafkaesque story, I mean it was about a vacuum cleaner but you could see what she was trying to do with it.

And Sylvia, these responses--they made me feel so reassured. Isn't that crazy? But I was really reassured there were so many people out there--people reading the personals, no less--who loved Franz too. It made me feel considerably less lonely.

Of course, like a heel I never answered any of them. I got too anxious about what would happen if I actually met any of these people. It's typical of me, to go to all that trouble and then do nothing about it. It also made me feel horribly guilty. These people had gone to such effort, and for what? For a whole lotta nothin'. They're all still out there somewhere, all those Kafka readers. Answerless. Adrift. Probably thinking the whole thing was a hoax. A Kafkaesque nightmare . . .

Now I can wait for your kind, piteous reply. Oh God, you're thinking, Hamlet is a sad loser geek. Even though thousands of people do it I have always thought people who do personals are so inherently sad and there I was, briefly, one of their number. It was humbling. Which, of course, is never a bad thing. But also I think I figured if I never wrote back it was like I hadn't really placed the ad in the first place; I could still count myself virginal in the personals department. Don't ask me why.

All of that was sometime ago, just so you know. I'm feeling very self-conscious about telling you this, obviously, but I thought one self-revealing K outburst deserved another.

Yours in 6'1" 30s SWM apprehension,
Hamlet

Re: Kafka Readers Anonymous
Hamlet:

It's true I've always thought people who placed personals were questionable. But: I also thought people who quit grad school were questionable. I also thought people who wrote on the computer to people they'd never met were questionable. So either I was right all along and it's just that I myself have joined the ranks of the questionable; or, the reality of the world shifts and fire changes your perspective and people's ability to connect with each other has been imperiled by the new post-industrial economy blah blah blah, in which case:

--You take your friends where you find them. Sadly those Kafka readers never became your friends though. Did you keep the letters? Do you ever think, "Well if all else fails I can always write the Kafka readers"?
Sylvia
PS I didn't even thank you for the aphorism. Franz is a favorite of mine too, but I don't think I've ever read that little morsel.

Re: Only connect
as Mr. Forster so masterfully said.
Dear Sylvia,
   You know, I did keep the letters. The good ones. Now
that you mention it, I'm slightly nervous that I might
not have adequately stashed them away. I have a friend
staying in my apartment right now and though she's a
busy, productive person, she's also got a curious
streak a mile wide and I wouldn't completely put it
past her to go rummaging through my papers.
   You're so tolerant! It's refreshing. Somehow I'm glad
one other human being out there knows about my Kafka
personal. That that doesn't have to be a fact I take
with me to my grave. I haven't been quite as burdened
as, say, Raskolnikov with his small secret about having
clobbered the old lady, but it has been something I
wanted to get off my virtual chest.
   But, no. I think I'm past writing the Kafka readers
back. I've got other kinds of writing to keep me busy.
And other correspondents, like your friendly self.

                                          Best,
                                          Hamlet

Re: My friendly self
   Well, the feeling is mutual. You also were tolerant.
It's been a while--months--since I've bent anyone's
ear, I suppose I should say eye in your case, about my
previous efforts in philosophy.
   I wouldn't worry about the Kafka letters. I'm sure
she'll be too busy to go plunging around in your papers
and find them.
   Other correspondents? Oh no! And here I was thinking
I had exclusive access . . .
Fondly,
S.

And then, for no obvious reason, there followed a silence that stretched for days.

ABBIE COULD TELL SOMETHING WAS UP.

She could just *tell*.

Before, Pi's limbs had been closed in around herself. She sat, she stood, she even walked with her arms folded, or her fists trapped safe and airless in the pockets of her jeans. Her head dipped, her fine face ducking behind the falls of liony hair; her sea eyes stayed lid-shadowed and distant. All those words she'd lost were sewn into silent pouches in her cheek, where she wouldn't allow herself to let them out.

Now Pi was beginning to climb out of her private asylum. She was releasing her hands and arms from captivity. Sometimes they went so far as to speak along with her, an open hand questioning or offering where before it would have hidden and clenched. She held her head higher. She didn't allow so many of her sentences to drain away into mumble. Her eyes held Abbie's now, in a way they rarely had before.

The change started sometime around that night when Abbie couldn't sleep and had gone downstairs to bother Pi. In her attic room Abbie had been lying in bed thinking of Abe. His image was where all long nights led, and she hated it. That night he seemed to her a muddy poison that still murked through her veins—like the build-up of alcohol or some drug you might get addicted to which clings to your body even after you've stopped taking it, won't leave your bloodstream but clusters in puddles and corners, blocking the way, refusing to go. Abbie had heard stories of chain-smokers giving up cigarettes and how for weeks afterwards black gunk coughed itself up out of their lungs and noses, as if surrendering finally to watchful authorities. She'd read about a weightlifter who'd gotten hooked on steroids, how a greenish ooze started leaking out of his skin, his body's late effort to clean itself out. Abe was like that. A kind of awful, sour silt, and when she was alone with night's insomnia she tasted his bad flavor on her sleepless tongue.

This was what he had become for her, the man she'd built a life with. Abbie still found the transition bewildering. She found it very hard to know in the way she had to to move her life forward, that this was how she now felt about the man she'd loved and fought with, the man who had charmed and cherished her, who had watched with a green-masked mouth and terrified brow as her self erupted into infinite pain and out of that blind moment arrived their daughter. He had been with her, then. Smart, broad-chested, fierce and selfish Abe had given himself to her then. And she had taken him in. He'd given her sensations she hadn't had before, an excitement and fury, an eagerness that kept her fit, busy, beautiful, *on*. When he'd left her, or rather when she'd discovered his infidelity and found it intolerable, she was shocked out of her love for him. Her spirit lost its passion and tolerance and she was left stripped, starved, empty, enraged. But the dregs of him still slowed the blood in her sometimes, made her midnight breaths short and shallow.

Abbie made herself get up. She listened to the waves. A restlessness itched at her. There was another adult in the house, after all. It had to be reasonable for Abbie to go down and try to draw a little conversation out of her.

So she went downstairs to bother Pi. Abbie was almost dissuaded when she saw the blue computer screen light spilling thinly out into the hall; she almost turned right around to sneak back upstairs. But her creaking footsteps had already revealed her. And just because Pi was sitting at the computer didn't mean—didn't have to mean—she was unmoveable by human contact.

Abbie had deliberately startled Pi by playing bold. She had an afterhours inspiration that the computer might be the item to crack if she wanted a way through to her troubled lodger. Abbie was still trying to rid her mind of the rancid thoughts of the divorce. So she invented flirtatious sentences, pushed the "Why don't you show me?" line with a near kittenish insistence. She hadn't really meant to come on so slyly—her body brushing close to Pi's was an instinct, not a plan—but it had the desired effect of throwing Pi off her guard. And, Abbie realized, it was Pi's guard being perpetually up that had become so wearing.

That she had tapped Pi open so quickly about her college lover had been an accident. An accidental pressing of the switch that reveals a door that opens and allows you in. Fran had told Abbie that Pi knew the famous filmmaker

Marie Jackson at college; she hadn't said they were lovers. Pi supplied that detail herself. She must have wanted to tell her. Abbie had guessed Pi was gay or bi anyway: people weren't usually so secretive otherwise. Though why Pi thought Abbie might be worried about it—she had lived in San Francisco for twelve years, after all—was mysterious.

But Abbie found, in spite of her lack of surprise, that the confirmation, Pi's stiff-backed tensing of admission, gave her a short, sharp thrill. Her own body jumped at the news. It also made her suddenly doubtful about this closeness she'd put between Pi and herself. She stilled the hand she had been running along Pi's rigid neck to coax her into relaxation. Abbie had been playing with Pi a little, to get a reaction out of her and because it was gratifying to see her flustered after these months of calm. But now the game seemed riskier. Abbie pulled away from Pi, against the wishes of her own skin, which had gotten hotter at the mention of Pi's past.

And then the alarm had gone off. It sounded like an alarm. Like the blip of a machine's cool eye, a tennis service machine judging a stepping over of the line. On hearing the warning noise, Abbie broke into a small sweat.

But it had been the computer—an alerting message that someone had sent something to Pi. The banality of the fact broke the moment. Abbie couldn't take these computer games seriously. She knew it was old-fashioned of her, and as a mother she felt it was probably her duty to keep up, to get a handle on this Internet thing. But it reminded her of those straggly nineteen-year-olds at Stanford who were addicted to pinball machines, who stayed up all night playing them in Tresidder Union.

Abbie moved away from Pi to ask her who her little message was from—she hadn't actually said "little," but she thought it. She had the weird sensation that she was asking whether Pi had any gentlemen callers. It was like notes left in lockers. Any new messages? Who from? Who's your secret admirer?

But it became clear that whatever this note might be, Pi was serious about it. She told Abbie it was probably a letter from Fran or another friend, but when Pi read the name of the sender Abbie saw her pale face pinken and her blue eyes grow genuinely bigger. She looked like a small surprised goldfish.

"What? What is it?" Abbie asked. By now the charge in the moment had gone. Abbie no longer felt wary, poised on an edge; she was merely curious about this odd woman before her who was clearly getting physically excited by something on-screen.

"It's Hamlet," Pi said, shrugging off an awareness of how absurd it sounded.

Abbie smiled. Now she was relaxed, though melancholy. She'd go back up to her attic room and try to get back to sleep, but around the darkness would be waiting the circles, the endless vulturing circles of her thoughts about Abe.

"Well," Abbie said, her eyebrow arched. "That sounds important. I'd better leave you to it." She touched Pi's shoulder. "I wouldn't want to get in the way of you and the prince."

And since that night, the unfolding.

The limbs and secrets coming out.

It was a strong, lean body Pi had. There was a rangy hunger in it, no matter how she swaddled it in sweatshirts and tube socks. Tube socks!—was actually what she wore around the house. She didn't really care, Abbie knew. She didn't want thoughts about clothes to distract her from whatever her higher calling might now be, now that she seemed to have left the ivory haven of academia. But in spite of Pi's feigned indifference, her body managed still to speak, though she tried to muffle it.

Abbie saw and noticed more now, which she put down to a number of different factors. The weather was warming. You no longer had to bundle up. There were days with enough sun, even in this shadowed house, that you could wear a slight T-shirt, a loose, long-sleeved shirt over. In that outfit, Pi's flat neat stomach was visible, you could read the angled wings of her shoulder blades, and her graceful neck bared itself when she pulled her hair back in a high, tidy ponytail. Her long muscled legs appeared in denim cut-offs. Abbie found herself admiring them—the way you do admire another woman, a woman who's got a nice shape and a freedom.

There was no doubt that Pi moved more freely these days. She was less timid. Abbie toyed with various explanations for the difference. Maybe Pi felt more open after their brief night-talk? Coming out had somehow loosened her movements? Or—could it be—she was flirting? There remained another less happy possibility, that Pi had a girlfriend in town and her secret messages had some connection with that. (Abbie didn't understand how the Internet worked; she thought of it as a kind of glorified answering machine.) Abbie kept an ear on Pi's nights, and was pretty sure there weren't any four a.m. exits or entrances; she was sleeping light enough that even all the way upstairs she was sure a shy, love-soaked footstep in the night would have wakened her. It seemed unlikely to Abbie that Pi had met someone in Mendocino, but her curiosity finally pushed its way to the surface and she translated her question into a tease.

"How's your prince?" she asked Pi one morning. Martha had left for school; Abbie and Pi were putting away breakfast. The kitchen was readying itself for a silent morning after the women succumbed to their respective employments. "—Hamlet, I mean?"

"Oh. He's fine." Pi kept her face turned to the refrigerator while Abbie rinsed dishes at the sink.

"So do you get to talk to some of the rest of them, too? Rosencrantz and Guildenstern? Are they all in there?"

"No, no." Pi smiled. "Just Hamlet. I know it sounds insane—"

"Not at all! It sounds wonderful. I'd love to be able to meet fictional characters. I can see why everyone loves this Internet thing if that's what it makes possible."

"Ah. Well, now you know. That's the secret. That's why people are hooked."

"Martha too? Has she gotten to make contact with . . . I don't know who would be on her wish-list. Louis the trumpeter swan, I imagine."

"Definitely. And Pongo and Missus."

"Of course. So that's what she gets out of it. I'm glad to know. I'm glad it's —educational."

"Oh, very. I wouldn't let Martha in on it otherwise. You know, I want to have a good influence on her."

"Of course you do. You and Hamlet both, I'm sure."

Abbie brought it up in therapy. She was still supposed to be working through her feelings about Abe, but sometimes her feelings about Abe bored even herself.

"I think I understand Pi better than I did at first," she said one day, faced with the bland prints and calming magnolia walls. "I'm beginning to feel fond of her. But something's been bothering me. I'm not sure what it is."

Faith wore her standard expression: soulful eyes framed by concerned brows; a slight persistent squint to show she was focussed. She also leaned forward to emphasize how carefully she was listening. And she nodded continually, to show that she understood everything you could possibly say. When Abbie had first come to talk to nodding, sympathetic Faith, she'd wanted to weep with the relief of having somebody listen to her.

"Do you feel threatened by Martha's relation to Pi?"

"No. I don't think that's it. I'm glad Martha has Pi to talk to, too. With everything else that's happening, I know I'm not always as attentive as I'd like to be."

"You shouldn't get down on yourself about that, Abbie. We've talked about this. You're doing what you can. You can't expect to be Supermom all the time, too."

"Anyway." Abbie waved her off. "Martha still tells me everything, I'm not worried about that. In fact . . ." Abbie's eyes strayed from her confessor as an idea came to her.

"In fact—?" Faith pressed.

"No. Never mind. The odd thing is I feel bothered even when Martha isn't down there with Pi, even when Martha is in her room doing homework and Pi's tapping away at her computer, writing letters or whatever it is she's doing."

"What you're saying is, there are times when your daughter has her homework and Pi has her friends or romances on the computer—"

"I don't really believe it's a romance."

"—And those are the times you would, in the past, have been with Abe. And so your feeling of loneliness, of vulnerability, is heightened, because that takes your thoughts back to Abe, and the emptiness you feel—that we've talked about—since he's gone."

"Well—"

"You feel abandoned."

"Well yes, or . . . maybe I'm jealous, in a strange way, of the attention Pi pays to the computer. Maybe—" she laughed. "Maybe I wish she'd pay that kind of attention to me."

"Sure you're jealous! Of course you are! It's just how Abe was with his work. Right? When you needed him, where was he? At the office. When you wanted to talk to him about Martha, where was he? Working. So the computer in the house is reminding you of all that *frustration*—all those times you couldn't talk to Abe when you needed to."

"Mmm," Abbie answered, out of politeness rather than conviction. "Maybe that's what it is." She didn't want to hurt Faith's feelings by disagreeing with her. Faith did not, Abbie knew from past experience, always deal well with contradiction.

In Martha's ears the gulls wheeled cries that reminded her of the sharpness inside her chest in San Francisco.

She had missed San Francisco when they first moved up here. She liked Mendocino, the feel of the sandy dust in her toes and the fact that the air had less buses and cars in it and the beach was so close by they could go all the time. In San Francisco you could see the water from the top of the hill—it looked like a large dark lake when it wasn't hidden by fog—but somehow going to the beach was complicated, it took planning, you had to drive.

But Martha missed San Francisco. Her school there. Her best friend Olive who had beautiful black curls and a fat, crazy laugh. The ice cream store around the corner. And she missed their neighbor Mrs. Delaney who lived next door, alone except for a pair of grey birds called cockatiels. Mrs. Delaney sat with Martha in the afternoons and played card games with her, Go Fish and Old Maid in her dim crowded living room full of paintings she'd done herself of flowers and hillsides. She had taught Martha a new game, gin rummy, before the bad summer began. Martha played a lot of gin rummy with Mrs. Delaney that summer, more than she was expecting to because they were supposed to go visit some cousins in New York but the trip was cancelled because of the bad summer.

And now San Francisco reminded her of the bad summer.

Mrs. Delaney let her birds fly loose during the day, Martha remembered how they flew in circles around the living room and sometimes one of them, Romeo or Juliet, would land on Mrs. Delaney's shoulder and chew on her earrings. Martha loved that. Sometimes one would land on Mrs. Delaney's hands and try to eat the cards. Mrs. Delaney said if Martha was a card shark she could learn which cards had bites out of them and could cheat that way, but she knew Martha would never try to get away with cheating. Mrs. Delaney had a song she sometimes sang when she was looking through the hand she'd dealt herself:

Do your ears hang low?
Do they wobble to and fro?
Can you tie them in a knot?
Can you tie them in a bow?
Can you sling 'em over your shoulder
Like a continental soldier
Do your ears—hang—low?

Martha had never understood what it meant, but she sang it to herself now and then to keep herself company.

It was just one of those things. Those were Mrs. Delaney's words. One of what things? Martha asked, sipping lemonade. Mrs. Delaney made delicious lemonade and sometimes, "just to be bad," she cooked them hot dogs after they were done playing cards. "Don't tell your mother. I don't think she'd like it. But Jack used to love them." Jack was Mrs. Delaney's husband, who had "passed away" years before. That, too, turned out to be one of those things. When Martha asked *what things*, she was hoping for a definite answer, like there was a specific category of thing Martha hadn't heard about that included Mrs. Delaney's losing her husband and Martha's parents' fighting all the time. But all Mrs. Delaney said was "It's one of those things that makes life what it is. It's one of those things God gives us to make us human."

Which was not, in Martha's opinion, a satisfying answer.

Martha wanted to see her that weekend. After Fran dropped her off and her father, surprised, had given her a big hug and nearly squeezed all the air out of her chest, Martha said, "Can we go see Mrs. Delaney?"

"Mrs. Delaney? But, sweetheart, you've only just gotten here."

Her father's eyes were red. His cheeks bristled. She had forgotten that he had a different smell from her mother. Smelling him again made her feel strange and faint.

"I want to see Mrs. Delaney."

"But I was all set to take you to the park today. And afterwards I thought, if you wanted, we could go to Ghirardelli Square and get a sundae." He looked at her and saw how she felt about it. He gave her shoulder a squeeze. "OK. Listen. I'll take you over there and you can visit Mrs. Delaney while I get shaved and ready. Is that what you want to do?"

She nodded. So in his jeans and a big flannel shirt and his sheepskin slippers, he took her by the hand over to Mrs. Delaney's and rang the bell.

"She sure will be glad to see you," he said. "She's always asking me about you. She's crazy about you, you know. Almost as much as I am."

But Mrs. Delaney didn't answer her doorbell. She wasn't there. Martha's father said she was probably visiting her daughter and grandkids in Fresno. It was just one of those things.

"Sorry, sweetheart. You'll see her next time. I'll tell her you sent her a big hello."

They'd padded back down to the street, over to his house, their house, their old house. Inside, Martha told her father she wanted to call Pi.

"The girl who's living with you in Mendocino? Why do you need to talk to her?"

She couldn't say why, but he let her anyway. He dialed the number for her.

When Martha heard Pi on the other end of the line, she couldn't think of anything to say at all. But it was strangely good to hear the sound of her voice.

The gulls were crying outside the classroom. The noise had reminded Martha of San Francisco.

Here she was in another classroom, but this time it wasn't school. Her school classroom had the alphabet up around it—regular letters, and the more attractive cursive. In this room she sat in front of a long table with a lump of mud in front of her. She was waiting for her mother to get back from the bathroom; she was too shy to start without her.

It wasn't really mud. It was clay.

"Do you want me to show you how to do it?"

It was the teacher, a man with frizzy long brown hair and a slightly squashed face.

"What's your name?"

"Martha."

"Hi, Martha. I'm Randy." He smiled at her. "Do you want me to show you how to make the coils? It's fun—like I said, it's like rolling a snake under your hand."

"Oh, hi. I'm sorry, I just stepped outside for a minute." Martha's mother was back, her face brighter—her lips vivid with a new shade of berry. "I thought it would be fun for us to do this class together," she said, "but maybe she's a little young for it."

"No I'm not!" Martha started to roll a lump of clay to prove she could make a decent snake out of it.

They laughed in that irritating way adults do when you've just said something perfectly normal, which they have decided for their own perverse reasons sounds "cute." Martha puffed a little at the insult.

"I guess she should know!" Randy said. "You're doing a good job there, Martha. Make sure you don't roll it too thin, though. It works better with snakes than with worms."

"I guess Martha's introduced herself. I'm Abbie."

"Hi, Abbie. Randy."

More smiles were exchanged over her head while Martha pulled off another lump and started rolling it. She wasn't about to let them distract her.

In fact, it was fun. The clay felt cool and soft under her hands, and her mother showed her how to move her palm along while she was rolling the clay so it didn't get skinny at the middle and fat at the ends. You wanted it all even. Her mother was very good at it. Remember that blue vase in the kitchen? It turned out she had made that, years ago.

Martha was enjoying herself. The task was to make a lot of these clay snakes, which Randy called coils, line them up on the table, and then start sticking them around a base—Abbie helped her make the circular base—and after that smooth over the connections between the coils. That way you eventually made a little pot. Randy claimed the Romans used to make pots this way. Martha was vague about who the Romans were.

It was as she was trying to stick the second coil on top of the first one that her mother started to ask her about Pi and the computer. She knew Martha sometimes did stuff with Pi on the computer, and if it was private Martha didn't need to tell her, but she was just curious about what they did, exactly.

The second coil wasn't going very well. You were allowed to use water to help make it stick, but Martha had used too much and now it was getting slippery.

She couldn't see anything private about it.

"We play this one computer game that has shapes that you try to line up."

"Here, honey, you want me to help you with that?"

Her mother helped fix it. She dried it, took off the second coil, mangled and sticky, and told her to use another one.

"I thought maybe you wrote letters to people together."

"Sometimes we do, to Fran. I tell Pi what to say and she types it and sends it and then Fran writes back."

"It's just—" Her mother sounded embarrassed. "Pi said something to me the other day about Hamlet, and I was wondering who Hamlet was."

"Oh, *Hamlet*." The second coil was going better now. Martha was more cheerful. "Pi told me about Hamlet. She thinks Hamlet is JD, who's the guy who told us about Minx and Pinx. Pi and me, we're making up stories about Pinx the dog, who lives on the Other Side. Pi does most of it, but I help. You want me to tell you some of them?"

Abbie had missed some key part of the connection, the part that would have explained Pi's newly open limbs and lively face; but she told Martha she'd love to hear one of the stories. And that's how they spent the rest of their time in the classroom, as they each coiled and smoothed their way into making two small round pots, and the gulls' cries were eventually lost to the chattery sounds of voices and industry.

Re: the new thinking
Hi again H--
  Did I ever mention that:
                  All the new thinking is about loss.
                  In this it resembles all the old thinking.
  --?
  Did I run through that with you before? It's a quote
from Robert Hass, a poet I've been reading lately.
That's the beginning of a poem called "Meditation at
Lagunitas," which I highly recommend.
  Thought you should know.
Fondly,
S.

Re: KRA
  By the way, as an anonymous Kafka reader I wanted to
say something about that aphorism you sent, which I've
kept--as I keep all of your letters, in the invisible
bank of my computer. It's odd, to think of having Kafka
sitting there in the shapeless chip of this unaesthetic
machine. It so seems the wrong shape for him. (Or does
it?) But anyway, that isn't what I wanted to say, what
I wanted to say, what I wanted silently to write, was:
  I've been thinking of that phrase, life "as a hovering," to recognize life "as a dream, as a hovering,"

It's a beautiful idea, and reminds me of what I used to dream of in my philosophy. The suspicion that the grabbable life right around us isn't necessarily what's true. That's maybe why surreal fictions, like Kafka's, get closer to a truth we recognize, almost instinctively, though it's so far beyond our conscious understanding of the world. The surrealism touches that place our stubborn senses cannot reach.
Do you know what I mean?
S.

Re: the gush
Hamlet,
  I'm sorry if I've veered into sentiment and gush here. I was just kidding about the other correspondents. I don't really expect to be your only one, obviously.

Re: the new thinking
  And, hello. Hello. Hamlet, are you getting any of these?
  Haven't heard from you in a few days, and I was just wondering.

Re: irony
  Of course, maybe we've lost the signal here, which would be kind of ironic, wouldn't it. I mean, given the Hass quote.

Re: Do you read me?
  Oh it's just me again, Hamlet. Merely me. So do you?
Sylvia

Re: So--
So Hamlet, where the fuck are you, anyway? Pardon my French.

Re: My French
  Whose idea was it anyway, though, to cover bad language with that euphemism about the French? I doubt
whether they appreciate it. Do you suppose when they
swear they say "Pardonnez mon anglais"?
  Another question for the soup.
  S

Re: The French, more generally
  Which puts me in mind of Europe, and all the big
questions there are about Europe. "All the new thinking
is about Europe. In this it resembles all the old
thinking." Doesn't have quite the same ring.

Re: Do you read me?
  Hello, hello. We are getting a faint signal here.
  Can you confirm identity, over.

Re: Say what?
  Is that you, Hamlet? Why the weird crypto-space speak?
  Anyway, if you're wondering if it's me, Sylvia, yes,
it is. Ich ich ich ich/mobyphobia/Julie Andrews,
manque--It's me, all right.

Re: Crypto-space
  Thanks. That was convincing.

Re: Beyond a joke
  Hamlet, what the hell is all this? I'm sorry to be
blunt, but it's just making me feel like I have turned
into a scary computer nerd after all.
  Sylvia

Re: Security measures
  Sylvia--
  Sorry. I know that must have sounded strange. It's
just that I came back to a twisted set of e-mails which

had me worried. They were from someone with the initials SP, and I thought maybe it was you in another guise. But they were weird enough that they had me really worried. I wanted to make sure you were in fact you before I launched back into our lovely correspondence.

   Sometimes, you just don't know whether to trust the print world, after all . . .

   But I promise I won't turn myself, or you, into a scary computer nerd. I haven't lost my mind--I can still tell a hawk from a handsaw, just about--and I haven't yet decided the CIA has planted receptors in my brain or anything. Though remind me to tell you sometime what it was like to get kidnapped by aliens.

Just kidding,
Hamlet

Re: Trusting the print world
Hamlet--
   Yeah, well. Story of my life.
   Know what I mean?
S
PS Sorry to hear about the twisted e-mails. I'll try to keep mine straight.

Re: Story of your life
Sylvia,
   God, I'm sorry. I know it's the print world that caused you such grief in the first place. That was rather grotesque of me to put it that way.
H

Re: Grief and loss and the whole damn thing
   Yep.
   By the way, did you get that quote about loss I sent you? I need to know, so I know whether you'll get witty back-references to it.

Re: g. and l. and the whole d. t.
   Yes I did get the quote about loss. Thank you for it.
How true that is (as Dan Quayle might say).

                                                        H

Re: Off the face of the screen
Hamlet:
   So--you vanished off the f. of the s. What happened?
Or would it be a breach of your new security regula-
tions to say?

Re: Once more unto the breach
   I sense something of a chill in your print, dear Sylvia. It's funny how words have a temperature, isn't it?
   You should know that my face going off the screen--
was nothing personal. My face was literally nowhere
near a screen, that was the problem.
   But it was a pleasure to come back to your series of
stacked messages--waiting, like impatient planes on the
runway, to take off.

Re: Absence makes the heart
Dear Hamlet,
   Partially thawed, already.
   But I missed you. If I am allowed to write such a
thing. I was worried you had floated off into the
ether. We were already fond over here (I've kept Martha
informed, in a general way, of my chattings with your
princely self, so I include her in the we), but in the
absence of any further communication we had grown
fonder. As the saying predicts.
Any hint where you went?
Sylvia

Re: Absence makes the heart
Dear Sylvia,
   I was missing our communication too. I'll tell you
more about the chops and changes later. You never

step in the same river twice, undsoweiter undsoweiter.

Pardon my German. That is in fact the only German I
remember from college, besides "als immer," as always,
which comes in handy often in descriptions of my life,
e.g., "I am full of self-loathing today. Als immer."

Yours H

Re: your German

Oh, all right, I'll pardon your German. I ought to, I
used to speak it myself, seeing as it was the language
of all those dinge-an-sich I was studying.

So which river was it? And why would you loathe yourself when you're a prince of a guy, except perhaps when
you go disappearing off without a word for days at a
time?

S

Re: dinge-an-sich

Taking your points in order:

Re: Where I went. I was abruptly called away from
matters before me to go to a funeral. Re: the self-
loathing: it's inevitable. I am the same person, my
life is still the same life, and with or without funerals it all goes on and nothing is solved, undsoweiter
undsoweiter.

Apologizing for the lack of cheer,

H

Re: With or without funerals
Hamlet--

Funeral? That makes all of my writings seem entirely
trivial and frivolous, with the possible exception of
the Hass quote.
Yours feeling sheepish and shallow,
Sylvia

Re: sheepish and shallow
My dear Sheep,

Here's your chance to make up for it. I want to ask you a question, a big one. It's the kind of question funerals sometimes inspire. It is this:

God, the existence of. If so, why; if not, why not?

Please think carefully before you begin, and give yourself enough time to answer the question. Don't forget to write your name at the top of each page.

Re: The question
God, the existence of

We're not necessarily well equipped to deal with this question. We're so busy checking the polls to see if Clinton's ahead, checking the weather to see if the whales are out, checking our psyches to see if we've processed our past pains successfully--all conspire to drive out niggling questions like whether or not God exists. But here's my effort:

If so--because otherwise, how could you explain the harmony of the world, the redwoods, the coastline, the Marthas, the Kafkas, the children's books, the look of love, the light in the eye and the stars and the sun and the wide, blameless sky?

If not--is easy. If not, it's altogether more possible to excuse the existence of smart bombs, dumb wars, race hatred, people standing in line to watch executions, bad TV, brainless blockbusters, pornography, the insidious fascination with serial killers--undsoweiter undsoweiter. If there isn't a God, all this is explainable. If there isn't a God, the existence of evil (always a tough theological nut to crack) poses no problem, since we can just say Evil exists, what can you do, c'est la vie. Pardon my French.

Is there a preponderance of evidence on either side, really? Well, but is it the kind of question you can answer with evidence? (The most truly sophisticated

exam answers, I'd like you to know, are the ones that
answer the question with another question.)
   Hope this sheds at least a sliver of light.
S

Re: Tough theological nut
Sylvia--
   Who are you calling a theological nut?
   You'd definitely be in about the 93rd percentile for
that answer. It lucidly, if briefly, lays out the basic
lines of the two arguments--though as you point out it
doesn't actually answer the question. We had to take
some points off for that.
   Your reasoning is not unlike mine when I've tried to
handle the hot potato that is this spiritual quandary.
Sometimes, in the most venial way, I think it would be
so handy to believe in God--I mean it clearly gets people through terrible shocks and yes losses, and I'd
guess that feeling suicidal wouldn't be an option if
you believed in God because you'd always have His glory
and sacrifice to pep you up when the going got tough.
   True?

                                                      H

Re: Pep factor
   I hadn't addressed the pep factor in what I wrote.
But this certainly seemed to be the case after the
fire, for instance. In that situation the religious
folk had a definite head start over us atheists. On the
one hand, they had someone very specific to be irate
with--God, damn it--but then on the other, given as you
point out God's glory and sacrifice, there had to be a
good reason for this having happened to them, which
must have been a comfort.
   For me, there was--what? Only the idea of the cosmic
joke, which let me tell you isn't very comforting. You
know, "Gosh, isn't it ironic that all my words and

philosophy became immaterial, given that I used to philosophize about the immaterial world. What a great
joke!"
  So funny I forgot to laugh.
  S

Re: Cosmic joke
  Wait, S, you referred to yourself as an atheist
there. Is that official?

Re: My official atheism
  I'd have to say it is, yes. At a push you could get
me to admit to some new ageish something or other--
hence the concern with ghosts, and otherworldly other
worlds. But God in the bearded guy on the throne sense,
no, I don't think so. How about you?
  S

Re: Bearded guy in the sky
  I don't know. A few years ago I'd have said certainly
not, what do you take me for, a moral majority nut?
(More nut imagery. Why do nuts and religion seem to go
hand in hand?) I was a good product of my separation of
church and state education, with liberty and tolerance
for all, so Jesus and Buddha and Allah and Yahweh and
everyone else were all up there in the same firmament,
along with Elvis Presley and the Stars and Stripes--all
man-made icons, unique and special though they might
individually be.
  But a close friend of mine lately confessed he's been
going to synagogue, which threw me. A synagogue, he
clearly said, not "the temple of Sigmund Freud and his
acolytes" which is where he formerly worshipped. In
this particular friend this is a change on an order I
can hardly describe--a 7, say, on the Richter scale.
  Meanwhile, at the funeral, there was a certain amount
of God talk going around. As you'd expect. It was the

Christian God, who leaves me tepid, but I did get a
spooky feeling in my veins while I sat in this church,
which made me think on a more serious order than usual.

OK, spot check--how embarrassing is this for me to
tell you? I feel that in this day and age it's so much
riskier to speak of religion than it is to launch into
a topic like "and which position do you like to have
sex in?" Not that I have those conversations often, I
hasten to say, and I have no interest in discussing
that with you now. But I don't know how far to go into
my own eccentric cosmology here with you. Kafka personals may be one order of embarrassment, but religious
flickerings of belief are altogether something else.

Apprehensively yours,

H

Re: Eccentric cosmologies

Are surely the only interesting kind. You could argue
that they are the only kind, given that each person's
spirituality is likely to be idiosyncratic. But that is
not a view in keeping with any organized religion, because the whole concept of organized religion suggests
you can connect people's cosmologies and fit them all
together, like a particularly successful line dance.

Wow. How did I get onto line dances? All you wanted
was for me to say I don't mind hearing about your eccentric cosmology. I don't, H, obviously. In fact, I
prefer it to talking about sexual positions.
S

Re: Eccentric cosmologies

OK. Well, it's not so different from what you wrote
earlier. I was having these thoughts recently when I
was beetling up this east coast of ours (by train) in
order to get to the funeral. And this train ride spells
it all out for you. Because it starts out with the
train skimming over large bodies of unnamed water--I'm

not just being coy here, I have no idea what they are--
which shimmer and shiver bluely and silverly, as bodies
of water are wont to do, stirring even in a small-
minded person like myself deep, rich thoughts, as bodies of water are also wont to do. In a way it was a
relief that I couldn't name this water--it made it seem
all the purer, all the more planetary, I mean if you
really got into it you could start drumming up some
baptismal imagery here but I don't want to go quite
that far.

Anyway. So here I was admiring this water and thinking that underneath the dread and self-obsession that
I, for one, seem to be stuck with much of the time,
there really is this spectacularly ordered, planned,
intricate, careful universe, you know the one I mean,
the one where water is beautiful to look at and also
has some lyrical molecular structure and at the same
time nourishes the fishes and is part of the weather
and the food chain and all those other good things.

And when you think about it that way, it does seem
kind of vain of us to assume that this just happened,
without anyone being in charge. I mean, it would be
like going into a room where there's this incredible
dinner, a feast, laid on the table--turkey and roast
potatoes and cornbread and carrots and salad (OK, it's
a Thanksgiving table, obviously) and pumpkin pie and
those amazingly tasty dinner rolls with lots of butter
on them--and going, "Gosh, how lucky that this fabulous
food organized itself for us! Let's tuck in!" You know,
without guessing that some benevolent Mom person was
really behind this feast and had planned and cooked it
all so it would appear on the table on time, hot,
ready, the turkey cooked through so no one gets food
poisoning, my mother was always paranoid about that.

Are you with me here? The Thanksgiving example is
meant to point up the vanity in thinking this highly
ordered world could come about without any planning being done by anyone. If you prefer a more macho meta-

phor, you could say it would be like the Superbowl
being staged without the NFL behind it.

So. Therefore, it would seem to follow that God exists.

HOWEVER.

Around this point in my thinking the train started
pulling through some of those terrible, blood-rust and
bitter-yellow-colored, trash-scattered stretches, those
smashed-window stretches, those--First World? Who said
this was the First World? stretches, that the train
also goes through as it snakes its way up the edge of
the Atlantic. You start to see water that runs dirty
with indifference, weeds that aren't scenic, are just
ugly and dead-looking, people with the dough-shouldered
sag of the sick and abandoned.

And at that point, I had to move on in my thinking.

Having made such a cool and incredible world, wouldn't
it be perverse (to put it mildly) for God to populate
it with a species capable of allowing hideous poverty
and environmental rampage, the destruction of everything
beautiful and nice? Or--on its bigger scale--genocide?
Hiroshima? Extinction?

So. Here's my preliminary idea to get around the contradiction here. Which as you mentioned has puzzled
thinkers for some years now. It seems possible to me
that God might have been here to start with, when everything was kind of dark and vague and claylike, and
that's when He got really creative, made amazing stuff
like birds and mountains and the printing press (and
possibly Tang; I'm sure God played some part in the
making of Tang). And then--too late!--He began to see
that there was a terrible, crucial design flaw in human
beings. They were greedy! They were small-minded! They
hated each other, for some weird reason! Which was
eventually going, God could see this as of course He
was able to see the big picture, to make the whole project go right to hell.

At which point God decamped to a different galaxy to

try again, figuring he'd leave us to muddle ahead as
best we could.

OK! That's the picture. The funeral helped me fine-
tune this view.

Yours fearing I've gone over the edge here,

H

Re: the edge

No, no. I like it. The "God as bumbling but powerful
DIY freak" cosmology. What I like in your account is
that it explains both ends of the paradox. On the one
hand, why order and loveliness; on the other, why despair and chaos. You've covered them both. That shoots
you way up into the 98th percentile, at a guess.

On a different subject, you've now, in that teasing
narrative way of yours, really piqued my curiosity
about the funeral. Do you want to tell me more about
whosoever it was?

I don't want to pry, but I want you to know that this
particular correspondent of yours is all eyes, if
you're in the mood to write it.

S

Re: All eyes
Dear Sylvia,

I didn't think I would, or should, before. To anyone.
It seemed to me too private. More private than Kafka
personals, eccentric cosmologies--even sexual positions.
I was beginning to think it unwise to write too specifically about people, for reasons that I don't feel
like going into but are related to the neurotic security measures we went through earlier.

But now a few days have passed. Life is calmer. Face-
lessness has relaxed me again. (It's such a good ther-
apy--burying your identity.) And I've realized you can
tell a story in a parable-like way, without naming

names, without getting specific. So that's how I'll
narrate this funeral.

A friend of mine, a woman, lost her son finally to
illness. He fell down the dark slimy well of disease,
and they couldn't fish him out again. We'll call him
the Son, you know, the way they do in parables. And in
this story, as you, S, might be sophisticated enough to
guess, there was at one point a brother, not that Bro
registered the death even by coming to the funeral. But
I did. I went to the service, though I'm no relation.

I'll describe it for you.

Little modern wooden and metal church. Suburbs. Green
around the place, many flowers, lilies and whatnots.
His mother would have killed to give him the real
thing, a Catholic funeral, but the Son was a stickler
enough back in the days he still had his mind and his
thoughts were his own, to get in touch with a minister
from the gay church, the MCC, to talk to him about doing the service and how he wanted it done. The Son
didn't want his being gay to be covered up, you see, he
wanted it to be part of what people talked about in
talking about him. An extra reason, if one were needed,
why Bro did not deign to make an appearance at the
event. But the mother, to her credit and though her own
Catholic faith goes so deep she probably doubts whether
any other kind of service (even a Protestant one) reg-
isters with God at all, honored her son's request. I
have a feeling that for her it was all mixed up together: her son being gay, her son asking some newfangled minister to do his service, her son dying from
disease at an age he should have been marrying and having his first kid--all these things were entirely outside her own cosmology, which has to do with the
Church. But when you've got a ferocious love for your
kid, the way this woman had, you just deal with it. And
how a woman like her managed to raise a Bro who didn't
get that simple point is beyond me.

Anyway. At the service the minister spoke, music was played, then a couple of the Son's friends got up to speak. Two guys and one woman. One of the guys was, I have to say this because you couldn't help noticing it, quite effeminate. He was striking, in fact. He had huge brown doe eyes and long lashes, this full, pretty mouth, and dark hair that was cut short in a boy bob. He was wearing black jeans and a tight, glittery shirt.

And this, approximately, is what he said when he spoke:

"If you love someone very much, the way we all loved our friend here, then even though you're sad--horribly, painfully sad--when they die, there is this great joy that stays with you, even all through a day like today, his funeral service, and all through all of your days. Because ever since you first met them, this person has been living with you, they have been with you in your mind and heart wherever you are, wherever they are. I remember when I first met him--I hope you don't mind me saying this--it was at a party and he was dancing with no shirt on and he was dancing so fast and beautiful, I couldn't help yelling out at him, this man I'd never met in my life, 'Go, girl! Go on!' because he was hav-ing such a great time dancing. And he just looked at me, he heard me through the music, and he gave me this SMILE. Oh, that smile! I almost fainted! It was an an-gelic smile, with a little mischief in it, too, and then he went back to his dancing, and I knew that later I'd meet him and talk to him and that this man would be in my life, no matter what, from that minute on. And he has been. And he always will be. And I don't care what happened to his body or what gets done with his ashes, nothing is going to stop me loving this man and talking to him and dancing with him and laughing with him--for the rest of my life."

By which point, inevitably, we were all weeping copi-ously.

And then the other guy got up, a clean-cut, all-American guy, and he shared more sweet stories about the Son, many of which featured playing pool. It seemed to me they'd been lovers, but I might be wrong. And then the girl spoke, the woman, but she was really a girl. She looked about sixteen. She had huge outrageous earrings and loud red lipstick and she read a poem she'd written for him called "You were like a brother to me," and while it may not have been a work you'd submit for publication in a national magazine, it was straight, and I do mean straight, from the heart, and it included the lines "When I looked up over the table/ I saw your face/and I knew I would be able/to tell you everything that was on my mind." Which was, in its way, also moving.

That was it for the friends. There should have been something from the family but his mother was too choked up. There were some aunts and uncles, and a heartbreakingly shrunken grandmother, but none of them spoke. I think it wasn't their kind of venue. And though I was tempted to stand up and shout over the canned organ music, "His brother should be here, God damn it!" I decided it would have been blasphemous and I managed to restrain myself.

I found myself praying for him, in a manner of speaking. For the brother dead; and also, uncannily, for the brother who has stayed alive.

Yours,
Hamlet

Re: Your parable
You were good to go to the service. The brother manque.
How is the mother holding up?
Otherwise, I'm not sure what to say, or write, except--I'm sorry. For you, for her, for the girl who he

was like a brother to, for the man with the glitter
shirt.
Yours fondly,
Sx

Re: The mother
    I'm worried about her, of course. She looked so very
small when I was up there. She's always small, but
she's someone with a terrific amount of energy, so she
can seem small but BIG, you know? Loud and funny and
just unforgettably there in front of you.
    But that day, she was so small she was almost smaller
than the tiny grandmother. I felt like a weird clumsy
giant. I couldn't figure out how to shrink myself down
modestly the way the occasion seemed to demand.

                                            H

Re: the friendly giant
H--
    I'm sure you were perfectly adequately sized. Not too
big at all. Your heart would appear to be big--but big
is good, in a heart.
Sx

Re: Big hearts and coronets
    But how big was it, though, to leave the same night
as the funeral? Which I did. For the pretty small reason that I found it too sad and depressing. I talked
with the mother for a while and did what I could to
comfort her, and then like the emotional coward that I
am I just split. Came back down here.

                                   Yours,
                                         H

Re: Big hearts and coronets
    OK, Hamlet. I'm going to say something--at the risk
of sounding clumsy giantish, myself. (Not to unbury my

identity here or anything, but I, like you, have an issue with my height.)

   This is more thinking about loss. Because for those
of us who have ever gotten lost, or thought about losing ourselves, I guess such speeches as people give at
funerals make you think what it does to the people who
love you. Partly I'm thinking about this in my situation, being up here away from it all. This excursion
was my own way of getting lost, maybe. If I put it that
way, it starts to seem selfish of me to have hidden myself on this unfamiliar edge, away from my friends, not
to mention my former colleagues.

   Me, me, me. Sorry. I actually wanted to talk about
you, you, you, but it began to seem way too presumptu-
ous. But: the havoc it wreaks on people, forcing them
to lose you.

   --Maybe in your own subtle way you know what I'm
talking about.

Sx

Re: Me and my subtle ways
   Yes, yes. I got it.
   Re: Something else entirely. Might we return to the
subject of the Glitter Shirt Man?

Re: Yours
Sorry if that was v. clumsy on my part. Go ahead--glit-
ter away.

Re: The Glitter Shirt Man
   Well I was thinking about what a strong presence the
dead man still seemed to be in Glitter Shirt's life,
and would go on being.
   And this made me think of my father, because I
started thinking that though my father is not to my
knowledge dead, not technically, he would seem to be
deader to me than that young man is to Glitter Shirt. I

mean, do I dance and laugh with my father? No. Do I
even think about him, except to hate him? Hardly. How
alive does that make him, really?

Not very, Sylvia, frankly. Pinsk's shade is more of a
real entity to me than my father. So are you, for that
matter: someone I don't even know, haven't met, don't
have a picture of. You too are realer to me than my
father.

And what, pardon my French, kind of fucked up situation is that?

H

Re: Knowing fathers best
Hamlet:
Were my life circumstances different, I'd be feeling a
philosophy paper coming on right about now.

Everyone thinks philosophy is so dry, but sometimes
ideas come to you as if you were a poet or songwriter
(let me indulge the comparison for a second) and you
think--I have to write about that NOW. So, for instance, I am beginning to think: I must look into the
questions of presence and absence; how absence of body
can sometimes have no effect on the presence of a person in someone's life. I suspect this would be a soft-
core paper for your general interest type of
publication, on which the academy frowns, rather than a
multi-footnoted job, on which the academy beams. I once
heard this great item on the BBC, on a learning English
program (I'm sure you know how cosmopolitan we are in
the Bay Area, listening to BBC radio, getting updates
on life in the former empire from all those fancy accents)--and some guy had written in from Calcutta or
somewhere to ask, "Can you please explain two English
phrases--'Absence makes the heart grow fonder' and 'Out
of sight, out of mind'? There seems to be a contradiction." It was entertaining to hear them try to explain
it. That would probably be the title of my paper: "Out

of sight, out of mind?" with a big question mark on
the end. (I might be tempted, as an example, to draw on
yourself, pointing out that, though you are perpetually, and by definition, out of my sight, you are
rarely, as it happens, out of my mind.)

Anyway. Fathers. I don't know what to say about them
--yours or mine or anybody's. If I had the equipment to
write a philosophy paper on the subject, I could come
back to you with a good answer. In the interim, all I
can say is: Fathers, can't live with 'em, can't live
without 'em. Hardly original, I know.

Re: Fathers: If so, why; if not, why not
Hi again S--
    And you? Do you live with 'em or without 'em?

Re: Fathers: If not, why not
    Without. I haven't mentioned mine because he's not as
effectively dead to me as yours apparently is to you.
He's alive, he's out in Phoenix, Arizona, I get letters
from him at Christmas and occasionally other times. He
doesn't keep track of my addresses so he sends these
letters to my mother's house, which is fairly tacky
considering their none-too-pleasant divorce way back
when. But that is the point of this notional father of
mine. He's a tacky guy. How tacky? I'll give you a
hint: the letters I get from him are XEROXED.

    Here, I'll invent a sample letter for you. They go
something like this:

    Hi everybody!
        It's the end of another summer and all Marilyn and
    John can say is . . . Phew! Thank goodness God in-
    vented the school year!
        Just joshing. We had a terrific summer with the
    grandkids--don't worry, not all at once! Bob and Di-
    ane brought Hayley and Christian over in June while

they went to take some well-earned R & R in Hawaii.
You probably know that Bob's been promoted to general district manager, which is excellent news and
well deserved. John is trying to persuade him to
spend the promotion bonus on putting in that new
jacuzzi they've always dreamed about. Hayley and
Chris are getting to be pretty big squirts, 9 & 11,
but not so big they can beat their grandfather at
miniature golf, to John's relief. (Not to mention
Marilyn's!) We had a great time with the kids here
and were sorry to see them go.

The dust had hardly settled when we had Tim and
Tanya here on their way up to Family Values Camp
[or some such]. We had them for one week before and
then again a week after, so they could tell us all
the things they'd learned to do, like silk-screening
and wilderness skills, and Tim could show off his
very impressive mosquito bite collection!

Donna's operation went real well though and the
doctors are proud of how fast she recovered. She
said everyone was great and spoiled her and thanks
to all of you folks who sent cards. Marilyn wasn't
sure Donna would be totally ready for Tim and Tanya
when she got back, but Tanya said she could bring
her new camp-survival skills to bear on helping her
mom convalesce. She and her brother both are very
good little helpers.

Hope all of you are well in health and spirit. We
miss you and hope you'll visit soon. Marilyn hopes
so especially--so someone can take John off her
hands and play some golf!

May God be with you, et cetera.

--And that, Hamlet, that third person John--that's my
father. I'm serious. Just to reassure you--the grandkid
chatter is about Marilyn and her kids, who have always
been more real to the guy than the not-so-treasured

daughter who somehow leaked out of his first marriage,
i.e. me.

I haven't told him yet about the fire, my loss of
livelihood, any of it. He'd probably think God was punishing me for being a philosopher, or for my generally
unproductive lifestyle. Anything that doesn't involve
marriage, procreation, and home improvement is deeply
perplexing to him. I'm pretty sure that for him graduate school comes under the heading "pointless navel-
gazing."

So I know what you mean about who's alive to who(m).
You know more about me now, even if you don't know my
name, than this guy who gave me half my genes. You at
least know something of my words and thoughts and humor; you know the scrabblings of my philosophy; you
know I have recently been reading the sequel to 101
Dalmatians to a sweet girl named Martha. He doesn't
know a damn thing. Sometimes when I have a stupid moment (as I do fairly often, like today at work when I
jammed the document feeder not once but THREE TIMES, in
the exact same way)--I blame my father's genetic contribution. I assume it's from him, as my mother is
pretty intelligent. How he and my mother remained married long enough to conceive me remains one of the
larger mysteries of life. To this day, my mother spits
at the mention of his name.
Sylvia

Re: Fathers: Worth the paper they're printed on?
My dear Sylvia,

I had no idea you came from a man who sends xeroxed
letters. My heart goes out to you. I'm sitting here
trying to figure out which is worse, no letters or xeroxed letters, though comparisons in these cases are
probably pointless. When was the last time you saw him?
I'm imagining Mr. Cleaver, more or less. Is that right?

My own father, as you might have figured out, falls

unhappily between the "Absence makes the heart grow
fonder" and "Out of sight, out of mind" schools of
parenting. Neither has worked for him: he's out of
sight, but hasn't successfully left my mind; he's absent, and yet the heart has not grown fonder. Now why
is that? With my mother, it worked--I became infinitely
fonder of Mom after I moved to the other side of the
country from her. Nowadays I think she's cute as a button and can even contemplate living in the same city as
her again. With my father, I do still want to kill the
guy, periodically. Of course I'm stepping out of role
here saying that because the real Hamlet is a dutiful
son, and his father was by all accounts a great guy. A
lot of filial piety going on there. Whereas if the
ghost of my father were to show up, I wouldn't so much
charge him to speak, nay speak, as I'd say--Fuck you!
Isn't it a little late for these theatrics?
  Pardon my Shakespeare.

Hamlet

Re: Your Shakespeare
H:
  Consider it pardoned.
  OK. Here's my effort to tackle the complex problems
raised in your previous e-mail. I will show how an alternative approach to the question of troublesome people in one's life (including fathers) can have
beneficial results for one's productivity and general
state of mind. I will use the work of Donald Davidson
and Bernard Williams to establish my argument. In con-
clusion I will discuss the ravages the therapeutic culture has wrought in America while also secretly
wondering if they have a point. I'd like to thank various famous people, including Meryl Streep, for their
assistance in the writing of this e-mail, not that I
know them personally but I've always admired their work
and this seems a good place to mention it.

Sorry, I just had a flashback to how I used to have to write philosophy papers. I was doing that for five years, Hamlet. Can you believe it? They brainwash you into thinking that's an interesting way to begin a piece of writing. Yikes. Sometimes I feel like I've escaped from a cult. Sometimes . . . I miss my cult.

Back to your Shakespeare. I wanted to go over something I've been thinking about as I've watched one of my co-habitants here in this northern town. The older one, that is, not Martha but Martha's mother, my employer/auntuncular confidante/social worker assigned to my case. As I've mentioned, she herself is going through a hideous divorce right now. It makes my mother's feelings about Pops look like sweetness and light. This woman--her insides are bathed in acid because of the horrors of this divorce. She thinks she's handling it, but unbeknownst to her, her distress shows up all over her body like a rash. She has no idea I've perceived this because she thinks I'm an emotional dwarf out of touch with my feelings and she's been trying to get me into therapy since I set foot through the threshold. But that's another story. (Her therapist's name is Faith. Don't you find that sort of comically poignant?)

The point is I'm watching this kind soul frizzle and fret over the ex-man in her life, and it's horribly evident to me that the pain of it is clinging to her like a poisoned spider. She can't brush it away. And she's such a good person, such a nice, warm-faced person, that I wish--me, the emotional dwarf--I wish I could somehow get her to let go of it. You know? I wish I could help her let go.

I'm a fine person to say this, I realize. It doesn't seem I've let go of my angst about parents--mere days ago I was ranting to you about my father (though if you really want to hear me get hysterical sometime, ask me what I went through with my mother in my early twen-

ties--the short answer is hellfire and damnation). But
with both my mother and my father, I did get to this
point somewhere where I just decided I'd have to let
them rest. In peace, preferably. Get on with my life.
With Pops that means reading his xeroxed letters and
refraining from sending him bitter parodies in reply;
on the other side, I'm lucky to have a benevolent stepfather as a buffer so it's all fairly painless. And to
their credit they were kind to me after my catastrophe.
They really were.

So now in the middle of the night this is my new man-
tra. Let it go. It's very nearly the lyrics to a Beatles song, so how off base can it be? I'm not about to
get a shrink--no amount of psychologizing is going to
explain away the fire and how its cosmic joke ate my
life--but I am thinking, maybe I can somehow stop
fighting against the loss. And, see, maybe this applies
to you and your father, too. When I hear you talking
(when I read you writing) about your father, I get a
terrible feeling that maybe his absence is wearing you
down. And you can't let that happen. You can't. I say--
find your own Glitter Shirt people in life, the people
who you'd dance with even in their absence, and don't
worry if they're not your father.

I only say this because I live in California and this
gives me the right--nay, the obligation--to issue
touchy-feely remarks of this kind. If such is possible
over the computer. This is, in short, my concession to
living--I'm a Californian, damn it! I have to at least
try--with a little magic, and a lot of style.

That, or I'm losing my edge and becoming a vapid new
ager.
Yours fearful that my self-mockery doesn't adequately
disguise my essential sentimentality,
Sylvia

Re: The vapid new age
Dear old Sylvia.
   Fuck.
   Fuck, fuck, fuck.
   This is not a response to what you wrote, by the way.
Let me make that clear. What you wrote was fine and
possibly new agey, but as you say you live in Northern
California and can't help it. Who's to say Kant was any
more to the point?
   There's more to be said about what you wrote, but S:
I'm in trouble. I'm resorting to the direct approach
here. I'm back at my sister's now--I came back down
here after the funeral. And I've just been hanging out
here writing, feeling very distraught on behalf of my
friend, the mother of the guy who died. I love her, the
mother. I'm getting into one of those states of mind
where I am feeling both despair and this great wave of
love for everyone. Do you ever get those? Even my buddy
who bosses me around telling me to write whale screen-
plays, who took me out to a lovely Italian dinner while
I was up for the funeral because he just got an NEA
grant, owing to the fact that his work does not feature
body excretions and is hence not controversial. But he
deserves his grant. I'm happy for him. I love him, too,
in my new wave of affection.
   Someone found me. That's what happened. Someone found
me at my sister's. Some scary guy named Steve Palin
knocked on the door saying he wanted to see me, and she
assumed he was a friend of mine from college or whatever so she let him in. And where does he know me from?
The fucking Internet, that's where. I should never have
started writing about this town. It was such a mistake
--this is too small and specific a city to get away
with writing about. How hard could it be to track me
down, given how much blather I wrote about my sister
and her friends?
   Sylvia, I've gotten too fucking deep in this. This

guy's obsessed--it's like he's a stalker. How glamorous! Apparently his handle is Abbie Hoffman, which if he didn't make me so nervous I'd find kind of cool. He told me he had plenty to tell me about therapy, antidepressants, and members of the quote unquote silent majority . . . I got rid of him as fast as I could, but I've been in a cold sweat ever since. I never wanted to be recognized. I never wanted to be found. That was the whole point. I wasn't trying to be a performance artist, you know. I was just trying to write.

I'm going to get out of here, Sylvia. I don't even know who the hell you are, as you recently pointed out, but I don't want to stop writing you. I love your messages, even the disturbingly new agey ones. You have a lot of magic, and not a little style.

But, listen. (Watch.) I'm going to have to hit the road again, me and my small friend. Not back to the city. I don't want to go back there. We're going to go West. It seems to be the thing to do. I hear the sun shines out there, and it will be a new dawn and all that. Hollywood was telling the truth all along! Who'd have thought.

That's it for now. Please keep writing me. I'll figure out a way to stay connected and get my mail. You see, in the fullness of my somewhat exaggerated state of mind, I have a great fondness for you, too, Sylvia. Me and the pup, both.

> With kindest regards,
> Hamlet

In most of the galleries there were dolphins. Also whales, seals, otters, pelicans, seagulls. Crafted marine life swam or flew in great schools out of local studios and into the many-galleried streets of Mendocino, and from there into the happy hands of visitors who wanted to live with shaped remembrances of their wildlife time here. These pieces made whole and graspable that glitter of light you thought or hoped you saw while you strolled or boated along the waves: that underwater fin or flipper, that furry face, that wing arc. Of course you might want to take home something so tangible from your vacation or honeymoon. Of course you might.

Abbie worked in a gallery that sold fine art. It was one of the few that didn't sell driftwood creatures and pretty lampshades—not that Abbie had anything against lampshades; she'd bought one herself. Nick Hancock's Gallery Place sold precious jewelry—he had to for his business to stay alive—but his passion was for oil painting and finely made furniture. Abbie liked Nick's eye in painting but believed that the best of his ambitious gallery (with two floors, it was Mendocino's grandest) was the work in wood. Improbably ancient redwoods stood half an hour from here, casting their cool shadows and implacable history across the town. Wood was the origin, the genius of this place. The forgiving ghosts of all those cut forests must have come back to haunt local people, because in the carvers' hands a piece of oak or cherry—bowl or table, shelf or ornament— was turned into a rich, smooth lyric.

Still, selling was selling. There were gallery tricks common to either end of the trade, like knowing at what point to let a customer watch and wander without your interference and at what point to sneak up on him like a predator. That was when you offered whispered details about the work he was looking at, subtly acknowledging his discernment in noticing it.

After minutes tracking him in her peripheral vision, Abbie approached a long-haired man who had been moving a rough, careful palm along the surface of an inlaid walnut table.

"That's made by a fascinating man who lives in Comptche . . ." She started her spiel before she recognized the teacher from her ceramics class. "Oh! Hi. Randy, right?"

"I didn't know you worked here, Abbie." From the copper glint in his eyes, she understood this to be a lie. Her cheeks colored with surprise. "In with the high end of the market. I've been after Nick for years to show ceramics in here, but he's still holding out on me. He isn't a pot man, he says. Not that kind of pot, anyway."

"But you show in town, don't you?" Abbie slipped out of her saleswoman voice. "I thought I saw some of your work in Horizons."

"Nice of you to notice."

"Well, I'm interested—you know, I did some pottery myself years ago. Back in the seventies, when every other person seemed to have a kiln or a wheel in their back yards."

Leaning into the gallery hush, they exchanged friendly ceramics chatter—wheels and glazes, firings and potters' marks—in voices that got warmer and easier and then a little warmer yet as the conversation turned (it was he who turned it) in a certain direction. Randy complimented Abbie on her adorable daughter. He teased out enough information to work out that Martha's father was not around; that Abbie considered herself unattached. That she hadn't been here long. The copper in Randy's eyes brightened. He talked of the town's famous restaurants, what a great place Mendocino was for food. Maybe they could enjoy a dinner at one of them, say Café Beaujolais, sometime together? Sometime soon. The sooner the better.

It had been so long since Abbie had played this game, she'd forgotten how well she still knew its moves. The divorce—specifically, the paralegal, that brutal thin knife of a girl—had slashed her confidence to a nothing, to a shred of itself. She hadn't thought she still knew how to move and slink under another person's watchful eye.

When Abbie and her husband were first married, he'd gotten bearishly, boorishly jealous of other men's attentions to her. Waiters who flattered her, the appreciative nods of his colleagues—even a museum guide, once, who commented on her beautiful hands—these men made Abe bark, angry as a dog at the garden gate. He wasn't like the mellow Daves or Phils in Abbie's life, friends who worked an uphill battle to adapt to the age's demands on men to be nice and egalitarian and speak in quiet voices. Her husband spoke in a loud voice. He wrapped a heavy arm around her. She liked the feel of its animal weight on her shoulders, around her then-trim waist. She loved letting him love her. She had shaped herself into the man's strong, passionate limitations the way she had shaped her whole body into his vivid and aggressive love-making; the way she had folded her soft limbs into his stocky, firm ones, after. Abbie had prized him for his righteous love of her.

Which was why, later, she was so much the weaker. Her shoulders seemed so light without Abe sheltering them; her whole body felt empty and sick and unclaimed. In the totality of Abbie's rage after her discovery of the paralegal—which somehow obliterated whole suns from the sky, and made her look at blunt, weapon-worthy objects with a new kind of interest—the betrayed, once-optimistic seventies girl had to wonder if the doubting Daves and feminist Phils had been right all along. They'd always thought (you could see it in their creased, concerned faces) that the man Abbie married was at heart a brute. That he wasn't "evolved," the way they were. This made the end of her nine-year subjection all the more humiliating. She'd put up with so much! She'd compromised so far! And all so that the unreconstructed male could leave her in the most old-fashioned way possible, classically, you might say, with her feeling fat and forty, a mother, a helpmate—while he ran off with some young insignificance, some girl who was mindless of such disastrous states, some unsullied sexiness who had neither history nor future.

It was only now, as she nodded and smiled and dipped her eyes, as she gave the right answers to this Randy, who was himself not bad-looking, with an open grin and wide-set brown eyes, though his face seemed slightly squashed—that Abbie realized this might be another means of punishing Abe, of killing him in her mad mind. Of course! Another man. It hadn't occurred to her before. She murmured yes to dinner at Café Beaujolais—it would be lovely, a real treat. Perhaps, she hoped, this gentle man of ceramics might be able to fulfill some part of her giant desire to annihilate Abe.

Who, as it happened, selected that moment to come into the gallery.

If she'd been in a black-and-white movie, she might have fainted. Certainly the earth stilled, the sea swelled, and she felt a sudden sharp pain in her sinuses as if she were about to have a nosebleed. The blood drained from her feet, leaving her sandalled toes cold and numb. "In the event of a sudden loss of cabin pressure," the reassuring airplane voices promised, "oxygen masks will immediately be released from above your head. Place the mask over your nose and mouth and continue to breathe normally." Abbie, airless, could have done with one of those handy heaven-sent masks.

Fortunately the men knew how to arrange themselves. Nick emerged from upstairs with his boyfriend Allan; Randy got a quick measure of the situation and left after a brief word with Nick but not before throwing an assertive sentence Abbie's way about looking forward to their dinner together. Abe may or may not have reacted to the remark, Abbie wasn't able to notice. Nick, meanwhile, had recognized Abe: in the old good days Abe had been a very valued customer. He'd regularly browse in the gallery for jewelry for his beautiful wife and once spent a couple thousand on one of the finest Californian landscapes —a passionate, textured piece—Nick had ever sold. Nick was a model of modesty and discretion to his former customer, sharing polite talk with him about the work they were currently showing before letting Abbie go off for as long as she needed to.

There was something in all of these machinations that infuriated Abbie. The men managed and organized her as if she were a child or a pet who could be corralled into obedient action. Who said she wanted to go off with her husband to talk to him? Why should she have to talk to him just because he'd made the dramatic gesture of appearing? What right did he have to spring such surprises on her? She was still trying to clear the clots and sputter from her head, to come up with some good, sharp line to express her resistance to this whole plan, as the once-couple walked the sandy sidewalks away from the gallery—when she felt his firm familiar fingers holding the base of her elbow, steering her towards the restaurant he had obviously already chosen.

"What are you doing?"

"Can I take you to lunch?"

"What are you *doing* here?"

"Taking you to lunch," he said, not loudly at all but gently; gently, with a certainty in his voice that made her want to shoot him. Abbie, the person who couldn't kill a moth or a spider—who always used the glass-and-magazine trick to peaceably rid the house of indoor insects—wanted to shoot her soon-to-be ex for his sly arrogance. For his cool confidence, his damned doubtlessness. She might have done it, too, if she'd had a gun in her purse: one of those cute pearl-studded revolvers they make for the ladies, an item Abe had once encouraged her to get after a rash of San Francisco street crime. If she'd listened to him, she might have shot her husband now with blind satisfaction, one more story for the evening news.

"There is only so much that gets communicated through lawyers," he said to her, while continuing to steer them lunchwards. "I think there are a couple of basic points you and I have to work out for ourselves. Face to face."

Abbie made herself look at him, to try to get an idea of just what that formerly loved face was proposing. But grief and rage stained her vision, made it too hard to see. She turned away. "You *are* a lawyer," she said. Her words were bitter, her tone acidic, but apparently she had no choice but to let him take her to lunch.

"You can't stay, you know."

"I wasn't planning to. I have to fly to Houston tomorrow morning for a meeting. I'm driving back to the city tonight."

They were walking back towards the house. They'd lunched, they'd talked, they'd succeeded in neither killing nor maiming one another. Perhaps they'd moved a short, short distance closer to each other. At the gallery after lunch, Nick had taken one look at Abbie's bloodless face and sent her home.

"I'd like to say hello to Martha."

"That's fine. But I'm having dinner with someone later."

It was a premature truth. Still, Abbie could tell from his grunt that the idea bothered Abe, though he tried not to show it. She counted it a small success.

Their slow feet edged them back to the house, and with the slowness came their separate memories of where it was they were going. The place they once gave life to together. It had been a love nest once. A retreat. A passion place, where one salty summer day their child was conceived; where later, with infant Martha asleep at the top of the house, they'd known raucous joy in the room below, tossing the bed around as if it were a rough rowboat on an unruly sea; where, when upstairs was too far away, they'd made love in Abe's toolroom, up on the counter, screwdrivers and wrenches and other nameless tools clattering to the floor to make way for this other more urgent domestic project.

"Pi's picking Martha up from school," Abbie said flatly. "They'll be back soon." She didn't want even a shadow of such remembered possibilities in the air.

"No problem. I'll wait."

Abbie forced her manner to become brisk as they neared the screen door. This was her home now, after all. She wanted him to see how it had changed since he'd last been here. How they lived without him. How she'd made the place hers.

But the first thing Abe took in, since you could see the doorway right from the kitchen, was that his toolroom was gone. He had taken most of the stuff down to San Francisco at the end of the last summer but had left a couple of decent saws up here, a vice, a box of screws and nails and other fiddly things. He strode over to survey the room's emptiness.

"What happened to my tools?"

"They're in the garage, Abe. Relax. I didn't get rid of them."

"What is this? Your study now or something?"

"It's Pi's room."

"Oh, right. I forgot about her."

He felt no bashfulness about standing in the doorway of the room he'd once made cupboards and bookshelves in, now a monkish cell with a computer sitting alone along the workbench, a few vague Xeroxes stuck to the walls. There were no photographs around, nothing.

"What's she like?"

"Quiet. She keeps to herself. But when she opens up, she's . . . funny. And smart. She can be charming. She and Martha get along famously."

"I gathered that."

"She's a good friend of Fran's. One of Fran's old friends from high school."

Abe let a wandering eyebrow express his feelings about Abbie's niece, which she was perfectly aware of, which was why she had mentioned the connection. Fran had always seemed wild to Abe, off the wall. Unmanageable. "She doesn't have much decorating sense, does she, this girl?"

"Pi lost everything she owned in the Berkeley fire."

"Oh." He sat down on Pi's bed next to Abbie. He shook his head. "I didn't realize that. That's tough."

"Abe. Listen. I don't want you to go home thinking it's decided. It isn't. I have to think it over."

He put up a hand and started to reply when there was a chattering and clattering in the kitchen. Abbie started up almost guiltily. The two girls were full of breath and words—both of which stopped, when Pi saw a strange man in her room and Martha saw her father.

"Daddy!" she said. But she stood where she was, confused.

"Hello, angel!" He got up to give her a big, ostentatious bear hug. He extricated himself finally to introduce himself to Pi, giving her a thick slab of a handshake. He explained that he had come up for the day and was only going to stay another hour or so—long enough to take Martha out for ice cream, if she wanted.

Ice cream often works.

"Oh, can I? Please?" she asked her mother. She had an instinct that her mother had to give permission for this now. Excursions with her father were not as free as they once were.

"Of course, honey. You go ahead with Daddy."

Martha was befuddled by the sight of her father in this house now, her mother here, too, the two of them not apparently fighting. A fierce, painful hope gripped her chest that it was going to be all right after all. The prospect of a double-chocolate-dipped cone with sprinkles only increased her excitement, and she practically skipped off with her father down towards Main Street. For the first time in an uncountable number of days, a small window of optimism opened a brightness onto the child's troubled heart.

"So." Pi was standing in the kitchen, arms folded. "That's the man."

"That's him." Abbie grimaced. "Was he different from what you expected?"

"Shorter. Shorter than I'd pictured. Though I know that's not the most profound observation."

"No, no. That's fine. It's helpful. He sometimes gets bigger in my imagination."

Abbie's hands were nervous around the counters, rearranging, arranging, finding food and hiding it again. Finally, she said, "Look, I know it's early. But I'm going to open a bottle of wine. Would you like a glass?"

"Sure."

Now that he was gone, she could let herself go. Abbie pulled up a few chairs—enough so she could put her feet up on one, sigh over a glass of just-poured lemony wine, and knock her head back in a long, relieved swallow.

"Was it that bad?" Pi asked.

"It's never good." Abbie closed her eyes. She moved a hand over the smooth curve of her neck.

Pi took her glass and sipped. "You weren't expecting him, I guess?"

"Absolutely not." Abbie rattled a shaking head. "Abe's always been very good on strategy, and timing. It's why he's so good in court. He has a great instinct about how to wrong-foot people. He does it with his manner, too. Today he was all—well, I won't say *all*—but he was very charming and chivalrous. Taking me out to an elegant lunch in the sun, keeping his voice down, speaking politely, asking me questions. When he wants something out of you, he has the smoothest tongue of anyone I've ever known."

Pi took a larger swallow. "And what was he using his smooth tongue to get, in this instance?"

"He wanted me to say we'd move back to San Francisco. So he can see Martha more regularly and she 'doesn't have to become one of those pathetic kids who spends half their weekends in Greyhound bus stations being shuttled back and forth from parent to parent.' "

Pi nodded. "Well, it's true. Those divorce bus trips are no fun."

Abbie looked at Pi more carefully. "Where is your father, Pi? I've never asked you."

"He lives in Arizona. I never see him. My mother effectively squirreled me away from him after the divorce. She squirreled me all the way over to Europe, in fact. We lived in London for two years with an old aunt of hers while she tried to make it as a painter, and I went to a hideously oppressive girls' school. Luckily she met Richard—he was over on sabbatical. We came back to the U.S. a happy family."

"And did you see your father again when you came back?"

"Well, my mother did hate him. Fairly intensely. She was casual, let's say, about keeping up contact with him. But I did take a few divorce bus trips to see him in Arizona. He had a new family by then, too, though, and it all somehow seemed a waste of time."

"And now?"

"We keep in touch. A little."

A silence stretched itself over unsaid thoughts.

"So what do you think? Do you think you'll move back?"

"I want you to know that whatever happens, Pi, you're welcome to stay here. For as long as you need to."

"Oh God, Abbie, don't worry about me. You've been so kind to me already."

"It isn't kindness. It's been wonderful for us to have you here. Martha's loved it—well, so have I, I've loved it. You're a pleasure to have around."

Pi took another draught of wine to hide the blush. "Anyway, I'll probably have to go back, too. It's been restful to pretend I live up here, but I have to go back to the Bay Area sooner or later. I can't imagine where else I'd go."

"Look, this isn't decided yet. I haven't said yes to Abe. I don't like him bossing me around. Of course, he knows that, too, so he presented it in the canniest way possible."

"Which was—?"

"Oh, to bribe me, in effect. If I move back down to the city, he won't sue for joint custody, he'll organize an alternative weekends plan. It's crafty. He knows I don't want to fight him in court. Anything that goes to court, he'll win. So he is doing me a big favor here, you see. Giving me a way out." Abbie sat up, and sighed. "It's very tempting to avoid the fight. But then I think of going back to that city, where we were—" Her face folded. "Do you know what happened to me today?"

"What?"

"The man who teaches that pottery class I'm doing with Martha came into the gallery and was flirting with me. He wants to have dinner with me."

"Well." Pi kept her face upbeat. "That's good, isn't it? Is he cute?"

"Yes, it's good, I guess, and yes he's cute-ish—I emphasize the *-ish*. I used him to make Abe jealous. That was the good part."

"So what was the bad part? Other people are interested. That sounds good to me."

"Let me tell you something." Abbie leaned forward, a tad unsteadily. "There was Randy flirting with me, and all I could think was, *Why is he doing this? What's wrong with him? How can he think I'm attractive?* That's what Abe has done to me."

"But Abbie—" Pi protested. "Of course he's attracted to you. You're beautiful. I mean, come on. If you don't believe that, what hope is there for the rest of us?"

"Oh, you're sweet." Abbie brushed long fingers through soft curled hair, and refilled their glasses. "I hope you don't think I'm a terrible lush, here."

"Of course not. You've had a stressful day. Your ex-husband showed up. People have been flirting with you. That's a lot to handle."

"But do you know what I mean about this? When you split up with Joe—Mike—what was that man's name?"

"Alan."

"—Wasn't your confidence shaken?"

"Well, I found out he was still sleeping with his wife, which I did find a little hard to forgive. That was a problem.—Oh my God. What have I just said? I'm sorry—"

Abbie started laughing, though. "Are you telling me you were the paralegal in this situation? I can't believe it!"

"No, it was different. They were already divorcing. Plus, you know, he was only about ten years older than me . . . Oh God. Help. Maybe I was the paralegal. Let's change the subject. I'm sorry."

"It doesn't bother me, Pi." Abbie reached a hand across the table and touched Pi's, briefly. "Really! As long as it wasn't Abe, I don't care. But let me ask you this. When you came up here, you were all closed up, closed in. I'm sure that Alan was still upsetting you then. But now, look at you. You're different."

"How do you mean? What's different?"

"You're glowing. Your face is alive. Have you met someone, Pi? Is it your prince?"

"Met someone?" Pi's face turned an unfortunate color and her voice, unusually for her, came out slow—stupid, even.

"Yes." Abbie watched her, puzzled. There was no reading that face, though, not now. It had ducked again behind layers of caution. "Is that a bad question? I'm sorry. Am I prying?"

"No, no." But the freedom in her movements was gone. "It's just—it's hard to say. It's hard to say. It depends what you mean exactly by 'meet.'"

Which was a mysterious answer, but not apparently one Pi was going to elaborate on, since a few minutes later she was making excuses and retreating to her room, saying she wasn't used to drinking so much on an empty stomach.

Re: Fuck, fuck, fuck
Dear Hamlet,
The feeling is entirely mutual, you know. Fondness, concern, regard, undsoweiter undsoweiter.

Your messages--doesn't that make you think of pieces of paper scrolled in a bottle? there should be a new word for them in this new paperless age--anyway, your messages are a locating factor in my odd life. That is a kind of irony, isn't it? There you are, apparently about to wander off into the wilderness, where the computer if you can hook it up will be your one familiar, predictable place. Whereas I am physically grounded in this house here, so I shouldn't need the computer to place me the way I do. But for various reasons I don't trust my environment here completely, so these messages of ours are an anchor for me, too. Crown and anchor me, as Joni Mitchell might liltingly croon, especially if I still had my tape collection to hear her croon it.

What I mean by that, Hamlet, is I have a lot of feeling for you, too. Even if I am an emotional dwarf. No disrespect intended to dwarfs there. I suppose that is a heightist expression, isn't it? You have to be careful with your phrasing in this day and age.

So: Fuck, fuck, fuck--as you yourself so succinctly put it. I'm sorry your space was invaded in such a gro-

tesque way, by Abbie Hoffman of all people. I'm ashamed
to admit I don't know much about Abbie Hoffman. Free
speech, long hair, a yippie, a hippie, a beatnik? It's
bad not to be clear about such things.

  Anyway what happened? What did you do? And, more to
the point even though it won't esp. show up here on-
screen--where are you?
Sylvia

Re: Wild blue yonder
Hamlet, my friend:
  I wasn't planning to write you again till you'd written back, but I'm afraid that plan has gone out the
window. You are apparently not there, wherever "there"
is (I feel a Gertrude Stein moment coming on), but I
take comfort in imagining that you are. I hope it's not
just that you're silently contemplating the sad fact of
my shared humanity with Abbie Hoffman and feeling that
all writers with sinister handles are to be avoided.

  I'd like to be able to write something comforting
about your having had Abbie H pounding on your head in
that city there, which for ease of reference I'm going
to go ahead and call Baltimore; but I don't know what I
can say without starting to sound like the same kind of
stalking fan he is. In fact this whole episode presents
a problem for me, don't you think? Doesn't it implicate
me in some insidious way? What I mean is, what's the
difference between me, Sylvia Plath, and him, Abbie
Hoffman, except that he lives in Baltimore and I don't,
and you now know he's called Steve and what he looks
like and you don't actually know what I'm called or
what I look like?

  I'm just thinking of that human hunger to see people
in the flesh. To press the flesh. Isn't it like my being thrilled the time I ate lunch in the same hotel as
Bette Davis? I was with my mother who'd come up to San
Francisco, and for an unremembered reason she wanted to

take me out somewhere Fancy, one of the Union Square
hotels. And who should be lunching there that day but
Miss "Fasten your seatbelts, it's going to be a bumpy
ride" Davis. My mother was very cool--all her "breeding" came to the surface--and she just leaned over and
said softly, "And if you look into the right corner by
the giant fern, you will see Bette Davis eating her
lunch." I swivelled around and it was true: in all
stillness and majesty, there she was, all alone but for
a Waldorf salad she was lunching on. It was all I could
do not to run up and ask her to autograph my martini
glass.

I'm digressing. What I'm wondering is: was Abbie
Hoffman/Steve's desire to meet you a simple hankering
after stardom? Or did he, as it sounds, want to tell
you his personal response to what you'd written? In
which case my worry is that I am not so different from
him, finally, with my ghost stories about Pinsk and my
insistence on sharing the dalmatian sequel with you.

This is too disturbing a notion to pursue. I'm going
to start feeling like some creepy Abbie Hoffman type
myself, even though I still don't know precisely who
Abbie Hoffman is. (He's somewhere between Allen Gins-
berg and Tom Hayden in my imagination.) So I'd better
take this opportunity to sign off, affectionately. But
not so affectionately as to alarm you--
Sylvia

Re: The Shangri-La
My very dear Sylvia,

You don't mind if I call you that, do you?

Hello from the Shangri-La, which does not actually
bear a great resemblance to my own picture of "Shangri-
La." I would have thought of "Shangri-La" as being, I
don't know, palm-filled, with happy breezes and
friendly faces. Kind of like Los Angeles, or the filmic
fantasy of Los Angeles anyway. A nice amount of green-

ery to run around, for the children and four-footed creatures among us.

In reality, the Shangri-La is a dump. The bed sags, the towels are made of crepe paper, the "free" soaps are the size and texture of bullets, and our neighbors are enjoying their own private but noisy Shangri-La La La LA, pardon my French, which is making it hard to concentrate.

Still, I've managed to sneak my white-haired friend in here against House Rules. He's under strict orders to be well-behaved and quiet, which he's complying with in the most sensible way by crashing out in front of the TV I have on loud to drown out the loud neighbors. I'm not really watching it, but I swear to God they just showed a video of the Rodney King beating again, because of the trial I guess. Can we ever get away from that damn video. The proprietor's probably taping it, he looked like the kind of guy who might watch it in his leisure time over a six-pack of Coors. I've now switched channels to something more restful, an old Western with guys shooting each other on dusty horseback. This can get me in the mood for my new adventure.

Re: Bette Davis, etc. I don't know. Maybe being hounded by my public will turn out to have been a good thing. After all it did get me out of my sister's house and who knows, if something hadn't gotten me out of there I might have become a permanent shadowy fixture in their home, doing domestic tasks for them till I was old and decrepit. One of them would become a famous scholar, the other a high-powered exec, and when people would come over and ask, "How do you two busy girls keep such a beautiful home?" the exec would answer, "It's my big brother. He never succeeded in finding a life for himself so finally we gave him one here. He wasn't good at cleaning his own apartment but we've found him very satisfactory, and he gets room and board in exchange so we don't feel we're exploiting him."

It is not to be, Sylvia. I have stalkers hot on my
trail so I am fleeing it all in Humbert Humbert-ish
fashion, but without the illicit underage sex to spice
up the chase. (My own travelling companion bears scant
resemblance to the luscious Lolita. Sadly.) I do have a
feeling of being pursued, partly because of Abbie Hoffman, partly because of "Sparky," my hot--or at least
warm, I'm not sure what his official status is--rental
car.

Abbie Hoffman, just so you know, was pretty well how
you imagined him. The real guy, that is. Noisy, rebel-
lious, into free speech, big curly sixties hair, cute
irreverent grin; author of "Steal This Book," which
among other things told people how to make Molotov
cocktails. He got into trouble for having a shirt made
out of the American flag, and he also had a quote I
always liked about freedom of speech being the right to
shout "theater" in a crowded fire. He was one of the
more surprising suicides, I felt. I think he and Jerzy
Kosinski went around the same time. It was one of those
stretches where lots of people you admire go down one
after the other, and your own mortality begins to feel
like a small drop in the bigger general bucket.

Re: the overall vexed subject of wanting to press
flesh. You may well be right that it's human, that hunger. It's just not what I was looking for. Probably I
have some deep-seated Problem with pressing the flesh,
generally. But if people strike you as famous--whether
they're Internet authors or the stars of classics such
as All About Eve--why in either case not leave them be?
I mean, look at you with Bette: you and your mother allowed her to lunch on serenely, you refrained from getting her to sign the martini glass, even if you half
wanted to. Similarly with me and the William Shatners
and Jack Nicholsons of my feverish imagination--I must
have some weird interest in these people, but I satisfy
it by sticking them into my dreams. A nicely uninvasive

approach, as it's no skin off any of their famous noses
to spend time in my head.

Sylvia, you have to believe me here: I didn't start
writing so people would want to meet me. I wrote because I had to; I had to put those words into print,
simply, frivolous though many of them were. OK, so I
did, I'll admit, want to see if there'd be an audience
for what I had to say. Yes I wanted people to read it.
I'd be an idiot, or a liar, to say anything else. But
wanting people to read you is emphatically not the same
as wanting them to knock on your door and ask you out
for a beer. Especially people like Steve. This sounds
terrible, because God knows I may seem like a lunatic
myself to respectable people, the hard-working single
mother secretaries or the Puffendorf followers. But
this Steve character, with his buttoned-up shirt and
nondescript shoes, his eerie, thin moustache and
butterscotch-colored hair--he had a glint in his eye
that I found disturbing. He seemed, in a Star Trek-ish
or maybe Star Wars-ish way, to represent the Dark
Forces threatening the Internet: the hidden pedophiles,
the stalkers, the schemers, the loons.

Not that I have to worry about him anymore. He ain't
heavy, and he ain't my brother. In fact altogether I
feel fairly burden-free now--I have that jazziness of
step that life in a car can give you. I'm sure you know
what I mean. It's forgetting, it's movement--that's
what's so joyous about life on the road.

And meanwhile, to interrupt my own lyricism: what
about you? What of you and yours? Any new visions of
young Martha you'd care to share with this Shangri-
La-er?

I haven't answered your "there" question yet. Do you
mind if I hold off on the specifics? "Shangri-La" is
as much as I feel I can say right now, and in a funny
way the Shangri-La is all of my universe, my microcosm
tonight in this room, where what makes up the place is

a simple small world--a blue night, a dead cowboy, a
sleeping dog, a finally quiet set of neighbors, a lone
man, a dove-grey computer, a worn bunch of bags, a
glitter of possibility, a low dread of nightmares, a
placelessness, a lack of fixed abode, a hope for a reply note, a spasm of affection, a warm taste in the
mouth, a sudden love of the small hours, a rare peace,
a tired eye, a faded light, a lateness, a delayed sentimentality, an understanding, a good night, sweet Sylvia, a good night.

Hamlet

Re: Shangri-La
Very dear Hamlet.
  Never mind about the there. Your words on the
Shangri-La were more than enough. And I don't mind being called dear, dear. Do you?
  So you've done it: cut loose, hit the road. I admire
you. That's what everyone thought I should do as a way
to get over my Loss. But I came here instead. To whales
and Martha and her mother and nonfat blueberry muffins.
Sometimes it's strange the turns a person takes, not
quite intentionally. (I was never that interested in
philosophical questions about intentionality, but maybe
I should have been: I've always had a random way of
making decisions in my life.) I didn't have a great
reason for coming up here, I just felt it would do me
more good than hitting the road. But see, I didn't have
a travelling buddy like you do. I'm sure I don't need
to remind you that my furred former companion is probably now ash. And it seems to me that a travelling buddy
makes all the difference; Lolita or not, you wouldn't
want to go through that alone.
  Also, you have a destination. Don't you? You are going, I'm guessing, from A to B. I, by contrast, would
have been travelling from A, through a lot of pretty
scenery and interesting backwaters, visiting far-flung

college friends across different landscapes and time
zones--merely in order to end up back at A again. Which
seemed pointless as a journey to embark on. Talk about
going in circles! And as we know, though I seem right
now to need to repeat it, there wasn't even an A at A
for me to come back to.

This is sounding weirdly defensive. I don't know why.
Maybe because there seems something passive about what
I've been doing--the gal thing of sitting around waiting for things to happen rather than the guy choice of
going out and making them happen. Or maybe I'm just
jealous of your Shangri-La, which despite your complaints about the frolicking neighbors sounds sort of
fun to me. I haven't been to a motel for years--since
an obscure time about four years ago, when I visited my
grandparents' graves in Sacramento.

It's funny--I haven't thought about this in a while.
Some delayed guilt had hit me about not having gone to
either of their funerals--they both died when I was
back East in college and too busy being self-absorbed
to come back for them. This later seemed callous and
bad. And it felt right to go to their graves alone, one
out of the blue day; it wasn't the anniversary of either of their deaths or anything. I think it was Presi-
dents' Day. I bought some not very lovely flowers at
the cemetery store there that sold all the accessories
you might need in such a place: cards, flowers, grave-
stones, veils. I spent half an hour trying to figure
out from the map where they were before I finally found
them. It wasn't the most peaceful spot in the world--
you could hear the freeway, which made me feel badly
for them, I mean imagine having to spend eternity listening to traffic noise--but there were some pretty
(parched) pine trees overhead, so at least they were in
the shade. As I'm sure you remember, in California
shade is everything. I gave them my chrysanthemums and
sat with them for a while. I told them I'd decided to

go to graduate school in philosophy. I don't suppose
they were that interested--these were my mother's parents, he was a doctor, she was a doctor's wife, though
a well-read one--but I think in a general way they
would have approved. They might have judged philosophy
a less obvious choice than, say, physics (they were
very pro my stepfather, who's a physics professor), but
they wouldn't have thought it was pointless navel-
gazing. I was glad to sit up on that dry hill and talk
to them about it. I cried, even. I found myself missing
them, for the first time in years.

And I stayed in a motel. It wasn't that long a drive,
I could have made it back to Berkeley the same day, but
I didn't feel like it. I was emotionally spent. You
know how that can be. I stayed in a place called the
Vagabond Inn, which seemed poignant to me in my heightened state, and I had an evening of thinking about families, and my mother, and then I watched cable shows I
couldn't watch at home. That's the real virtue of the
Shangri-Las and Vagabond Inns of this world, in my
opinion: cable TV. Do you have cable there?

One other fact about the Vagabond I liked. They
served "Continental breakfast"--complimentary Continental breakfast, I should say--which snobbishly I found
very funny, as it consisted of coffee in a thermos and
stale apricot danishes. I just couldn't imagine "Continental" people really recognizing this as their kind of
breakfast, but like I say that's a hoity-toity thought
on my part. "Hoity-toity" is the kind of phrase my
grandmother would have used.

Not that a close textual analysis will show that you
asked me, H, about my maternal grandparents, or for
that matter about the last time I motelled it. I'm
free-associating. Your specific question concerned the
young Martha, whom I've neglected to mention recently.
Let me try to redress the balance, and stop talking
about myself for one damn minute.

Martha. What can you write about Martha in the time
allotted, being careful to cite your sources?

Martha will be eight in a month, something she's
quite aware of because of course eight is a major step
up from seven. I loved those birthdays when you were a
kid, when each age seemed a whole great project: you
know, this is the year I'm going to figure out what being EIGHT is all about. It'll be a new plane of existence. Seven--seven will mean nothing to me soon, seven
is for little kids, seven is the past, eight is the future. (I don't know how old you are H but I recently
turned 31, a non-descript age if ever there was one.
There's nothing epic or interesting in 31.)

At a guess, I'd say Martha will be glad to put seven
behind her because at a guess, I'd say seven has been
the worst year of her short life so far. It's seen the
break-up of her parents, a cataclysm at any age; having
to change to a small coastal school, for reasons never
made clear to her; and sharing living space with an obscure fire-dimmed person, who all but burst into tears
one evening when she read the word "metaphysical" in
one of the girl's books. I've also recently learned
that another negative of life in exile here is the
missing of a grandmother-ish figure in San Francisco, a
babysitter/neighbor named Mrs. Delaney who taught Martha
how to play gin rummy and had pet birds that flew
around her living room.

On the plus side: She's learned some good stuff. Native American songs, at school; all about the Lorax, at
home, not to mention what Swooshing is; how to make a
coil pot, in a pottery class she's taking with her
mother. She also, as you know from the very beginning
of this e-pistolary friendship of ours, has learned
about life beyond the visible, and who's who on the
Other Side.

I hope such knowledge is a comfort to her now. You
know--sometimes knowledge helps, sometimes it doesn't.

Martha's father breezed by for a visit two days ago,
which as you'd expect has changed the arrangement of
the atoms in the atmosphere here. Since that night,
when Dad took Martha out for a double-dipped chocolate
fudge cone, which she came back with glued to the corners of her cute little mouth--the poor girl has been
moody and dour; while her mother has been, by contrast,
jumpy and excitable. I don't know where it will all
lead. (My guess is: back to San Francisco.) I hope that
while nerves are fraught and uncertain Martha may find
some solace in otherworldly places, or at the very
least from her books. It's what I used to do myself,
when the domestic going got tough. The age-old solution: read your way out of it.

    Is there room for this cluttered narrative in your
dove-grey computer? I wish I could honor the goodness
of your good night with something good of my own. But I
hope you'll trust and believe my less poetic warm
wishes, sent to you there in the Shangri-La land of
your dreaming.
Sxx

Re: The Sleeping Giant
Very dear melancholic Sylvia
    Oh listen, you're poetic too. Don't pretend for a
minute that you're not. You are poetic not least about
the fragile young Martha, her perilous journey through
seven into the hopefully more cheerful and vibrant
eight. Thank you for your long tale, for your local
color, for your maternal grandparents, for the flowers
on the grave. Thanks for the Continental breakfast.
Maybe one day I'll have one myself--but not I think
here at the grim Sleeping Giant, where I'll be lucky to
get some bitter chicory drink in the morning.
    I'm sorry if this will sound strange at first. I've
been driving. Entirely too much. Tomorrow I'll have to
do less. Driving is so odd. Do you find this? It's got

to be one of the most American activities around--right
up there with playing baseball and firing a handgun--
and yet it does strange things to your head. It may explain why we're such a fundamentally weird and paranoid
group of people: we spend altogether too much time in
our cars.

Today's drive took me someplace unnerving. Not just
through jungly dampness and accents murk-thick as the
bayou. Not just through improbable foods and unlikeable
insects, people who I didn't see and who didn't see me,
because in a car you're invisible.

The strange place I went to as I drove was the tangle
of suicide. It's a word I hardly use, in its simplicity. But sometimes it isn't a bad idea to look at a
thing directly, to look at it over the miles, the miles
and miles. The way driving lets you do.

I tried talking to my passenger about it, first. He's
a good listener. And I feel he has a right to know
where I stand on the issue, since he's so implicated in
the result should it happen.

What I told him amounted to this.

I wasn't kidding when I started to write my Diery. It
wasn't a big tease to get people going. Anyway, people
had already set up ED 536, there was a group of people
talking about suicide and books, making jokes in questionable taste about offing themselves and generally
airing that perpetual question depressives have on
their mind, namely how to keep going, how not to stop.
So that question wasn't one that came from me first.

But I was serious about it. I meant it. When I
started posting my now-infamous chronology I genuinely
thought it would be my way of writing to the end of the
line. And as you know (I said to my travelling buddy),
you smelled it in the air that night, being a perceptive dog--that particular night I was on the brink of
doing it. I would have done it--it seemed so simple, so
pure and inevitable--if it hadn't been for you, pooch.

You and my sister. Who, in her own short-haired way, had perceptive inklings too.

But now, now that I've written so much, something weird has happened to me, which believe it or not I never predicted. Namely--my Diery being public has changed me. Because now I somehow can't think about doing it. I don't honestly know why I didn't anticipate this. But here's the thing: I may be egotistical but I'm not an exhibitionist, and if ever I did off myself, my whole desire would be to go somewhere quiet and do it unobtrusively--no mess, no noise, so no one would notice. I understand the fallacy in this fantasy (no one would notice?); but what's the point of fantasies if there can't be fallacies in them?

Do you know what I mean by this, Sylvia? I'm changing voices here and talking to you. My driving companion answered my ramble in the way I'd expect from him--with the wisdom of silence. A slight whine of question, followed by the deep black eyes of affection.

But from you, of course, whoever you are, I might get more of an answer. So tell me something honestly, straight from your heart, wherever your real heart may be. When you used to read my words were you tuning in, voyeuristically, to see if I'd do it? Is that people's fascination with suicides, finally--to see if we gloom-mongers have the courage of our dim convictions?

What I'm trying to figure out is whether I am finally creeping out of the lightless pit I was in then, whether in some snakeish way I'm finally shedding that skin--the skin of those words, of those months of jokey jokes of despair. In which case, you see, I have an odd writerly qualm. I'm not saying this to be precious, you've got to believe me, this is something that truly preys on my mind. My qualm is, is everything I wrote before fundamentally untrue? Not about the dinner party at my sister's or the dying son and his mother--nor about my two dear comrades in arms, the director and my

co-opera-goer--but about what I started with, namely my
ambition to go.

Maybe this is the blind paradox a potential suicide
enters, once he gets trapped in the not-so-fun funhouse
of distorting depression. Not hinting about the feeling
is the wisest if your greatest wish is to go through
with it, because then you can do the job quietly, without anyone paying much mind. (That was Lili's point,
that afternoon on the phone.) Whereas if like me you
end up making a big song and dance about it--maybe even
out of some quiet suspicion that they won't let you get
away with it--it's all the harder to follow through.
Then you get trapped in a fear that you only mentioned
the despair in order to get some attention, which seems
so humiliating and shameful that the only way out of it
is to prove that you meant it--to stand up on the ninth
floor and do the swan dive to your death.

Have you ever contemplated it, Sylvia? Like--when you
first found out that the fire had eaten your life, did
the morbid thought of ending it ever cross your mind?

This is doubtless an insensitive question. If it
weren't for my junglesome surroundings here, I might
not be tempted to ask it. But we're at that stage in
our e-pistolary friendship, as you call it, where
there's no point in being anything but real with each
other. Do you agree? And this, right now, is the
"realest" thing I can write to you.

I am sorry, believe me, for the sheer weight of all
this. But I need to talk this through with someone, and
this is the only kind of talking I feel I can do, and
you're the only person with whom I feel I can do it.

Yours,
Hamlet

Re: The Sleeping Giant
Dear, dearest Hamlet.

There's something so reassuring about calling people
dear. It's not like calling someone "sweetheart" or

"darling," which seems so loaded. Dear's more old-
world; more timeless, more classic.

Listen. (With your eyes, I mean. Listen with your
eyes.)

Re: The Diery. First, I never tuned in to see if
you'd done it yet. It horrified me to think that you
might. I tuned in to find out what you'd say next.

Second, about your question, if I've understood it
right, whether in posting your suicide notes, in writing at large about your despair, you succeeded somehow
in writing your way out of it.

This seems possible to me. Why shouldn't it be? Isn't
writing an honorable escape route? Isn't writing your
way out of the pit better than shooting your way out of
it, or pep-pilling your way out of it, or pardon my
French fucking your way out of it? That's got to be the
whole point of being a writer, or one of them: that you
can turn your dark internal shapelessness into something crafted and worthy. If my professional perk as a
philosopher is being able to turn private quandaries--
what can I count on, and how can I count on it?--into
important discussible questions (not much of a perk,
admittedly, but it was enough to string me along), then
yours is being able to turn blood and guts into poetry.
Or narrative. Some kind of story other people will follow.

But this seems absent from your bayou-induced gloom of
yesterday (which I'm not trying to dismiss or belittle,
I hope you understand)--"this" meaning your acknowledg-
ment that you're a writer and hence exempt from more
standard character critiques. Exhibitionism and ego-
centrism have different meanings for writers, don't
they? I'm not saying writers are never exhibitionists,
of course they are--though personally I don't have much
time for the ones who coke-habit their way into the
gossip pages, behave as if they are movie stars, which
they emphatically are not. But as a piece of exhibitionism, I hate to tell you, the Diery has not scored

high: you never did clarify whether your mother tormented you with kitchen utensils, and you haven't told people which sexual positions you prefer. (Don't worry, I'm not asking you to name them.)

Egocentricity isn't a problem either. Here, I'll do a little philosophy for you to illustrate the point. Egocentricity of a kind is analytically part of being a writer. That's a Kantian phrase just meaning that egocentricity is inherent in the concept of "writer." Right? You have to be willing to look at yourself, or what's the point? If you can't be honest about yourself, why not be a journalist instead--or a philosopher for that matter. Writing seems to me one of the few professions which excuses a degree of self-absorption. (Maybe also acting: let's consult Meryl Streep on that.) Again to compare my situation: I might use philosophy--I have used it--as a way of giving verbal life to my private phantoms, and the philosophy I do might reflect something of my mind and my psyche; but I could never squarely use philosophy to look at myself. Which is just as well, since I'd much rather stand in the woods with my eyes wide open to the sky and think of the air and what's in it. Which, no doubt, explains in part why I'm an emotional dwarf, but that's a separate issue.

I'm getting into a polemic here, for which my apologies. But your words have prompted me to defend you against your new attacker--namely yourself.

Why shouldn't you write about feeling suicidal? Why is that any more dubious than writing about big white whales or sex with a thirteen-year-old? Incidentally, it's a good thing Nabokov didn't post Lolita on the Net, can you imagine the ugly flood of enthusiasm he'd have received in reply? The Steve equivalent for Vladimir would have been some overcoated individual knocking on his door, flashing photos of girls acquired in the underground slave trade.

Back to the point. I think your only real concern here is about having posted your words rather than hard-copied them safely into some clean well-lighted place to buy books. The degree of separation that old bound option offers would have earned you more privacy. Maybe next time you want to write out your weariness you should do it the old-fashioned material way, black ink on white paper. Though on the other hand, if you'd done it that way, I'd never have known about you. I'm still not going into bookstores: my own iconic book remains the only one I own. So if your conversation hadn't had this bodiless nature, there's no way I, for one, would have been able to partake of it.

All of which is paradoxical. Which reminds me of Zeno's paradoxes, which reminds me of Zeno, my cat that is, not the original Greek. Which reminds me of the fire which reminds me of your question: Did I ever, have I thought of it, have I wanted to, myself--? Has the ravenly thought ever nevermored its way across my bereaved mind, making me want to put paid to my life?

Only in an academic way. I don't just mean that as a bad pun, either. I remember one day after the fire, when I was walking around San Francisco feeling generally numb and bewildered, I did have a detached thought: "Some people in my position, presumably, would kill themselves. People have died for less." It was a rational assessment: some people would find self-slaughter the logical response to the loss of their livelihood, everything they cared about in a life that didn't happen to have kids or spouses to bolster it. But I had another thought twinned with that one: "Some people in my position would march right back into their department, meet with professors and students and advisers, and demand time, mercy, money; charity, help, comfort; so my philosophical life and career would go on." You see, people in my department were eager to help me. I don't know if I mentioned this fact to you before. I might have overlooked it in my eagerness to flaunt my self-pity.

Anyway, I wasn't having either of these responses. That's one reason I felt so icy cold the day after I talked to my former landlord, who called to inform me he no longer had any land to lord over. I was cold because I knew I couldn't do either brave thing: meet the fate squarely and charge back in there to fight it; or meet the fate squarely and commit self-slaughter in protest at the unfunny joke of the gods. I was cold because I realized--Oh God, Oh Christ, I'm going to have to live this new life somehow, for some poorly argued, inadequate reason: because a spark lit, a wind blew, a drought happened, fire-fighters went home one night, thinking they were done, leaving things smoldering; and the next day, all orange, burn, and heat, the fire woke and roared and chased us out of our lives. No reason at all for it. No good reason at all. It was--you know, at heart, this is what I believe--it was just one of those things.

So there's your answer, H. That I'm sending to you not knowing when and where you'll get it--in what state, in what lobby, with what neon sign flashing out-side above VACANCY. I hope you don't hate me for not contemplating suicide. I've done the done thing and read The Bell Jar, I find the subject as compelling as the next guy. But if it hadn't been for the Diery, I'd never have become a regular checker-in at ED 536. In fact I never went there for anything else, once I found the Diery. (Other people's writings did nothing for me.) I like the Dickinson poem that started it--well "like" is a feeble word, I mean it's a tiny mournful masterpiece--but it doesn't strike a deep chord in me. I feel almost shallow saying this. I feel like a Hall-mark card. Life is for living. Well. Isn't it?

Not for everybody--I realize that. The smartest kid in my high-school class, a beatific-faced young man named

John, who tended to get paired with me in math and English as the other big grade-achiever: he went off to an ivy league college, like I did. People expected greatness from him. He was also interested in philosophy. I'm mentioning John because John threw himself under a subway train when he was nineteen. Apparently he was under the influence of an Indian guru at the time; I never got the whole story. But when I heard about John, truthfully, I did not feel: Oh God, me too, I know why he did it. I felt: Poor John. Poor smart, troubled John.

Do you hate this? Maybe it's terrible to get a note from someone who doesn't have the bent to self-destruct. But as you mentioned, realness would seem to be important between us--if I can't tell you what's real, what is the point of our words?

Sending, if it's not too shockingly sentimental, love to you out in whatever wilderness you're in,
Sylviaxx

Re: Domino Lodge, in whatever wilderness
Very dear Sylvia,

It is shocking, yes. But there's a place for shocking sentiments in this world. Furthermore, thank you for the honest answer to my question. Probably I was assuming the land of suicide thoughts was one you'd taken a quick tour through at some point. But now I find it more comforting, oddly, that you haven't.

Sylvia, what a long strange trip it's been. And I'm only halfway there. I'm now on the cusp of that giant ten-gallon state, the one where everything is that bit bigger than you're used to. It's true, it's not just a story people tell. The first meal I had here--a plate of ribs, it's the kind of state that makes you go all carnivorous--seemed to contain the meat from a whole school of cattle. (Or is it flock? or gaggle? What word is it that dumb beef cows gather under?)

In truth I'm still getting over my brief pass through the Deep South. It was scary, Sylvia. For instance at the Sleeping Giant I discovered after I woke up (I'd pulled in under cover of night) there was a big old Confederate flag flying out front. This did not sit well with me, but I was too much of a coward to say anything. I paid my bill the next day like nothing was wrong, when the proprietor volunteered the fact that his policy was not to let colored guests stay there. He said this to me. To ME! Didn't he suspect I was a Yankee liberal whom such an idea would upset? He probably did. I don't know how I turned out so naive about such things. I must have inherited some of my mother's world-view, that this is essentially a happy land where people are nice to each other.

So I'm wondering. Is it too late for me to make this journey deeply symbolic of our collective history and the building of our nation on the foundation of slavery, which we try to suppress but which comes back to haunt us like the ghost of Hamlet's dead father? I know this is a new departure for us, e-pistolarily. Maybe it's knowing we may be electing a new Prez this year and being aware that the jolly Arkansan I'm likely to vote for, who's supposed to rescue us from eons of Reaganism, recently put a black man to death in his home state, a man with an IQ of 50 or so. He "had to" do it, we're told. Public opinion gave him no choice. Some public. Some opinion.

But enough about me and the fundamental division at the heart of this great nation! Let's talk about you.

You've written such depths about your life these days, and I've yet to return something worthwhile. But I do have one prediction. I think your one iconic book might prove to be the thin edge of the wedge of a new life of books. One book is a lot closer to many books than no books is. Do you know what I mean? Does this have any relation to Zeno's paradox about time?

Sylvia, what have you been doing besides not going
into bookstores? Tell me some stories.

Yours tripping on a high dose of beef ribs,

Hamlet

Re: Dominoes
Dear Hamlet,
   You asked me what I've been doing? I'll tell you.
   It's four in the morning, to give you the up-to-the-
minuteness of it. I can't sleep. Which is not so unusual these days, I've written you other letters at
2 a.m., generally when I've been up avoiding bad
dreams. After all this time I have started, though it
seems trite even to me, to dream about the fire. Usually I manage to rescue some objects, most commonly my
dissertation, from the flames. These dreams jolt me
awake, always at first with that horrible sweet relief:
"It's OK! My dissertation's saved!"--before I succumb
to the later dread of recognition. I can't believe
that this many months later I haven't gotten the message through my weak brain; that my consciousness
is still resisting the truth that it's all long
since gone. I'm losing sleep over it, at this very late
date.
   But today I seem to be losing sleep over something
else, something to do with present tense material.
Since you're not here I may as well tell you about it.
   Now I should say first that if stylistically this is
somewhat looser than usual (is it? One is not always
One's own best critic) I should go ahead and tell you
that we were sharing a drink together, me and the boss.
I do sort of think of her as my boss, which is not accurate. I think it's because it's been so long since
I've had a real boss--dissertation advisers aren't
bosses, they're like your parents, checking whether
you're presentable and well-spoken, hoping you'll make
them burst with pride at the upcoming recital. My ac-

tual boss in the advanced xeroxing position I hold in
this town can't remotely take himself seriously as a
boss so we have a postmodern relationship, a jokey pas-
tiche of the classic boss-underling dialectic. (He'll
say to me, "Miss P, how's that coffee percolating?
Would you care to bring me a cup?" and I'll respond
with something like, "Certainly, Mr. Tate, is my skirt
short enough for you today?") Whereas real, authentic
bosses give you specific instructions: "Jones, I want
that report on my desk by tomorrow morning." Or
"Piper, I want you picking my child up at 3 p.m. on
the dot, Monday through Thursday. Is that understood?"
Bosses are bossy. That's the whole point of them. My
dissertation adviser was never bossy. He was just silently full of expectation, which is different.

Maybe I shouldn't be talking to you about bosses,
given your past. God, put half a bottle of wine in me
and I'm tactlessness personified. I'm sorry. The only
reason I'm bringing up bosses now, Hamlet, is because
my boss has been flirting with me. I think. Maybe I've
even flirted with her. I did tell her that as a divor-
cee I thought she owed it to herself to start smoking,
because that's what divorcees are supposed to do and it
makes them irresistibly attractive. Perhaps this was an
overly flirtatious remark.

This diversion is going to open the whole ugly can of
worms that is modern-day sexuality--which, H, you and I
have thus far scrupulously avoided. But staying off the
subject is beginning to seem coy to me, so I'm going to
go ahead and mouth off to you about it. So to speak. I
hope you don't mind.

I don't imagine you'll be shocked by my mention of
sapphic undercurrents. After all, in this day and age
almost any girl worth her salt has at least tried the
soft option. Obviously, a certain bookshop-managing
sister comes to mind. Lord knows when I was in college
everyone was doing it--the movie stars, the daughters

of movie stars, the would-be movie stars, the sleepers-with-movie stars. (I never slept with that particular star everyone always asks about, but only because she never asked.) I had a serious sapphic love, an intense yearslong thing, in college.

What may be more shocking to you, my dearest H, is that I have the other kind of tendency too. Isn't that the darnedest thing? Before my life blew up in the fire--actually it ended just before the fire--I had this nice boyfriendy person named Alan. We took scenic walks on campus together, we did teenage things like make out in the bushes (this man was a junior professor! What was he thinking?), he made me tasty Indian dinners and we rolled around through the night together. Do you mind me telling you this? I promise I'm not going to get into sexual positions, the details thereof. Still, I realize I'm crossing a boundary here, stepping over a line in the electronic sand. Confiding something extra personal in you, dear impersonal Hamlet, who given the identity issues involved in this kind of medium are for all I know a woman, or a dog, or a drag queen, or two people, or from Azerbaijan.

Any of which would be fine. I'm not prejudiced in any way.

Can I tell you something about tending both ways in one's sexuality? Not in a self-piteous vein, I mean, just to keep you informed of the facts. Everybody hates you. I mean it. It's a curse. The lesbians hate you for obvious reasons: you're a sellout, even if a million of them are doing it too, and the other million are getting inseminated by anonymous syringes in lieu of the old-fashioned method. One gay friend of mine used to refer to Alan as "that person" while I was dating him. Occasionally the phrase "heterosexual privilege" got spat in my eye, which made me feel very Marxist and seventies.

Furthermore, your straight friends hate you because

it's too damned confusing. They've just gotten used to
being all supportive of your being gay and even pretending for your benefit that they've occasionally been
attracted to women themselves, boring you at great
length about the crush they had on their little league
coach when they were twelve. They've even come along in
cute tops to dance with you at gay clubs, to show how
cool they are, and then here you throw it back in their
faces by suddenly sleeping with the same kind of speci-
men they sleep with. It's irritating for them! Under-
standably. Plus, what if this now means you're
competition for the guys they're after? What if you're
suddenly not SAFE around their boyfriends, which was
the whole beauty of it previously because you didn't
need to be watched like a hawk every minute the way
straight girls did and now they're going to have to
start being all vigilant?

Even shrinks hate you for it. I know this because
contrary to popular belief I have in fact consulted a
shrink in my dark past, for a short while in the year I
was having a complete nervous breakdown about my
mother, not too long after she'd recovered from hers
and was spewing all kinds of bile at me for being gay:
blaming her breakdown on me, telling me it was worse
than if I'd been a heroin addict, undsoweiter undsoweiter. Fun stuff. I was quite fucked up at that point,
had various eating problems, basically got skinny and
cadaverous, which happened to coincide with my doing an
excessive amount of coke with a trashy babe I was dating at the time--do you want to know all of these sordid details? Probably not. All I'm trying to say is I
was seeing a shrink. And the shrink tried to untangle
my predilections, but once I mentioned I had both kinds
she hit the Freudian ceiling, explained it was all a
horrifically immature stage I was at of sexualizing
both parents blah blah and it was symptomatic of my
deep unease with myself blah blah and my inability ever

to make decisions in my life blah blah BLAH. Shortly
thereafter I did make several big decisions: to move
back to California; to stop seeing the trashy babe;
and, crucially, to stop seeing that shrink. A suitable
amount of time later I was enrolled in philosophy graduate school--and the rest is history. (Get it?)

And men. Men. Who knows what men think about the ambi-
sexual option? Perhaps, Hamlet, you'd care to speak
to this, in due course? I can't imagine you're of the
"I love it, if you'll let me watch" school, though I
have met various men of that ilk, they are not merely
a feverish invention on the part of lesbians. I
slept with a guy like that, before Alan. A poet. Wrote
erotica, don't you know. Mr. Erotica wanted gals like
myself to be aware of the male option. And basically
he was a nice guy, a considerate lover. Which is more
than you can say for some of the gals, it's a myth
they're all sensitive and lovely. Some of them are
brutes! Putting their hands in all kinds of inaccurate
places.

Is it obvious that I'm drunk?

I'm drunk. Hope that doesn't offend you. I snuck another bottle of Zinfandel into my cell here.

Anyway. Alan, just to continue with this fascinating
theme for another instant, didn't seem to mind. About
my Lesbian Past I mean. He was too mild-mannered to
care. He was just so friendly and mild-mannered sometimes you wanted to rub him all over with steel wool,
just to see him get mad. Rest assured I never did it.
Curiously, H, the man who seemed the most irked at my
change of allegiance was a gay friend, Ryan. Ryan was
full of doom and gloom, he insisted Alan was going to
go back to his (ex-) wife eventually. It turns out he
was right about that, but wasn't it weird of Ryan to
care?

I'm going to crash shortly. Me or the computer,
whichever goes first.

OK, here's the breakdown, Hamlet. I sense that it's time to sum up here, to present my closing arguments. In conclusion--

MEN have, to their advantage--

1. Height. Another heightist remark, but I love people being taller than me, which is all too rare in the girls because I'm nearly 5'9". Tallness is a gift. Be tall, and the world laughs with you; be short, and you laugh alone. A new saying. The New York erotic poet was tall and had strong, long limbs, and I revered him for it.

2. Cool shirts, that you can borrow if you're nice to them.

3. A more sustained interest in reading the newspaper, which is a relief after the mealy, self-obsessed conversations you're sometimes forced into with the ladies.

4. More aggression in bed, which can in its way be charming.

5. Cute feet, long hands, an endearing inclination to want to fix things when they're broken.

6. The knack of getting dressed quickly.

7. An appealing sentimental side that can make you want to kiss them though that embarrasses you both.

WOMEN, by contrast, have--

1. Breasts, which speak for themselves. (Bet you didn't know that did you?)

2. Soft skin, which is nice if you're very delicate and sensitive as I obviously am myself.

3. Superior capacity to gossip--an irksome or delight-ful trait depending on your state of mind.

4. Better bath products, which you can borrow.

5. The ability, when they're serious about something, to acquire a mystery in their eyes which can make any feminine face look radiant and beautiful.

6. Wombs, which have advantages and dis- that I don't need to list for you here.

7. An appealing sentimental side that can make you want to kiss them which in turn makes them very happy.

   That is my final word on the subject, Hamlet. I'd better go sober up. Please hurry up and get this, will you, in whatever damned state you're in? Since this is about the realest thing I've ever written in my life, with the possible exception of my no-longer-real dis-sertation, I'm eager to get some critical feedback. You're allowed to tell me I'm a monster. You're allowed to tell me that it's time for me to grow up. In short, you're allowed--you're encouraged, Hamlet, obviously, at this key point in the conversation--to tell me some truth.
Love
Sylvia

Re: Blue Moon Motel, whatever damned state I'm in
My sweet insane Sylvia,
   You make me laugh, you know, which may not be good for my digestion but is fun nonetheless. You've also given me plenty of food for thought to go along with

the food for stomach I just had--an uncontinental, un-
complimentary breakfast of a huge stack of pancakes and
oodles of fake maple syrup, in the motel's attached
coffee shop.

I'm getting slowly through the big state in small
hops: driving less per day so I don't end up exhausted
and killing myself in a car crash, which would be
ironic really after everything I've gone through. So it
was accidental that I got your message soon after you
sent it, I guess--I was sitting in my room reading it,
wired on coffee and sugar, while out in your state you
were probably passed out in a purple Zinfandel stupor.

Incidentally, I wasn't offended. By your louche behav-
ior I mean. As long as you are not my mother and about
to launch into melancholic confessions about my father,
I don't care how much you drink. In fact, while you
were good enough to express infinite tolerance for
whatever my "real" identity may be behind the electronic mask, I think we have hit on one serious boundary problem for me: if you did turn out to be my
mother, it could be the end of a beautiful virtual relationship. I just wouldn't experience the same degree
of trust and openness. Sorry, Mom.

However. Let's assume that you're not my mother. The
biographical details you've revealed so far, if true,
do not square with my mother's; certainly if Sally has
had sapphic episodes it's news to me. Though she, unlike your mother by the sound of it, has generally been
pretty chipper about my sister's choice of lifestyle.
There was a short blip at first when she ran around
saying Cindy had unresolved anger at my father and that
was why she was going for girls, but eventually she realized we all had unresolved anger at my father, not
least Sally herself, which made that a poor argument.
By now she's fine with Jane, we have Christmases together from time to time and everybody's incredibly
L.A. about it, exchanging lots of hugs and respect and

lines like "I'm just glad to see you so happy, honey."
My mother scored highly the first time she met Jane, by
which point Mom had had a few years to adjust and join
P-FLAG and everything. Sally got bonus points by giving
the girls her room to sleep in, which had a waterbed in
it. Can you believe it? I mean, can you believe my
mother was that generous but also can you believe she
still had a waterbed? They're so seventies. They're
like lava lamps.

Onto the subject of sapphic love in your own life. My
feeling is: I love it, if you'll let me watch. Just
kidding. Though since we're on the subject, I have to
tell you a shameful story of sapphanalia one night at
the girls' Baltimore pad. What happened was just this:
I went down to the kitchen late at night in search of
snacks, rather quietly evidently as I caught the gals
there in mid-smooch. Not mid-peck, not mid-sisterly
hug, but mid-SMOOCH, something certainly involving some
wetness and tongue action and raunchy hands beginning
to wander. This was weird for me, to say the least (Big
Brother is watching you!), and all the more unsettling
as I discovered it turned me on. HORROR. Cin was
clearly freaked out too but Jane just said, "Hi, luscious!", cutely, on seeing me, and "Night, luscious!"
when I promptly retreated. And I think we should draw a
veil over the rest of that solitary evening of mine upstairs.

So. You are not a monster. You are [Elephant Man
voice to be employed here] a Human Being! I mean, re:
the Victor/Victoria predilection--you're not saying anything Sigmund didn't say years ago, are you? Even if
you find little public endorsement of bisexuality as a
way of life, the Herr Doktor said it was the natural
order of things. So just wave a copy of his works at
people next time they harass you about it.

I particularly enjoyed your comparative list--some of
which seemed familiar to me, some of which was fresh

and original. For instance, I hadn't put together the
toiletries argument for myself, but I can see where
you're coming from there. My own bath products at home,
back when I had a home, were always very distasteful to
someone like Lili. (The sleepovers were too polite to
mention it.) Lili used to say that Dial soap and Prell
shampoo were not good enough in the enlightened consumer age of the nineties, but I told her Minsk had
never had any complaints. The Prell especially got to
Lili. How could I explain to her the appeal of using
the same shampoo I've been using since I was 12? Plus,
that green color--who can resist it? Lili buys shampoo
made of coconut bark and lime juice, exotic island in-
gredients--I checked the next time I was at her place.
Nowadays my bath products all come in handy dwarf-sized
portions, one of the free pleasures of life lived in
motels.

As far as I'm concerned, if people want to go forth
and multiply, they can go ahead and get together the
old-fashioned way as you call it, Adam and Eve style.
If it's companionship they're after, then why a man
should be preferable to a woman or a dog or a drag
queen or someone from Azerbaijan is unclear. Companionship would appear to come in all shapes and sizes, no?
From handy mini-samples to industrial-size. And similarly with sex partners--I'm not trying to set up a
lewd joke about sizes here, actually I was more wanting
to point out that variety's a fine thing, different
strokes for different folks . . . No, it's no use, when
you get into the territory of sex talk it's innuendo as
far as the eye can see.

Now, re: sex. I mean, sex qua sex. The stuff itself,
the grunting and thrusting. For me, just to get up
close and personal for an instant, which is about how
long I can stand to: Well, it's a great institution,
and I love it, but I seem to suffer a willed amnesia
about it all immediately afterwards. At heart, I'm a

falling asleep a nanosecond later kind of brute, terrible to admit, which is why on a generous, open-hearted night I do my sensitive man routine first (Mr. Erotica's got nothin' on me, bud)--because otherwise my sex partner will merely be stuck, poor thing, with a dead weight in her bed for the rest of the night.

But I'm not completely clear whether it was sex or love you were talking. My own take on the love question --which since we've done God, fathers, and suicide, was bound to rear its vexed head one of these days--is: If so, why, yes. If not, why--Not.

What I mean is I wish people would acknowledge that Not is a viable option. I'll let you in on a trade secret. I do occasionally read the postings in ED 536. You've had a chance to figure that out, I guess. Anyway, that whole series about "Should JD get a love life?" I found irritating. Why confuse depression with loneliness? They're very different kettles of fish. (Another iffy phrase in this context, but one I've always enjoyed.) Suicidal yearnings or no, I'd like to insist that I am within my statutory rights in choosing to live as a bachelor.

After all, there have been some notable bachelors in history, haven't there? (Not only suicides . . .) Franz K was a bachelor--and what's good enough for Franz has got to be good enough for me. It used to be a perfectly respectable choice, and not only in England I mean where probably they were all privately entertaining young boys in their homes and reliving the sexy floggings of their schooldays. People didn't used to bug guys for going the bachelor route, or gals for doing the spinster thing, living with their sisters with whom they'd open riding academies or run the local branch of the Salvation Army or what have you. They just became "old Mr. Baines" or "old Miss McGillicuddy," and everyone would wave at them on the street and children would bring them candy and their pet dogs would be the favorites of the neighborhood. That's how it was, wasn't it? I grew up in the same Norman Rockwell fantasyland as Ronald Reagan, obviously.

The point is I've had girlfriends, and they have never really done it for me. It's like in the eighties when various people were doing a lot of coke. As you yourself were, Sylvia, apparently. I tried coke and it never did much for me either, except make me twitchy and broke. The effects, I have to admit, are uncannily similar.

Now it's true that the girlfriends I've had have mostly been short-term. Once in college I went out with someone for a whole year. A pretty, slight, doll-like woman who had a steely intelligence under her floaty hair and skimpy dresses. She was cool, and beautiful. I had a lot of fondness for her, and she was attractive, God damn it, in a murderous way. Less attractive was the difficulty she had which emerged after a while: a difficulty in sleeping exclusively in my bed. She sampled Krieger's too, for instance, and it was hard to have the same je ne sais quoi joie de vivre Chanel No. 5 for her after that. Don't even bother to pardon my French.

Not that I'm a Frailty thy name is woman guy either. I did dump her soon after the discovery about Krieger, it seemed the only way to salvage some pride, but I might have done that in the end anyway. She was too clingy. She was too all around me. It was like her arms and hair were wrapped around my head and I couldn't breathe. And this in a woman who was notoriously independent, feminist, and doing her own thing, viz. the sampling of alternate beds. Some local expert in female psychology like my roommate Lars said she did it to make me jealous and pull me back in, but if so it backfired. She dated Krieger for a while after that, which had a mercenary, twisting the knife in the wound feeling to it, but he soon left her for his Hedda Ga-

bler of the time and I will admit to experiencing a
small thrill of delight about that. He and I managed to
stay on course with each other without exchanging much
but some unkind remarks about her hair, and the whole
thing blew over.

It is not like Krieger is so different from me in the
love department; he just dates people for longer than
me. I too am serially monogamous, but each relationship
only lasts two weeks. He dates them for a year at a
time and they get all serious and occasionally move in
together and then he goes to a theater festival in Con-
necticut or Vancouver and falls for someone else there
and the cycle starts all over again. But people don't
seem to make the same tsking noises over Krieger they
do over me. Why is that? Maybe because Krieger is a director and it's assumed he knows what he's doing,
whereas I am unemployed and it's assumed that I don't.

Who knows? Maybe I'm wrong and one day I will surprise myself, and she'll surprise me, and we'll surprise each other, and some sort of love thing will
ravage me. I mean, while strenuously defending my right
to remain a bachelor, I have to say it's not like I'm
against coupledom in principle. Not at all. I don't
necessarily see it as the pinnacle of human achievement, but I can see it has its charms. It's not like I
don't weep in the movies where the guy and the gal finally get it together after the hundred obstacles and
hardships that have kept them apart. It's just when I
look ahead and imagine me, JD, in the future (a novel
idea, in any case, and one I'm still getting used to),
I literally can't see it. I can't see me speaking those
very ordinary throwaway lines: "Honey, I think we're
running out of bran flakes, we'd better stock up"; or
"Did you set the machine to tape the movie while we're
out at the Finkelsteins'?"

That's my thinking on the question for the moment,
Sylvia. Hope it's as true as you were hoping it would

be. I have to go put some miles between here and the
next place, with the combined horsepower of all three
of us--me, Sparky, and Minsk. Imagine us in one of
those comedy buddy movies; and I'll imagine you in your
tallness and hangover, bathing in superior bath products, while that fond shade of mystery lights your
bright eyes.

Hamlet

Re: The morning after
My very dear Hamlet,
    You are so right. I do have a hangover. A headache. A
nausea. And an embarrassment, for I have a feeling it
was highly indiscreet, whatever nonsense I sent you.
Luckily for me I didn't save a copy of it, so I'll
never have to know the gory details.
    I've just woken up and read your reply. It was humane
and canny, as usual. You have a way of writing about
things that makes my own writing to you seem thin and
dry, like some sort of health wafer. I like your story
of bachelorhood and spinsterhood--who knows, maybe Reagan was right after all and that Norman Rockwell world
really is still out there. If so, you're the guy to
find it.
    Your letter of love and not love also reminded me of
an obscure book I studied in college, which I will
briefly mention in order to recoup some dignity after
last night's rant. It was by a Russian formalist writer
in the whenevers, teens I guess or twenties, Battleship
Potemkin era, called Viktor Shklovsky. He was exiled in
Berlin along with other Russians at the time for some
obvious historical reason that escapes me, and the book
consists of all these lovely letters he wrote to his
beloved about Berlin and his life and observations and
philosophy. It's called "ZOO, or Letters Not About
Love," because his beloved had forbidden him to write
to her about his love for her.

This, in any case, is neither here nor there--a
phrase that has a nice aptness these days. And speaking
of which, I can't help being aware that having been
writing me from There all this time, you are getting
closer and closer to Here. Does this fact strike you at
all?

Hamlet, will we ever meet? Is what I am wondering.
Yours,
Sylvia

Re: Figments and figmentation
Hi again Hamlet.
I know. It hasn't been long. Just a day! A day in which
you did your lone-starred miles and saw the lone-
starred sights--you, Sparky, and Minsk. I'm not surprised if you didn't have time to write.

But I'll confess something strange about not hearing
from you. It has caused some old neuroses of mine to
come flickering to the surface, like so many goldfish
at breadcrumb-feeding-time. The neuroses in question are
ancient, primal ones, ones I used to have about my
mother for example, back when I was a troubled child of
divorce. It's the most basic fear I'm talking about
here, the What if something has happened to you? fear.
It happens when you get a fake sense of premonition
about someone--you start reading all sorts of signs and
think you know they're in trouble.

And this silly anxiety has led, domino-style, to a
whole series of other doubts. Namely: How would I know
if something had happened to Hamlet? Who would tell me?
Who in his life even knows I exist? Which led to: Well
it works the other way, too--who in my life (besides
Martha) knows he exists? And then, what if he doesn't
exist? A disorienting thought occurred to me: what if
you were a figment of my imagination all along? Worse,
what if you're a collective hallucination by us sad
people in ED 536 who are trying to create some writer-

hero figure? Such spiraling suspicions are what happens
when you lock me and my imagination up in a room together, with nothing like a philosophy book to keep us
all occupied.

This may seem incredibly offensive, of course. I might
get touchy if someone started to doubt my existence.
But recently I've been having some "issues" around
doubt, as we say in California. I've been wondering how
we know when we're sure of things--and feeling unconfi-
dent that I've got a grip on the answer.

I know that you're out there. I feel sure that you
are.

Nonetheless, as an idealist philosopher who lacks
practice and encouragement in her craft--or maybe as
someone who's gotten out of the habit of trusting my
metaphysical instincts--I wish there were a way you
could give me some small proof. I know this gets me
dangerously close to the Abbie Hoffman category of person, and I am worried about the impact such a question
may have on you, but I have to ask again.

Is there any way we might ever meet?

Yours,

Sylvia

Re: Figmentation

Dear Sylvia,

This one will be a hard one for me to write. Believe
me.

I've moved beyond the lone star state now. I'm in the
southwest. Where peach and teal are the preferred decorating colors, and it's possible to get damn good beans
and rice and cerveza.

I'm sorry my not writing put some doubt into you.
It's weird, isn't it, the effects these electronic
words have on our hearts and minds? One day someone
will have to come along and philosophize about how this
medium is changing human relations. Maybe in fact it

will be you, Sylvia, who will do that. That seems to me
a suitable post-fire project: detailing the shape of a
new world mediated for us through electronic lines; a
world where presence and absence are shifting their
meanings. What do you say? I have no doubt you could
write a hefty NY Times bestseller on the subject. The
Metaphysical Touch: How our hearts and minds are now
moved by beings unseen. Getting global and millennial
about the new kinds of existence. You might include a
passing reference to the great Puffendorf somewhere in
it. I think the time is right for this, Sylvia. It'll
be big. The kind of thing that will get you profiled in
People.

Part of your book, I imagine, might be an exploration
of those doubts that you mentioned. Doubt's your department as a philosopher, isn't it? For myself, I want
to tell you an important fact: Yes, I am here. Wherever
here happens to be. That is to say--I exist.

But, Sylvia. This is difficult. I don't think our
Heres should collide. Not materially, anyway. You'll
think I'm a coward, maybe--it's perfectly possible I am
one--but I don't feel a face-to-face meeting would be
right. But saying that is, at least in my twisted mind,
a way of valuing our connection in print. That's how it
seems right to me--knowing you in this way. I like the
way you exist for me here. I do incidentally keep copies of all the letters you've sent me, they inhabit
their own neat Sylvia file; so while you might not have
a copy of your rant about love, I myself have it to own
and re-savor. I'm a big believer in print, you know--as
you obviously are too, fire or no fire. (Come on. You
know you are.) A very bad song from the seventies or
possibly early eighties comes to mind here. "I like you
just the way you are." That bad song itself is all
about hair-color and so forth, but for me it means: I
like you this way. In words.

It gets worse, though. I am trying to make a great

change, Sylvia. There are many flippant things to be
said about a move West; I myself have said several of
them. But there are some serious things too, and one of
them is--I think I need a period free from the computer. If life is for living, as you my very dear Sylvia did say yourself, then it may be time for me to
unplug for a while.

  Not necessarily forever. No no no! I don't want to
rob myself permanently of you, my comrade in words.
Just for a while. While I rebuild a life for myself.
And you write your metaphysical masterpiece. And one
day again, someday, our letters, our words will meet up
again. And more pleasure can be had again from this
sweet meeting of minds.

love.
Hamlet

Re: Letter not about love
Hamlet--
Re: Your last. You're not really going to unplug, are
you? Forsake this world of print?

  Even if we don't meet, Hamlet--and I'm sorry, maybe I
was wrong to suggest that to you, maybe hopes of pressing the flesh are always misguided--that doesn't need
to mean an end to all this, does it? Are you really
issuing that old cliche, you of the vivid, new shaping
of language: We can't go on meeting like this?

  Surely this flesh, this collision of Heres--this metaphysical touch--is a right one. But then, I can't speak
for you. Obviously I can't speak for you; I can hardly
speak for myself, given the silence of this medium. But
I can write this to you: it is these words, dear H,
that have given me faith in the world again. Fuck it,
I'm just going to say this now. What's the point in being coy? I will tell you how it is: my head and heart
were all dead till I read you. I'd lost the point of
the storyline. No, I wasn't close to ending my life,

that's not how my temperament goes. But my mind, usually so full and busy, was empty and quiet, and it was
hard to recognize myself in that state. I didn't know
where I was; I didn't know where I could go. Then I
read some poetry. Then I read you. Then I read Hamlet,
and the Lorax. And then I read you some more; and I
fell for that person in print.

Was it the ghost of Pinsk who said, "Isn't learning
to read each other one of the main tasks?" How right
he was. I have felt, for the first time in--oh, let's
say a mythical amount of time, some great quantity of
time, since I breathed my first library--that I've
found someone, your princely self, who was able to read
me. And, at the risk of sounding vain, I thought I had
the same relation to the words you were writing, i.e.
to you.

Was I wrong about that, Hamlet? Was that a delusion?
I can drop the idea of meeting you; really, consider it
dropped. I have no desire to be like Steve Palin, make
you recoil in horror. Only tell me, please, Hamlet,
that you won't cut off our words.
Yours with love
a girl known as
Pi.

But, to her blank amazement, when Pi later checked in, she found her own
letter bounced back to her. Along with the computer's few cold words of rejec-
tion.

BAD ADDRESS FILE. MESSAGE RETURNED.

SHE TUMBLED THROUGH THE DOOR EXPECTING DARKNESS AND NOTHING, ONLY to find lightness and someone. It was Pi. She was still up, solemn in blue jeans and tube socks, pensive at the kitchen table.

"Hi!" Abbie's voice sounded overloud, even to her own ears. She suspected her face was probably the worse for wear. "I didn't expect you to be up."

"I couldn't sleep." Pi seemed sheepish. "I didn't expect you to come home."

"On a first date?" Abbie said. "On a first date that will probably also be a last date?"

"Didn't it go well?"

"No. It did not really go well, no." Abbie began to unpack herself from her dinner-date clothing and then stopped. "You know what? I feel like going for a walk, to clear my head. Do you want to come?"

Pi straightened, a little hopeful, a little more alert. "Well sure. I'd love to. Is it OK to leave Martha?"

"It's so late," Abbie said, smothering her mother-voice. "I'm sure she's sound asleep. We'll just go around the block or so. We'll only be a minute."

Abbie changed from restaurant shoes to boots while Pi stood and stretched, cat-like, and found an old leather jacket to shelter her from the elements. It had been Abe's, which made Pi reluctant to accept it as a hand-me-down until Abbie told her she looked dashing in it, like Amelia Earhart. That convinced her to wear it.

The night yawned dark and cavernous as the inside of a whale. They might have been the only two swallowed by it, so empty were the small town's streets, so thin the lights that gilded a few spare houses. Abbie took their path out towards the headlands, instinctively—down the brief stretch of road that led out to that edge.

Pi asked her about the date. Abbie gave her nice version first: Randy was a good guy, bright, self-centered maybe but not in a terrible way, and in fact that had made it easier for her; it meant she didn't have to talk as much. They just didn't quite hit it off. With some encouragement from her lodger, Abbie went on to admit she had found him a bit boring, maybe even irritating, the way he'd gone on in a near monologue about himself and his troubles. Finally, her housemate probed further, and Abbie spilled into a short diatribe.

"Well, you see—" Her hands moved like pale fish through the dark air. "It turns out that poor Randy is getting over a heartbreak, too. He was jilted by his ravishing young girlfriend, who threw him over for someone her own age instead. But instead of just admitting that this is upsetting him, he turned our delicious Beaujolais dinner into a complaint about the whole *system* which sets men up to think younger women are the greatest acquisition, conferring the highest status. You see this conspiracy causes misleadable people like Randy to fall into a *trap* of trying to please these younger women, when really they should be looking for a mature, grown-up relationship with someone they can *respect* (this is where I got a meaningful look, which I was supposed to find flattering), who's had lots of experiences in her life (this was where I felt very aware of my wrinkles) that she's eager to share with someone else (not that he ever got around to asking me much about my life, that would wait for another day). And furthermore—this was the best part!—he has come to realize how important it is to find someone who understands that a deep connection goes beyond the purely physical."

"Which you presumably would have transcended by now, given your great age and experience?"

"I think that was the idea." She laughed. "Actually, it's funny. Sort of. After all, the food was good. And he chose a nice wine. He drank most of it, but what I tasted was delicious."

"That's no doubt something his younger girlfriend wouldn't have been sophisticated enough to appreciate."

"Probably not."

"Oh my God!" Pi stopped in her tracks. "I know about him. I know about this man! His young girlfriend—Claudia—is currently dating my boss."

"What boss?"

"Xander. The guy at the Xerox store. You know, he's told me about Claudia's ex—Xander's not the most discreet person. Under cover of the Canon's loud noises, he's told me all kinds of intimate things. He likes to talk to me about sex, basically. It's entertaining. Anyway, so this Randy apparently—well. I don't want to put you off."

"It's too late. I am already off. He did it himself."

"He was into some kind of mild SM. Restraints, I guess, mostly. And Claudia wasn't. It all got too heavy for her, according to Xander."

"I thought there was some glint in his eye. It doesn't surprise me. So are the young lovebirds happy together? Tell me they are."

"They're very cute together. Xander's a sweet guy. He's teaching her to fast. That's his idea of a good time. Their first major date was a weekend camping down in Van Damme State Park, doing a carrot-juice fast and taking a five-hour hike together. She looked a little pale when they got back, but Xander said it was excellent."

"So they're happy?"

"They seem to be. They can hardly keep their hands off each other. The Xerox store has become a pretty steamy place to be. It gets awkward sometimes for us deep types, who are less interested in the purely physical."

"You don't need to put yourself into the same retired category I'm in, Pi. It's polite of you, but age-wise you're closer to juice fasts and paralegals than great reams of experience."

"I wasn't being polite. I was just trying to establish the fact that I, too, am on the side of sophistication and transcendence."

"Oh, I've never doubted that. Not for a minute."

They walked on into the crash and the cavern. They were nearing the sounds of the water, which rolled and rocked and soaked the air with fresh fictions— siren calls and Nautilus, talking dolphins and mermen. Tales old and new flickered beneath the invisible black waves. From where they stood it was everywhere, the sea—they couldn't see it, but they could feel and hear it, and smell it in the loud wild fragrance of its wave breaks.

"Do you want to walk off the road?" Abbie asked. "Take one of the paths?"

And Abbie led them farther onto one of the winding grassy paths, towards the noise and the salt, the froth and the majesty. It wasn't something Abbie would usually have done; she had her own fears in the dark, along with a voice in her ear worrying that her daughter was at home alone, and though a note was left and the door locked, they shouldn't linger, they should go back soon. But before she turned back around, Abbie had a strange urge—not for her own sake but somehow for the sake of her housemate, her au pair and her lodger: her niece's friend who maybe, by now, was her friend too. Abbie wanted to take Pi somewhere out of herself, out of whatever pessimism had shrouded her face by the kitchen table. She wanted to bring Pi into the expanse that was a night's moment by the cliff-edged sea: when all that was small became smaller, the Randys and Alans subsided into the sanded ebb, and only what was great would be left on shore. Whatever was great in Pi—and Abbie didn't know her well enough to know what it was—must meet this air and ocean and help her spirit leave its private cage. Abbie believed that was what the sea was for, to uncage you. For herself, her most obvious greatness was her love for her daughter; that was what was purest within her, and the only passion big enough to brave the night's unstarred scrutiny. If there were other greatnesses within her, she didn't know about them yet, though she might still learn to discover them.

Martha's dreams had not been kind.

They had tempted and teased her so she awoke not knowing which parts of them were fiction and which true. Sometimes her dreams righted the world completely, taking her back to San Francisco before the bad summer. Sometimes her father tucked her into bed. But once she found her father and Pi in the kitchen, in embrace. That one was a nightmare.

The morning after her father had come on his surprise visit to Mendocino Martha had a moment of startlement. Did that really happen? But she knew it must have because her hands were still sticky from the chocolate ice cream cone.

And now. Tonight. Was she dreaming now that there was no mother above her head? The girl's instinct was that some order was all wrong. The house felt black and hollow, like the fearful pit at the base of her stomach.

"Mom?" she called out into the echoing hall.

There was no answer.

"Mom?" she repeated. "Pi?"—a sharp anxious call like the gulls'.

Again, no answer. Martha crawled back into bed and hid there, staring at the invisible ceiling. *Maybe she's just gone outside for a minute. She'll be back soon.* Some guardian voice, like the memory of Mrs. Delaney's, tried to calm her panicking heart.

There was one thing Martha had recently been finding a comfort in when she had trouble or worry in the middle of the night, which happened too often now. She added to the story she was making up about Zeno and Pinsk. At school she was drawing pictures to go along with the story. But she had kept it a secret from her mother and Pi. Her ambition was to make a whole small illustrated book—her teacher was going to help her with the writing—and then present it to her mom, all at once, a surprise. A whole book! Written by Martha.

> The Ghosts of Pinsk and of Zeno the Cat
> One day Zeno the cat was sitting perched on a tree. Sitting next to him was his friend Pinsk the black poodle. You may think it's strange that they were in a tree, like birds, but they were ghosts and ghosts have a different set of rules.

She had drawn a picture of two black creatures sitting on a tree branch.

> Suddenly Pinsk saw an old friend of his down on the beach. It was Hamlet! Pinsk flew down to meet him on the sand. (That's another thing about ghosts—they can fly.) Once he got to the beach they had a big reunion.

A picture of a blue line of ocean, and a person and dog walking on the beach.

> Pinsk and Hamlet started playing a game. It was called "Fetch." But instead of Hamlet throwing the stick, Pinsk threw the stick for Hamlet! Like I said, when you're ghosts you follow a different set of rules.

This picture needed work. It wasn't completely clear. The guy held a dark line (it was a stick) while the black dog-creature sat on the left of the picture.

> Suddenly the sky got dark. It started to rain. The cats and dogs had to stop what they were doing. They had a job to do. They had to get up in the clouds to make the storm happen. And what did Hamlet do when it rained?

So far, this was as far as she'd gotten. She couldn't yet answer that question. The fun thing about its being private was it kept her in a kind of state of suspense. She started to look forward to the nights to see what ideas she'd come up with next. It was almost like reading a book by someone else. However. It was getting complicated, keeping the different stories straight. By now there were so many different ones to keep track of: her own about Zeno and Pinsk; the new Narnia one her mother was reading to her at night; and sometimes, though Pi told her less than she used to, what was happening with Hamlet and Minsk in another state somewhere. Then there was the other story, the true one. About what they were going to do: whether they'd stay here or go back.

Martha knew perfectly well that decisions were hanging in the air, waiting to be made. You'd have to be an idiot not to feel it. You could hear people holding their breaths when she came into the room. Looks were obviously being exchanged over her short head.

The girl still had stomach-clutching moments when she suddenly believed, was suddenly absolutely *sure*, her mother and father were getting back together. That would explain why her father had come up here, taking her out for her favorite kind of ice cream. As he watched her eat, her father had asked her:

"Sweetheart—do you ever wish you and Mom could move back to San Francisco?"

Martha's heart had stopped.

"I don't mean back into the house," he said quickly. "I just mean—your mother and I have talked about you two finding a new place to live back in the city. That way, you see, sweetheart, I could see you more often. Which would make me very happy. What do you say about that, pumpkin?"

She, to play it safe, had shrugged and hadn't answered him. Like what happened didn't make much difference to her one way or the other.

Because there was a steely side of Martha shaping up, too. There had to be. She had figured out last summer that you had to learn to be very calm and accept everything because there was nothing you could do about it. You couldn't change what went on. This steely side of Martha had a different interpretation of her father's visit. *They're not getting back together again. Forget it. This is just one more of their weird changes of plan.*

Not that anyone ever felt it was important to give her a good explanation of what was going on. It infuriated her. It was like last summer—all the best information ended up coming from Mrs. Delaney, who would explain things to her that her own parents just skipped right over.

Martha wondered whether the parallel person in this set-up was Pi. Pi, even if she seemed distracted these days, might actually tell her some of the things she wanted to know.

So she prepared her questions. She'd ask her one afternoon on the way home in the car, where Pi couldn't hide or run, where she'd be trapped into answering.

Pi, Martha would say, to get her attention.

Mmm? Pi would be vague, watching the road.

Can you please tell me what is going to happen?

A LIGHT TOUCH ON HER NECK. A TASTE. A SMALL, COOL THRILL. AND THEN A strange, almost primitive sound: buffalo on the horizon, a faraway moondance. Abbie looked around with some wildness in the purply air—Pi was near her, but not right beside her, and she was facing in a different direction, towards the sound of the drumbeat. Another touch, and another, on her cheek, which felt damp.

It was raining.

First softly: a spring melody that blended in with the sound of the ocean and brought out the sweetness of the headland grass. Then it became heavier. Then it became very heavy. Soon it was pouring, a hard and serious April rain that was determined to drive out drought memories and leave the world muddy and renewed.

"We'd better go."

"Let's go."

"I'll follow you."

They made a cautious way back to the road, and on the road the wetness turned absolute and cold and no longer something to be savored.

"Help! Can we run back?"

"Yes!"

They ran. And there is that particular unbridled pleasure in running in the rain, if it's not to catch a bus or desperately to avoid a ruined hairdo—there can be a simple joy in the feeling of movement in rain, a wetness knowing it's soon to be dry, a chill that will shortly be burned off indoors. It brightened both women, so that by the time they made it into the warm, well-locked home, where a child was safe still upstairs, their breaths were proud and exhilarated; their cheeks were alive and their eyes wakeful as diamonds.

"So much for calm night-time contemplations."

"It feels great, though," Pi said. "To be outside, even to be rained on. I've been inside too much lately. I love the rain. Somehow it's always good news, now. Means everything's that bit less flammable."

Abbie shook her coat off, bent over, and scattered rain from her head in a brief shower. Pi shed the soaked leather jacket, apologizing for any damage done to it.

"He won't miss it," Abbie said. "We got it on our honeymoon. I imagine he's happy to forget it."

Their coverings off, a silence struck, which became almost awkward. A hesitation hovered in the quiet room.

"It's late," Pi offered. "You must be tired."

"Not really. I'm feeling strangely awake. Youthful, even. Shall I make some tea?"

Instead of sitting at the table, taking up her breakfast or dinner position, Pi perched on the edge of it close to Abbie, watching her.

"Martha and I have a story about the rainfall, you know," she said shyly. "About who's behind it."

"Is this one of the stories you've been secretly telling each other? She told me you had an ongoing tale about a dog named Pink who had died and gone to heaven."

"Well, it's like heaven, this place, but closer to hand. The creatures there have jobs, like people do. The weather, for example. Some of them are in charge of it. So they'd be behind a big rain like this one. Pinsk and, so the story goes, also my old cat, the one who died in the fire, Zeno."

"You and Martha enjoy your stories together, don't you?" Abbie's back was to Pi—she stood over the stove, as if to test whether a watched kettle could really resist boiling.

"We both enjoy other worlds," Pi said. "Worlds beyond reach. I think that's what Martha and I have in common."

"And what about the world within reach?" Abbie asked, turning then to find what she thought she might—Pi's Pacific eyes wide with a sudden light, understanding the chance before her, the body, the warmth, the pull. Abbie moved slightly towards Pi, and from that brief no man's land Pi pulled her over to her own side, close to her, where she was still propped against the edge of the table. She took Abbie's face in her hands and kissed her.

She kissed her.

Her soft lips opened Abbie's gently, slowly first—a question, an experiment-

—and then soon the mouths met the way mouths love to do, moist and willing and inspirational, the bodies drawing closer together and a person's legs (Pi's) wrapped around the waist of the other (Abbie), pulling that nice waist closer and warmer while the kiss kissed and the mouths opened and a hand moved through another's hair (Abbie's) and another hand touched lightly a knotted shoulder (Pi's) and someone uttered something like a moan; and there was some rainwater in with the kiss and an eyelash or two were damp, but whether with rain or a sentimental tear would be hard to say. And all the while the heat rose within them both and their hands started to move more boldly, freed of their doubts, and the two women were speaking in tongues, in that foreign language everyone should learn to speak sometime in their lives as it's the only one that expresses love wordlessly, with the possible exception of certain kinds of music.

The kettle shrieked.

"Help!" Abbie said and stepped away, flicking off the gas and moving the irate kettle and looking guiltily to the door to see whether the cry might have wakened her daughter. She waited there a moment before sidling back into Pi's welcoming arms.

And there was a part of Abbie, how could there not be?, that thought calmly: I am kissing another woman. I have spent my life kissing men, and now here I am kissing a woman. How was it different from what she'd known before? Not much. It was strangely familiar. The sensation reminded her of nothing so much as being nineteen, when Abbie selected boys to date largely on their ability to kiss. Their looks hadn't mattered so much to her. She remembered Kenny McAllister—a name she hadn't thought of for a couple of decades. What a tasty, full mouth he'd had, what a sensual way with his lips.

And on they kissed. Till blindness came and judgment was a quiet stifled thing and the desire was not the kind you could ignore or skip over. It was at that point that Pi murmured, "Should we leave the kitchen?" and Abbie said, "We probably should," though a late fear hit her that she might not know what came next. Here she was, forty, feeling like a teenager, a late virgin, some kind of spinster. She let Pi take her by the hand to Abe's former toolroom, the monk cell, where the messageless computer was still and no light was coming out of its square smooth eye. There was only the steady calming patter of the April rain, a rhythmed sound to go along with whatever rhythm they'd make up themselves.

"Are you sure about this?" Pi whispered to Abbie, in a voice that temporarily chilled Abbie's heart—there was such a thin, deep sadness in it.

"I am," said Abbie. "I'm sure. Are you?"

The woman's pretty eyes lost their focus for an instant, and Abbie sensed them travelling to whatever pessimism had captured them earlier.

"What does it mean to be sure?" Pi said, with what looked in the darkness to be a rueful smile. Then, as if to answer her own question, she pulled Abbie with her onto the narrow bed, and surrendered her smile to the sweeter meeting of their nightlong embrace.

Part 4

WHAT WOULD THE WORLD LOOK LIKE IF WE COULDN'T SEE IT?

This was the first line of a paper Pi had once written. She liked her openings to be sharp and vivid—like a new flavor. She wanted to make a reader sit up straighter, wipe the sleep from his eyes. There was nothing worse, in Pi's opinion, than those mealy-mouthed papers that began drugged and rambling, with a long summary of some previous academic's argument and the humble yet defiant assertion that the current writer would be suggesting something . . . a little different.

This particular paper had been on all the aspects of the world we know and picture without having direct experience of them. The point Pi wanted to make with the opening joke was how much of our world is constructed by us; how much we build with our minds. (Her eventual answer to the opening question was: *Much the same as it does now.*) The commonsense model, Pi wrote, is that we move through our world passively, receiving information, simply taking in what's there as if we were empty vessels. In fact, ninety percent of the world— she had liked the absurdity of assigning it a number—we don't see, though we feel we know it, nonetheless. We go by what we've seen before, or what we've been told, or what our culture holds to be the case. If I am in a city, emerging from a subway station, I will not turn a corner and find a grove of redwoods; I will turn a corner and find another street. I know this, even if I have never turned that particular corner. So much knowledge is actually unfounded, hopeful belief. *Imagine the faith involved in a single telephone call*, Pi wrote, *in a network of unknown connections.* Still this was a sentence of hers she liked. It was one of the sentences she remembered.

Pi was lying underneath the skylight in Abbie's bedroom, naked and sated.

What world she could see from there was the purest one possible: it was sky and light pouring down into her eyes, as the skylight did its job of pulling the morning down into the room. As Pi lay there she felt for a strange moment that she could have been anyone, anywhere, under that egg-white a.m.; there was so little to remind her of what she knew. So Pi did what people do. She constructed the world. She heard the spray of water on tile and knew Abbie was downstairs in the shower; she felt the hum of her own body and knew that they'd made love again, in a rush after Abbie got back from taking Martha to school; she felt the scratch of tiredness behind her eyes and knew an uneasiness of spirit had kept her awake in the night. And she knew the uneasiness went along with the fact that her mind was not altogether in the same place as her body. Her mind was worrying at something beyond here, something far away from this small, skylit, satisfied room.

The spray of water stopped. A door opened and closed. Morning muffles crept out from the bathroom, padded upstairs to soften Pi's ears. When Abbie came in, Pi saw her olive lovely body wrapped in a light blue towel, with a matching towel wrapped around her head, turban-style, trapping Abbie's wet washed hair. It was Abbie of the Nile, Abbie to whom Pi in a former life might have fed peeled grapes and honey tangerines.

"What are you looking at?" Abbie smiled, shy.

"You," Pi said, waving a hand at her. "That outfit suits you. It's like a kind of fetching traditional garb."

"Why—thank you." Abbie moved around the room, gathering creams and bracelets, earrings and make-up, the wearable items of her feminine self. "I'm glad you like it. It's native to this region." She stood before the mirror donning accessories, keeping an eye on Pi's reflection there.

Gradually, Abbie's face became artfully shadowed and ornamented, her wrists belled with silver, her distinctive light perfume touched behind the ears. Her trick seemed to be doing the last details first, before shedding the traditional garb and putting on the day's costume. Pi found the sequence fascinating. Her own was usually so slapdash: pulling on jeans, finding a bra and some no-challenge cotton shirt, a brush through the hair and a thin underlining of eyes so that she looked awake, at least, if not glamorous.

"Do you think I could learn to do that?" she asked.

"What?"

"All those feminine things—powders and jewels and everything. Why don't I know how to do any of that?"

"Does your mother?"

"No."

"That's why. You learn it from your mother."

"So Martha will get it, then. She'll inherit the knack." Pi sat up, wrapping the sheet around herself. "Maybe you could teach me. Do you think it's too late for me to learn? Do you have to learn frills early or not at all?"

"Frills? You can hardly call me frilly."

"Certainly I can call you frilly."

"Oh, I don't think so. Not frilly. If I'm going to teach you anything at all, you're going to have to show me some respect. I'm your elder and better, after all."

"I know that! You're entirely better than me. For which fact I have the utmost respect," Pi said. "So go ahead. Teach me one quick thing about frills. For instance—that stuff you put on your face first. Is that really necessary? What does that do, exactly?"

Abbie was now nearly complete in the mirror. If not frilly, she was certainly lavender and amethyst and rosebud and summer rain.

"Now really." She turned around to face the sheet-wrapped Pi. "You're lovely just the way you are. You don't need to learn about blush and foundation and lip liner. I promise. You do wonderfully without it. It isn't necessary. Not for you."

" 'Just the way I am'? Is that what you said?"

"I know it sounds trite—"

"No, no. It doesn't sound trite. Not trite."

And Pi lost the world again, suddenly, to the quandary at the heart of her.

"Pi . . ." Abbie sat down beside her and looked into her face. "What is that? What happens to you when you get that look in your eyes? Are you thinking of someone? Who?"

Pi clambered out from under the covers, gave Abbie one fond thumbstroke on her fragrant cheek, then performed her own minute-and-a-half dressing routine. Her words were scattered by moving clothes.

"I'm not sure who I'm thinking about," she said. "Isn't that nutty? How can a person not even be sure of that?"

Abbie's expression retreated now back into that kindness she used to wear when she was first talking to her lodger. But their loving, of course, had changed everything; there was an edge and a worry in the current between them. Abbie stood up and turned to fetch some last touch, a scarf or brooch, to make her complete.

"*I* know who it is," Abbie said. "I recognize your expression."

"Really?" Pi stopped, mid-sweatshirt. "You do?"

"Pi." Abbie stepped back, out of the sun-square: the sky that fell between them had brightened suddenly, a brief gap in the clouds. "Don't you think it's time you told me about your imaginary friend?"

The look on Abbie's face was now sturdy and undeniable. Pi didn't try to deny it. But she did shelter her eyes with her hesitant fingers.

"Yes," she said in a thick voice. "I probably should."

In the old days, Pi would have enjoyed working on such a question. The pleasure in it. It was like one long game of Frisbee for the brain—you took an idea, a problem (*what is it to be sure of something?*), and you threw it around with a bunch of friends, maybe with Rob and Tamar, for example. You were serious, the problems behind the ideas were serious, but in the end it was play. When you quit for the day, you were ready for pizza and beer. Ready to read the papers. Find out what had changed meanwhile, out in what academics and academic-haters alike called "the real world," for reasons never made entirely clear.

It might have gone like this:

"Is being sure not admitting of any doubt?"

"No. I don't think so. Doubt is what makes surety *sure*. If you don't allow doubt, or the possibility of doubt, you're just being stubborn. Or stupid."

"But how does 'being sure' differ from just knowing something, then? There's less doubt. That's the difference. I may know something, like that two plus two equals four, but when I'm sure, that's different; that's more like—I'm *sure* I'm sitting here talking to you right now."

"Oh come on, aren't you sure that two plus two equals four? I am."

"Well, no. I don't think I'm sure of it. I could be made to doubt it. I could be led to believe that somewhere, on Twin Earth, say, two plus two equals five. I could believe that."

"Don't bring Twin Earth into it. That's so bogus. We don't *live* on Twin Earth. We live on *this* Earth. And on this Earth, two plus two equals four. Right?"

"Oh yes, don't get me wrong. I do believe two plus two equals four. I'm not about to argue against that."

"That's a relief."

"All I'm saying is I feel like—"

"Uh-oh. She 'feels like' . . . This isn't promising."

"I could be made to *doubt* two plus two equals four. Because of the way that I know it. I'm not sure of it, the way I'm sure that I'm sitting here."

"I can't believe you're saying that! So are you saying you're more sure of things you know from your sense perceptions? That's really going to get you into hot water. Your sense perceptions are nothing to count on for surety, pal. They're lyin' cheatin' things. Think hallucinations, think phantom limbs. Think brain in a vat. How do you know you're not just a perceiving brain made to *think* you're sitting here talking to me? Et cetera. So let's try this again. Do you really want to say sense perceptions are what make you sure of something? Think it over. Take your time here. Don't rush."

"Okay. Here we go. When we say 'I know something,' we don't usually mean '. . . that may be untrue.' There's a certainty implied in the phrase. We mean: 'I know it.' Unless we qualify it. So I know two plus two equals four. Why? Because that's the way the world is, that's the world as we know it, that's one of the geometrical forms of this world in the noumenal realm, to use the Kantian . . ."

"Now there's no need to bring Kant into it. You're using Kant as a crutch. Throw it away! Walk free of the crutch! Say what you're saying without reference to Kant!"

"Fine. All I'm trying to say is surety isn't actually a different *way* of knowing something, it's not a special epistemological category: maybe it's a feeling, a sensation that goes along with knowledge. And I might even venture to say—I'm not sure about this, and you're going to scream, but even so—I *might* be willing to say that what different people are sure of varies. That's the Rorty angle here, see. The relativist point creeping in. So you're sure that two plus two equals four, because at heart you're a mathematician and science worshipper and you think logic is beautiful. But I'm not a science worshipper, you see; so what I feel sure of will be different. Specific to me."

"What is what? That you're sitting here talking to me? Are you really going to throw your lot in with the sense perceptions? Is that what you're surest of?"

"Well, now, I think sense perceptions have been given a bad name. I'd like to give them some credit here. If they were good enough for Bishop Berkeley, they ought to be good enough for me."

"But Berkeley had God on his side. That was a huge advantage, you've got to admit."

"And what makes you so sure I don't have Him on my side, too?"

"Oh! Gosh, I'm sorry. I didn't realize. In that case, you win. With God on your side, you definitely win."

Of course there wasn't anybody up here to play such games with, which was why Pi hadn't been playing them. Up here in the "real" world such questions moved through her head uncaught, unanswered, wheeling across the sky of her mind in undescribed arcs.

Pi missed it. She missed her teammates. Her brain muscles were unexercised. Comic banter with Xander was not the same. It was, in comparison, like playing Ping-Pong or badminton or any low-impact game: you never worked up anything like a sweat. It improved your wrist action, maybe, at best. But Pi missed the full, flat-out sport of the real thing.

There was a small person whose feelings were on people's minds, but who was never given a chance to speak for herself. One day she'd go to college, make good friends, and grow funny and cynical about her upbringing, whatever her upbringing turned out to be. One night in the future (sometime in the next millennium, when life before computers would be a faint folk memory), she'd get drunk with a friend and have a startling insight that would help clarify her past. There would be therapy, or not. After years or months of a fearsome anger at one parent or both of them, or somebody else altogether, she'd come to a peace about this past and would learn to live her own life free of it.

But in these days, these Mendocino days, that to-be-clarified past was still in Martha's future, and it was being presided over by people invariably taller than she was who were quite satisfied to talk to each other over her head or behind her back or—worst of all—when she was altogether out of the room. People who let slip tiny details, hints and clues, that Martha took back into her room to gnaw on like a squirrel over its private hoard.

For instance. One night before dinner Martha was sitting unobtrusively at the table while Abbie and Pi pulled pasta and salad together, and she distinctly heard Pi calling Abbie "my Better," which she then transformed into "my Bet." It was hard not to notice this. Especially since when Pi said "my Bet" Abbie's cheeks turned a pinker shade of pink.

"Why did you call her that?" Martha asked. "Why did you call Mom 'Bet'?"

"Well . . ." Pi hesitated. Her hands were busy ripping up lettuce leaves—eagerly, as if they were illicit love letters. "It's like calling you Martles. Why do I call you Martles?"

"It's a nickname."

"Right."

"But 'Martles' comes from Martha. 'Bet' doesn't sound like my mom's name at all."

"You're right." Pi pointed a salad tong at Martha. "You're absolutely right. If you were a philosopher, you could say I'm begging the question. A phrase I've never completely understood, actually. How did begging come into it?"

Which was supposed to qualify as an answer. Martha was losing faith that Pi would be forthcoming with any information the way she'd hoped. Nonetheless, it was worth trying. Any strategy, at this uncertain date, with the world ahead of her blank and unforeseeable, was worth trying. So after dinner that night, Martha asked Pi to read to her. It was something she hadn't done for a while.

"Sure, Martles. What are we on these days? Narnia?"

Martha nodded, not that she had any intention of letting Pi read. It was all part of the scheme. She went upstairs, brushed her teeth, got into her pyjamas, and came down to say goodnight to her mother, then trekked back up, with Pi flapping along behind her. She got into bed and waited till Pi had sat down, found the book and the page they were on, asked for a quick recap on the story to date, and was opening her mouth to read the first sentence.

Then Martha spoke.

"Pi. Can I ask you something?"

Pi looked up. "What's that?"

"Do you know what's going to happen?"

"You mean in Narnia? Actually, I don't know, it's been so long since I've read it. But it's more fun if we find out together, anyway."

"Not in Narnia. I mean about San Francisco. Are we moving back there?"

Pi's face clouded. "Well—I don't know, really. It's—"

"My dad said we were."

"Oh, he did? Well. Would you like that?"

Martha shrugged. "I miss Mrs. Delaney. And Romeo and Juliet. What would you do if we moved back there?"

Pi narrowed her eyes to an inscrutable squint. "Who knows? I've thought about moving back to San Francisco, too. I might live with Fran again, or something. We could all go rollerblading together."

"We're not moving back in with my dad, though." Martha looked hunched. "He said we weren't living with him anymore. He and my mom don't want to live together anymore."

"Did he say that?"

Martha nodded.

"I'm sorry about that, Martles."

"You knew that. Didn't you?" Martha's voice was pointed, sharp—a little arrowhead. She was not about to let Pi play dumb.

"I guess from what your mother's told me it does sound like they won't be living together anymore. But they still care about each other, you know, and they love you a lot—"

"Why aren't you married, Pi?"

"Me?" Pi blushed. "You've never asked me that before. Why are you asking?"

"Well, why aren't you?"

"I guess I haven't met the right person," Pi said blandly. Then she shook her head. "No. That's not quite right. You know, Martha, I may not ever get married. Maybe I'm not the marrying type."

"Why not?"

Martha made her bright eyes burn a hole right through to Pi's private, tiny soul. She needed someone to tell her the truth, for a change.

"I don't love people the way you're supposed to for a marriage," Pi said, looking steadily back at her. "There's a way you're supposed to love to get married, and that's not what I've done. So far."

Martha looked away. "Oh," she said. "So then what about Hamlet?"

"What about him?"

"Did you think about getting married to him?"

"Martles!" Pi laughed. "I've never met Hamlet. I've only written to him. You know that."

"Why haven't you met him?"

"I don't know where he is. Come on." She tried opening up the book again. "That's enough debate about marriage. Shall I read you more about Narnia?"

"Wait." There was a school of questions that darted around under the surface of Martha's mind. She was trying to figure out which one to catch—which to ask. Which shimmering, opalescent sentence was right for now. She didn't want to ask one that would turn out to be dangerous. Some, she suspected, had hidden teeth.

"Couldn't you find out where he is?"

"Who, Hamlet?"

"Yeah."

"You never know," Pi said to her. "You never know, Martles. I just might." She opened the book, as if to signal a final end to the conversation.

"I don't want you to read to me tonight," Martha said.

"You don't?"

"No." Martha shook her head. She reached up and took the book away from Pi. "I want to think about another story instead. Guess what?"

"What?"

"I'm writing a story with Pinx and Zeno and Hamlet in it. All by myself. They're playing fetch, on the beach. Do you want to hear it?"

"Really?" Pi was impressed. "That's very cool. Of course I would."

"I'm writing it down and everything. And I'm drawing pictures. My teacher is helping me. But don't tell Mom. It's a secret."

"OK. I won't tell her, I promise."

"It's going to be a surprise. Can you turn off the light? I want to tell it to you in the dark. But you can't tell Mom."

"Don't worry. Your secret will be safe with me."

Before Pi turned off the light and heard the story, she tucked Martha into her own soft sheets. She kissed her on the forehead with an unusual gentleness; and Martha noticed as Pi leaned over her a sharp glitter at the edge of her eyes, and a look on her face that seemed, strangely, a lot like love.

When Abbie came back that afternoon, Pi was all booted up and ready to go.

"Where are you off to? Where's Martha?"

"She's having dinner over at the Abernathys'. I told them one of us would pick her up around eight." Pi was jittery. "I thought we could go for a walk, maybe. In Russian Gulch. While it's still light."

Abbie was a little suspicious, but she agreed. She seemed to feel she was being set up for something, and maybe she was. Pi didn't know precisely the shape of her own urge, she just knew that some clarity was important, some openness, and an instinct told her it would be easier to be open in the tall and shadowed woods.

Pi had a familiar route in Russian Gulch by now. It was her problem-solving path. It didn't occur to her to consult Abbie. Her solid, confident feet just started on the way under the trees they were used to, her hands jammed in their familiar place inside her jeans pockets. Her thoughts stretched themselves comfortably in the scattered sun.

The air was quiet, fresh with late spring dampness. The trees held their familiar dignity, refusing as ever to offer any definite opinions. Abbie seemed happy to keep a companionable silence: she understood it was Pi's words they were waiting for.

For half an hour the path was peopleless. Then they heard a rapid thudding joy of young shoes, and two teenaged girls appeared coming towards them, startled to see unknown adults here.

"Hi," Abbie greeted them.

"Hi." They looked blank. "Are you guys going to see the waterfall?"

Pi nodded.

"How is it?" asked Abbie.

One of the girls shrugged. "It's a waterfall," she said. "Come on, let's go. Bye!" She grabbed her friend and started jogging with her again back down the path.

"It's true, though," Pi said after they'd left. "What else can you say about it?"

"I'm not looking forward to Martha being that age. I'm glad we have a few years to go before I have to cope with adolescence."

The path started to climb more steeply. "You know, Martha asked me last night about your plans. About you two moving back to San Francisco."

"Is that what you wanted to talk to me about?"

Pi stopped. Breathed. Unfit, her body told her: *You are unfit for this kind of life.* "No," she said. "I'll get to that. But I thought you might want to know about Martha. She seemed worried."

"I know she is." Abbie was breathing, too. She blew her hair out of her eyes, a child's gesture, a cuteness. "I wish there was something I could say to her. What can I tell her? She wants to hear that Abe and I are getting back together. That's what she wants most of all, of course. It breaks my heart not to be able to tell her that."

"Really?" This was about the most conciliatory thing Pi had ever heard Abbie say about her husband.

"Of course. I want everything to be right in Martha's world. I passionately want that." A sigh came up from the depths of her lungs. "Still. It will be righter, I think, if we're there at least. Back in the city. I talked it over with Faith, and that's what she thinks, too. I called Zack at the Hayes Gallery, and it was true, what Abe said to me. They're eager to have me back there. So," she said, "I think that's what will happen."

"And . . ." Pi said. Usually this was not her. Usually she was not the one asking this particular, clumsy question. "And where would you say our little interlude fits in to that plan?"

"It's not necessarily little, Pi."

"Next to the big picture, it is. You're talking big picture."

"I'm talking about the future, and how to organize it so it's least painful for my daughter."

"I understand that. I'm just saying it sounds like that future will probably be organized without—"

She paused, looking for the word, the right phrase, the appropriate euphemism.

"You don't have to give it a name," Abbie said. She shushed Pi's mouth with her own, and for a long minute they were pulled into a kiss that seemed already sweetened by its own nostalgia.

"I don't think we should try to give it a name," Abbie said again. Her grey eyes were shining with an ocean light Pi hadn't seen before; and they weren't even close to the water here. They were sheltered by a stand of redwoods, close to the dark bark floor of the forest, close to the moving white song of the nearby waterfall. Abbie pulled Pi down so they sat together in the fading light. Pi watched her in a funny astonishment.

"What?" Abbie said. "What are you staring at?"

"It's just strange. I assumed you wouldn't be happy with something so vague. I thought that was why you called me an emotional dwarf—because I was never definite about anything."

"There's nothing like the end of a nine-year marriage to make you wary of being definite," Abbie said. "Besides. When did I ever call you an emotional dwarf"?

"Maybe you didn't use that exact phrase. But you implied it."

"How," she laughed, "do you imply 'emotional dwarf'?"

"You know, because I wouldn't go into therapy."

"Pi." Abbie collected Pi's hand and laced Pi's fingers through her own. "That was about the fire. That had nothing to do with your emotional life, about which I know next to nothing because you've always been so private. I had been thinking about how it must have felt to lose everything you own. To have lost your calling. I may know nothing about what you were studying, but it was obviously devastating to lose it. Fran told me the same thing. She said before you were always busy and energetic and that the fire seemed to have . . ." She paused; she was trying to avoid the word "extinguish." "Anyway, I thought it might be a help for you to talk to someone about all that. About what it meant to you. That's all."

Pi found Abbie's hand a comfort. She held it tighter. It had been a long time since someone had done just that—held her hand. It was odd how the simplest gestures, the most basic kinds of touch, were often the ones that got to you.

"I did find someone. That's the thing. I did find someone to talk to about it."

"Of course you did." Abbie closed her eyes, leaned back against the redwood, the ancient straight-backed sentry of this land. "You found your prince."

Pi shuddered in an imagined chill. She waited for the woman with the wise and silvered head to ask her more, to press the point, but she was wordless. Instead, still holding Pi's hand, she stared up through the redwoods at the darkening, vertiginous sky. She did not seem to be in any hurry for anything at all.

And that was how Pi was finally able to tell it—unasked for, unpressed. She took a clean breath of forest air and she started to speak. About the man and the myth: the guy or the character. Whichever he would turn out to be.

And Abbie, in her goodness, listened.

The next day Pi was trying to get Xander to discuss the mind/body problem with her. She idled against the counter while he sat staring at the computer screen, trying to fit "Jed Wilkes, Contemporary Arborculture" onto the format for a normal business card.

It had come up, Pi told Xander, when she'd talked with Abbie about this odd state she was in, in which her mind and body seemed to be weirdly separated. Pi neglected to tell Xander a key element in this story, about girls kissing under redwoods—the feasting of their various sense perceptions. She felt she could make the story work without that detail.

"So what was her take on it?" Xander asked.

"Abbie told me I had a restless mind. That my thoughts wander, all the time."

"I can see that." He moused and maneuvered.

"And that my body doesn't seem to keep up."

"Why? Where's your body?"

"My body is here, but may be going back to San Francisco."

"OK. And your mind?"

"My mind is somewhere on the way to L.A."

"L.A.," he said. "Yikes. What's there?"

"Xander, I'm insane. You have to tell me I'm insane, because Abbie was too nice to say it. Someone I know over the Internet is in L.A.—we've been e-mailing. I was thinking about going there to try to meet him. Just to meet him, nothing else. I want to *see* the guy, but it's not a romance or anything. Still, it's crazy. Right? Abbie seems to think maybe I should go, get it out of my system. So your job is to tell me it's crazy."

"Why crazy? Because he might be a psychopath?"

"Well, that. Right. Or even just—even if he wasn't, I mean, maybe he doesn't exist at all, right? I mean how can I be sure he's really even out there?"

"Well, who is the guy? What do you know about him? Someone must exist, I'd say, or you probably wouldn't be getting e-mail from him. Not that I'm a philosopher with your sophistication, of course. That's a layperson's view."

"It's the guy I've been writing to. I told you I've been corresponding with someone."

"You did."

"Well, him."

"But you've hardly told me anything about him. You've been very secretive. You should have been a spy, really, Pi. You're so damn discreet."

"What can I tell you about him? I don't know what he looks like."

"How'd you hook up with him?"

"I was searching around one day in some poetry section and I found a group focussing on Emily Dickinson. Specifically on one poem—a dark little ditty on suicide."

"You're not talking about ED 536?"

"Do you know it?"

"Pi! Of course I do. That's so funny."

"Why 'of course'?"

"Practically everyone I know cues up ED 536. Because of the Diery. So what happened, you started writing someone from there? Who? If that's not probing too much. This is so funny. What's your handle?"

Pi wasn't quite keeping up.

"You've read the Diery?"

"Oh come on! Everyone has. I mean, a lot of people I know have. Someone from the fasting group told me about it. I've never posted anything there, I've just gone in to read the Diery. So I probably wouldn't recognize your handle anyway. But you don't have to tell me if you're too embarrassed. It's weird, I know—like someone turning the lights up abruptly at a party or something. Having this other identity revealed. I remember a friend of mine who uses this comic-book group I'm in telling me he'd figured out that I was the Incredible Hulk. Which I was. I'd written a lot of bullshit as the Incredible Hulk. It was humiliating. And there was no point denying it. He knew me too well, and could tell."

"I've only posted there once or twice myself. Mostly I've been writing privately to this guy."

"So who is he? Or I guess I should say, Who does he say he is?"

"He calls himself Hamlet."

Xander smiled. "That's good. Picks up on JD's fixation. Though, strictly speaking, Hamlet's not a suicide. He dies by tragic, preventable circumstances. 'If it be now, 'tis not to come; if it be not to come, it will be now' and all that."

"Since when do you go around quoting Shakespeare?"

"Since we read *Hamlet* in our reading group. Thanks to your suggestion. I'd been hoping for Philip K. Dick."

"Xander." Pi hesitated. "It—it is JD. It's JD I've been writing to. It's him."

She felt a surge of excitement as she said it. This was so different from telling Abbie, who had no idea what she was talking about. Telling this to Xander was like being able finally to tell someone that you've had an encounter with some-one famed and impossible—Elvis, maybe, or Immanuel Kant.

But Xander merely slid a skeptical face her way. "Really? What makes you think so?"

"I know it. It's obvious! It's his voice. It's JD."

"But how can you be sure?"

"Because he's been telling me everything. About travelling across country with Minsk, about going West—everything."

"It might be somebody pretending to be him. It wouldn't be that hard to fake it."

"But he's been telling me all these specifics. Like about Gloria's son's funeral, and how sad it was . . ."

"Interesting." Xander nodded noncommittally.

"It's not just interesting!" Pi spun Xander around in his chair to make him face her, not the screen. "It's *him*! Listen. I'll tell you what I think. I think he's been writing me instead of posting the Diery. There's been a gap with the Diery, right? That was because he's been writing to me. When was the last time he posted any of it?"

Xander smiled. Infuriatingly. "I take it you haven't gone to ED 536 lately."

"Why?"

"You should check it out."

"Why? What's there?"

"A new section of the Diery." His smugness was palpable. He spun back to the screen. "There's a new section posted. Called 'The Millionth Man.' "

"What . . . ?" Pi was outraged. How could Xander know something about JD that she didn't? "When was this? As of when?"

"Two days ago."

She couldn't believe she hadn't checked. "Well, how do you know it's him?" She tried to throw him off.

He shrugged. "I don't. Nobody does. Who's to say each piece was written by the same guy all along? It just sounds like it is. And this sounds like JD. It's his farewell."

Pi leaned against the counter to absorb the news. She felt almost faint. Then something occurred to her.

"Xander, tell me something, if you've been checking ED 536 regularly. Did someone named Abbie Hoffman write something about meeting JD in Baltimore? Going to his sister's house and meeting him?"

He thought it over. "Abbie Hoffman? Not that I know of."

"Anybody? Did anybody write something about actually meeting JD, in Baltimore?"

"I haven't seen anything."

She closed her eyes. Now she was losing her mind, for sure. There was no evidence that if you put a hawk and a handsaw in front of Pi right now she'd have any idea how to tell one from the other.

"Tell you what, Miss Piper," Xander said to his employee. He had spotted his love interest—Claudia was approaching the store. "You're looking a little pale there. Perhaps it's a problem of a feminine nature? Might I suggest—"

"I'm not getting you a cup of coffee, if that's what you're wondering."

"Miss Piper! I'm not out to exploit you. I was going to suggest you take the morning off, go home, make yourself a soothing drink—and read 'The Millionth Man.' Miss Jansen here will take over. Why hello, Miss Jansen! Aren't you looking nice today!"

"Hi, Xan."

"Really?" Pi asked Xander humbly. It was true, she was itching to get to her computer. To read what was there. "You wouldn't mind?"

"Go ahead! Go," he said. "Me and Miss Jansen here—" He beckoned Claudia over. "Between the two of us, I'm sure we can handle this arborculture guy." He pulled Claudia onto his lap to make their co-working easier.

Pi got ready to fly home to re-meet her screen. But before she left Xander's

Xerox for the last time, she thanked him and apologized for her bad manners. Her once and soon-to-be-former boss shrugged off her apology with his own kind of graciousness. He left her with a truly kind word, one she wouldn't understand until later that morning.

"Hey, maybe it is true, Pi. Maybe it is true." His face was free of irony, for a change. "Who knows? Maybe you're Horatio."

D I E R Y

The Millionth Man

FIRST THINGS FIRST.

I returned the car.

For all the thousands of you out there suffering vicarious anxiety, thinking, Jesus Christ, when is he going to return the damn *car*? The answer is, well not by any stretch of the imagination on time, but it is nonetheless taken care of. And if anyone's wondering—so what do they do to people who hold on to rental cars, besides charge the hell out of their credit cards? I can't tell you the answer, because I chose the coward's return method, which the sharp-sighted among you may recognize from my college days: I snuck over there after hours, at about midnight, parked the car outside the office, and then just posted the keys through the door in one of those little envelopes they're nice enough to provide. I didn't bother noting down "ending mileage" because I think that number will be irrelevant in the bigger scheme of things. But I did fill it up with gas, to show my basically good will. It was the least I could do. And I left a little note on the dashboard, in true JD style, expressing a sentiment which believe it or not is heartfelt: SORRY FOR ANY INCONVENIENCE I HAVE CAUSED.

I should explain that I probably have caused these Zippy Car people considerable inconvenience, more than you might imagine. Not only by hoarding the Taurus for lo these many weeks—I was supposed to return the car three weeks ago—but also because I did not return the car to its original home, my nameless city of residence. I just sort of granted myself the right to do a "driveaway" rental or whatever they call them. I drove away. Off into the sunset. And I didn't stop until I was several sunsets into the journey—all the way out here, the land of Willa Cather's archbishop and Georgia O'Keeffe's dead deer skulls, and Native Americans pretending they enjoy selling turquoise trinkets to tourists. The only reason I stopped here is because I happened to drive right by a Zippy Car Rental outlet and I figured the car rental deities were sending me some message from on high. So I waited for the appropriate hour, i.e. when no one would be around to yell at me, and then cruised back and dropped off the goods. From that dark spot I walked back to our motel with my four-footed escort.

To tell you the truth, I feel a lot lighter now. The guilt was beginning to wear me down. Not that I hadn't grown pretty fond of the Taurus, which had earned itself the nickname "Sparky" as we got to know each other. Minsk had made a happy nest for himself in the back seat, which had taken on the comfortable, greasy shine of our mutual belongings: Minsk's food and water dishes, my supply of Coke which I seem to have gotten re-addicted to ever since that post-suicidal Chinese food with Krieger, my quote unquote briefcase (like I am really the sort of person who needs a briefcase), a dishwater-colored eco-friendly JavaBooks bag full of books Cindy was kind enough to provide me for the journey—including a few snuck-in titles like *100 Things You Can Do to Fight Depression* and *Life Goes On!* or some such. All of these items made Sparky feel like home to me. But it was such a guilty home, it wasn't worth it. You know? The very panels of the vehicle breathed accusation. It was like knowing you'd buried your father under the floorboards of your apartment—like that Poe story where the guy's driven crazy by the accusing throbs of the dead heartbeat in his ears. It was the same for me. It got to the point where I could hear the cling! of an imagined cash register every time another mile on the mileometer clicked by, and a light trickle of sweat would creep down my worried brow. I'd rather be guilt-free and homeless than driving Sparky forever, checking the rearview mirror for the flashing lights, getting ready to spreadeagle myself against its dusty sides while Minsk barked his alarmed insistence that they not send me to jail, not at least without reading me my rights.

Why homeless? you may ask. What's wrong with the ninth floor, once Lili vacates it and returns to Nirvana songs pounding miserably out of her own roommatey apartment? If I've had to leave Baltimore, as I apparently have since last posting my tragicomedy here on your screens, why not just go back where I came from?

Well that, if you take the long view, is exactly what I'm doing.

I'm heading home.

There's always a fine line, isn't there, especially here in the Land of Opportunity, between "running away" and "striking out." Not striking out in the baseball sense, in the pioneer sense I meant and I refuse to make a baseball joke at my own expense, even though I just set myself up for it. But striking out is always seen to be good and adventurous, while running away is cowardly and pathetic. So we grow up being told the Puritans were heroic to take on this new country. But who's to say they weren't just refusing to be manly and face the music at home when they Mayflowered their way over here in the first place? How many people think Columbus was just avoiding commitment when he ran around the world seeking out native peoples so he could call them dumb inaccurate names and pave the way for their massacre? Same goes for all those pioneers, forty-niners, and the rest. Everyone idolizes them. No one accuses them of running away from their personal lives.

I'm just trying to make a simple point—that it is possible to have different interpretations of the same event. Maybe I'm running away; or maybe I'm making a smart call about a new start.

If I sound a tad defensive here it's because I am. So would you be if you'd had Lilian Hofmeister hollering at you the way I did earlier this evening. I called her from the motel lobby—not a dignified place to have a major emotional run-in with someone. I felt like a runaway teenager. Dear Lili accused me of being a coward for not coming back and promised she was going to go to that concert with Raul Quesadilla instead of me after all. I said to her, Come on you must be pleased at least that you get to stay in my apartment for a while, away from it all up on floor number nine? And she said being pleased about the apartment was like a mosquito next to the elephant of displeasure she felt at the fact that I wasn't coming back. I thought that was quite eloquent. She asked me—with a snarl really, I thought that word was just literary fancy but Lili did issue a genuine snarl—just how long I was planning to be gone on my orgiastic voyage of self-discovery. I told her I didn't know. It depended what happened. She said did I realize how Californian and seventies I sounded, and how it would serve me right if I ended up joining some Patty Hearst–style liberation army and calling myself Harold Haroldson and wielding an assault rifle, or failing that that I should at least do something mildly interesting like come out of the closet after all these years. I asked Lili, What, you too, you think I'm gay? What is this? And she said No she didn't that's why it would be interesting. She said if it made me feel any guiltier, which she hoped it would, she had been promising a date with me to some singer she met that she really liked named Arabella. She had thought we'd hit it off. I said, first of all, *Arabella*? Be serious. And second I said, I thought you liked this woman, why get her in touch with a gloom-monger like myself? And she said, If you have to ask that question, you deserve to go to L.A. and end up living in some godforsaken suburb like Tarzana and spending the rest of your life wearing sunblock and fretting about muscle tone. I'm not even going to tell you where Lili told me I could put all the Beverly Hills palm trees. By this point I was holding the receiver close to my ear in case any innocent lobby-goers might accidentally catch some of Lili's terrible invective.

We will, I am sure, have a more affectionate conversation soon, Lili and I. That one was rough going. It turns out—as someone warned me, only recently—that people get very upset if you go away from them.

Krieger on the other hand didn't bat an eye when I told him my plans. I could tell this even over the telephone. He had a very open-eyed, accepting tone of voice.

"I think that's a good call," he told me. "What's here for you right now? Nothing except bills and latkes and the prospect of humidity. The job market sucks. I'm sure it sucks in L.A. too but it'll look different. It'll be good for you." He cleared his throat and then said besides had he told me he was going to be in L.A. soon, too? A college pal, one of the ones I've managed to lose touch with, is a big honcho at one of the major studios—he always was an overachiever not to mention a champion networker, this guy. He saw that Krieger won an NEA and was wondering if he wanted to come out and meet with some people in "creative development," or one of those Hollywoodisms, sitting around a pool coming up with million-dollar ideas. So Krieger's going to beat me out there, probably—by the time I get there he'll be tan and have lost forty pounds and be wearing sunglasses that cost several hundred dollars rather than the kind you buy on the street for ten. I imagine they'll sign Krieger up to direct, you know, "Krazy Kat—the Live Action Movie," and all talk of the bard will be safely behind him. "Oh what a falling-off was there," I nearly said to Krieger, but I wasn't sure he'd have a sense of humor about it; he's never been great at taking jokes about himself.

One person who's a hundred percent behind this California plan, who is in part sponsoring it, is my sister Cindy. I never told Cindy about my scam with Sparky. I have obscured the criminal basis of the expedition, which I'm sure you can understand. But Cindy insisted, to my grotesque embarrassment, on giving me some money before I left and I, to my even more grotesque embarrassment, accepted it—largely because I knew the illicit Sparky was going to eat up my credit cards and without a credit card there is just so very little you can accomplish in this world. So I took the cash. She was very gracious about it.

She said, "I'm not going to tell anyone, even Jane. I'm just doing this so you don't have to worry." I believe this to be a well-intentioned lie; ever since I found out that Cindy and Jane tell each other *everything*, right down to reports on ear pustules and hangnails and detailed accounts of what they ate for lunch, I have not had any faith in their ability to keep secrets from each other. But it was certainly kind of Cin to be alert to the fact that I might still have a smithereen of pride about it. That's about exactly how much I do have, in fact—a smithereen—otherwise I wouldn't be sitting here blabbing to all of you. But it's important to be honest, you know? Otherwise, why bother writing. Why bother writing, "Well everybody, I've just signed a great contract with a military engineering firm to handle their personal software, I'm getting back on my feet again now and am relocating to Colorado Springs where I can get married and raise a family, and so thank you for your support, you've all been swell, Yours faithfully"? I mean, how much satisfaction would writing such a fiction give me? None. Not even a smithereen.

But this does lead to one other metanarrative question here about my decision to go West, to head out there in a blaze of glory, into the sunset, off a cliff—whichever Western cliché you prefer. I know you think what I write here is all very artless and confessional. It probably is. And I'm sure you think I don't consider my audience, which let me tell you after a certain incident that occurred in Baltimore concerning a boundary crossing encounter with One's Readership is no longer the case. You see secretly, like a parent, I have been careful in the information I've given all of you, in the story I've told. I've been selective.

And I was thinking, since I want this edition to be the last installment of my Diery: how interesting would it be for me to return to my nameless city of residence, after some random episodes in Baltimore, including the spilling of red wine on my shoe and the spectacle of three white chicks singing "Respect" down by the harbor? It wouldn't have a good narrative arc. I can see that. I bet even the wandering Joe, with his presumably inferior narrative instincts, would have noticed that. You need movement. You need change. You need the hero to go somewhere else for there to be a sense of resolution.

So I am going West. To the city of my birth. To the place, don't imagine I have forgotten, where my mother lives, but I don't believe that is the hazard it might once have been.

Now, I may have let slip a nasty item or two about my mother Sally in here and I'd just like to take this moment to retract them, if I may. The woman drinks, yes, and she carries a chest full of regrets about my father around with her all the time even though she is now dating that eligible divorcé Cin mentioned, the Kirk philanthropist fellow. But the fact remains, when I told Sally that I was thinking of heading back to California for a while, she said—I mean the *first* thing she said to me, on hearing this, was:

"Oh, JD, that's such good news. Do you think you could help me, when you're here, to sort through some old boxes of your grandmother's things I still have in the garage? I want to get rid of most of it. I'd ask Walter to help me but he has a terrible back, poor dear, he can hardly lift anything heavier than a paperback."

I guess to some normal adult people this could seem an insulting response to my news about my big life change, taking the bull by the horns, etc. But I found it very appropriate. Uplifting, even. You know, at least I can be useful. My mom must be one of the few people left right now to whom I can really be useful. And as we all know, it's important to feel useful. It's nice to know I'll arrive in L.A. with one concrete task ahead of me, just to get me going.

And now I'm going to disappear into the deep night with the tolerant but restless Minsk. We'll go count the stars. An unexpected side benefit of returning the car to Zippy Car Rental: a night of stargazing here in the clear, cold Southwest, where the rusty strange earth seems like a new planet. I'm planning to look up into the brightness of April constellations, to see how infinity changes my take on things. Minsk is planning, as far as I know, to discover a new world of smells, a fresh taste of geography. To marvel at a place without dog runs or leash laws, where the size of the sky makes him feel a very small white poodle indeed.

Beautiful. Beautiful! I feel it's all coming together now. I've got that *rush* you get from narrative momentum.

Last night, post-stargazing (there were thousands, they were glorious, they left my eyes full of new light), on returning to our not luxurious but adequate pad in the Motel Rio Grande—I had a short, calm night. Minsk slept on my feet. The room was blissfully quiet, in comparison with other recent motel rooms I could tell you about, except in this case for the occasional truck noise, which reminded me of my apartment in the city and so made me feel right at home. Best of all, I dreamed well. I had a heart-swelling dream about . . . Paul McCartney.

There are so many Beatles songs out there to choose from. Really, one for every occasion—births, deaths, weddings, high-school graduations. There's always one that seems to fit. From my point of view the Beatles are, if not bigger than Jesus, at least likely to be the best thing that will turn up on your car radio when you're driving cross country through deep, strange states you've never quite heard of. On the whole the radio tends to be filled with voices hammering on about Mexicans and blacks ruining the country; or someone describing their prostate problems in unhappily vivid detail for a celebrity radio doctor. Musically you're most likely to get a twangy lady crooning, "I love your cheatin' heart/I love you yes I do/You can kick me in the face/But I'll still be true to you" or some such stirring Nashville sentiment.

The point being. The last song I heard before I turned in old Sparky was "Hey Jude." And while, as I say, there are plenty of great Beatles songs—"While My Guitar Gently Weeps," "One after 909," "Eleanor Rigby," and so forth and so on—"Hey Jude" was an excellent one for the DJ to select at that moment. I'm not about to quote the words to you, you know perfectly well how they go. Just imagine me (if you can imagine this) sitting in a dark Sparky with all the lights turned out, Minsk wondering what the hell is up, and me crooning along in my surprisingly tuneful voice to the earnest longer-haired Paul M. of that time. I was practically crying. If a policeman had come along right then, it would have been perfectly reasonable for him to arrest me on suspicion that I was about to commit some sort of unspecified felony.

So there was Paul! Last night, in my dream. Playing a new song for me. He was explaining something quite poignant: that because he was Paul McCartney, an ex-Beatle obviously but also with hundreds of hits since then, even if half of them are well-meaning drivel like "Ebony and Ivory"—because of all that, people assumed every song he wrote would be fantastic and that he'd never have anxiety about writing anymore. How could he? He was Paul McCartney. But, see, he confided in me (because he could trust me; I was sympathetic, and I'd be discreet) he could still lose his nerve, writing. So he wanted to play his new song for me to see what I thought. And he wanted me to be honest; that was important. If it was fluffy nonsense, I had to tell him straight out. I promised I would, and he started playing.

It was beautiful. It was a moving beautiful song, and I told him so.

That's all I remember about the dream, luckily for you. I know how tedious dream-sharing is: Cindy and Jane, to my horror, spend half an hour *every morning* telling each other their dreams. And even I don't need someone to tell me what Paul signifies here. I mean, he's a figure of regeneration, isn't he, triumphing over adversity because look how he picked himself up after the Beatles split up? And I'm aware that it's square to like Paul, that anyone worth their weight in hipness likes John because he's mystical and dead, or George because he's mystical and still around, or even Ringo, who's so goofy that there's a kind of double negative which winds up working in his favor. But I want to put in a good word for my man Paul. He's stayed married, first of all. Always admirable in a man and father. He also remains puppy dog cute, even if he is sixty or whatever by now. Besides, as I now know, he has crises of confidence, which makes anyone lovable but especially someone as famous as Paul.

I didn't need dream interpretation on this one. But Paul did make me think of Gloria, of her sprightly readings of life and how a touch of her voice this morning might do me good. It was early where I was, but because the East Coast is so much farther ahead of the game than the West I knew she'd already be at work.

There's something you don't know about Gloria, due to a transmission error in your copies of my Diery, i.e. that I haven't written for a while. You don't know that Gloria's son Daniel died. You won't be surprised to hear this, because last time you saw him he was thin as a sheet and as pale, and no longer speaking in sentences. Most things like words and the personality that words create had slid right out of him, and he was just body and spirit, but not even that much of the former. A few weeks ago he made the transition, and now he's entirely spirit, and as spirit he still lives for Gloria and for other people who knew him. I went to the service. It was the least I could do, having played the part of his brother in the last months of his life. I never met the real brother. He didn't show up at the funeral. So much for man's humanity to man.

So I've been worrying about Gloria recently because of that. As you would if the last time you saw a person they were hunched into a fifth their natural size, raddled by grief. Bereavement had compressed her into a tiny figure of choked sobs and shaking shoulders, clothed in a simple dark dress that could not stretch itself around an infinite loss. I hugged her and her shudders moved through my frame, causing my own body to quake. What else could I do? But since then I've been trying to call her regularly to check how she's doing.

"JD!" she said this morning when she heard my voice on the phone. Gloria's one of those incredible people who always makes you feel important, even when the story of her life crushes the story of yours. "How are you, honey?"

"I'm fine. I'm in New Mexico."

"New Mexico! What are you doing there?"

"Calling you," I said. "To find out how you are."

"How did you know to call me? You must have known. Something must have told you to call me. Did you have a dream last night?"

"In fact, yes, but I didn't call you about that. I just wanted to find out how you're doing."

"JD, you're sweet. What did you dream?"

"Well, it's hard to see the relevance of it. It was about Paul McCartney."

"Oh!" She actually laughed. This crazy wonderful woman actually laughed. "You are blessed with your dreams, do you know that? Don't forget it. Paul McCartney! Do you know what he was telling you?"

"I had a few ideas. But yours will be better."

"That I'm going to be a grandmother."

This was so far from what I was expecting that I did a kind of triple take. I was trying to figure out—could her son Daniel have gotten someone . . . before he . . . ? But then wouldn't the baby have been . . . ?

"Really?" I said, to express my confusion.

"Tony's wife, Diana, is pregnant. Three months, already! They were keeping it a secret at first. The baby is due at the end of October."

"Gosh, Gloria, that's—"

But see, I hate the brother. It's hard for me to want him to reproduce. He doesn't deserve to, is my feeling. Do you know what I mean? Does the world really need the offspring of cruel, bigoted people? My feeling is not. But this merely illustrates the fact that Gloria, as if anyone could doubt it, is a much bigger person than I will ever be. All five foot two of her.

"It's a blessing, JD. God is blessing me. If it's a boy—Diana wants a girl, but I'm praying for a boy!—they're going to name him Daniel. Diana and I have already agreed, Anthony can't change our minds about that."

She made some noise that translated over the phone lines as half cough, half laugh. You could hear the weeping in her voice still. It soaked her words. But you could also tell that this news had brought her a deep and obvious joy; it had given her a new future.

"I can't stay on the line," she said. "I'm sorry, honey, I've got to get back to work. JD, are you all right? You're not in trouble?"

"I'm not in trouble. I'm moving. I wanted to tell you. I'm moving back to California. To Los Angeles." I hadn't wanted to break it to her before, but now I felt I could.

"To be closer to your mother!" she said. "Oh, that's good. That's good, JD. I know she's missed you. Oh. *I'll* miss you. I'll miss you—"

"I'll come back." I swallowed. I hate goodbyes. "For visits, and everything."

"Of course you will. Of course. I've got to go, honey. Mr. Lieberman needs these figures by noon. Noon! He's nuts. I still wish you were here to help us. Just the other day Cheryl couldn't figure something out . . . Oh, JD! I'll miss you. You be good now."

"I will. Bye, Gloria. Bye. Goodbye!"

So that was good. That was sweet, if mournful. It was all I could do not to burst into tears after talking to her, she sometimes has that effect on me. But maybe she was right. Who knows? Gloria's always been several steps ahead of me. Maybe that is what Paul showed up to tell me. That Tony's wife, Gloria's daughter-in-law, was with child. That Diana had done the decent thing, the only thing you can do in a terrible situation: she had taken a sad song, and made it better.

I thought I'd mention one other question about my destination that was raised by another of our dramatis personae, namely Jane. Jane thought the going West idea was fine. But she wondered: Why City of Angels? Why not City by the Bay? She knows, so she claims, more nice people living in San Francisco than you "could fit on the head of a pin," her phrase. She even promised me that some were perfectly heterosexual, in case I was imagining a big batch of homos. (Well you do, don't you.) She said San Francisco's cleaner, safer, easier, and more breathable than L.A. She said there are better bookstores. She said it had decent public transportation. She said it was the home of Peet's coffee, arguably the best coffee on the planet. She said, What does L.A. have, to compete?

I had to tell her.

Hamburger Hamlet, for one. Our gramma, Sally's late mom (the one with the boxes in the garage), used to take us there for cheese blintzes and German apple pancakes when we were kids. She had German roots, we used to suppose, though she never confirmed this. She was always vague and hidden about her background, the way formerly poor people from faraway states sometimes are.

Anyway, not only that, I said. L.A. has orange trees and movie stars. Movie stars! What are we saying? L.A. has *Meryl Streep*.

In fact L.A. as you know does get hideous press. There's hardly anyone who will stick their neck out and tell you what a swell town L.A. is. People from the metropolis I used to live in sometimes pretend they're going to move there for a big change, but from the outside everyone thinks both cities are violent, dirty, polluted, and on the brink of civil war. Not, in short, to be touched with a ten-foot pole. L.A. at least has beaches, but you can imagine for someone like me —a case of melanoma just waiting to happen—that's not the big pull.

But the more down on L.A. people get, the more sure I am that I want to go there rather than the Bay Area. People are so damn smug about the Bay Area. You know? Forgive me, because half the small batch of people reading this may live in Silicon Valley and I admit you all rule the world and created this technology without which I wouldn't be here today filling up screen time. But I believe you're just a little too pleased with yourselves. Going with L.A. is like voting for the underdog. It's like wanting the Dodgers to beat the A's that World Series year when the A's had won everything and Jose Canseco had spent the season blasting home runs all the way to Baja. You want the losers to win. It's human nature. People say L.A. is going straight to hell? People say all the nice rich white folk are leaving in droves to move to calm homes off Seattle and Vancouver? Get me on down there! Get me over to L.A. right now!

Besides: white people leaving Los Angeles. Is this such a tragedy? People tell you this like it's the equivalent of saying the polar ice caps are melting. "Whites will no longer be the majority in L.A. within twenty years" or whatever that statistic is. (Like it wasn't the Spanish who colonized the town in the first place, ¿verdad?) This is the global warming of America's racial demographics. Our nonwhite ice caps are melting, and soon us whiteys are going to be drowned by all those minorities, who we won't even be able to call minorities anymore because the term will be incorrect!

Let's face it. White people are becoming obsolete the world over. Our moment has passed. If we insist on kicking drunk drivers nearly to death on video and producing politicians who send mentally handicapped black men to the gas chamber in order to get votes—who's to say our time isn't up? L.A. is the cutting edge of a phenomenon that's taking place the world over. Which unlike global warming is not, in my opinion, such a terrible thing.

Oh, what the hell do I know. I'm just ranting. That last section was brought to you courtesy of Cindy Levin, with whom I lived for a good month, long enough for her to implant a silicon chip in my brain containing her top five political analyses. All I wanted to say is I'm going to stick up for L.A. L.A. can't help being fake and stupid. They make movies there. What do you expect? It's like Tang. L.A. is like Tang. Better yet, L.A. is instant coffee, the Bay Area is Peet's. I can't think of a better way of putting it.

Furthermore, which one do you think I belong in, really? Think about it. Here, I'll give you a quote as a hint: "He shall recover his wits there; or if he do not, 'tis no great matter . . . 'Twill not be seen in him there; there the men are as mad as he."

I don't suppose I have to tell you which play of 1604 that snippet is from. Of course in the original we're talking England, not Los Angeles. It's a fun line that allows the English audience a laugh at their own expense, which unlike Krieger the English have always been good at.

Still I think you can substitute L.A. for England, JD for Hamlet, and you get the picture. And you see why it's got to be the best idea.

There's one other loose end I'd like to tie up before I get ready to board the Lone Ranger or Hiyo Silver or whatever kitsch name Amtrak has come up with for their service to L.A. Did I mention I'm going by train? Cinematically speaking, it would have been preferable to hold on to Sparky all the way out there so we could have had the obligatory shot of the "You are now entering California" sign with dead flat desert all around, the sky full of its yellow ambitious gleam that shines right into the squint of your eyes. On the train you don't know when you're in one state and when another except by deducing it from the timetable. So I'm just going to slide into California without knowing it, I'll probably sleep through the great transition and wake up blankly in the state about which some wit once said, "It's a great place to live—if you're an orange."

OK. The loose end, careful readers will recall and have been tipped off about by the quote, is Horatio. What happened to the search for Horatio? Have I been looking up Levins in every city I've been through so I could have a fabulously coincidental reunion with a guy who also had the wandering Joe, nominally, as a father? Surely that's what would have happened in the film of the book: a meeting with Joe's other son in some improbable outpost. Why did I never, as Cindy kept hoping, at least have dinner with one of my clucking red-haired aunts so I could ask them what they know? Or was I kidding about the Horatio notion all along?

The answer is: I found Horatio, without having to do any of that stuff. I found Horatio! Which is one reason, as you might have guessed, I haven't posted any Diery for quite a while. I've been otherwise occupied getting reacquainted with my old soul mate, my old friend the philosopher. Horatio—or I do forget myself.

One thing to reveal right off the bat. Horatio turned out to be a woman. Weird, eh? We were expecting a boy, but no. Still, it's nothing that would have surprised Will Shakespeare. His plays always have men dressed up to play women who are disguising themselves as men. Old Will was the original gender bender. Our first Queer Theorist.

But the fact that she's a gal does contradict my original notion that it was a real brother I was looking for. Krieger would seem to have been right to express skepticism about that. (Don't tell him I said that, it'll just make him more swollen-headed than he already is.) Not that my search was metaphorical, exactly, just that what I was looking for was a brother *under* the skin. A kind of blood brother. One where we could prick our fingers and touch them together, if in this disease-ridden age that weren't such a fraught, impossible ritual. I found someone who was a little less than kin, and more than kind. More than kind.

She is a charming soul, this Horatio. Let me take a moment to tell you something about her. The first thing to know is that she has a surprising access to the shadowed world. I have no idea how she got this—it's some kind of uncanny knack she has. This lets her play with creatures from the world beyond this one. Fantasy creatures, dead creatures, creatures from a parallel universe; creatures that live but don't speak our language. If we were in Salem or other old, superstitious days, she might have been called a witch for her talents and dumped in the river, but in our enlightened age the word for it is nothing scarier than *philosopher*.

Am I making her too much a hero? Aren't I supposed to reserve that role for myself? Ultimately, even with his inaction, his handwringing and self-hatred, who's the one who fights the duel? Who's the one who kills the king? It isn't Horatio, is it? It's the other guy. It's Hamlet.

But this Horatio is a great gal in her own right. Worthy of her part, even if she never was given enough lines. Like the original, her main quality is that she's a good friend. She's the kind of friend whose words improve your life by making it a better-described place. She gives you slices of the world on a page, and they're slices that feed you, that still your hunger. She puts into her print enough of the unseen world to keep you curious, enough of the seen world to remind you where you are so you don't lose your bearings. You know what literary metaphor comes to mind here? She is Charlotte to my Wilbur. You remember how horribly sad it is when Charlotte dies at the end of *Charlotte's Web*; we all cry at that part no matter how old we are or how many times we've read it. But it's the good kind of heartbreak. E. B. White knew what he was doing; he knew kids could take it. Kids have to be told the truth, and the truth is sometimes even your favorite people like Charlotte have to die.

Anyway. The point I'm trying to make is that there's a line towards the end of *Charlotte's Web* that is something like "She was a true friend and a good writer, and it's rare to have a friend who's both." The same could be said about my Horatio.

Friend. Are you sure? *Friend?* I know the romance readers among you are breathing a steamy, panting sigh of anticipation and are waiting for me to describe pulling her willing body close to me, feeling her mouth melt into mine as I devour her soft lips, as I feel my stiff resolve press against her soft and waiting femininity . . . The romance readers are chattering happily, I knew it! It had to happen! He's in love!

You silly people. I'm sorry, but I have to say it. Romance has never been the point of all this. It hasn't been the point of my despair, or my restlessness, or my desire to write a story, or the substance of the story that I wanted to write. This has been a tale about purposelessness: what happens when the bottom drops out of your place in the world and you try to find a way to get back some ground.

Certainly when there are Horatios in the world you don't feel so alone, because there is someone who will see through the madness you pretend to others. Who won't necessarily think you're committable. Who'll laugh at your jokes. Minsk, to be fair, has done his best on that front, but there is that barrier between us of not sharing a language.

No other person can fill a hole in your life. If I've posted this Diery for any reason at all other than a self-aggrandizing desire to see my own words in print, it's to point up the fallacy in that small catastrophic idea. It leads to so many errors. So many unwise divorces. So many unwiser marriages. It leads to long, fraught searches—up to and including the placing of personals—for that one perfect person who will make living worthwhile.

So, see, finding Horatio, rewarding though it's been, isn't the thing that gave me the big boot to get out of my former city and come out here to L.A. Who knows what it was, really? My sister Cindy lending me a generous amount of cash? Reading a couple of good novels at Cindy's place, deciding that a world that included *The Book of Laughter and Forgetting* couldn't be such a bad place after all? Or going to Daniel's funeral, seeing the floodwaters of grief there, and realizing in a pretty serious, straight-ahead way that that is not something, even in my periodic waves of self-pity, that I'd care to inflict on my family, on the people I love. If you start living through that ritual in your imagination, you have to come up against the truth that it is laughably selfish, the idea of putting them all through that loss. Just because you happen to find going on difficult. (Credit where credit is due: it was Horatio's clear eye that helped me see this crucial point.)

I'm cautioning you against the big resolution. I know you'd like me to tell you I found God, or love, or the Beatles, or even employment. There would be a tidiness if I could at least reassure you exactly how this ends. We American readers are fond of our endings.

I'll never forget an assignment I had in a college Lit class. We were reading Kafka. I was coming to understand the extraordinary luck I had being born in an era when we have Kafka on our bookshelves—and the luck we've all had that Max Brod didn't burn all that genius into ash the way Franz had wanted him to.

Anyway, in this class we were reading *The Castle*, which as you may know Kafka never finished. It's officially unfinished. It ends with the landlady yelling something about a new dress to a character named Gerstäcker. Which, admittedly, is none too conclusive. So what was our professor's assignment? Write the end to *The Castle*. Is that insane or what? First of all, the idea that any of us squirts could even begin to write like the Master; but more than that, the idea that *The Castle* needed an ending! In my humble judgment, it's perfect as it is. It just stops, the way life sometimes does, not even at the end of a paragraph.

What I'm saying is I've always valued the ambiguous in narrative. I think we need to quell our desire to know exactly what goes on. So if I unplug now, if I unplug here in New Mexico, it is to allow all you readers to choose the ending you want for me. I mean you can just sit tight and imagine it, whatever you prefer or think is likely. A great emotional funeral at the end, in spite of what I just wrote, with angels (and Minsk) singing me to my rest? (In which case, let me state for the record, I'd like to leave my poodle and books to Horatio; my rent-controlled apartment to Lili; and my laptop to Krieger. It's about time the guy learned how to use one.) Or a casting agent who spots me in the street, discovers some long-buried talent of mine and helps me to make it big, changing my name to Brad Stone or something so I sound more square-shouldered and movie starrish?

Everyone has to find a reason for living. You know that old chestnut, "Why are we here?" I think the millennial person's response to this question, if he or she has been to college, survived adolescence and the dysfunctional families or drug-riddled streets of home—is to answer paradoxically: "To find a reason for living." I don't care what it is for you. A job, a cause, a dog, a book, or a kid. Something to keep you putting one foot in front of the other.

I'm approximately the millionth man so far this year to go through these machinations in order to reach this resolution. There will be a million more after me who'll have to go through the same calculations for themselves. And some other number—one I won't name, it will only depress you—who won't get to the end of these thoughts, who will make a swan-dive deep into their grave first. There are a lot of guns out there ready to satisfy those whims. There will always be bridges to jump off of. (Another good reason for me to stay away from San Francisco. Too many bridges.) Plenty of pills waiting to be taken in over-big doses.

When I'm in L.A., I'm going to look seriously for work. I'll probably end up flipping burgers. That's OK. At this point, I'll take it. I'll move Mom's boxes from the garage. I'll let Krieger "lunch" me. I'll find some little shack in West Hollywood to live in with my few belongings. I'll do the things you do to prove you plan to participate.

I think about Joe sometimes. I do. I think about Joe. But I try not to hate him quite as intensely as formerly. I don't know. He must have his own problems. It's hard to forgive him just dumping his genes on us and then leaving, but then I guess at least he did *leave* the genes: otherwise I might never have the sardonic streak that I have, or the ability not to drink myself into oblivion, or the not-so-hidden ambition to shoot my mouth off in print.

Of course I still hope, I'm bound to, that he's "doomed for a certain term to walk the night/And for the day confin'd to fast in fires/Till the foul crimes done in his days of nature/Are burnt and purg'd away." You know how that goes. I'm still mad enough at the guy to hope that for him. But in reality, wherever old Joe is, he's probably in the same boat as I am. He's probably out pounding the pavement. Looking for a job.

And God knows how things change, over time. God knows my cynicism may not be warranted. Our Joe—our moping, meandering Joe—for all I know, he may have already found one.

JD.

The receiver sweated in her palm.

She would ask for *JD*. Of course, what if that wasn't really his name? It might not be. For all she knew he was really called Archibald, and this late effort to reach him might end in a joke, a humiliation, a nothing. "JD," she'd say to a silent indifference at the other end of the line—and her piled-up hope and curiosity would vanish into ash.

As Pi started dialing, her hands got sticky with nervousness. She got through to the bookstore, and a woman's voice, Western and sensible, came on the line.

"Is that Cindy—Cynthia Levin?"

"Who's this?"

"Hi—you don't know me. I'm a friend of your brother's."

"Oh, Jesus. Is he in trouble? What is it?" Her voice, this unknown voice, became brittle with panic.

"No, no." Pi needed to be clear. "I'm sorry. I don't know where he is. That's why I'm calling you. I just wondered if you might know how I could reach him."

"I'm sorry, what did you say your name was?"

"Well . . ." How could this be such a hard question? "He knows me as Sylvia."

"Sylvia?"

"But that's not my real name. My real name is Emily Piper. People call me Pi."

"And how did you say you knew my brother?"

"I didn't say. It's just—it's hard to explain. You see, I've been writing to your brother for the past couple of months. We've been corresponding, and then something changed, and I couldn't get in touch with him . . ." She realized the story that might sound best. "And so I was worried about him. I wanted to make sure he was all right."

The woman on the end of the phone sighed.

"Listen, Sylvia—"

"It's Pi, actually."

"Pi. I appreciate your concern about JD. I do. I don't know how well you know him, but, you know, we all get worried about him when he disappears the way he sometimes does, because you just never know with him. I mean— you just never know."

Pi kept a respectful silence.

"But I couldn't help you track down his physical whereabouts right now even if I wanted to. All I can tell you is he should be showing up in L.A. pretty soon."

"So he is definitely on his way to L.A.?"

"Well, 'definitely' as far as anything ever is with JD."

"And . . . Will he be staying with your mother once he gets there? I don't want to pry—"

"He should be, yes. Listen. You do sound worried. I'm sorry, it's just there have been all kinds of strange people—I mean, no offense—trying to find out what's happening with him, because of all the Internet stuff. He told me about it, or tried to. I find it all bizarre, I have to admit, but I'm probably a dinosaur. That's what JD tells me. I still believe in books, real books—that's how old-fashioned I am. I read hard copies of stories, on actual pages! Crazy, right? Anyway. Do you want me to give you my mother's phone number? That way you can at least call him there when he arrives."

"That would be great. Thanks."

As she took the number down, Pi tried to shake off the feeling that she was somehow swindling this gullible sister into giving her the telephone number.

"I really appreciate it," Pi said. "And I'll do as you suggest—I'll call him there just to make sure he gets there OK."

"Good idea." The voice on the other end of the phone hardened with sibling impatience. "It's typical of my brother you know—to go back to L.A. now. Jesus. What timing."

"Right," Pi said vaguely. She wasn't thinking about Cindy Levin anymore. She was staring at this phone number and wondering if it would take her to him. Would she drive there? Would she find him? Would he be who he said he was?

The emptiness on the phone seemed to be one Pi was supposed to fill. "Timing?" she echoed. "Why? What do you mean, exactly?" "Haven't you been following? L.A., by the looks of it, is getting ready to burn."

Wednesday.
My dearest Bet,
My first letter to you. Always a key moment in any connection. Here it goes.

I am going. And I am coming back. But I am going, because there is something I have to find out, and I can't find it out from here. And I am going now, because I have a weird feeling that time is of the essence in this. You were right in something you said to me in the woods. It sounded harsh but it was true: I have to know my own mind. Who'd have thought that was such a tough task?

When I come back, things will be different. You never step in the same river twice, as they say. I take it you will be making your plans about moving back to San Francisco sometime over the summer. I'm probably headed back there, too. I found myself saying to Martha that I might try living with Fran again for a while, and it sounded true as I said it.

Who knows? Maybe we'll be neighbors. Maybe we'll go skating together. Maybe I will learn certain frilled arts from you, or maybe I will teach you a few of my own. We will find out, I guess, if there is any kind of name to attach to what happens between us.

Thank you, Abbie, for your kindness. You pretend you haven't been extremely generous to me, when in fact you have been. What I'd most like to do is quote for you my favorite Joni Mitchell line. In some obscure way you remind me of her, something in the purple prettiness, I guess. In your traditional garb. This line is from *Miles of Aisles*, her live album, and one of the tapes I have probably missed the most. It's the end of the concert, and everyone is applauding Joni ecstatically and she is almost overwhelmed by how much people love her (as you should be), and she says with a kind of awestruck laugh, "Thank you for your presence—and for being here, and everything."
I feel the same way.

love
Pi

PS Sometime soon, you'll be blessed with a surprise fiction from a small, unexpected quarter—I hope you enjoy it.

That's what it all led back to in the end. All roads, in the end, lead back to life on the road.

Her car, without Martha in it, seemed oddly unpeopled. The car had taken on a new identity as mini blue school bus to an active near eight-year-old. Marthaless, the car reverted to what it had been before—a tight blue box for the voices of Pi's life.

Pi started with an experiment: silence. Radio was so good at luring your inner ear away to somewhere else, someplace imagined and heard about: the grimly perpetual "war-torn" Bosnia or an edge of election campaign trail, brought to you by human NPR voices. But on this drive Pi thought maybe she should let the surroundings themselves keep her company.

She drove first along Highway 128, a weaving thing that drew you away from the coast, through the Anderson Valley and back to 101, the so-called Redwood Highway. As Pi drove through a hamlet called Boonville she remembered Xander once telling her that Boonville had the distinction of having created its own language, called something exotic like Boonglish. Xander was full of information that seemed highly unlikely to be true and yet later proved to be. Pi was convinced it was probably just some kind of pig Latin gone haywire, which offended him. "If you'd ever read," he told her, with a surprising edginess, "I'd get you a book about it from Mary's bookstore." It was the kind of story she would have run by Hamlet, before. Before he pulled the plug on her.

The blond hills curved away from the road as it spun in and around patches of dense dark oakery. It was the first time in months that Pi had driven more than a few miles up or down from Mendocino, and it felt good to encounter her state again. Its scattered vineyards. Its craft joints and sandwich galleries. Its yellowness and heat. Pi rolled down the window and inhaled the dry scent of burnable grasses and sagebrush. There was no sound inside the car; she let the baked, rich land speak for itself.

What does driving do to you? He'd said something about it. He'd said it made you feverish and unbalanced, but Pi felt otherwise. Driving made her strong. She'd forgotten the authority a person had behind the wheel, when you controlled your vehicle, however humble and Japanese it might be—when you had a surety of pace and direction and, yes, destination. Of course, Pi thought. It was a linear activity—going from A to B—and she had always enjoyed a straight line of argument.

Within hours Pi had moved swiftly on, and the freeway was cluttering with malls and commuter towns, a widening of lanes. The road pressed on inexorably to the city and its great orange icon, and Pi realized for the first time, squarely, that there was no way this journey could avoid San Francisco. City by the Bay. It was flat in the path of any person traveling from Mendocino to Los Angeles, there was no getting round it.

Unless. There was an alternative. Pi made the decision spontaneously on seeing the sign. She changed lanes and drove to the Richmond Bridge instead.

No one much mentions the Richmond Bridge. It's not one of the ones that you hear about. It hasn't the crowds, the glamour, or suicides of the others. (The Golden Gate is your number one suicide bridge in the area. You can walk along its open invitation as you can't along the others.) The Richmond Bridge is basically just a long bridge, nice enough, that sways unnervingly under traffic and brings on earthquake anxieties in the slightest breeze. It takes you from yachtsome Marin County to forgotten industrial Contra Costa, enabling you to bypass San Francisco. People use the Richmond Bridge who have to. People don't choose it for aesthetic reasons. It takes you over the water everyone has to get over, and drops you off a short number of miles above the educational mecca of Berkeley.

Pi was on the bridge before she'd had a lot of time to think about it. It was a clear day and the bay beneath her was a steamy slate. She swallowed and breathed. And she drove.

It is so strange, she reflected, when you shatter your own mythologies, finding them as breakable as movie glass, the bottles cowboys crack over each other's heads in Westerns. You thought their breaking would be dramatic, sending dangerous shards all over, when in fact they yield with nothing more than a moderate *clink.* Pi had thought it impossible to drag her mind and body back across the bay—and here she was in her Honda doing it. Her heart wasn't even breaking: it was murmuring merely, a gentle commentary. *This is a place you once lived in.*

Time is of the essence, she'd written Abbie, but suddenly it wasn't. There was time for this rediscovery at least. From the freeways she took the Ashby exit to Berkeley, scuttled up through the low-housed modest suburbs towards the hillier greens where she'd once had a home. Driving up Ashby, Pi could see the hungry yawning emptiness of the dull uncolored hills. It reminded her of that vast pit in her stomach after the fire. The hills were still dark and unlived on, bare and protesting.

Pi didn't allow herself to drive all the way up. She was not going to drive to where La Vista had been or possibly still was. What would be the point? She was not posing for a photograph—herself squatting over the desolate landscape where once had sheltered her many intimate books.

Instead she pulled over and parked on College where people and storefronts, bagels and coffee, would bring her back to the present. To material life as it was pleasantly lived here, to well-looked-after, nice-faced moms and their children, and longer-haired students in shorts who bore an uncanny resemblance to her old friend Rob.

It *was* Rob.

"Rob!"

She grabbed his arm—to hold him, see if it was really him, not let him escape.

He stared at her, taking in the news that she was here—his once colleague and friend, she who'd vanished in a puff of smoke. "Hey," he said. Not quite smiling. "Is it you? Or a figment of you?"

"It's me."

Rob, floppily black-haired with wide ears and pale skin, was as familiar and as eerie to Pi as a character from some childhood TV sitcom. A surge of affection lightened her limbs, which she flung around him, in a sudden effusion.

"It's so good to see you!"

He still looked bemused and bewildered. "Wait a second. Are we on Twin Earth here? I assumed you'd left us for a higher plane." But under his trendy squared glasses—new since she'd last seen him—a warmth crept into his intelligent eyes.

"I know—I've been terrible. I'm sorry I've been so out of touch. And you were so kind to send me the modem and everything—it was terrible of me."

He nodded. "You're right. It was terrible." Rob was never one for empty politeness. "So what are you doing here, besides scaring people to death? Have you moved back?"

"No! God, I would have told you," she said, and ignored his skeptical look. "I'm just passing through. I'm on my way to L.A. I just stopped by for a minute, just to see it. You know, I haven't seen it since—since I left."

He looked up to the hills. "It still looks like shit. Everyone's squabbling. It's a mess. It'll be years before they pull it together again." He returned to her. "So, listen. I'm supposed to be meeting Tamar at Cody's five minutes ago. Let's go together."

"Oh—I'd love to, but I can't. I've got to hit the road. I'm trying to get down to L.A. by tonight."

"Come on, Pi. What's the hurry? Where's the fire?" He stopped, and squinted up at the sky. "Nope. That was poor taste. That was a joke in very poor taste."

Pi touched his arm again. It was so pleasingly solid. "I haven't missed your good taste, you know. It's been your bad taste I've missed. Look, I'm parked right here—let me give you a ride over there, at least."

He jumped in. "Aw. You've missed me? That's so sweet," he said, as Pi drove them over the all-too-known roads down to Telegraph. The hairs on the back of her neck rose at the memory of her last time on Telegraph. It was where she and this small car were in the original moment of loss. As they approached the bookstore, Pi was beginning her goodbye when Rob yelped, "Parking place! Grab it!" and, like a former Berkeley resident, she instinctively did.

"Rob, you don't understand," she said as the car stilled. "It's great to see you, but I've got to go. I can't come to Cody's with you. Time is of the essence."

"That's a totally empty phrase." He jumped out and fed the meter with quarters. Pi had forgotten how hyper Rob could get. "Come on! You've got to see Tamar. She won't believe me if I just tell her I saw you. She'll think I've had a caffeine-induced hallucination."

"How many cups are you on these days?"

"Four espressos this morning already. That's good. That's down from six."

He spun through the glass doors of the bookstore, leaving Pi no time to explain she couldn't go in, she didn't do bookstores anymore . . . She had no choice but to follow him. Inside, she had one sharp intake of new book smell —and, like Pavlov's bell-happy dog, she felt that old urge in her fingertips. The desire to browse. The readiness to buy.

Pi saw Tamar before Tamar saw Pi, as she gave Rob a nice kiss to greet him. Lingeringly. On the lips. She kissed him the way a lover kisses and Pi realized that this was what Rob had wanted her to see. He surrounded Tamar with a proprietary arm and said, "Look what I brought to show you."

Tamar looked.

"Pi!" she exclaimed. She laughed. "How have you been? Where have you been?"

"Twin Earth," Rob said. "She's been telling me all about it. It's very interesting."

"It was a research trip," Pi said. "You know, maybe I'll write it up. I've been looking for new material."

Rob and Tamar, Pi was thinking. Why didn't anyone think of it before? Seeing them now—her small red-haired shape snug in his gangly long-limbed one—they looked so right together. So permanent and inevitable, the way successful couples do.

"There's so much to catch you up on," Tamar said. "Come have lunch with us."

"She can't stay. She's got very pressing business in Los Angeles, which is much too important and secret for her to reveal to the likes of us."

"It's a Twin Earth thing, you wouldn't understand," Pi said. "Listen, it's great to see you both. Really. You look—you look great."

"Are you moving back here, Pi?"

"I don't know. I haven't decided."

"The brooks are still babbling. They're singing your name." Rob gave her his version of a bear hug. Boy-friendly, joshing. "Well, listen. Keep in touch, you old idealist, you."

"This time," Pi said, "I will."

And she left them, fueled by a new unruly joy. Joy at discovering neglected friendships still alive and kicking; at realizing that she hadn't, after all, burned all her bridges.

Hours passed. She made it through the trapped freeway tangle of San Jose and the hot stretch of points south. She began to drive through endless miles of speeding-by agribusiness: great plains of corn and tomatoes, uncountable pear trees, infinite lettuce. At times whole patches of air were thick with the sweet smell of garlic.

Pi was nearing the Pacheco Pass. The Pacheco Pass—quite apart from its romantic name, which brought to mind hungry pioneers and men riding on horseback—was a significant part of this journey, as in Pi's mind it marked the place where you left Northern California behind and started the drift to the south. It was also the site of the crucial watering hole, the Casa de Fruta.

Pi's first encounter with the Casa de Fruta had been a disappointment. She and her mother and Richard had been driving down to Southern California to visit Richard's relatives for the first time. It was an important meeting for the adults, who conferred mumblingly in the front. Pi was left thirsty and bored in the back. Finally she asked her mother plaintively, "Can we stop soon?" and her mother answered, "We'll stop at the Casa de Fruta. How about that?"

"What's that?"

To which Richard, new parent figure, answered helpfully, "It means 'House of Fruit' in Spanish. Doesn't that sound fun?"

For the rest of the hour it took to arrive at this fruity oasis Pi, little Emmy as she was then, pictured a Hansel and Gretel–type operation: a small tasty cabin made not of gingerbread but of orchard fruits. Apples, apricots, peaches, plums; blueberries and strawberries, oranges and cantaloupes. What a wonderful place this would be. What would it smell like? How many bright colors would it have? And—a small practical part of her worried—how would they keep it fresh and cool in this terrible heat? After two hours in the car her own bag of apricots had grown sour and warm.

In fact the Casa de Fruta turned out to be nothing more than a mini emporium of gift items: crystalline nuts and dried fruit arrangements, fancy foods that had no interest for her whatsoever. For the kids there were donkey rides out back, which were not what young Emmy had had in mind. Ever since, Pi associated the Casa de Fruta with that jolt you often experience as a child when you come to realize that your fondest fantasies have no corresponding reality in the world. Nonetheless, it was a ritual of hers to stop there. She loaded up on marinated artichokes, soda, and corn chips. On her way out she passed a pay phone. Why not? On an impulse she dialed a familiar number.

"Hi. Fran?"

"Hello?"

"Hi! It's me."

"Pi! God. You scared me. You sounded like this crazed woman I've been counseling lately. She calls me constantly, she thinks I'm having an affair with her husband. Sorry if I sounded strained. How are you?"

"I'm fine. I'm at the Casa de Fruta."

"That's nice. And where is that?"

"You know, the place on the way to L.A. Olives and fruit leather, pineapple salsa."

"Oh, there." Pi heard a cigarette being lit, the first exhalation. "So what are you doing? Are the girls with you, Martha and her dear mother?"

"No. Why should they be?"

"I don't know. Company. Are you all right? You sound a little weird."

"I'm fine."

"Has Abbie been acting up again? Have you had some kind of altercation?"

"No, no. Nothing that simple."

"What do you mean?"

"Nothing. I'll tell you about it some other time."

"You're being very mysterious. So why are you at the Casa de Fruta? Are you coming back from a visit south? Jesus—it's awful, isn't it?"

"What's awful?"

"The King verdict."

"They announced it?"

"God, Pi. Where have you been hiding? I thought you said they get NPR up in Mendocino."

"I haven't listened to the radio today. So how many years did they get?"

"The cops got off. Totally acquitted. People are going nuts."

"The cops got *off?* How is that possible?"

"Don't ask me. People are evil. What can I tell you? It's unbelievable."

"That's just what Cindy said would happen."

"Who's Cindy?"

"Cindy—Oh, it's a long story. She's the sister of this guy I've been writing to over the Internet. He's the reason I'm trying to get to L.A."

"Pi—you're not having some kind of weird computer affair, are you? Is that why you're being so mysterious about everything?"

"No! It's nothing like that. We're friends. We've become good friends. But— I need to see him. He's called JD. It was his sister who said L.A. was getting ready to burn."

"Wait a second. 'JD?' 'Cindy?' "

"Yes. JD's why I'm going to L.A. I know it's crazy, but I want to meet him."

"Pi, hold on. You're not talking about JD—you don't mean JD as in the Diery?"

"You've heard about him too?"

"Heard about him? Peter and I talk about him all the time. There was just a thing about him in *People*, and Peter is doing a story on him for KQED. The cult of the suicide writer."

"Oh." The excitement Pi had felt telling Xander had evaporated; this new recognition only made her feel tired. "Well, I've been writing him. We've had a whole correspondence."

"You're kidding! This is so exciting. Peter will want to talk to you about it. He's fascinated by the way JD's writings have pulled all these people into a silent community, creating a sort of new extra-literary literary world—"

"Fran, I'm sorry. I can't think about this right now. I'm not thinking about the cultural ramifications of JD. I'm thinking about *him*. The actual guy."

"I can't believe this. You and JD! It's so glamorous. It's like having an affair with a movie star."

"I'm not having an affair with him!"

"But even so, even though it's glamorous, you can't go down there. I'm sorry, but you can't. It's not smart. You've got to turn around."

"I have to go. I'm going to go. I'll be fine."

"This is too weird. How did you get involved with JD? Come back here and tell me all about it. I'm serious. You can't go to L.A."

"You know," Pi sighed into the mid-state heat. Suddenly she felt like crying. "Part of me agrees with you. Maybe it's wrong to try to meet him. If I were a good idealist, I wouldn't need to. He'd be real enough to me as it is."

"Now, now. Philosophy bullshit has nothing to do with it. I thought you'd foresworn philosophy, anyway. I thought that career was behind you."

"I'm reconsidering."

"Listen, I'm sorry living with Abbie isn't working out. Why don't you come back to the Bay Area? We'll find you an apartment. Life can be good here. Peter knows some great people in radio. Voice is the wave of the future."

Pi nodded, sending a mute smile into the fumes around the Casa de Fruta.

"Pi, you can't go to L.A. Just come back here like a good girl. OK? Go to L.A. next week, or the week after. Go when it's clearer how much of it is left."

"But I have to go now. I have to see him," she said stubbornly, checking the sky for signs. The steep sun brought water to her eyes. "If, that is, there is anyone there to see."

What is it like to meet a friend you don't know? How does it go? How do you construct a person out of the print you recognize him in? It was like going to pick up Kant from the airport. How would you know the guy when you saw him? (By the intelligent bulge in his forehead, no doubt.) It was JD's voice that she knew. The written voice. Who knew what he sounded like? It was perfectly possible he spoke in a squeak. She thought of those traumas with radio announcers—the personalities you knew intimately through the patterns of their speech, whose photographs when you saw them left you shocked and dismayed.

All she knew of him was how he wrote. All she knew was the sound of his print in her ear.

Hey Sylvia.

He might have written her now. If he had written her now, she knew how he'd sound.

Hey Sylvia.

You're probably wondering where I am. Aren't we all. Minsk asks me the same question every couple of minutes. I don't know what to tell him, except the one obvious item: We're not in Kansas anymore. Not that we ever were, for very long.

I've got my eye on you, Sylvia. Don't worry. I'm keeping my eye on you.

Kind of like God, though we never did satisfactorily resolve whether or not He exists. A less exalted comparison would be Santa Claus, I guess—someone who sits up there and keeps checking on how people are doing. It's so cool! I've finally found some work to keep me busy. Though to do either job right I really ought to have a white beard, which I lack.

Sylvia, you've heard me talk, ad nauseam, I dare say, about the old chestnut that is unemployment. But let's change the subject slightly. We know my history, paltry as it is: worked on a weekly paper, bummed around, wrote half a bad novel. Discovered I was able to understand computer systems, hence got a decent support staff job. Worked for several years. Gained a feeling of self-respect. Paid the bills. Bought a couple of dogs. Joined the quote unquote real world, acquiring material items which gave me a stake in the overall system. Then, abruptly, through no fault of my own the recession hit, and I got FIRED. Haven't been able to pick up the pieces. Look forward with my dog to starting again in Los Angeles. Am 6'1", 30s. SWM . . . Oh, you remember those details.

But you. You! You the dead poet. You the philosophy girl, named strangely after the chick who will always be remembered for sticking her head in a gas oven. I never understood why you didn't call yourself Socrates. Hemlock seems such an infinitely cooler way to go. Green, cool, goes down easy. And it would have picked up the scholarly angle, obviously.

You, Sylvia! What are you doing?

I know, I know. You used to philosophize. This we've heard. This we know about. And though dapper John in Arizona might consider academia an indulgent and ill-paid form of navel-gazing, my own sister goes out with a gal who does the same thing. So I have to respect it. Besides, the people I know who are skeptical about grad school, myself included, are probably just jealous. Lili, before she hooked up with the preemie donnas and met the up-and-coming tenor Raul Hot Tamale (I'll stop; very soon I will stop with these tasteless jokes)—used to threaten to go to grad school in Spanish and write a new translation of the *Quixote*. And Krieger always had a small chip on his shoulder for not having gone to drama grad school, though why he would need to I couldn't say. Even me—absurd, sloping-shouldered, pet-owning me—even I in my wilder moments used to ponder the graduate school option. More books to read! Lots of sitting around drinking coffee! The ability to go on protests about one social ailment or another and get very self-righteous about the people who don't show up for them! The right to have office hours, affect people's GPAs and their futures!

But, as you well know, Sylvia, the graduate school option leads inexorably to—teaching. Committee meetings. Clawing your way after tenure. Being in a private institution, teaching spoiled brats who drive BMWs and wear distressed yachting shoes; or being in a public institution, where the race wars may be closer to the surface and everyone's out for each other's blood because they're all underfunded. Is this the life you were after, Sylvia? Because I will let you in on a state secret, you can believe or ignore it at your peril. *You could still do this.* Yes, Sylvia, you could. You could rewrite your dissertation. Certainly it would add time on to your toil. It would qualify as a huge pain in the ass, and you would attain a kind of scholarly martyrdom for doing it. You'd be awarded the Purple Heart of academic valor. But I bet somebody out there has a piece of print of yours, some old Kant writing to start you out with again. And you can't pretend the ideas aren't still clocked in your head. I know you well enough to know you've been philosophizing in the dark, when you think no one can hear. The thinking is still in you, it didn't go up in flames. Besides: you know people at Berkeley would help you. Your colleagues are still there. It's a life; you could reseize it.

Just felt I had to let you know. I've got your best interests at heart here. The world is your oyster, Sylvia. I'm sure you don't need me to remind you. Personally, I'm still holding out for the nonfiction blockbuster on metaphysics, to keep all the *Times* readers up to scratch on what's what with reality, in this day and age. I'd like to see you write the kind of book everyone feels they ought to read, like A *Brief History of Time*, though I'd prefer it if people actually read yours, rather than just buying it and leaving it on their coffee tables—always a danger with the big-brain bestsellers.

OK Sylvia. That's it for now. I know you've missed my voice. I'm sorry I haven't written. I'm sorry I haven't written. I would have, you know I would have, it's just that . . .

But Pi couldn't supply the rest of the sentence in her mind. The voice only went so far, and no further. After that, there was nothing; and it was the silence that chilled her.

For the rest of the way, Pi played the radio. As the miles went on it exuded more and more urgent alarms. At first Pi assumed it was the hysteria of the news media, turning the story of one lit match into a great arsonist's fantasy of destruction and chaos. But slowly, as the accounts built of broken windows and raging fires, of frequent gunshot, of free-for-all looting—Pi began to believe the scale of what was happening. This was a big one. This was going to be one of California's greater disasters. It might even surpass her own, in dollars cost and newsprint spent, afterwards, explaining and probing.

She drove closer to the smoking city. Los Angeles had always seemed such a featureless place to her before—you couldn't tell that war lurked inside it. You couldn't even really tell when you were *in* it, L.A., the sprawl around was so infinite and indistinct. Gertrude Stein might have written of Oakland because it was her home town, but Pi had always felt that Los Angeles was the city where there was no *there*.

Soon the traffic police were warning drivers not to go within a two-mile radius of downtown. Names of streets and intersections, freeways and neighborhoods that meant nothing to Pi, were rattled off on the radio. She just wanted to get to Pasadena—to a phone booth, a telephone number, a voice that might tell her she wasn't crazy; which by now, with the alarms all around her, she was beginning to suspect she was. Why hadn't she taken Fran's advice, come back in a week or two? She didn't actually want to die over this quest of hers. Time was of the essence, she had felt since the moment that morning she'd finished reading "The Millionth Man," but now, here, on the edge of civil unrest, she was beginning to agree with what Rob said. If you looked at it carefully, the phrase was an empty one.

Pi took a Pasadena exit and pulled over on a wide street at a small metal box. She dialed the number Cindy had given her, leaned her head into the booth, and waited.

A man's voice answered, which she wasn't expecting. The voice was low and calm, with a faint implied question, a suggestion of self-doubt.

Was that his voice?

"Is that JD?"

"No, it isn't. Who's calling please?"

"Yes—I'm a friend of JD's. My name's Pi, or—or Sylvia. I've just driven down to L.A. to see him, and I wondered if—he was around." The words fell out of her mouth.

"He isn't here right now." The voice was oddly lugubrious. Suddenly it departed from her, issued a sentence in some other language, fast and cough-like. It was the tone used with a small child. "Here," he returned to her in English. "I'll put his mother on."

"What? Hello?" This one was bright and impatient. "Hello? Who's this?"

"Hi." Pi tried again. "I'm sorry to bother you. My name is Pi. I'm a friend of JD's, I've driven down to L.A. because I was hoping to see him . . ."

"Oh. Well.—Honey, no, don't climb on that. Leah? Could you get him off that? It could break.—Hello?"

"Yeah. Hi."

"Where are you, Pam? Where are you calling from?"

"Pi.—I'm in Pasadena somewhere."

"Oh! So close. That's good. Don't go any further in, will you. They're telling people to stay away from downtown. It's terrible, like a state of siege! We're worried about JD. He was supposed to be coming in on the train, but—I just hope he has the sense to call, and someone can go and get him from wherever he is. You say you're staying in Pasadena?"

"Not exactly staying. I've just driven down from the Bay Area."

"Well, Pasadena's a good area to stay in. That's where we are. We're just waiting for JD to call, you see. Cindy said—Oh, honey? Honey? No. No, you can't go in there. No, you can't. Mabel? Thanks.—OK, sorry. Pat? Are you still there?"

"I'm still here."

"Because I'd better get off. What if he's trying to get through? We don't have call-waiting here, you know. The only telephone in Los Angeles without call-waiting. Now. Do you want to call back a little later? Or, I tell you what, do you just want to come over? It's not safe out there. I hope JD'll find his way. Why he had to pick today of all days to arrive, I don't know. Why don't you just come over here and wait with us? At least it's safe."

Worry pounded at Pi's head. The sun warmed her back. All she'd wanted was to see him. To talk to him once. She hadn't meant to arrive in time for the race wars, to take shelter from them in the comfort of strangers.

"That's so kind of you," she had to say. "I'll be right over."

When she arrived, it was like a dream.

She met the faces the way you do in a dream, all of them looking and seeming familiar, though later you can't begin to describe them. The home seemed to be part of a complex called La Playa, not that la playa itself was within view. It was a group of cheerful bungalows gathered around a central lawn area in an arrangement that if she'd had the mind to concentrate might have made sense. Pi was sure there was order everywhere, and logic. It was just that she couldn't see it.

She was greeted at the door by a woman with a comfortable, weathered face: a face riven by warmth and comedy and the deep gauge of alcohol. She welcomed Pi with a worn, intimate smile that suggested they'd been expecting her—for years, possibly; that Pi was in fact the guest of honor, and all this alarm and ceremony had to do with none other than her.

"Pam, dear! Come in," said the nest-haired woman, opening a door into a loud and crowded house. "I'm Sara Levin. Come in. We're all glued to the television. It's just awful. I shouldn't be sitting here smiling at you when terrible things are going on. Come in now."

She led Pi into the busy improbable cocktail party environment that seemed to be going on inside, with voices (it seemed to Pi) of many different times and places. Tucked in and around drooping dusty palm plants and a battered acid-colored sofa were the characters Pi recognized by name if not by face. (It was like watching the movie version of one of your favorite novels: Oh, no, I never pictured Karenin looking like *that*.) A white-headed elfin lady was introduced as Sally's neighbor, Mabel McGillicuddy. She was seated with a plastic bowl in front of her at a Formica dining table towards the rear of the room near the kitchen, shelling peas. She waved a pea-pod at Pi in greeting. A distinguished gentleman in his sixties mentioned to Pi that his name was Walter Kirk but people called him Jim, as if there were nothing funny about this. And perhaps there wasn't: after all, his stalwart face seemed the kind you might very well entrust with the commanding of the starship *Enterprise*, or indeed any other starship. Later in conversation Pi learned that he was on the board of the environmental group Sally worked for, and it occurred to her that Jim Kirk was the philanthropist swain.

To everyone she was introduced by Sally, who had from somewhere found a full wine glass to hold on to, as "Pam—an old college friend of JD's visiting from San Francisco," a phrase so dense with inaccuracy that Pi didn't dare try to fix any of it lest the whole thing disintegrate. She smiled a lot. Smiling helped.

There was another cluster in the party too, and they were dark-haired and honey-skinned and seemed to belong together. The shapely young woman Leah had a great swoop of blackness piled on her head and wore her Lycra effortlessly, as though it didn't cling to her or make her hot. Her red mouth looked capable of serious scolding and was often busy proving it with a small wrapped quantity of noise and energy called Eyal, who was an age childless Pi could not guess. Whatever age that was after walking and running and being able to wreck things but before speech made it possible to negotiate and explain. Attached to these two, not by proximity since he was sitting in a leather wing chair in the corner, with a yellow pad on his knee and a pen hovering over it, his head cocked towards the television; but clearly attached to the other two nonetheless, since when they addressed him often in another language (Pi realized it must be Hebrew), he raised his heavy horse eyes up from the television and over to Leah, particularly, though he didn't answer, he just nodded to show her he'd heard her—

Was Joe.

Joseph Levin, he was introduced to Pam as, and the introduction earned a vague smile from him and a brief nod of the head, which Sally, for one, did not seem to feel was adequate so she clarified the introduction.

"This is JD's father, who happens to be here with his new family—by coincidence, really. He's here covering the trial for one of the Israeli magazines. Imagine the story he'll send back to them now. What a terrible thing."

As if the remark were a signal, the low ebb of chatter died for a minute and they all turned, including Eyal, to the television's talking heads. They were muttering and decrying and looking stern while their safe studio selves were periodically intercut with aerial shots of fire and mayhem and thick obscuring smoke. In a rational state of mind Pi would have listened to the television and had some reaction to it, but the noise made her mute for a minute and she listened merely, slack-jawed, half waiting for the well-paid pundits to issue the kind of random brilliant remark they would have in a dream, something like "R-E-S-P-E-C-T: Find out what it means to them," or "Well, Bill, as they say: I am not my brother's keeper."

All hell was breaking out on television. That much Pi could see. But she couldn't make herself believe the disaster was real. She expected more people to come and watch television with them: she was waiting for the whole crowd to come back out the way they would for the final curtain—everyone, even the guy who died way back in the first act. The final image would have them all huddled around the bright star-glow of the violent television, watching as America's second city tore itself to burnt and rageful pieces. Krieger and Lili would be there, their arms loosely wrapped around each other in friendship; and Gloria and her sons, both sons, even the bad and unforgiven one Tony, because he never meant to be so callous, in his heart he still loved his sick brother after all; and the minor characters who were only ever on for a few minutes—scary Marcie, Paul and Susie, Mr. Merkelson the neighbor. Even Miss Aerobia from the fourteenth floor.

The telephone rang.

Everyone looked at Sally, whose hand went up to her loose-skinned chest in alarm but who made herself say brightly, "I've just got to check on the chicken. I don't want it to burn. Can you get that, Joe?"

Tall, stooping Joe did the manly thing and answered the phone. When Pi heard his molasses-heavy voice she knew it was Joe she'd spoken with earlier from the side of the road.

"Yes?" he said.

The room inhaled—a twitchy, news-greedy silence.

"He's not here right now. Who's calling?" A general group breath of relief. "I see. No. We expect him later. Would you care to call back? Yes, I will." He placed the receiver back carefully, then tried to retreat. Eyal intercepted him, wrapping his plump arms around the lean suited legs. Joe looked down with some bemusement and addressed the child with a few words of Hebrew, and as she listened to the unknown language, Pi started to hear a known one in her inner ear.

So that's him. That's the guy. Can you believe it? That's the guy who gave me half my existence. He hasn't aged that badly, I suppose. I was always doubtful about his attractiveness quotient, even if Sally does tend to mention it when drunk, but here he is having landed himself a very good-looking younger wife, so there must be something in it after all. He must have hidden reserves of charm that he rarely expended on his progeny—

"That was David Krieger," Joe announced. "JD's friend. Calling to make sure he got here all right." He made a spidery, long-limbed production of getting back to his chair, commanding everyone's attention as he did it. Jim Kirk resumed a conversation with Leah on the Gulf War, and Sally sat next to Mabel McGillicuddy to help her shell peas. "Will you stay for dinner, Pam?" she called over. "I can't let you go back out there. Look at the television! It's mayhem. There's plenty. We're just having drumsticks. Why don't you stay?"

"Thanks—I'd love to. That's kind of you. Thanks."

They seemed to be the first actual words Pi had spoken, and they managed to break some spell. There wasn't anywhere obvious to fit in so she sat on a crooked footstool near the wing chair with Joe in it. He seemed to be safely absorbed by his scribbling.

You don't need to be scared of him. He's harmless. I'm sure he's never hurt a flea, unless you count sustained emotional damage on the two kids, though as we have demonstrated one recovered admirably and exhibits her distress only in having chosen to live in Baltimore; it is only the older one, the fuckup, who never managed to readjust and occasionally fantasizes about suing for emotional dam-

ages in the enduring American tradition. Anyway, you should talk to him. Why not? The worst that can happen is he'll make some horrible anti-Arab remark. Israel, eh. So it was true all along! I always thought that was just a fanciful rumor stirred up by the apologetic aunts and that we'd discover him living up in Northern California somewhere and he'd, you know, turn out to have been Thomas Pynchon or someone fun all along and that was why he was always vague on his whereabouts. Wishful thinking. And now it turns out the guy did rediscover himself after all. A journalist! Do we believe it? Should we ask to see his press pass, or would that be too rude? But who would ever listen to what the wandering Joe had to say about anything? The idea boggles the mind.

"So Pam," he said, still scribbling. "What do you do?"

"You know," Pi confided, "my name isn't Pam. It's Pi. People call me Pi."

"As in Apple, à la Mode?"

"Well—more as in 3.141589, et cetera."

He laughed.

And his laugh was strangely joyful. Next to the mournful appearance of him it had a catchy, world-weary element that suggested that in all of his long, tiring travels, he'd never experienced anything quite like the absurd pleasure of meeting someone named Pi.

"How did that happen to you?" he asked her.

"Oh—my last name's Piper, and I've never much liked my first name . . . It started in college, with a math joke that got out of hand."

"They so often do," he said, which intrigued her. Suddenly he scribbled something down from the television, mumbling to himself.

"You're writing about—?" Pi gestured at the television.

"Riots," he helped her. "They're going to be riots."

"Cindy was predicting this all along," Sally suddenly called over from the pea-shelling station, which had turned into a salad production line. "She knew it. For weeks she's been telling me this would happen. She knew they wouldn't convict, and that people would go crazy."

"How can Cindy in Baltimore see what's happening in Los Angeles?"

"She knew, that's all I can tell you," Sally said. "She has a special interest in minorities. Minority issues. She's very attuned to them."

Minority issues. Why doesn't someone tell the guy just how "attuned" my little sister is, and why? Don't let him off easy! I mean, you've got him here, the Invisible Man. Confront him with something. Or ask him something challenging. It's like the Presidential debates—make use of your question time!

"And why—what—" Pi floundered. What could she ask him? "Where's the name Eyal from?" was all she could come up with.

"It's the name of Leah's brother. He was killed two years ago. A soldier." He scribbled some more. "Names are important. JD—like you, he took a nickname. That's always bothered me. What's your first name? Your Christian name, so to speak?"

"Emily."

"Like the poet. That's nice. If I were you, I would have stuck with Emily." He laughed again. "Apple Emily, à la Mode."

Now for God's sake don't let him charm you. Don't give in to the mysterious dark eyes, the sweet smile of melancholy. It's a shtick! That's all it is. He's been doing it for years. He's had a lifetime to perfect it. And it works! That's what I can never believe. It works, on the ladies anyway. People feel sorry for him. Oldest trick in the book. But don't you fall for it. Don't let him work his treacherous magic on you. Before you know it, you'll be lending him money and agreeing to move to Tel Aviv to be his au pair and buying him extra pairs of socks because his are looking a little worn. This is what the guy does. This is how he always gets people to do things for him. I'm here to testify, to tell you it's not too late to turn away . . .

"So Apple Emily." He put his pen down on the heavily scrawled pad and cracked his knuckles, a brief scale of snaps and crunches. "Are you also a writer, like Joseph?"

"Like who?"

"Joseph." He clarified. "My son."

"Your son's name is Joseph?"

"Yes. You're not supposed to do that in the Jewish tradition. Never after somebody living, only to remember someone no longer alive. I couldn't persuade his mother. Couldn't! She was there, and boom! Joseph David, is how it ended up on the piece of paper. What could I do. Emily, are you a writer?"

"I'm a philosopher," she said. "Or was. I was, until—"

"Oh no, if you're a philosopher, you're a philosopher." He shook his head. "That never changes. I should know, my own father was a philosopher, of a kind. And now I understand 'Pi' a little better. Pi is a good name for a philosopher. It's a lousy name for a writer."

The telephone rang again. Once again Sally looked up, hand to chest. This time she couldn't think of an excuse. "Could you please answer it, Joe?" she asked. The light in her eyes was the frightened, yellow kind, and he couldn't refuse her.

"Excuse me," Joe said to Pi as he got up again. He's not such a bad guy, Pi was thinking, as she heard him answer the phone. She only half listened to his words while he talked. They were brief and uninformative. "Yes? Yes it is. I see. Where? All right. Thank you."

But when he hung up, the hush in the room was murk-thick and dread-filled, and the baffled sounds from the television suddenly seemed impossibly loud. Joe himself didn't look at anyone. He pulled his body tightly together, and pressed his long, elegant fingers hard against a dark, breaking brow.

This time it was not an innocent call. It was the call everyone who knew JD had always worried they'd one day receive; though it would be long minutes before his father would find a way to put the fact into words.

D I E R Y

The last installment

IN THE MOVIES, OF COURSE, OR IN *HAMLET* FOR THAT MATTER, EVERYONE GETS the lingering death moment. You can see why. The audience feels so cheated otherwise. What—the guy just *dies*? That's it? Doesn't he get to say anything to anyone? I mean, we haven't sat here for three and a half hours for Christ's sake for the guy just to die, pop!, like that. Give us some entertainment. Give us some drama. Geez!

And I don't know the stats on how often in real life such dramatics are possible. I have no head for numbers like that anyway. I imagine nine times out of ten people just go, they disappear, they slide under the surface just at the point when someone really wanted to tell them one last thing they thought they should know, or was planning to break down and tell the guy how much they'd loved him all along. Just when some important person had a key word or two to drop in his ear.

That's how it was in my case. Sudden. Quiet. Unsurrounded by my nearest and dearest. And, I hasten to tell all of you, it was unintentional. Not by my own hand! Is that ironic or what? I'm sure you assumed that if I did go I went the Anna Karenina route in the end and threw myself under Amtrak's Hiyo Silver Express, or that I took a swift pull of an iced double hemlock with skim, or that I found the nearest bridge or high building and plunged off the edge. You didn't believe any of that hopeful crap I laid on in my supposedly "last" Diery installment, did you, about how I could never do this to my family et cetera? The guy's just saying that, you thought, to make us feel better. He's trying to be a role model for us unstable types because he's had to realize that he's in a position of responsibility, people read what he writes and so if he wrote, "Oh fuck it, let's just get it over with and drink the poison Kool-Aid" we might do it. So he wrote all that upbeat stuff about looking ahead to the future, went to L.A., composed a last will and testament, then stuck a gun down his throat, and pulled the trigger.

Not true! I have to correct your ideas on this point. I may be gone—I am gone, in point of fact—but not by my own pale hand. I went swiftly and stupidly, by somebody else's. And I'm not saying there's any justice or moral in it happening that way. I'm not going to pretend for you that it makes any sense. It's just, as the saying goes, one of those things.

Don't think I'm not sad as I write this, either, because I am. You have no idea—no one does—what was going through my mind on what would turn out to be my last day on earth, as the Hiyo Silver rolled into the City of Angels, my once and future home, which I had not intended to become my final resting place. The train slowed to a stop, jostling all of us train folk into a state of excitement. You've got to try it yourselves one day. Find out what Amtrak is like, that odd bunching of fellow travellers—consisting of Native Americans and Nam vets, cardplayers and college kids and people suffering from plane fear. It's an experience. On the longer trips, along with self-important uniformed conductors, you somehow become one big American family for the duration of the journey, the way you only really can with people you've shared group sleep and small bathrooms with. When the train arrives there's a weird moment of grief, at the prospect of leaving the nest.

Nonetheless. The moment of nostalgia passes, at which point you become aware of your need to smuggle out of the train your smuggled-in poodle, and so along with the flood of humanity you drain your way out into the orange-lit station, allowing yourself one random moment in which to honor long-forgotten ancestors—on your father's side, obviously—who had not such great experiences with trains in a much-discussed event earlier in the century known as the Second World War.

But out you get, climbing down into the station and blinking your eyes at all that orange, and finally letting your small white friend run free. And it's around then, in this unlikely spot, the train station in downtown Los Angeles—who'd have believed L.A. even *had* a train station—that you finally, stupidly realize that something is UP.

There's a certain amount of hysteria sizzling the air. People are talking very fast and not necessarily in languages you know. News is alive all around you, and everyone has a different take on it, but the gist seems to be that *there's trouble.* Finally someone says a word you hadn't heard yet that day, a technical word which doesn't always mean turning point and crisis, but in this case, in this year, in this city which people no longer feel they belong to, it does. *Acquittal.* That's the word. And for acquittal, read: The city's on fire.

OK, OK. I'm getting very dramatic here but didn't you want me to? You wouldn't want me to downplay it. And if I go easy on the eyewitness details, which would be what would really have street value in an account like this— did you see anyone get beaten? stabbed? wrenched from their car? better yet, killed?—if I omit such details, it's only because I had the rotten luck of getting killed myself.

Now it's debatable whether I got killed as a direct result of the riots. People will argue for years over this. (A self-important journalistic phrase I've always wanted to use. I love the grandiosity of it.) Actually people will argue for at least a couple of weeks, because at some point they have to put together the body count on the riots so the world media and police commissions and handwringers everywhere can have something concrete to discuss. Inevitably in such a ghoulish numerical task there are going to be some borderline cases, aren't there? That is, any gunshot-inflicted deaths anywhere near the famed intersection of Florence and Normandie are going to count for sure; you can be damn sure any police deaths are going to count, even if it was actually some old cop choking to death on his donut in a parked car in Encino; the woman burned in a fire in a liquor store in South Central is going to count, even if it takes investigators a week or two to come up with her human remains. But what about a male, white, thirty-three, killed in an automobile accident on Sunset Boulevard along with a male, Chinese-American descent, forty-five, who was driving and also killed? The two bodies are found crushed the way only auto accident bodies can be, but even crushed there is an odd way in which they look as though they had shared some last embrace. Traces of alcohol, though not an illegal percent, are found in the blood of the driver. The driver was a resident of Glendale, to which he was presumed driving with his hitchhiker passenger. The wife of the driver had spoken to him an hour before the crash, at which point he had been downtown weeping at a pay phone near the train station, where he had just seen off his brother who had been visiting from San Jose. He had been weeping not because of the farewell to his brother, who by his wife's account was a good-for-nothing who'd come to L.A. to chase after some girlfriend—but because he said the city was destroying itself and he didn't think there'd be anything left when it was over. He was frightened, his wife said later. He loved Los Angeles and hated to see it destroyed. His wife said she was shocked that her husband would give a ride to someone, it was completely unlike him, he was so cautious and he'd sounded so frightened on the phone, but when she heard that the other man had had a dog with him, a poodle, she'd understood. They had poodles too, the driver and his wife, grey toy poodles that they loved very much, called Santa and Barbara because Santa Barbara was where they'd spent their honeymoon twenty years before. They had no children. She was unable to.

Incredibly, the passenger's poodle survived the crash.

That was one of those unexplainable things.

The police said the dog must have been on the back seat, sheltered by the driver and passenger seats on impact, and though the animal was clearly in shock it had stayed at the scene, unusual in a traumatized animal, and though they would not go so far as to say the poodle was sitting howling by its master's cooling body, they certainly gave the impression that the dog was wide-eyed and mournful and understood perfectly well, as well as anyone could, what had happened. This in any case was the account presented by the police to the survivors.

I'll get to the survivors in a minute.

First I want to backtrack to the point about whether or not this is a riot-related death. Just to keep the reader informed of the facts. Because there was a chase, a genuine car chase—you think they only happen in the movies but they happen in real life too as it turns out. Cop cars, flashing lights, screeching tires, a disreputable BMW—this had it all. And the cops were racing down what can only be described as Sunset Boulevard, which our driver was on because he had some theory as to its being better to take a weird backroad route to Glendale, thus minimizing time on the freeways. Which as we see turned out to be a flawed theory. Because there were the cops, a glimpse of a flashing light ahead and then immediately after that the realization, too briefly to qualify for the word, that the car being chased had crossed over the center divider, not hard to do on parts of Sunset, it's a treacherous road when it comes right down to it, so the car was coming straight towards our innocent bystanders, aiming at them right between the eyes you might say, so that though our driver valiantly swerved, thus saving the chased car, his own car went straight into a low-speed palm tree, which was enough to mangle and permanently damage the car and both bodies, leaving two innocent bystanders dead, the chased car free, and one poodle remaining strangely, one is tempted to say miraculously, intact.

But is anybody ever really an innocent bystander? Are all bodies really "victims" of the riots in some sense or of the items which caused the riots in the first place, namely the sick and splintered structure of the city of Los Angeles? Are we all victims, none of us innocent, of the Rodney King beating and its aftermath?

Ask Cindy. That's what she'd tell you.

Myself, I think it's gruesome to dwell on the details of the coroner's calculations as to whether myself and Alan Liu should make it into the official count. I think Cindy—not that she'd appreciate my lay psychologizing, and it's ironic coming from anti-Freudian me—but I do think she needed some aspect of my death to fixate on to comfort her, and the coroner's report turned out to be it. Cindy will tell you she has the mental health issue licked, but sometimes if you see the obsessive way she pursues things like this coroner's report you can tell that we must be related, and that there are certain cracks in her sensible sensibility.

And I feel sorry for her now. How can I not? She's lost a brother. We know how painful *that* is. Your brother: your right-hand man: the guy you'd call when you were in trouble, the guy you'd joke-punch on the arm after an especially bad pun, the guy you might lose your temper with and it wouldn't matter, the guy you could roll with, play-biting and barking; that creature whose smell you knew as well as your own. He could infuriate you, no question about it—Oh for Christ's sake, stop being such a pain in the ass, you'd think to yourself more often than not—but you'd wind up realizing tearily in the middle of the night that you loved the guy, after all, that nothing and no one could replace him. That in some peculiar fraternal way he gave life to your life and heart to your heart, that ultimately he wasn't heavy—I'm sure you know the quote but I can't resist it—he was your brother.

So I think it's Cindy I feel sorriest for.

It should be my mother. Right? What can be worse than a mother's grief for her dead son? There is nothing worse. Believe me, I've seen it. It doesn't bear thinking about. It's the kind of thing you just have to turn your eyes away from, they can't even look. I would feel sorry for Sally, of course I would, if I could bear to even think of her, which for the moment I can't.

Of course I might have felt worst for my dad. In spite of all the bitterness, I mean, you might expect me to feel an odd posthumous floodgate of grief for my father. You know the guy I mean. Joe, Wandering. Last seen over a tuna fish sandwich several plot lines ago. All but given up on. As it happens though, coincidence and the global village being what they are, Joe happened to be in the same town, same place as his erstwhile son at the time of the latter's death. Uncanny, eh? Claiming to all and sundry that he was a journalist these days for a Tel Aviv magazine, which veneer of respectability encouraged the once wife to open the door to himself and the current wife and current child, a cute little fellow by the name of Eyal.

But a clarification. The real reason he came to L.A.—he genuinely was writing an article, but he angled for the assignment—the real reason he showed up, I have it on the authority of someone he spoke to at the funeral, was: He wanted to check out his son. Chip off the old block! Someone had wised him up to the cultish Internet writings of a lad named JD who, incidentally, had a habit of kvetching about his father, and apparently this pricked at old Joe's conscience, an organ some of us were not aware he possessed. He read the stuff, recognized himself—That boy means *me*!—and rather than hiding his head in the sand as you might have expected, he hopped on a plane and came out to the old homestead, taking along with him his wife and child to improve his credibility and probably to provide him some comfort, since women and children generally can relieve you of some of your guilt, even if the guilt is towards the original batch of women and children.

So I should weep for him now, not that dead people can weep but if we could. I mean, imagine how mortified the poor guy must feel, never got to say he was sorry, never got to say to his son, "You did good, kid," like he would have in the film, never got to shuffle and hem and go, "Well, son, I'm proud of you," while the audience sits there and holds back their tears. "I'm going to do better this time around," he might say, gesturing at young Eyal, across whose face a hopeful future would be written large while some background music symbolizes an end to the Middle East conflict.

I should weep, we all should, that this touching reconciliation never had a chance to take place. But as I say, I can't weep, all I can do is stand out here on the beach playing Frisbee with my new man Pinsk, and reflect that while erring has always been human, forgiveness is said to be divine. And in the fresh salt breeze of my life in the afterworld, I can reflect on whether my own qualities will ever stretch to the divine.

The truth of the matter is I feel sorry for everyone. Not least—myself. It's no picnic, being gone. I thought I'd be into it. You remember: I was lusting after this state, for God's sake, not so very long ago, and now I've achieved it it's already beginning to pall. Isn't that always the way it goes? You finally get what you think you wanted all along only to discover that you didn't really want it at all. I had that experience back when I was a kid with a game called Kerplunk! I *really* thought I wanted it, I'd seen the TV ads, and nothing seemed remotely as fun as this ridiculous game called Kerplunk! My mother, dear Sally, was finally pummelled into submission and bought it for us for Christmas. Cindy and I settled down joyously to play it, only to discover that Kerplunk! was a completely lame game involving toothpicks and marbles that you tired of all too soon. It's the same story with death. Here I am, gone, and my big and only joy is being able to play Frisbee on an abandoned beach with that dog-gone old dog of mine, the other one, Pinsk, as the inevitable gulls cry and forage around us and a few stately pelicans skim prehistorically past.

But I want to tell you one last story here, before I head out. It's a story from my youth. My medium here, my friend the channeler (Horatio, or I do forget myself), wanted to make sure this got into print.

This is something my mother would like you to know. All of you. It's some writing of mine she dug up for the service—it's amazing how morbid so many metaphors turn out to be, isn't it? But of course none of you virtual folk were able to make it to the service, not being aware of the death of myself. So here's a sampler to aid you in your grieving. It is a piece I wrote when I was nineteen. The urge is to go *Mom!* Geez. D'ya have to be so embarrassing? I was nineteen, for Christ's sake! But funerals are heightened affairs, where you can get away with melodrama, not to mention gobs of sentiment, which I've always been a sucker for. I'm not saying it wasn't a little thorny that she read this, or for that matter that she could get through it without crying. But that merely added to the effect. And in this case, though it goes against the grain to say it, I believe that in choosing this passage to read my mother made the right call.

A Place I Once Visited

There is a lake not far from here. It seems unlikely, I know. In these brown hills? These stark, carved shapes, growled at on the edge by a blue sun-spilt sea? Why would anyone bother with a lake? The land isn't made for it. This is beach country, swimming pool country, a place where you might now and then find the odd river. There couldn't be lakes here. Why would anyone bother with a lake, with all the turquoise-bright pools scattered around?

Nonetheless, I believe there is a lake somewhere not far from here. I would say I can remember it, except that I seem to be the only one of the alleged players in this memory of mine who believes in the place. My sister, who was there, disclaims all awareness of this lake. It is her opinion that I made it up. Of course, she is an adolescent and believes scarcely anything anyone tells her. What she can't see is the image in my mind's eye of herself in her bright purple Speedo of that era—we're talking sometime in the early seventies, a year when she was maybe eight and I a couple of years older—and she's sitting by the edge of the lake, on the little pier, with a stick, poking around at possible, hypothetical fishes. My sister's counter-claims to this are extravagant: she categorically denies ever owning a purple Speedo, a denial which is patently ridiculous as nearly everyone did at that time.

There are no photographs to resolve this dispute one way or the other. It's her word against mine.

On this particular afternoon I was talking with a tall man about girls. Or to be more accurate: he was talking to me about girls. There was some notion that we were there to fish, and I did have a small toy-like rod and reel, with some slimy salmon roe stabbed through their hearts by a tiny hook. I sat at the reedy edge of the purple lake because I had an idea that that was a likely place for fish. It seemed to me that if I were a fish on a hot day I'd go doze in the reeds and try to stay out of trouble, and the man I was with was too ignorant about fish to correct me on this point. The man I was with had utterly a lack of interest in fishing, though he made a minor effort to pretend. Until, that is, I got out the glass jar of salmon roe, which caused him to jump back a few yards in repulsion. Once the bait was on and I'd made my cast, and the offending berry-like blobs were safely drowning in the lake's cool depths—the man crept towards me again, squatted on his haunches, and talked to me about girls.

Specifically, he told me about Cheryl. He told me a few key facts about her: that she was twenty-five and an airline stewardess, that she had long, shapely legs. This man had met Cheryl when he'd taken a recent flight up to San Francisco, for reasons no one was sure of, though there was some suspicion that he was trying to meet one of his favorite writers there. I distinctly remember (my sister thinks this is ridiculous) the man saying to me, "And when Cheryl came up with her drinks tray and the line, 'Coffee, tea, punch, or bouillon?', that was it, right there! I was hooked."

I stopped fishing for a while after that. The fish weren't biting, and it was tiring to sit there holding the rod. I trapped the rod under a rock and let it fish for itself. My sister couldn't have cared less whether I caught anything or not. She was busy with her own project of counting out pebbles and arranging them in elaborate patterns on the jetty. And the man we were there with—he didn't even like fish. He was a pastrami man. He wanted me to talk to him about girls. He asked me were there girls I liked in my class. (I was twelve years old.) I told him, I don't know why, it wasn't true, that I liked a girl named Sally.

"Sally," he said. He shook his head. "What a crazy coincidence. Sally. So what's she like, your Sally? Anything like Cheryl?"

Instead of answering him I got up and went for a swim. It was very hot. Did I mention this? The day was hot as a furnace. Insects ticked in the air, but slowly, lazily, like it was too hot even for them to rub their legs together and make their small song.

I jumped off the small pier. Not before pushing my sister in, I might add. Even *this* she doesn't remember. Under hypnosis, I feel sure she'd at least get back the part where I push her in. Not that she did much about it. I was expecting a big fun waterfight, but she was in a disdainful mood and so after one surprised yelp she just climbed out and sat back on the pier, mostly turned away from me but keeping a thin edge of her eye on my whereabouts in case I snuck up on her to pull her back in. Once she was positioned, though, she sat not saying a word. It was deeply frustrating for me, who had been trying to create some drama or conflict. She didn't even call me a "jerk" or a "dork." She just sulked.

So to fool her, I dove underwater. Instead of sneaking up on her. Instead of hollering something to the man we were with, who was watching us both from the bank, looking at his watch and at the sun overhead and at his Chevrolet, which was going to be a hot plastic hell when we got back inside of it. Instead of showing off or doing anything, I just swam through the brown, fishless murk of the lake.

I swam and I swam. I don't know how I swam for so long. I started to feel like a fish myself, flickering my feet like they were silver fins. But as I swam, I wasn't really thinking of what I was doing. I was just thinking about Sally, about the girl I had lied to the man about, a girl who called herself Sally.

I very nearly never came up for air. There was a moment underwater, when the atmosphere was cool and heavy and the touch of the water so soft—the sounds of the world so distant and meaningless—when I suddenly felt incredibly sleepy. I felt I could just curl up then and there and fall asleep; and that if I did, my dreams would be spectacular, they'd more than reward me for my brave dark-water adventure.

But eventually I surfaced. Some hidden instinct—a hunger for oxygen, a yearning for sunlight—pulled me upwards. By the time I was coming up my lungs were on fire. I was airless. I needed to get out.

You do feel like a fish when you do this, because when you emerge, the world outside is poisonous at first. It hurts you to breathe. I was coughing. I spluttered. It wasn't pretty. I was probably some very unattractive shade of blue.

But there on the pier were the two of them. My sister, and the man we were with. They were standing together. He had a hand on her shoulder. I don't think I'd ever seen them standing that close before; they never got along very well. For the first time in my life I could see the resemblance between them, and I finally believed they were related. (I'd always had my doubts, before.) The look on their faces was identical.

It was the shock of loss, like a sudden slap in the face. Both of them were white with grief, even under all of that suntan. Their eyes were round and hollow and disbelieving. Their bottom lips jutted slightly out, a tiny defensive expression against what they were sure had just happened.

I saw them there, rigid with fear and what even I knew had to be love, and I laughed (once my lungs were full enough to laugh again). It was cruel of me. I had played a terrible trick on the two of them, and I knew that was bad. I think I realized, in spite of my laughter—it was nervous, defensive laughter—that it isn't right to play jokes with death.

I did understand something that day. I acquired a new piece of information, from the happy taste of lakey relief in my mouth. That there are times when something plain as air is delicious.

THE END

Tears wetted her face and made it hard to read the last sentences as she copied them from a sheet of paper to the screen. But she got to the end of them. And she typed those words, THE END; it seemed overdramatic, maybe, but otherwise she wasn't sure she could make herself believe it.

She looked out the window, stilling herself, stilling herself to the truth of the fact. The tears in her eyes jewelled the bay there—made it shimmer, made it shiver and change. The bay always changed. That was the beauty in watching it, as it moved back and forth between the Golden Gate and the Bay Bridge.

In a large white room with no memories, boxes of books waited in cubed cardboard for her to unpack them. She would get to those later. First she reached a hand down to scratch the white curly hair of a mournful poodle. He was sitting obediently at her feet: her feet now were the ones he was learning to follow. The dog seemed to have some intuition that the moment was an important one, that it had to do with someone he'd once loved, dearly. Pi murmured soundless words of comfort to him and wiped her face again to free it from salt. Then with one decisive finger she pressed the SEND button. She watched as the machine devoured the message, and the screen in front of her faded to blank.